TROUBLE IN
BAYOU
SABINE

THE BAYOU SABINE SERIES

TROUBLE IN BAYOU SABINE

The Bayou Sabine Series

LAUREN FAULKENBERRY

Blue Crow Books

Trouble in Bayou Sabine is a work of fiction. Names, characters, places, and incidents either are the product of the author's imagination or are used fictitiously. Any resemblance to actual persons, events, or locales is coincidental.

This book was previously published in 2015 with the title *Bayou My Love*.

Publisher's Cataloging-in-Publication Data
Faulkenberry, Lauren 1978-.
Trouble in Bayou Sabine : A Bayou Sabine Novel / Lauren Faulkenberry.
    p.____ cm.____
ISBN : 978-1-947834-40-8 (Pbk) | ISBN: 978-1-947834-41-5 (eBook)
1. Women—Louisiana—Fiction. 2. Love—Fiction. 3. Louisiana—Fiction. I. Title.
813'.6—dc23

Blue Crow Books

Published by Blue Crow Books
an imprint of Blue Crow Publishing, LLC, Chapel Hill, NC
www.bluecrowpublishing.com
Cover Photograph by Pexels
Cover Design by Lauren Faulkenberry

First published by Velvet Morning Press 2015
First Blue Crow Books Edition 2017
Second Blue Crow Books Edition 2019

Author's Note

This book was previously published in 2015 with the title *Bayou My Love*.

Praise for The Bayou Sabine Series

Beautifully descriptive and engaging. A delightful story about learning to let go of who you think you need to be and take a risk on happiness.

-Orly Konig, author of THE DISTANCE HOME and founding president of the Women's Fiction Writers Association.

Faulkenberry is a gifted storyteller with the ability to capture the most human side of relationships. *Bayou Whispers* is a rich and emotional story that will draw readers into the heat of the bayou and leave them wanting more.

-Tina Ann Forkner, award-winning author of THE REAL THING and WAKING UP JOY

I'd read this book again, and I recommend it to others who love a fast-paced romantic mystery. I give this book five stars.

-Dayna Leigh Cheser, author of the TIME series

I loved this book. It has so many different dimensions that you will literally be glued to the pages...There's mystery, intrigue, and unexpected pieces to the story. PICK UP THIS BOOK. It's a MUST READ.

-Pretty Little Book Reviews

From the moment Jack spoke in that French/Creole drawl he and Faulkenberry had me hook, line and sinker. I was a goner, and I didn't surface until the novel's end. I may be in love.

Faulkenberry creates a world of magic, suspense, and desire. An engrossing romance with just the right amount of heat!

for Andrew

Chapter One

I KNEW when I strode into my father's office—before he'd had time to drink his two cups of coffee—that I was asking for trouble. But I was furious.

He glared at me, the phone cradled to his ear. His upper lip twitched in the way that usually sent people running with fear. As I sat down in the chair across from his desk, I could hear the muffled voice on the other end of the line. Judging by the way he scribbled on his notepad, nearly piercing the paper, the conversation wasn't going well. If I were a more dutiful daughter, and less hacked off at him, I might have come back later. But he'd been ignoring me all week. I needed a straight answer about my next job and was tired of waiting.

My father has a knack for taking roughed-up houses and making them look like they belong in the glossy pages of architectural magazines. I'd started working for him when I was in college and discovered I had a knack for it too.

This fact puts him in a tough spot. On the one hand, he'd like his progeny to take over his company one day. On the other hand, his progeny is me: a hard-headed thirty-one-year-old woman whose general presence aggravates his ulcers. I don't do things the way he does, and he's a control freak. This often puts us at an impasse.

Most of our jobs work out OK. Because I get bored easily, the short-lived challenge of a new house-flip appeals to me. My father sleeps a little easier when his daughter has steady employment and is not too close to his office. He likes to micromanage me, though, and that's where things get hairy.

Still on the phone, he leaned back in his prized Mission-style chair and shook his hand at me to say *shoo*. I crossed my arms over my chest and raised my brows. He pointed to the door more emphatically. I propped my feet on his desk.

His eyes narrowed as they rested on my beat-up cowboy boots. They were my favorite pair, vintage brown and white with tulip and bluebird inlays. He grimaced whenever I wore them and called them unprofessional. In the beginning, he'd expected me to dress more like a real estate agent, in a nice skirt suit with heels. But skirt suits were completely against my nature. I was a tomboy through and through, perfectly happy in my jeans and plaid shirts. I usually took five minutes to pull my hair back in a ponytail and could sometimes be bothered to put on a little mascara, but that was the extent of my preening. My curvy figure and wildly curly hair had made for an unkind sprint through adolescence. My father was of no help in feminine matters, and my mother was long gone, so I'd fumbled my way through my formative years and came out the other side with zero appreciation for makeup or fashion. Heels put me just over six feet tall, and even though I had my mother's soft face, I intimidated most men.

It seemed more beneficial to focus on beautifying houses.

"I'll get somebody else over there immediately," my father said, slamming the phone down. He turned to me. "Honestly, it just can't get any crazier around here. I hope you're not coming in to tell me you're quitting too."

"I've been thinking about Grandma Vergie's house," I said.

"Enza, I don't have room for that on my plate right now. We'll get to it in a few months."

"I know you don't. That's why I have the perfect solution."

He stared at me over his glasses.

"What if I went down there myself and handled it?"

He chuckled like I'd told him a joke that wasn't all that funny.

When Vergie died a couple of months ago, she'd unexpectedly left her house to me. Dad suggested flipping it, despite my suggestion to keep it as a rental or a vacation home. It was on a stream in southeast Louisiana, just a little north of New Orleans. Bayou Sabine was a beautiful area, but my father scoffed at the idea of another property to maintain. He wanted to turn it around as fast as possible. There was no room in his heart for nostalgia.

"I'm serious," I said. "I want to handle this one."

"Your first flip should be local."

"I've been doing this for years. Give me a chance."

The phone rang again, and he answered before I could finish. "Hang on a sec," he said into the phone. To me he said, "You can take the next one."

I was so tired of hearing that line. I'd been patient, doing all the dirty work he handed me for five years now. House after house, he'd had me doing clean-up and demo, filling dumpsters with all the garbage left from houses that had been auctioned. We were based out of Raleigh, a city where a lot of houses went to auction. Most days, I felt like I needed a haz-mat suit, because people who left pissed off or in a hurry, well, they weren't concerned with what they left behind. Piles of dirty clothes, rotting garbage, refrigerators that had reached DEFCON 1—nothing surprised me any more. Some days I thought he was making me do the grunt work just to scare me off. He knew I had a weak stomach for filth. What he didn't know was that there was no way I'd give him the satisfaction of seeing me fail.

My father delighted in watching failure.

Occasionally he'd toss me a compliment and say I had a good eye for architecture, or I had more patience than he did—but he still couldn't let me loose. Sure, he loved me, but sometimes it felt like he was trying to make me prove I was in this business to stay. He considered training me an investment, and his investments needed to bring returns. Turning my grandmother's house around would go a long way toward making him see me as more of a professional and less of a wayward daughter.

When I stood, he didn't shift his gaze to me. I reached over and held my finger down on the phone, breaking the connection on the line.

"Enza!" he yelled. "That was a contractor!"

"I don't want to wait for the next crummy house in the wrong part of town. This one's important."

"That sort of sentimentality is going to cost you a fortune," he said. "And by extension, cost me a fortune."

"This isn't about sentimentality."

He sighed, tapping his pen on the desk. "It's nothing but a swamp down there," he said. "The house won't be like you remember." He had a strange look on his face, one I couldn't quite decipher. Usually I could read my father well, because he's a straightforward guy and doesn't have time for things like subtext. This look wasn't anger or fear, exactly, but he was definitely hiding something.

I shook it off, focused on winning him over. "I still want to go," I said.

It had been years since I'd been down to that little corner of Louisiana. When I was a kid, I spent summers with Vergie. But when I was sixteen, shortly after Mom left (no one ever told me why, and eventually I gave up asking), my father told me there would be no more summers with Vergie. *She doesn't want you to visit any more,* he said flatly. Being a teenager, thinking the world hated me, I took that to mean Vergie hated me too.

It never occurred to me until years later that my father might have lied.

Sure, I could have sought Vergie out. But part of me believed my father and thought she really didn't want to see me. After all, she was my mom's mother. They had the same blood. Could they not have the same tendency to abandon me for no reason? I was scared that if I did go to see her, she'd turn me away and confirm everything my father said.

I couldn't take that kind of hurt again.

Years passed, and I shoved those memories to the back of my brain. I hardly thought of Vergie.

But then she died. Alone, for all I knew. And then I hated myself for not visiting her. Dad wouldn't even go to the funeral with me. I stood in the back of the church because I didn't want everyone talking to me like I knew her so well, her only grandchild. The little chapel was packed with people—easily a hundred—all fanning themselves in the heat. The whole time I felt like an impostor, and I had a headache for days from the tears. I didn't go to her house because I knew all those people would be there, swapping stories over dinner. I couldn't bear hearing all the things about her I'd missed out on.

We didn't find out until weeks later that she'd left the house to me. I thought the lawyers were mistaken, but it was true. And that made me feel worse than anything.

Dad was probably right to want to sell it—when would I ever be down there? The truth was, I didn't care about flipping it to turn a profit. I felt like I owed her: Repairing her house would be a kind of homage. The potential profit was just a way to get my father on board and let me use his resources.

Besides, it would do me good to get out of town for a while and go back to a place that had good memories tied to it.

My father's eyes narrowed. "You aren't going to go down there and get all attached are you? We don't have time for nostalgia."

"I want to turn this house around just as fast as you do."

"Then you won't have a hard time parting with it," he said, pushing his glasses up on his nose. With his gelled hair and oxford shirt, he looked like he belonged more on a used car lot than in a remodeling business. "I know you like to hang onto things that need fixing," he said, his eyebrow arched.

True, I took in strays. I dated men who were broken, hoping to mend their fatal flaws. Everyone has one, of course, but while my father chose to write people off because of their flaws, I urged my partners to overcome them. I took a lot of risks and failed more than I succeeded (with men, not renovations), but there's a science there, right? A law of averages. You fail enough, you succeed in the long run. Dad liked to hold this habit over my head. He wanted me to settle down with a reliable guy who could balance his checkbook and pay a mortgage on time. But every time I sought out reliable, it backfired. My last boyfriend had been a banker, but then he quit to be a writer. I'd let him stay with me, rent-free, while he tried to build up a freelance business, burning through his savings. I thought I was being supportive, but my father called him a moocher. When we finally broke up, my father said, *See what a waste of time and money that was?*

My father thought my propensity to fix people was a weakness. But he thought my inclination to fix houses was lucrative.

Houses were easy because you figure out what's broken, add the cost of materials plus the cost of labor, then factor in a little patience over time. Unlike men, renovations were something I could calculate.

"You said yourself you've got too much going on up here," I said. "Besides, we'll have squatters if we wait too long."

He stared for a long moment, then leaned back in his chair. Those were the magic words. My father despised freeloaders. "Fine. I'll give you six weeks. That should be plenty of time for that house."

"Six weeks," I said, wondering if he would actually trust me to finish on my own. A perfectionist to the core, he loved to show up halfway through a project and take over completely, arguing that his way was more cost-effective, more efficient. I hated that about him. Sometimes it was easier on everybody if he just came into the project in the beginning. It would save me a car load of aspirin and whiskey. But I was hoping this time he would leave me alone.

"This will give you the chance to see if you love this job as much as you think you do," he said, chewing on the tip of his pen.

I wanted it to spill blue ink down his lip.

"And this way you get to be the boss." He winked, then circled a day on his calendar. "Now, let's get your flight booked."

"Fair enough," I agreed. "But no planes—I'll drive."

He frowned and gave me a look of zero faith. "Right out the gate, wasting time."

"Saving money," I said. "No rental car."

"Try to stay focused down there, will you? Don't get distracted by anything else that needs fixing."

"Will do."

He reached for the phone and said, "Would you excuse me so I can get back to work here?" He was already dialing before I got to the door.

I stopped. "Why do you think she left the house to me?"

He sighed and laid his glasses on the desk. "Who could ever explain Vergie? She was nutty as a fruitcake." There was that unreadable look again. What was he hiding?

"I'll call when I get there, Dad."

"Bonne chance," he said, arching that eyebrow again. "You're gonna need all the luck you can get."

The door slammed behind me. I didn't need luck, and I was going to prove it.

CRANKING the radio up was the perfect antidote for a conversation with my father. I couldn't carry a tune in a bucket, but I figured that's why they made car radios—so people like me can blow off steam while driving through four states that look exactly alike and try to forget our fathers' lack of faith in us.

I'd spent the night somewhere in east Mississippi, in a motel that served moon pies and instant coffee as continental breakfast. It was a blessing I was exhausted when I checked in—I didn't notice much about the place and was able to sleep the peaceful slumber of a person ignorant of potential health hazards. Ordinarily, I wouldn't stay in a place like the Teddy Bear Motel, but around midnight, I'd finally gotten too tired to keep driving. It was the only place around. So I'd stripped the comforter off the bed, skipped the shower and brushed my teeth quickly, not staring too hard at the sink or counter. Too much scrutiny of that place and I'd itch all the way to Bayou Sabine.

A little after noon, it was already scorching. I cursed myself for not getting the Jeep's air conditioning fixed back in the spring. With the windows down, I tried to convince myself the heat wasn't so bad, but my clothes were sticking to me. The land around me had shifted from rolling hills to marshland, and at last I felt like I was out of my father's orbit. I was thinking less of him and more about those summers I'd spent at the big blue house on the bayou, Vergie teaching me to play poker while we sat on the porch. Starting in grade school, I'd visit her for nearly three months every June when school let out. It was my favorite time of the year. I could run around barefoot and go swimming in the creek at night, and I didn't have to be ladylike—ever. With Vergie, life seemed more magical. Anything was possible when I was with her.

As I opened the last moon pie I'd smuggled from the motel, I was hit with a flash from years before.

Vergie and I were sitting on a quilt in one of the old cemeteries, back in a corner under an oak tree with limbs that undulated along the ground like tentacles. She was telling me ghost stories while we had tea and beignets, the powdered sugar clinging to our noses. We sat still as tombstones while a funeral procession passed, the people dancing as music filled the whole sky.

"Why are those people having such a good time?" I asked. "Isn't that a funeral?"

"That's the grandest way you can say goodbye to someone," Vergie said.

Vergie's own funeral had been tame compared to the scene

that day, and now I felt bad that we hadn't given her a send-off like that one. She would have appreciated that, and I would have remembered if I hadn't stayed away so long.

Why had it taken me fifteen years to come back?

I turned my thoughts back to the house as I crossed the state line. Six weeks wasn't much time.

I pulled off the interstate onto a smaller highway. From there on, the roads would get narrower until they carried me into the little community of Bayou Sabine. I vaguely remembered the way, but with all the canals out here, the roads start to look the same. It's beautiful—don't get me wrong—but if you were to turn me around three times and plop me down in the middle of this marshland, I'd likely never see North Carolina again.

I checked the GPS on my phone, but the road wasn't showing up.

"Oh, come on," I said, swiping my thumb across the screen. The red dot that was supposed to be me was now off the nearest named road. According to the GPS, I was in a bayou. I glanced up at the road, trying to get my bearings and not swerve into the water for real.

Signal lost, it said. I groaned, restarting the app. When I looked up, an alligator was lumbering across the road—all six feet of him stretched across my lane.

"Oh, hell!" I slammed the brake to the floor, flinching as the tires squealed and the Jeep fish-tailed. I bit my lip so hard I tasted blood, and I called that gator everything but a child of God. I expected to hear a terrible thud at any second. Swerving, I missed him by just a few inches, but I was close enough to see his catlike eye as I shot across the opposite lane and onto the shoulder. Off to my left, there was nothing but swamp and black mud. I gripped the wheel, fighting to stay on the hard ground.

The Jeep stopped on what felt like solid earth, the weeds as high as the door handle. My heart hammered in my chest. Vergie used to tell me old voodoo legends about alligators, how they were tricksters, always causing trouble.

Please don't be stuck. Not out here.

My foot eased the gas pedal down, and the Jeep inched forward. The tires spun as I pushed harder. "This is not happening."

A rusty pickup rumbled toward me. The driver gave me a long look, but he hardly slowed down. I nudged the Jeep into four wheel drive and turned the tires as I hit the gas. It rocked a few times, then lurched forward and caught hold of the grass before crossing onto the pavement. I glanced back to where the alligator had crossed, but it was gone.

"Welcome back," I muttered to myself.

THE OLD TWO-LANE highway cut the land in half, with swamps on one side and pastures on the other. With the black water so close, I felt like the earth might open up and devour me at will. The trees were full of moss, the water creeping up their trunks like it was swallowing them.

I passed Vergie's driveway the first time, not recognizing it until I caught a glimpse of the pale blue goose she'd left by the mailbox like a sentinel. The paint was peeling, but the goose stood firmly in a patch of daylilies, just as it had since I was a girl. I turned around and eased onto the dirt drive. I felt the hollow in my chest expand, the void Vergie had left.

Cypress trees lined the road to the house, their limbs curling toward the ground. The breeze tickled the drooping leaves of the trees, and in the distance I heard the faint clink of glass, like a wind chime. Just beyond the house stood a spirit tree, bottles hanging from its branches like Christmas ornaments. It had been there long before Vergie, but she had added a few herself after drinking pints of bourbon and gin. She used to tell me those bottles captured evil spirits, kept them from roaming through the bayou and attaching themselves to good folks that lived nearby. I'd never really believed they held ghosts, but I liked the sound of the wind whistling over the lips of the bottles. Now, as the light glinted blue and green in the leaves of the tree, the sound felt more melancholy than soothing.

This place had a wildness that was hard not to like. It smelled sweet like magnolia, bitter like the swamp. Egrets dotted the trees like blooms of cotton, preening themselves in the slivers of sunlight. The driveway wound back into the woods, hidden from the main road. Patches of gravel mixed with the soil, packed hard from the heat and drought. When at last I pulled into the yard, I was surprised at how small the house seemed compared to my memory of it. It was still plenty big at two stories high, but it was a paler shade of blue than I remembered, and the roof was missing some shingles. The porch was cluttered with potted flowers, strings of lights hanging from the eaves, and a hammock strung between two corner posts. I could almost see Vergie's silhouette in the rocker, and I knew then that I was going to prove my father wrong.

I had to. I owed it to Vergie. This place was a part of her, and it was a part of me now too. I had to do this right.

It wasn't until I saw a pair of feet dangling from the hammock that I noticed the truck parked under a tree at the edge of the yard. A small dark pickup with patches of rust like spots on a horse. I squinted at the feet, thinking surely I was seeing something that wasn't there. But there was no mistaking the shape in the hammock, the lazy swinging motion.

I leapt from the car and slammed the door so hard that a head rose above the banister. My father had dealt with squatters once or twice, but I hadn't thought they'd move in so fast. Striding toward the steps, I cursed myself for not coming by when I was in town for the funeral.

I tried to cool my temper and concentrated on the sound of my boot heels pounding the dirt. There was no turning back now, because the man had definitely seen me.

He sat up in the hammock, and I swallowed hard as I reached the steps.

Chapter Two

THE MAN'S hair was rumpled, as if he'd slept in that hammock all night. His shirt, rolled at the wrists, was pushed up just enough from his pants that I could see a thin band of tan skin above his belt. He appeared to be only a few years older than me, but had tiny wrinkles around his eyes and lips that suggested he'd spent more time in the sun. And he looked familiar. My mind raced, trying to figure out where I'd seen him before.

"Hi there," he said, sitting up straight. "Are you lost?"

"No," I said, planting my hands on my hips. *Be calm,* I thought. *This doesn't have to get ugly.*

"I don't get too many visitors. I figured you took a wrong turn off the main road. You'd have to be lost to end up out here." His drawl made my ears tingle in a nice way, but the way he lounged in the hammock like he owned the place made me want to push him out of it head first.

"How about you tell me who you are," I said. "And what you're doing here."

He sat up straighter, running his hands through his dark hair. It was short, but stood out in tufts, as if the wind had pulled it through the holes in the hammock. "I believe it's customary for the interloper to identify herself to the current inhabitant," he said, half-smiling. "Not the other way around."

"This is my house," I said, trying to hold my temper down. "So that makes you the interloper."

He chuckled. "Darlin', I think you've got me confused with somebody else that lives in the middle of nowhere. Who are you looking for?" His tone was even, as if this kind of encounter happened every week.

"I'm not looking for a who," I said. "I'm looking for a house. This house. And last I checked, I didn't have any long-lost cousins living in it."

He glanced around him. "Well, one of us is in the wrong place. And it ain't me." His dark blue eyes held me in a warm gaze that in any other situation would make me want to lean in closer.

"This is my grandmother's house," I said, no longer caring when or where I might have seen him before. The priority was my property.

He cocked his head. "You mean Vergie?" His eyes lit up. "Well, why didn't you say so, darlin'?" He eased out of the hammock as slow as a river. Even his voice swaggered, and I imagined what it would sound like against my ear.

I shook my head to erase the thought.

When he stood, he smoothed his shirt down against his body. Tall and muscular, he towered over me, and I'm no small woman. His shirt was snug against his broad shoulders, pulled taut across his biceps. He held out his hand, smiling like I was some long lost friend, and in spite of myself, I shook it.

"I'm Jack Mayronne," he said. His big hand squeezed mine, and I swallowed hard as something that felt like static electricity rippled down my arm.

"Enza Parker," I said, struggling to keep my voice firm. "You knew my grandmother?" The nagging feeling returned. Where had I seen him? At this house when I was a teenager? Recently, when I was back for the funeral? I'd blocked so many of those images from my mind, and right now was not the time to try to recover them.

His thumb slid along my palm, and I saw a tattoo peeking out from under the sleeve of his shirt, a black curve like a snake. I wondered how far up it went.

"Sure," he said, holding my hand a little too long. "She was a fine lady. And if you come from that stock, I guess you're all right."

"That still doesn't explain what you're doing in her house."

He grinned, shoving his hands into his pockets. He looked like he could have come from a rodeo, in his faded jeans and plaid pearl-snap shirt. "You're just as feisty as she was, aren't you? I always liked that about her."

I felt my cheeks redden, and I hoped he didn't notice. Maybe he'd think it was the heat. After all, summer in Louisiana feels like being inside an oven.

"I've been renting this place for several months now," he said. A dog crossed the yard and trotted over. It lifted one ear toward the sound of Jack's voice and then sat by his feet. "Hey, jolie," he said, bending down to pat her on the head. She was stocky, and speckled brown and gray like granite, with expressive ears and a docked tail. Her eyes narrowed in my direction, and she let out a half-hearted bark.

"A Catahoula," I said, holding my hand out for her to sniff.

"Yeah," Jack said, and she snorted.

"The lawyer never mentioned anyone renting this house," I said.

"Probably didn't know. Vergie had only been living in the city for about six months. She let me stay here for practically nothing, just so it wouldn't sit empty."

"In the city?"

"She was staying in New Orleans with a friend," he said, still stroking the dog's fur. "Didn't you know?"

"We were out of touch for a long time."

"I was awful sad to hear about her," he said. "They broke the mold when they made Vergie."

It bothered me that he knew more about my own grandmother than I did. And it hurt when I thought about how I'd avoided this place for so long, how I'd gone so many years without seeing the woman who had been like a second mother to me. I pushed the regrets away to stop my voice from cracking. "I spent every summer here when I was a kid," I said, sitting down next to him on the porch steps.

Ordinarily, I wouldn't let my guard down with a stranger, but the drive and the humidity had left me weak. With no breeze, the air was stifling, and I was grateful for any patch of shade.

"Me, too," he said. "I mean, I used to work for her. Started when I was about seventeen."

"Really?"

"Yard work and odd jobs. She was trying to keep me out of trouble, I think."

I smiled, wondering if that was true.

"Strange," he said. "We could have met years ago. Wouldn't that be something?" He stared at me for a while, like he might recognize me.

Maybe that was it... I glanced away.

The dog pressed her nose against my thigh. She squinted at me and then dropped her head on my knee as I scratched her ears.

"You all right?" he asked. "You look a little pale." He set those eyes on me again, and I felt like I'd burn up right there on the porch. He seemed to genuinely care, despite the fact that I'd accused him of trespassing.

"It's the heat," I said. "I'm not used to it any more."

He smiled, revealing dimples that were made for disarming people like me. "Where are you coming from?"

"Raleigh." My eyes drifted to the inside of his forearm, to his tattoo. I had a soft spot for tattoos—especially the kind only partially revealed by clothing. I didn't want him to catch me staring, though, so I looked back to the dog, who had started to drool on my knee. Apparently she'd decided I was no longer a threat.

"How about a glass of water?" he asked, touching my arm.

"Sure, thanks."

He stared at me like he thought I might faint. "It's a hot one today. I'd bring you inside, but the A/C units have been acting up, blowing fuses every chance they get. I'm trying to give them a rest."

I leaned against the stair railing, feeling light-headed.

"At least out here there's a breeze," he said. He disappeared into the house, leaving me on the porch. I pictured myself sitting in a rocker with Vergie, sipping tea and eating macaroons. It didn't seem possible that someone else could live here now.

"Here you go, chère," Jack said, sitting next to me again.

chère. I fought back a smile, thinking that was likely his way of getting anything he wanted from a woman. There probably weren't many that could turn down the likes of him.

Jack's knee brushed mine, and I instinctively moved my leg away. "You know you have to leave," I said. I tried to be as nice as possible while standing my ground. Being a landlord was not anywhere on my to-do list.

"Usually it takes longer for women to tell me that."

"Sorry," I told him. "I'm no good at evicting people."

"Then don't," he said, his voice light. He smiled again.

"I'm not in the business of renting. I'm here to fix this house and sell it. I'm afraid that means you have to leave."

"But I live here," he said. "You know how hard it is to find nice places out this way?"

"Didn't you think that when the landlady died, you should start looking for a new house?" I leaned against the banister, fanning myself. "I'm sorry that this comes as a surprise to you, but I've got no other option."

He shrugged. "I'd paid Miss Vergie up through the next few months. I figured I had a couple more weeks to worry about moving."

I tried to wrap my head around the logic of that. It was hard to give him a firm glare when he gazed at me with those woeful eyes.

Like a calf in a hailstorm, Vergie would have said.

"How about if I refund your rent?"

He ran his hands through his hair. "How about you keep renting to me," he suggested.

I laughed but then saw he was serious. "I'm no landlord, Mr. Mayronne. I don't have time for that kind of responsibility."

"How hard can it be, chère? You just collect a check now and then."

"I don't live around here. I can't keep this place up."

"I've been keeping it up just fine." He sounded insulted. "You think I called Miss Vergie every time a pipe burst? I've been fixing things up all the while. You wouldn't need to be nearby."

The place did look OK, but he'd done some half-assed repairs. A couple of boards on the porch were unfinished, recently replaced. The paint on the door and window sills was fresher than the rest, making the older paint look dirty. The inside was probably peppered with spots that needed a matching coat of paint or a few finishing nails. People were constantly doing do-it-yourself repairs only halfway, which always meant more work for me.

"You'll have to find another place," I said.

The dog sat up, ears flat.

"But Enza, you can't just kick me out." His eyes were bright blue, but they flashed darker as he became flushed. When the light hit them, I saw little flecks of green, and I wanted to lean in for a better look. I was helpless around good-looking, charming guys like him, and I knew if he caught on to that, he'd try anything to stay.

I set the glass of water on the ground and stood so I could glare down at him. "I'm the owner, Mr. Mayronne. I can do whatever I want." He might have been a friend of Vergie's, but that didn't mean he'd have her roof over his head for the rest of his life.

The dog growled, deep in her throat, and wiggled her haunches. Jack pointed a finger at her, and she stopped. "Come on, chère," he said. "I don't want any trouble. But I don't want to be out of a home, either."

"Look, this isn't personal. This is running a business."

He stood then, rising a head higher than me. "This is not what your grandmother would want," he said calmly.

I climbed to the top step to look him in the eye again. "How would you know what she'd want?" I leaned closer. "How dare you."

"Because she was thoughtful and considerate," he said, standing so close I could see those stupid green flecks in his eyes, "and she wouldn't kick a man out into the cold."

"I don't think you have to worry about the cold around here."

He leaned against the banister. "I signed a lease, you know. I'm supposed to have a few months left."

"There's a loophole for death of the landlord. Those are standard." I glared at him until he finally looked away.

He paced across the porch. His broad shoulders drooped as he shoved his hands in his pockets. I felt bad for the guy, but there wasn't an easy way out of this. As Jack Mayronne scratched his stubbly chin, he reminded me of the last man I fell in love with. He used to scratch his chin like that when he was deep in thought. I could still feel the roughness of his cheek against my skin. The thought made me shiver.

I shoved the thought away. Right now I needed to focus on fixing this house and proving my father was wrong about me. *You've got no follow-through, Enza,* he liked to say all too often. I told myself that was just boredom—if I could finish projects fast enough, then I wouldn't push details aside. Even though Dad was a big-picture man, he loved zooming in on the details and using them to point out my weaknesses.

I hated him for that, but I feared he might be right. Fixing this house, though, would prove I wasn't as weak-willed as he liked to think. That would be one delicious moment.

But first I had to get rid of this man who seemed as rooted here as the cypress in the backyard.

"Surely we can come to some kind of agreement," he said.

"Yes. You can leave as soon as possible."

"How long will it take you to fix this place up like you want it?"

I studied the peeling paint, the hedges that were overtaking the rails. "What difference does that make?"

"Come on. Humor me."

"I couldn't say without seeing the inside."

"So let's take a tour." He pushed the front door open and motioned for me to go in. The dog raced through ahead of us.

Before I could argue, he led me inside by the elbow. He could easily bash me over the head, but if I wanted to see the house, my options were limited. This seemed to be the only peaceful way. And I felt it would be a mistake to get him angry. People often get defensive about their homes, and I needed to stay on Jack Mayronne's good side.

"How about you let me stay—just while you fix things up," he said. "That should give me enough time to find another place."

I barely heard him as we walked down the hallway into the kitchen. I saw myself at twelve years old, sitting at the table playing checkers with Vergie, both of us wearing frilly old dresses, sipping imaginary mint juleps and fanning ourselves with antique lace fans. The room was plainer now, with straight lace sheers over the windows. But the old table and chairs remained.

"Most of her stuff is still here," he said. "She rented it furnished, and I travel light."

I felt a pang of guilt. How could I not know she was living some place other than her home?

"So you're Martine's daughter, then?" he asked.

I stopped. "How do you know my mother?"

He turned toward me, biting his lip like he wished he could take those words back, then said, "Just from Vergie talking about her sometimes."

The thought of him knowing about my mother left me dumbstruck. I followed him through the house in a trance, sorting out what was real and what was not.

He led me through the living room, the back bedroom and the sitting room, and I tried to remember the last time I talked to Vergie. The few times I'd prodded my father to explain why I couldn't see her any more, he had quickly changed the subject. After my mother left, the summer visits had stopped. Why had I cut all ties simply because my father had? At sixteen, I could have called her. I could have written letters. I could have stood up to my father.

Why had I never stood up for what I wanted?

The dog was at my heels, her eyes fixed on me.

"Don't mind Bella," Jack said. "She's just trying to herd us."

"What?"

"It's what old swamp dogs do. Stop you from getting lost forever."

Her bobbed tail wagged.

I followed Jack as he climbed the stairs, distracted by the sway in his shoulders and his hips. He had an easy way about him, but he seemed as solid as the earth beneath us. His hands were solid too—those of a man who knew exactly what he was capable of, exactly how he could mold bare materials into what he wanted.

I loved feeling hands like those on my skin.

"There's a good bit to be done here, I guess," he said, pausing in the upstairs hallway. "I helped her with small things, like the cabinets and floors, but I didn't get into any big projects."

The banister was cool under my fingers. It was as big around as my thigh, carved in a Victorian style with simple lines. The spindles were square, not those dainty round ones that most people went for.

"I could probably be done in a couple of weeks," I said,

peeking into the first upstairs bedroom. The bed was made up with a patchwork quilt, an antique desk and chair by the window. The curtains rippled like water in the breeze. It looked like it had been empty for years.

He laughed, shaking his head. "A couple of weeks? You won't find people around here who'll work that fast."

"No people. Just me."

He stopped cold. "You're going to fix all of this by yourself?"

"Sure." I wandered through the next room, a makeshift study and library. When I turned back to him, he was slack-jawed.

"What, you've never seen a woman fix a house?" I get a kick out of watching people's reactions when I tell them what I do. It was like the idea of a woman wielding a hammer and paintbrush for purposes that didn't include hanging pictures or painting with watercolor was too much to fathom. "I do this for a living," I said.

His mouth curled into a crooked smile that must have broken half the hearts in the parish. "Guess they don't make many like you any more, either," he said.

"I was sort of a tomboy growing up."

"Could have fooled me." His eyes drifted down to my feet, then back up to meet mine.

That look made me more aware of how my clothes stuck to me in this relentless heat. Not expecting to meet a soul today, I'd thrown on a thin camp-style shirt and an old pair of jeans with holes in the knees. Clothes were one of those details Dad claimed I overlooked. I rolled the sleeves up higher and placed my hands on my hips, staring him down.

"I wouldn't have taken you for the manual labor type," he said.

"I still like to get dirty. Some things never change."

He smiled and motioned for me to follow him down the hall. I noted the cracks in the plaster, the ancient light fixtures with their painted glass, the way Jack's broad shoulders strained the seams of his shirt.

His playfulness was disarming. He was so good-natured, even

when he was about to be evicted. It felt easy to be with him, and
for me that was rare.

"I think I have the answer," he said, leading me toward the
back bedrooms. "It's win-win. You'll like it."

"Go on." One of the remaining bedrooms had a bed and
dresser, an antique highboy with ball-and-claw feet. The last room
was empty of furniture but full of boxes.

"How about I stay here while you do whatever work you need
to do, and then you can turn me out into the cold, gator-infested
bayou. While I'm here, I'll help you with the repairs. I'm pretty
good with hammers and miter saws and whatnot."

"What makes you think I need any more hands?" Especially
those hands, which I too easily envisioned gripping my hips
instead of a hammer.

He led me back down the stairs. "Simple math. If, instead of
you doing all this by yourself, you have me, then the work gets
done twice as fast."

"Assuming you can take orders. And assuming your work is
top-notch."

"Well, of course. And I figure you're going to need somebody
who knows all the locals—what if you need a plumber or an
electrician? You need a sub-contractor who can tell you who's
reliable and who's gonna rip you off."

"Good point, but there's still one problem. I was going to stay
here while I worked."

He raised an eyebrow.

"I can't stay here if you're here. And hotels will cost a fortune.
That's not in the budget."

He nodded toward the upstairs. "You can stay here. It's not
like we're short on rooms."

I laughed. "Stay here with you? Not a chance."

"What? I won't bite you, chère." He walked back onto the
porch, pulled a cigarette from his pocket and lit it with a match.
"Miss Vergie trusted me. You can trust me too."

"Bless her heart, but Grandma Vergie was a little bit nuts," I said.

She used to take in strays too—hell, that's probably where I got my inclination. She was one of those kind souls who never locked her doors and always trusted everybody to do right. I was slower to trust people and let them get close. I'd learned over and over that when you let people get close, they hurt you. They leave you. Friends said I was guarded, but to me that was just watching out for yourself. It made life less painful.

He shook the match, and the scent of sulfur and cloves filled the air between us. "I'll make you a deal," he said, holding his hand up in a Boy Scout salute. "If I misbehave, you can banish me to the couch at the firehouse. That's incentive enough to be good, believe me."

"The firehouse?"

He nodded. "Engine Six. On the other side of the canal."

"I wouldn't have taken you for a firefighter."

He stroked his chin. "Why, because of my squeaky-clean exterior?"

I tried to picture him in a fire truck. He seemed too laid back to squeeze himself into a state-regulated uniform.

"Can't a guy look a little rough around the edges on his day off?"

When I didn't reply, he said, "I get it. You think I'm just another hooligan trying to pull a fast one. You want to see my shield?"

"Actually, I do."

He pulled his wallet from his back pocket and flipped it open. A flash of brass caught my eye.

"Still, I don't even know you," I said, leaning against the porch rail. "I'm not in the habit of moving in with strange men."

"Well, I'm not accustomed to taking in strange women," he said. "But I'm willing to concede in order to help both of us out of a sticky situation. This way, you get to do your job, and I keep a roof over my head."

"Can't you stay at the firehouse for a few weeks?"

His eyebrows rose as he took a long drag on the cigarette. "It's kind of crowded right now," he said. "Got a few guys in the dog house and such. Happens about this time every year."

"In June?"

"I don't understand it, either."

"You have a copy of the lease?" I asked.

"Sure," he said. "It's around here somewhere."

"I'd like to see it."

He nodded, crushing the cigarette into the step. In the kitchen, he rooted through a drawer by the stove.

"I can't do this if I don't know anything about you," I said.

"OK," he said, thumbing through the papers. "Fair enough."

"I have questions."

He smiled. "I have answers."

I poured myself another glass of water. He stepped away from the drawer just long enough to pull a chair out from the table for me, like it was a reflex. The gesture struck me as tender, and then I realized why he seemed familiar.

"You were at the funeral," I said. Even though I'd banished the details from my mind, at unexpected moments, they would come pouring back.

He glanced up from the stack of papers and fixed his dark blue eyes on me. I remembered those eyes.

"You gave your seat to two little old ladies," I said.

He cocked his head and smiled. "You're the one that ran out in the storm. I was talking to your friend before she went after you."

I cringed at the memory. I'd been overwhelmed thinking about my mom leaving, Vergie dying and the possibility of running into my mother there. I'd dashed out of the church into a thunderstorm and stood on the lawn in the pouring rain until my friend Kate came out and dragged me to the car.

"You cut your hair," I said. "I didn't recognize you."

He shrugged. "It's OK. I didn't recognize you dry."

"I can't believe it's you," I said.

"I believe you had some questions for me."

It was easy to see why Vergie liked him. He was one of those guys who made you want to bake him a cake, who made you smile at bad pick-up lines. Some people just have a way about them that makes the world seem a little brighter. Vergie had also been one of those people.

"So you've been working for Vergie since you were seventeen?" I asked.

"Off and on." As he leaned against the table, it squeaked under his weight. "Started out doing odd jobs, then did more repairs when I got older. I'd come by and check on her a couple times a week and do whatever she needed done."

I watched his eyes to determine if he was lying. I was a good judge of character, but I'd been wrong once or twice, and it had made me gun shy, particularly when it came to smooth-talking, good-looking men.

"How long have you worked for the fire department?"

"Six years."

"Why did you come check on Vergie every week?"

"She looked out for me," he said. "So I looked out for her. It's what we do around here." He handed me the lease. "Here you go."

I turned to the back page and found Vergie's signature. Indeed, he had paid in advance. I searched for a clause that would void the lease upon the landlord's death, but there was none.

If what Jack said was true, how had I never seen him at the house all the summers I'd visited? He couldn't have been more than a couple of years older than me, and I would have remembered a teenage guy hanging around the house—especially when I was so boy-crazy I could hardly see straight.

According to the lease, he'd been renting six months. "What do you do besides fight fires?" I asked.

His fingers traced the stubble on his neck, until they disappeared in the collar of his shirt. When he spoke, he stared right at me, as if he was reading me just as carefully. "For work or play?"

I wondered if those terrible lines worked on women down here, or if they were reserved for out-of-towners who could be lulled into anything with a wink and a drawl.

"Either," I said.

"Nothing that's too embarrassing or impressive, chère." He half-smiled and opened the kitchen door, leading me back to the porch. We sat down on the steps. "But listen," he said, pulling a cigarette out, "you'll be safe here with me. And believe me, if you weren't, everybody in the parish would know about it, because everybody knows everybody's business out here on the bayou."

"Think I could bum one of those?" I nodded toward his cigarette.

"You're in luck… My last pack and then I quit."

He tapped another out, then leaned close as he cupped his hands around the match and lit the clove. I glanced up and caught his eyes for a moment through the smoke.

Clearly this had the potential for disaster—the kind that had nothing to do with the house. "Thanks," I said. "You were making me want one."

"So do I pass?"

I liked his quiet confidence. His eyes had a sleepy look about them, but there was a sharpness behind them as well—something that said I shouldn't mistake his easygoing manner for ignorance.

"Did you spend much time with her?" I asked him.

He smiled. "When she started renting to me, she came by to see me every Sunday. She said she was checking on the house, but I knew she was checking up on me. Your grandmother made a mean chicken pot pie."

"You knew her better than I did in the end." I wondered what they talked about, what he knew about her. If I let him stick around, I'd find out. That thought finally swayed me.

"I don't have much family of my own," he said. "She adopted me, you might say."

I could have been the one hearing all of Vergie's stories, instead of Jack Mayronne. If only I hadn't been so scared of my father.

"Come on, Enza," he said. "People here have boarders all the time. You're just renting me a room like anybody else would do if they had a big old house like this to themselves."

I took a long drag on the cigarette, watching the line of smoke rise toward the white porch ceiling. If Vergie trusted him to help her around the house, then he must be a decent man. She was always looking for the good in people, but she could spot the bad as quick as she spotted potato beetles in her garden.

I made a silent plea, hoping that wherever Vergie was, she could reach out and intervene if I was about to do something stupid. I waited for an instant, just in case a pipe burst or a vase went flying off the mantle as a kind of thump on the skull from the great hereafter. But there was nothing.

"Here's the deal, Mr. Mayronne. You help me with repairs, and I'll give you six weeks to move out. If we finish before then, I'll refund your rent for the remaining days."

"What if it takes longer?"

"It won't."

"I could help you if it does," he said. "I owe a lot to Vergie. I'm not saying I can work for free, but I'll do you a better deal than anybody else around here."

"Six weeks is all I need," I said. "But if you like, we'll leave that option on the table."

"Fair enough," he said, extending his hand.

When we shook, his fingers tightened around mine, and a ripple passed through my arms and chest, like when a pebble is dropped in a pond.

He smiled. "This'll all work out fine. You'll see."

I almost believed him.

Chapter Three

AFTER HAULING my tool box and suitcases into the foyer, I paused at the bottom of the stairs to give the banister a shake. It was sturdy as a water oak. That was the thing about these old swamp houses: The plaster was cracking, and the walls weren't straight any more, but the woodwork was solid. The floors were made of heart pine boards eight inches wide. The ten-foot ceilings downstairs had carved crown molding that made my heart flutter. The upstairs bath had a clawfoot tub and a stained glass window that I wanted to cut out and take home with me. If those details had registered with me as a teenager, they'd been lost in the ether of young adulthood. In my memory, this had been a quaint little farm-style house—cute, but nothing special. Now, seeing its pocket doors and hand-carved moldings, I was smitten.

Stop, I told myself. *This has to be just another flip.*

Jack walked in behind me and grabbed my suitcases. "Let me give you a hand with that."

I followed him up to Vergie's old bedroom. Of the rooms upstairs, this one was the most furnished. It had the dresser, the highboy and the four-poster bed. Framed pictures hung over a vanity by the closet door, and books were stacked on the shelf of the nightstand.

Jack set the suitcases by the dresser and then opened two windows to get a cross-breeze. "Sorry it's so stuffy in here," he said. "I'll put the extra window unit in here so you won't melt."

"When I was a girl, I used to sneak in here to play," I told him. "I don't know why it seemed so magical at the time, but it was like Alice's rabbit hole."

Back then, I'd rummage through the closet and pick through the dresser drawers, but Vergie didn't mind. Her room had been a shrine to her travels, the shelves filled with trinkets from places I'd never heard of. Now, as I studied the dark wood and faded wallpaper, it looked like any old bedroom. The mystery had slipped away.

"I left everything in this room alone," Jack said.

"How come?"

"She told me to box everything up in here when I moved in, but I couldn't bring myself to do it." He leaned against the post of the canopy bed, ran his fingers along the carved vines. "I didn't need the space."

A collection of pictures sat by the lamp on the nightstand: a couple of me, and two black and white photos of my mother that I hadn't seen before. To me, my mother was a ghost. It was as if she'd vanished—*poof!*—like a dove under a magician's handkerchief. Dad refused to talk about her—ever.

I didn't forget about her, because how can you, really? But I tried.

After she left, Dad found ways to keep me busy in the summer so I wouldn't have time to think of those summers with Vergie. Jobs, college prep courses, internships. He scared me into thinking I needed all of those things to even dream of success, so I did what he told me. He said I was too old to do nothing in the summer, that if I didn't start working toward a goal, I'd end up as lost as my mother.

He used my mother as a threat.

Now, standing in this room that both was and was not Vergie's, it made me wonder: Had Vergie ever tried to see me, or had she quietly given in to my father's wishes? He could be cruel. He could sniff out people's weaknesses and drive them away, and he could have easily done that to Vergie.

I felt the pang that comes when you know you've done something terrible, and there's no real way to fix it.

I traced my fingers over a patchwork quilt that Vergie had almost certainly made. It was mostly blue and green, the log cabin pattern. The floorboards creaked when I walked across the room to the closet, where a half a dozen dresses still clung to wire hangers.

"This seemed bigger when I was a kid," I said.

"Things always do." Jack opened the drawer of the nightstand and handed me a key. His fingers brushed over my palm as he placed it there. "In case you want to lock yourself in."

"Thanks." I slipped the key into my pocket.

"I've got some leftovers downstairs," he said. "Nothing fancy, but it's better than going into town after driving all day."

"You're cooking me dinner?"

He smirked, heading back to the stairs. "I'm reheating your dinner. I'd take you to one of the local haunts, but I don't think you're ready for that crowd yet."

"Just as well," I said. "The last thing I want to do right now is get in a car." I followed him down the stairs, watching as the light caught flecks of red in his hair.

In the kitchen, Jack pulled a chair out from the table and motioned for me to sit. The floors were scuffed from these same spindle-backed chairs being dragged out from the table over the years. It was a small kitchen, but it had a walk-in pantry with floor-to-ceiling built-in cabinets. You just didn't see that any more.

Jack leaned over, rooting through the refrigerator. The clatter of pots caught my attention, but what held it was the way his jeans strained ever so slightly on his frame.

He put the pot on the stove and caught me staring.

I quickly looked away, my cheeks burning.

"Hope you like chili," he said. "I cook pretty simple."

"I won't complain when a guy's cooking dinner."

He stirred the chili and pulled two beers from the refrigerator. "Care for a drink?"

"After that drive today? You bet."

He hooked the caps together, popping both off at the same time like bartenders do when they're trying to impress. He passed me the beer, clinked his against it and said, "Here's to homecomings."

His knee brushed mine as he sat down across from me. His eyes looked as blue-green as the bottles, and I found myself staring too long again.

"I know this must be little strange for you," he said.

"It wasn't what I was expecting."

"Few things around here are."

The white cabinets were chipped and stained, but the appliances were still in good shape. The sink was original—a huge one that extended into countertops, with grooves to channel the water from drying dishes back into the basin. The old pie safe was still in the corner, where Vergie used to keep her pies, and later her cookbooks. Patterns of stars and triangles were punched in the tin panels.

"I miss this place," I said. "Didn't realize how much until today."

"When's the last time you were here?"

"I was sixteen. I can't believe it's been fifteen years." The dog, Bella, wandered back into the room and sat down at my feet. She stared at me, as if still deciding whether I was a threat. "I should have come back to visit more. I should have ignored my father."

He cocked his head.

"Long story," I said, waving my hand between us. "He forbade me to come back here, and I was too young and stupid to rebel."

"It's hard to see what's really important when you're that age. Sometimes you still can't see it when you've grown up."

"Is this where you tell me your family's just as messed up as mine?"

"My parents died a long time ago."

"Shit. I'm sorry. I only meant—"

"It's OK," he said, getting up to stir the chili. "It just taught me you have to get your priorities in order. Be honest in your relationships."

"Did you grow up around here?"

"Yeah." He sounded relieved to change the subject. "Down in Terrebonne. Moved up here and went to high school, then left for college. I bounced around a little but came back here to work at the fire department a few years ago." He filled two bowls with chili and brought them to the table.

"I thought firemen lived in a firehouse."

"Only when I'm on duty. One day on and two days off."

"I'm lucky I came here on your day off. You would have given me a heart attack if you'd showed up in the middle of the night."

"You and me both." He grinned. "You gonna start this work tomorrow, you say?"

I took a long drink of the beer. Lately I could never turn off my working self—too much of my father had rubbed off on me. I thought about lumber prices when I sat down to dinner, estimated shipping costs when I lay down to sleep.

"First thing," I said.

"You don't waste any time, huh?"

"Not with houses. All those people that told us time is money —they were right." Already I was calculating how much paint it would take to cover the kitchen, how long it would take to refinish the hall floors. The old wallpaper needed to be stripped, and all the rooms needed a fresh coat of paint. People loved these houses with hand-carved woodwork because it made them feel like they owned a piece of dying history, but they expected a combination of historical and practical. They wanted hot tubs, updated kitchens and walk-in closets. I wasn't planning to knock out walls, but this house needed a visual overhaul that would preserve the best parts of the architecture while bringing it into this century.

"How's the chili?" he asked.

"Spicy."

"Need a glass of milk?"

I laughed. "I haven't been away that long."

He grinned, finishing his beer. "Tomorrow we'll go to the hardware store across the canal. I know the owner."

I had a credit card with one of the regional chain stores but kept quiet. He was making a nice gesture.

"Great," I said. "I'm on a tight budget."

After that, a silence settled between us, like we were two teenagers on a blind date, neither knowing what to say. I tried not to stare at Jack, but it took all of my willpower to avoid his eyes. A friend once told me I was intimidating because I stared too long. *It's no wonder you don't have a boyfriend,* she said, *You stare men down.* Ever since then I'd made myself look away every so often.

So I forced myself to break his gaze. He smiled once when he caught me looking at his hands, as if he knew I was imagining what they would feel like against my skin.

I shook the thought away. I'd avoided getting too close to men for a long time, keeping them at a distance even as I let them live in my house. My penchant for distance came from my father. After my mother left us, he'd blamed it on her being heartless. He'd convinced me that if you let people get close to your heart, they'd hurt you. I was tired of being hurt, so I chose relationships that on some level I knew would only be short-term. They were predictable: I kept the guy close but not too close; I liked him, but I was detached. When we inevitably split, I was lonely but not heartbroken.

The pattern I'd learned was this: When you let people get close, they love you, then they hurt you, then they leave you. When they disappear, they take a part of you with them, and you can never get it back. It had happened with my mother. It had happened with friends. Boyfriends. Vergie.

If I'd spent more time with Vergie, I might be more trusting. Less cold. My father resented her because of my mother. I could see it in the way he bristled when I mentioned coming here that last time when I was sixteen. *Your mother turned her whole family against us,* he'd said to me. *Those bridges are burned.*

And because he was the one who didn't leave, I trusted him.

"Hey, Enza, you all right?" Jack Mayronne was staring at me like he thought I might break at any second.

"Sorry," I said. "I'm not good company tonight." Those thoughts had been pushed so far down for so long that now it felt like they were tearing through my skin to get out.

"It's OK. I won't take it personally." His smile was warm as he stood and gathered up our dirty dishes.

"I'm just tired. I think I'll turn in for the night."

He placed the dishes in the sink and said, "So I'll see you bright and early?"

"Crack of dawn." I pushed my chair under the table and took the half-empty beer with me.

"Good night, chère. Sleep tight."

The dog whined, sitting on her haunches.

"Bella will protect you," he said. "It's one of her favorite things to do."

"Good night, Jack." I trudged up the stairs, hoping this wasn't another huge mistake. The sound of his name on my lips had sent a shiver along my skin. *Get a hold of yourself.*

The clatter of toenails on heart pine rang in my ears as the dog bounded up the stairs behind me. She paused at Vergie's door.

"Planning to spy on me?"

Her ears pricked forward.

"Git," I said, turning the doorknob.

She snorted and slinked back down the stairs.

I peeled off my sticky clothes and tossed them onto the rocking chair. On the wall above it was a grouping of framed photos. In one black and white picture, a five-year-old version of me was riding a billy goat, one hand grasping the fur on its neck, one hand up in the air like a bull rider. Barefoot, my hair in pigtails. Closing my eyes, I could feel the coarse fur in my fingers. Harold the goat had served as a pony back then, bucking as I rode him around the yard. By the end of summer, I'd been covered in scratches from the blackberry bushes where he threw me. Even now, standing in the musty bedroom, I could feel the wind tickle my ears, hear the goat's hooves pounding the dirt beneath them.

I made up the bed with the sheets Jack had left stacked on the dresser and opened the window higher. I locked the door and laid the key on the nightstand. The cool sheets soothed me as I climbed into bed. I didn't expect Jack to creep upstairs in the middle of the night, but still I listened for footsteps on the stairs. He seemed like one of the good guys, but how could I be sure? What if he had another key? I flipped off the bedside lamp and tried not to think any more about Jack, thinking instead of those long forgotten summers. With my eyes closed, I felt the salty breeze warm against my skin, heard the pounding of goat hooves in a thicket, growing closer, as if to carry me off into a distant memory.

Chapter Four

IT TOOK me a minute to remember where I was when I awoke. The bed felt funny, and there was barking—so much barking. I covered my head with the pillow, but the sound reverberated in my skull until I rolled out of bed. I pulled on the clothes I'd worn the day before and unlocked the door, giving it a shove when it stuck. After stopping in the bathroom to brush my teeth and pull my hair back, I hurried down the stairs. Judging by the way the light was streaming through the windows, I'd slept much later than planned.

My eyes wouldn't open in the harsh light. At the foot of the stairs, I collided with what I thought must have been the doorframe and cursed.

"Hey," a voice said. Big hands planted themselves square on my shoulders, and I yelped. Staggering backward, my foot banged against the bottom step, knocking me off balance. But a sturdy arm gathered me around the waist, righting me before I could land flat on the stairs.

"Jesus," I said. I looked up at Jack, who still hadn't let me go. "You nearly gave me a heart attack."

"Sorry," he said, not sounding sorry at all. "But you were headed for a crash landing."

I blinked at him. My mouth was open, but no sound came out.

"Didn't mean to scare you, chère."

My heart banged against my ribs so hard they hurt.

"Come here, have some breakfast." He dropped his arm, and I felt cold.

I trudged into the kitchen where the table was set for two. Steam rose from a skillet on the stove.

"You cooked breakfast?"

"I thought you'd be tired after your trip."

"I try hard to be a morning person, but I've never succeeded."

He half-smiled. "So I see. I got up early, thinking you'd already be up and going. Then I figured I might as well make breakfast."

I was starving. And delighted. But I couldn't let him think I was too easy to please.

"Your bacon's burning."

He went to the stove. "Sit," he said, motioning toward the table. "I'll get you a coffee."

The magic words. I sat.

He eased the cup in front of me, moving slowly like you do with a stray you're afraid might bite you.

I inhaled the sweet scent of chicory. "Thank you."

Outside, the barks turned to howls. I rested my head in my hands.

Jack Mayronne, unfazed by the barking, brought two plates of eggs and grits to the table. He wore a threadbare T-shirt that clung to his upper arms, as if unaccustomed to their size. I could see the chiseled muscles of his chest, and my eyes kept landing there as they tried to focus. I pried them away when I realized he was looking right at me.

"Sorry," I said. "I get a thousand-yard stare in the morning."

The look on his face said he didn't believe that for a second.

When he sat down, I saw the tattoo spilling out of his sleeve, winding along the inside of his arm. It looked like the long tail feathers of a bird. The darkness of the ink showed through his shirt at his shoulder, but I still couldn't piece the image together.

"What's with the barking?" I took a sip of coffee and winced.

"Bella's out getting into trouble," he said, pushing a bottle of cream toward me. "Probably chasing a squirrel or some such thing. Did you get some rest?"

"Yeah," I said. "What time is it?"

"Nearly nine."

"Jesus. I should be painting by now."

He laughed, sipping his own coffee. "Take it easy. You just got here."

"I don't have time to take it easy," I said. My father would probably call in two days for a progress report.

"You count nails instead of sheep at night, huh? Dream of spackling and whatnot?"

I frowned, focusing on the coffee.

"You're in the Big Easy, now, chère. You got to slow down a little."

"I take it you have the day off."

When he grinned, his dimples showed. "I go in tomorrow. Today I'm all yours."

I sipped the coffee, hiding my smile. Jack could be a distraction, no doubt. But he could also be an asset. It would be a struggle to finish these repairs, and it would be foolish to turn away a capable man who was not only willing to work for me, but duty-bound to do it right.

I just needed to stay focused. He was clearly used to his charm getting him anything he wanted.

Fortunately I got the distinct feeling he could be charmed too.

"How about that trip to the hardware store you promised?"

He leaned back in his chair. "Sure, we'll go down to Buck's. He's got everything you'll need." The glint in his eye suggested he thought I was in need of something you couldn't get at any hardware store. But I couldn't linger on that thought. With my father waiting for me to screw this project up, I had no time for distractions. No matter how chiseled and charming they might be.

Replacing tile. Repairing floors. Repainting bedrooms. Those were the things I needed to focus on. With Jack around I was going to have to concentrate on the details to make sure my brain and body were too tired to think about him. Those arms of his were nice to look at, but they also looked like they could operate a circular saw just fine.

God, this was going to be exhausting.

JACK DROVE us in his pickup, claiming we could fit everything we needed in the back. Despite my protests, he drove with the windows down so the wind flapped my hair against my face. "You need to get used to the heat," he'd said. The humidity was going to turn me into a frizzy mess—one more reason to hurry up and get out of Louisiana.

"You look like you're thinking pretty hard over there," he said.

I smiled. "Just thinking how fast we can do this, if you're as good as you say you are." My one worry was this: His movements thus far were as slow as honey dripping from a spoon. That could certainly be admirable in the right circumstances, but for repairs, he was going to have to speed up. I was accustomed to a tight schedule with no time wasted.

The truck lurched as Jack shifted into fourth, then hung his elbow out the window. I caught him stealing glances at me while he was driving, and I couldn't decide if I should be flattered. Was it crazy to drive around with a guy I just met, letting him get so close so quickly? My father would have told me this was a terrible idea, that men like Jack couldn't be trusted. To him, Jack would be another broken guy taking advantage of my kindness.

BUCK'S HARDWARE STORE—SIMPLY called B's—was tucked in a corner of the swamp off the main highway. Wood paneled with a green roof, it blended right in with the grove of trees surrounding it. In the dirt parking lot, a man wearing baggy jeans and no shirt was sitting on top of a rusted-out tractor, his feet propped up on the hood. He was reading a newspaper and gave us a lazy nod as we got out of the truck.

Inside, Jack strode straight to the counter. "Buck, how you been?"

Shaped like a pot-bellied stove, Buck had pink cheeks and a graying beard. His face was marked with hard lines. "Fine, you? Who's your friend?"

"Enza," he said. "Vergie's granddaughter."

"Nice to meet you," I said, shaking Buck's hand.

"Vergie's granddaughter? Well, I'll be. She was a sweetheart, all right."

Buck gave me a long look, but if he gave me enough of a discount on the lumber and supplies, I didn't much mind.

Jack read my expression. As we turned down the first aisle with baskets in hand, he said, "Buck's my uncle."

I tossed in packages of nails and tubes of caulk. "Well, of course he is."

He laughed. "Small town, chère."

When he snatched a pair of pink gloves from a display stand and dropped them in my basket, I said, "Really?"

"Thought you might need these," he said with a shrug.

"Very funny."

He laughed and put them back on the shelf.

There were only a few other customers in the store, but they all stared in that way people in small towns do when they're trying to be sneaky. I'd been in enough places like this to know that we'd be the subject of local scuttlebutt for days. At first I thought they were staring because they weren't used to seeing a woman in a hardware store, but then I realized it was because I was there with

Jack. I didn't miss the winks that passed between a couple of the men, the whispers exchanged over paint cans.

While I thumbed through the paint chips, Jack lit a clove cigarette, blowing smoke rings above his head. They widened as they rose, like wobbly halos. This kind of store was like a barber shop, where men came to stand around smoking and chewing tobacco, regaling each other with stories they'd heard about their friends through the week.

"I figured you'd paint it all white," Jack said.

I held two chips up for him to see. "White's too sterile. Colors make it feel like a home. Which do you like better?"

He plucked a light blue one from my hand and smiled. "Virginia Beach. For Vergie."

A voice came from behind us, ragged and deep. "Well, look what the ol' cat dragged up."

Jack's eyes narrowed. The look that came over his face chilled me.

A man with shaggy blond hair stepped around me and slapped Jack on the shoulder, though the gesture hardly seemed friendly. He was as tall as Jack but heavier and with broader shoulders. "Mayronne, don't you know gals like this don't belong in hardware stores?" He winked at me. "Didn't anybody teach you what to do with a woman?"

Jack ignored him, his jaw rigid as he stepped past him. "Come on, Enza."

"What? You too good to talk to me now?" the man said. He wore jeans that were snug and striped with grease, a plaid shirt and work boots.

Buck leaned against the counter, pulling his hat down on his forehead. "Keep moving, Remy," he called. "Ain't nothing you need on that aisle."

Remy turned to me, his eyes roaming from my face to my feet. His grin made me bristle. "Sugar, you're wasting your time with Mayronne," he said, gesturing toward Jack. "Why don't you let me show you how we have fun around here? You're new here, *non*?"

When he winked again, his lip curled into a sly grin that made me want to clock him. He had hollow brown eyes and a square face that looked like it had taken its share of punches. But he was handsome, no arguing that. I didn't want to stir up trouble so early in the day, so I turned back to the display of paint chips like I was just brushing off another hackneyed pick-up line.

Jack stepped between us, pausing inches from Remy's shoulder. "Leave her be," Jack said, his voice like gravel.

"What's the matter? Afraid she'll prefer my kind of fun?" Remy looked at Jack with a cocky glint in his eye.

Then Remy leaned closer to me, and said in a low voice, "Darlin', let me show you why they call it the Big Easy."

I plucked a paint chip from the rack and brushed past him. "There's a line I never thought I'd hear down here," I said, and headed to the paint counter.

"Well, ain't you a firecracker," Remy said. "That sass looks good on you, sugar."

"See you 'round, Remy," Jack said, and strode past him to follow me. Buck watched from the front of the store. He pointed a finger at Remy, then motioned toward the door.

"What?" Remy called. "Last time I checked, hardware stores were open to everybody."

"Then get what you need and get out," Buck said, "before I regret making it that way."

"Well," Remy said, looking my way, "I'm trying, ain't I?"

"You know," I said, turning to him, "why don't you take your—"

Jack interrupted, saying to Remy in a cool, even voice, "You don't want to start this here. Trust me on that."

Remy stared at him, stone faced.

"Hey," Buck yelled. "Am I going to have to drag you out of here my own self? I ain't going to bother the sheriff with this nonsense again."

"Guess you don't have what I need after all," Remy said, turning toward the front of the store. "Watch out for those fires, Mayronne," he said over his shoulder. "Be a shame if you got burned up in one."

I turned in time to see Remy's smirk turn to a sneer as he ambled down the aisle to the door. On his way past the stock boy, he said, "What are you staring at?" and knocked a box of screws from his hand. They clattered as they tumbled across the floor.

"Hey," Buck called from the counter. "Next time I don't ask nicely."

Remy laughed, shoving the front door so the bell clanged.

The door slammed behind him, and Buck shook his head.

"Sorry about that," Buck said to me. "Every place has its trash. Can't keep it hidden, no matter how hard you try."

"It's OK," I said as I handed him my credit card.

"Sorry, honey," he said, pointing to a sign beneath the cash register that said *Cash or Check Only.*

I sighed. There was more than four hundred dollars' worth of supplies at the counter and less than thirty in my wallet. "I don't suppose there's an ATM around here."

Jack gave Buck a nod, leaning against the counter. "Just add it to my bill."

"That's not necessary," I said.

He smiled down at me. "You can pay me back later."

Buck pulled a receipt book with carbon paper from under the counter. After scribbling some numbers, he passed it to Jack to sign. "All right, son," he said. "Y'all need a hand getting this in the truck?"

WHEN WE WERE out of the parking lot, I turned to face Jack.

"What?" he said, his eyes on the road.

"Who was that guy?"

"Remy? Just a hooligan with nothing better to do."

"Seems like he knew you pretty well."

Jack raked his fingers through his hair. "Everybody here goes back a long way," he said. "Hardly anybody ever leaves."

"What's he got against you?"

"He's got something against everybody. He never could seem to keep on the right side of the law. Or the right side of anyone in general, for that matter."

He bristled, though he was trying to stay calm. There was something specific between the two of them, but it was clear that Jack had no intention of revealing it to me.

"Buck, though," I said. "I like him."

"Yeah, he and my aunt, Josie, took me in after my parents died."

"You're lucky to have them."

"Don't I know it. They should have turned me out a dozen times, but they never did." He winked and said, "I was a bit of a troublemaker."

We sped along the road by the canal, windows down to let the marsh breeze in. With so many deep bends in the creeks and so many bayous, it seemed there was more water than land here. It was as if we were on a series of islands with secret connections.

"You didn't have to spot me back there," I said. "I could have gone back later with cash."

He smiled that crooked smile. "Well that would mean losing even more time that you could have been painting or caulking or staining. And I wouldn't want to get you behind schedule."

I stared off into the marshland. There was going to be trouble if he could read all of my thoughts that easily.

Chapter Five

VERGIE'S HOUSE needed more than I could actually do in six weeks with my limited budget. The trick with a flip was that you had to fix the biggest problems that would be the deal-breakers for buyers, but not improve so much that you drew attention to dozens of smaller things that needed updating. Otherwise, you were in an endless cycle of repair that would burn through your budget.

For example: Vergie's front porch had three floorboards that were obviously new. If I repainted the entire porch floor, then the peeling banisters would look even worse, the blue exterior would seem more faded, and the front door would look dingy. Before long I'd be painting the entire exterior because of a few floorboards.

My solution: Paint those new boards a matching color, then do a wash on the whole porch to blend it together. Scuff it up a bit to make it look "farmhouse chic," and it would go with the rest of the exterior. Historic farmhouses were supposed to have scuffs and scratches—but they needed to look like those flaws had been protected like memories while the structure held its integrity. That way, the flaws were called "character" and not "disrepair."

My way took more creativity than your average contractor had. Others couldn't be trusted with those details.

We started with the downstairs study. My favorite part of the room was the floor-to-ceiling bookcases filled with Vergie's books —travel guides, Creole cookbooks, and a slew of paperback westerns and romances. I pulled a book off the shelf and wondered if Jack had ever peeked inside one.

Those built-in shelves meant less wall space to deal with. A blessing, because the peeling wallpaper had to go. I had chosen a neutral buttercream that wouldn't make the ceiling look dingy and would be a nice complement to the dark wood of the bookcases and trim. The floral patterned sofa and green wingback chair had enough vintage appeal. They would stay.

"Did you ever meet the friend Vergie was living with?" I asked.

"Yeah, George I think was his name. Sweet old guy. Worked over at the jazz museum in New Orleans."

"Vergie moved in with a man?"

Jack shrugged. "They'd been together a long time."

I'd always assumed she was living here alone, because she was alone when I visited in the summers. It had never occurred to me that she could have had a boyfriend.

It made me happy for a minute, thinking of her with a beau.

We moved the furniture into the center of the room and covered it with drop cloths. First we had to strip the walls of the green paisley wallpaper. Jack brought a radio from his bedroom and tuned it to the clearest station while I filled a bucket with water. I dunked a sponge into the water, then wiped down a small section of paper right by a seam. With a putty knife, I worked a seam loose and tugged until a chunk of damp paper peeled away.

"That's all there is to it, then?" Jack asked, grabbing the other sponge.

Prying a corner loose at the chair rail, I pulled until the strip grew wider, crawling toward the ceiling like a serpent. "We'll have to go as high as we can reach, and then go back around with the ladder to moisten the section above."

He carefully worked a seam open and tugged the paper. A chunk no bigger than his hand came off. He frowned and slid the putty knife under the damp paper to pry it loose again. "This is tricky."

"Here," I said, wiping the sponge over another section. "Give it more water and pull slowly, at an angle."

He watched as I repeated the steps, then tried again.

"Just don't pull so hard the plaster comes off," I said. "Water is your friend."

He smiled, loosening another corner. "I'll try to be gentle."

We pulled the paper off in broad chunks and let it fall around our feet like shed leaves. It felt strange doing this in Vergie's house. All my other flip houses were just studs, walls and floorboards. But here, it felt like I was stripping away the last pieces of Vergie.

Jack hummed along with the radio, occasionally singing along in French. I loved those old zydeco tunes and could always tell the ones that were all about love—even if I couldn't make out the words.

The steady tearing of paper from plaster began to blend with the music. It was a rough sound, like fingers on a washboard. We'd started on opposite ends of one wall, and before long we were shoulder to shoulder. I pulled the last strip as high as I could, a couple of feet above me, but lost my balance and crashed into Jack.

"Whoa," he said, catching me in his arms.

"Sorry."

"Don't be," he said. "We should take a break anyway." One of his hands had landed on my waist. He placed his other hand in mine, singing along with the radio.

Before I could protest, he was leading me around the island of furniture, nudging me into a two-step. The curls of wallpaper rustled under our feet.

"We should really finish before the walls dry," I said.

His hand squeezed mine. I could feel his breath on my skin.

"Don't make me call my union rep," he said. "Even line cooks get fifteen minutes every three hours."

He grinned when our bare feet thumped together.

"I'm not very good at this," I said, my cheeks burning.

"You're thinking too hard. And trying to lead."

"Right," I whispered, stumbling against him again.

"Let yourself go. One two, one two, one two." He twirled me by the bookshelves that I hoped to God we would not have to paint. "You got to feel the rhythm, darlin'. You're faking."

"I'm not faking."

"Believe me," he said, his voice low, "I know when a gal's faking." His hand tightened on my back, pressing me so close that the length of my arm was right against his, my other hand resting on his shoulder.

I liked the feeling of his arms around me.

When he twirled me again, his hand tightened around mine, and he pulled me with such purpose that I thought I'd crash into him. I over-corrected, and we tumbled to the floor. Jack landed on top of me, his hands on either side of my shoulders, his face an inch from mine. He smelled like cloves and sawdust. I tensed beneath his weight, though the warmth of his chest against mine made my breath catch in my throat in the most delightful way.

His eyes, blue-green as glaciers, were steady on mine.

"Grace is my middle name," I said. "Probably should have warned you."

He smiled. "I bet you think that was a move. But I swear, I'm not that creative."

I smirked, thinking of course he was. "Right, Mr. Mayronne."

His tone was playful. "I'm not some sleazy guy. But I'd be lying if I said I didn't like you." His breath tickled my neck, making me shiver. Surely he could feel that shudder against his own skin.

For a second I thought he might kiss me, but he just stared at me, like he was trying to read my mind. I felt my cheeks blushing again, thinking of how his lips would feel against mine. It was hard to push those thoughts away with him resting on top of me, but I had to. My father used to say that all work and no play would have made someone a rich man. Even though part of me wanted to stay exactly where I was, I said, "All right, Casanova. Quit goofing around, and let me up, will you?"

His lips close to my ear, he muttered something that sounded vaguely French.

When he stood, he pulled me to my feet and plucked a strip of paper from my shirt.

"You want to start washing the walls down?" I asked.

He half-smiled, little crow's feet forming at his eyes. "Yes ma'am."

I opened a tin of paint and stirred, thinking of the way his face looked only inches above mine. I was about to pour the paint in the tray when I realized I'd opened the blue instead of the buttercream.

FOR TWO HOURS WE PAINTED, the radio fading in and out as the clouds passed overhead. Jack didn't say much, just hummed along with the music like I wasn't even there. I wondered if I'd hurt his feelings but didn't want to make things more awkward by pressing him.

After finishing the last wall, I stopped to take in the room. It was brighter all right. The afternoon sun streamed through the window, making the pale buttercream look more like a warm yellow.

Jack was painting around the bookshelves, streaks of paint smeared across his nose and cheek, and a smaller brush sticking out of his back pocket. With short strokes, he flicked the brush back and forth like a small flapping bird. When he realized I was watching him, he stopped.

"Something wrong?" he asked.

"No, we finished quicker than I thought we would. You're fast."

"Don't go spreading that around. Folks might take it the wrong way."

If he could do other repairs that fast, and that well, I might make my deadline.

He dabbed at a couple more spots, then stood back to survey his work.

"Looks great," I said.

He shrugged, holding the brush out to his side. "Not my first rodeo."

I smiled. With most men, as soon as you expressed the slightest bit of doubt in them, they wouldn't stop until they proved you wrong. I'd gotten myself out of a boat load of unsavory tasks that way. All it takes is, *You think you can strip those shingles off all by yourself?* or *That bathroom demo might be more than one guy can handle.* Works every time—but you've got to play your part too. You've got to express the right amount of gratitude.

"Clearly I underestimated you," I said. "It's a good thing you were available to help."

"Well, that was our deal, right?" He wiped his hands on his jeans. "I'm good for my word."

He walked toward me, and I instinctively took a step back. Reaching past me, he laid his paintbrush in the tray.

"I really make you nervous," he said, resting his hands on his hips.

"Not at all." Not for the reasons he thought anyway.

"Listen, chère," he said, "I'm sorry about before. I wasn't trying to—"

"I know."

"I mean, I don't want you to think—"

"I don't. It's fine. I haven't danced in a long time."

He smiled and then, in response to my gaze, said, "What?"

"You've got some paint here." I touched my cheek.

He wiped his face, but the streak was still there.

"No, here." I stepped closer and wiped the paint away with my fingers. There was another spot on his neck and flecks in his hair. "A little here too," I said, sliding my thumb over his neck.

He leaned over so I could reach.

"There," I said. "Got it." But as I pulled away, he dropped his hand on my hip and kissed me.

I stood still, my hands by my sides.

He stopped as quickly as he'd started, and eyes widened, took a step back.

Without another thought, I kissed him back. He tensed as my hands gripped his waist. For a second I thought he'd push me away, but then he slid his hands through my hair and kissed me harder, his tongue parting my lips.

I pulled away just to take a breath, and he tilted my chin back with his fingers. His lips grazed my neck, and my heart pounded, as if willing him to slide his tongue along every inch of my skin. His hands moved to my hips, and he nudged me backwards, pinning me against the wall. I loved the way he tasted, loved the way his chest felt pressed against mine.

I laughed as his chin grazed my neck.

"Ticklish?"

"Nope."

"Liar," he said, his voice husky as he tickled me with his scratchy cheek.

I laughed harder, squirming in his grip.

His lips brushed my ear as he said, "I like a woman who laughs in bed."

Catching my breath, I murmured, "We're not in bed yet."

His finger slid along my neckline, and he said, "God, I love the way you say *yet.*"

The tacky paint would surely stick to my clothes, but I loved feeling his tightened muscles against mine, and I thought, *Hell, what's one more coat of paint?*

"You feel incredible," he said.

Before I could say anything, he kissed me so hard that I felt the blood in my head rush to my feet.

As his hips pressed into mine, I felt him hard against me, and I wasn't doubtful any more. In that instant, he was all I wanted.

As I reached for his belt buckle, he held my hand above my head. "Not yet, darlin'," he whispered, his lips brushing my ear. "We take things slow around here."

My breaths quickened as I pictured exactly how he might take his time with me.

He unbuttoned my shirt so slowly it made me shiver. I thought at any second he'd rip the blouse from my shoulders and scatter buttons all over the floor. But he seemed to want to stretch this moment out as long as he could. I leaned into him, dragging my fingers down his back.

"So stunning," he said, as he dropped my shirt to the floor. "I can't decide where to start."

My heart hammered in my chest. His lips moved over my collarbone, and I struggled to undo the snaps on his shirt while my hands were free. He let me push his hands away just long enough to free them from his sleeves, and he grinned when I pulled him against me again.

He somehow knew exactly where I wanted to be touched, and I laughed a little, thinking that maybe I needed to offer up another challenge just so he didn't think I was too easy to please this way, either.

"Can I tell you something?" he asked.

"What is it?"

He slipped his hands down over my hips. His lips moved against my neck as he spoke, and I shuddered. "I've wanted you ever since you walked into this house. Does that scare you?"

"It takes more than that to scare me," I said, grasping his hips. "Show me how much you want me."

He lifted me then, pulling my legs around his waist. He sighed when I squeezed myself tighter around him, and kissed me harder. Still holding me against him, he moved away from the wall and stumbled down the hall to his bedroom.

We landed on his bed in a tangle, and I unfastened his belt, unzipped his jeans.

"I knew you'd drive me crazy," he said, raising up enough to strip off his jeans and toss them to the floor. He pulled my shorts and panties to my ankles, tracing his tongue from my hip down to my knee as he went. My breath caught in my throat, and I wound my fingers in his hair. His lips grazed my thigh so deliberately that it made me ache. I'd never wanted so badly for a man to keep touching me, keep trying to get closer.

Jack, it seemed, couldn't get close enough.

Why he was so different and why I could let my guard down with him didn't make sense to me—but I pushed those thoughts aside. His tongue, his teeth, his hands roving over every curve of my frame—that's what I preferred to concentrate on.

"Jack," I breathed, "Stop this teasing."

His lips moved against my inner thigh as he said, "I want to take my time with you."

I trembled as his tongue slid along the curve of my hip, and I tugged on his hair until he brought his face back up to mine. I kissed him hard, and he grunted in surprise. I couldn't feel enough of him, taste enough of him. I clutched his shoulders as if I was about to fly away and he was the only thing anchoring me to the earth.

His grip tightened. Then a buzzing filled my ears. I thought it was because of his cheek sliding along my collarbone, but when he leaned over me and reached for his jeans on the floor, I realized it was not.

He was stretched across me, holding me down as he dug through the pockets and pulled out his cell phone.

I tightened my leg around his waist, and he groaned, reading the number on the phone.

"What is it?" I asked, my breath ragged.

Still halfway off the bed, he held the phone to his ear and

listened. Then, all business, he said, "Yeah. Be there in drive time."

I relaxed my grip on him, and he settled back over me, placing his forearms by my ears.

"I'm sorry," he said. "This makes me a real bastard." He hovered over me, kissed me lightly on the lips. "I have to go."

"You're joking."

"It seems I gotta go put out somebody else's fire."

I covered my face with my hands and groaned. "You did not just say that."

He climbed off me and fumbled to get his pants on, wincing as he zipped them. "God, you're beautiful. I hate my job right now." He slipped his boots on and grabbed his shirt, never taking his eyes off me.

"What happened to your day off?"

"It's a big one," he said. "They need everybody that's around."

I sighed, falling back into the pillows. My skin already felt cold without his against it.

He smiled that crooked smile. "Don't worry, darlin'. I'll be back soon."

I propped my head in my hand, still dizzy, wishing he'd pretend he didn't get that call and climb back into bed. Then I felt guilty. After all, somebody's house was on fire, and right then, they needed him more than I did.

But only slightly.

He leaned over and kissed me, a slow, delicious move that made me want to stay all tangled up with him for the next three days.

"Hey," he said. "Don't forget where we were."

He jogged to the door, and I called out, "Wait!"

"What is it?" he said, leaning against the door frame.

"Be careful."

He frowned. "That's like saying *Macbeth* in the theater, chère."

"Shit," I said. "Well, break a leg, then."

"You get one free pass. Then the gods start raining irony and brimstone down on all of us."

He winked at me as he dashed out the front door.

I LAY BACK against his pillows, listening to his boots thumping down the porch steps.

What the hell had I been thinking?

I vaulted from the bed, and scooped my panties and shorts up from the floor.

"Jesus, Enza," I muttered, retracing our steps to find my shirt. Back in the study, I marched straight to the wall that now had the faint texture of cotton blouse and denim shorts embossed into the surface. I frowned, grabbing the roller and dunking it into the paint tray.

Was I out of my mind, climbing into bed with a man I just met? I couldn't even blame it on the paint fumes because my paint was top-quality water-based. I rolled a thin coat over the smudges, careful not to make the first layer peel off. It was too soon to add another layer, but those smudges needed to be smoothed away. Immediately.

I dug through the hall closet until I found a box fan, then aimed it toward the touched-up wall. I collected the last bits of wallpaper into a garbage bag and took it out to the porch. Bella was stretched out on her side under the hammock. She opened one eye and stared at me dubiously.

With Jack gone, I could finish up the room. Erase all the evidence that the last hour ever happened.

The drop cloths were splattered with buttercream, but the floor was clean. It could use a quick polish, but I'd wait to do them all at once. I uncovered the furniture, put some scraps of cardboard under the feet of the chairs, end tables and the monstrous floral sofa, and shoved the pieces back where they belonged.

I willed myself to forget Jack's husky laugh and the way his lips felt moving down my belly, over my hip. I would not think of the wrinkles that formed at the corners of his eyes when he smiled his easy smile. I would not think of his big square hands holding me under him as he told me he couldn't wait to taste me. I could will myself to forget the way his lips had felt on mine.

Thank God that building had caught fire.

When I woke, I had the sinking thought that I was in Jack's bed, but no—I was on the couch downstairs. It must have been hours since I'd sat down with my glass of wine, my reward for finishing one room and swearing off all future physical entanglements with Jack Mayronne. The house was as dark as the inside of an ink bottle, with just a faint hint of moon outside. When I reached for the lamp, there was only the click of the chain. No burst of light. I tripped over my tool box, then slammed my shin into the coffee table and cursed as I reached the far wall. When I flipped the light switch, nothing happened.

"Great. Something else to fix."

Lightning flickered outside, casting the room in a blue glow just long enough for me to navigate into the hallway and stumble into the kitchen. While rummaging through the drawers to find a flashlight, I heard the dog's toenails clacking on the floorboards. Barking, she ran into the hall. There was the sound of a key in the lock.

I froze, though I knew it could only be Jack.

The door squeaked open. There was the flip of a switch, then a groan.

"Hey," I called, "the power's out."

"Jesus," he said, dropping his keys. "I didn't know you'd be up."

I could barely make out his silhouette as lightning flashed behind him.

He brushed past me and opened the pie safe, where he fished

out a small flashlight. "It's probably just the breaker. Happens a lot when the window units are running at the same time. Power surge."

Down the hall, he opened the closet under the stairs and checked the breaker box. After a couple of clicks, the lights came back on.

He ambled toward me, like he thought I might bolt. For a split second he looked like he'd kiss me, but he stopped short. He smelled like a candle just blown out.

"Hi," I said.

"Hi, yourself."

"How did it go?" As soon as I said it, it seemed like a ridiculous thing to ask.

"I'll tell you over a beer," he replied, walking into the kitchen. "You want one?"

"No, thanks. What time is it?"

"Nearly eleven."

I sat on one end of the couch, studying the way he moved toward me. He looked like he felt bad about earlier and wanted to take it back too. Even though it was disappointing to think of him feeling that way, it was for the best.

"It was a warehouse," he said. "Burned right to the ground. After two hours they called us off." He stretched out next to me, propping his feet on the coffee table.

"What caused it?"

He shook his head, his hand resting next to my thigh. "No official word yet. The chief thinks it's squatters. I think it's something else."

"Like what?"

He took a long swallow. "Like an arsonist."

"Damn. Was anybody hurt?"

"No. We got lucky."

"You've been there all this time?"

He nodded, taking a long pull from the beer. His eyes were dark.

"You must be exhausted."

"Nothing I'm not used to," he said, sliding his hand over my knee. "What did you get into around here? I know you didn't just sit here eagerly awaiting my return."

I felt a ripple of warmth pass over my skin. "Mostly finished the study."

He stared at me, his fingers squeezing my knee. "You're all I could think about."

The starving, wanton part of me wanted him to pick up where he left off, slide his hands all over me. But the practical, rational part of me said I should get a hold of myself. Be professional.

"I figured you thought it was a mistake," I said.

"Why would you say that?"

"Well, you did leave me naked and alone."

He brought my hand to his lips. "You're going to love the way I make that up to you."

I took a drink from his beer and said, "I've been thinking about that."

He grinned. "Not as much as I have."

Easing back to my side of the couch, I said, "I think we should cool it for a while."

He stared at me like I'd just slapped him.

"Let's take care of the house first," I continued. "There's a lot riding on this for me. And it's going to be impossible to do if I'm thinking more about you than this job."

"You can't multi-task?"

"I'm serious, Jack. We could have a good time together—that much is obvious. But I think we should call a time-out."

"Look, I'm sorry I had to leave." He leaned closer, his hand on my thigh. "But that's my job. I wasn't trying to be an ass."

"I know," I said. "It's not that."

"I wasn't trying to make you feel bad."

"I'm supposed to be down here working—not having a wild fling on the company tab."

"That's cold, chère."

"I don't mean it to be. I just think we need to keep this relationship professional."

He sighed, folding his hands in his lap. "So you still want my help."

"Well, that was our agreement."

He nodded. "Work first, then?"

"Seems to be our way."

It took him a minute to realize what I meant. Then he laughed, but he wasn't amused. "Next thing I know, you'll make me sign a contract."

"The thought crossed my mind."

He laughed again. "Lord, chère. Can't you take a man at his word?"

Truth was, I couldn't.

I hoped Jack wasn't one of those things I would regret in days or years to come. He was clearly upset, but I couldn't be sure it was because he wanted to be closer to me. After he'd left, a hundred thoughts banged around in my head like marbles. And in the swirling fragments, there was one that stuck.

What if he was trying to con his way into keeping the house?

This could very well be Jack's way of trying to secure the roof over his head. He hadn't struck me as the calculating type in the beginning, but the more I thought about it, the more it seemed possible he'd planned to seduce me all along, to make sure I didn't kick him out. He knew the effect he had on me, and that would make me an easy mark. Then he'd be just another person who left me and took a part of me with him.

There was no way I'd let that happen. I was not gullible, and I would not be conned. As tempting as Jack Mayronne was, I needed to put distance between us.

"I should get some sleep," I said, standing. "And I know you need it too. We don't have to start too early in the morning, but the parish building inspector's coming at nine."

"OK," he said. "Me, I'll just go dream about all the things I was going to do to you to make up for leaving you in such a state."

I tossed a throw cushion at him, and he raised an eyebrow.

"Mmm," he said. "Guess you'll have to lie awake all night wondering."

"Get some sleep," I said. "You'll need it."

He laughed, and I trudged up the stairs, cursing my brain for being so damned logical. This was going to be a long six weeks.

Chapter Six

WHEN THAT BRIGHT orange hearse rumbled down the driveway the next morning, I thought I'd finally reached my quota of strange. Jack's bedroom door was still closed when I came downstairs, so I'd perched on the porch steps to drink my coffee. The car sputtered when it stopped, and a man in dark blue coveralls climbed out, dusting himself off. With a clipboard under his arm, he walked to the house in that same slow way Jack did, as if he weren't bound by time like the rest of us.

When he was halfway up the walk, he said, "You Miss Parker?" He had flecks of white on the front of his coveralls and a streak across his nose. Powdered sugar from beignets, I imagined.

"I'm Enza," I said. "You're here for the inspection?"

He shook my hand, squeezing too hard. "I'm Grant Carmine. You talked to my assistant last week." When he yanked his cap off, his blond hair stood straight up in the air.

"Right," I said. "Interesting choice of vehicle."

"Low miles. Lots of room. Hell of a deal."

"Come on in. I haven't done much besides painting."

"If you don't mind, I'll start outside," he said, pulling a pair of horn-rimmed glasses from his chest pocket. "Before it gets too steaming hot."

To keep out of his way, I sat on the porch, skimming the headlines of the local paper. Every few minutes I'd look up to see him scribbling in a small notebook, the dog following behind. He'd whistle at her every now and then, and she'd lie down and stare at him.

After a while, Jack wandered onto the porch wearing only a pair of jeans, his hair standing up in tufts. "Morning," he said, sipping his coffee. I could tell from his dopey expression that he'd showed up half-dressed to make me regret leaving him on the couch last night.

It worked.

I pretended not to notice he was missing a shirt, even though it felt ten degrees hotter on that porch. I just said, "Good morning," and handed him half of the paper.

While he was reading, I studied his tattoo—a bird with long feathers that trailed down his bicep. Black and grey with hints of green. I was dying to get closer and see what kind of bird it was, since I'd been too preoccupied to get a good look the day before. The feathers rippled as Jack turned a page, and I quickly averted my eyes.

Once again, he'd caught me staring. The tiniest smile touched the corner of his mouth, and I raised my section of paper to shield myself from his gaze.

AFTER AN HOUR AND A HALF, Grant handed me a list of things not up to code. He seemed a little too chipper about the number of shortcomings.

"It looks so solid, you wouldn't think it would have all these problems," he said. "Sorry to be the messenger with bad news."

"Give me the three most critical," I said.

He pulled a pencil from behind his ear and marked his list. "Mold in this downstairs room, dry rot in the west corner of the roof, leaky pipe in the downstairs bathroom."

"Any estimate on that?"

He shook his head. "I couldn't say, ma'am. But it'll need a new roof too. Probably before the end of the year."

The dog trotted over and stopped at his feet. She looked at him, then dropped something from her mouth.

Grant stared at the tiny object by his shoe.

"What is that?" I asked.

He picked up a small fabric pouch tied with string. "It seems somebody lost their mojo," he said.

I stared at the little bag in his hand. It looked like something that might contain a piece of jewelry, some souvenir a tourist would take home.

He placed it in my hand before I could object. I cringed at the dog drool and laid it on the porch rail.

Grant handed me the bill and smiled like he was at a funeral. Perhaps he'd picked the right car after all. "You have a good day, now. Good luck with the repairs."

I sighed as the hearse sputtered and wheezed down the driveway. I'd known the house would need some work, but this was more than I'd expected. My plan was to come down and spruce the place up with some paint and a few upgrades—not repairs that would run into thousands of dollars. I could call my father, but as soon as he heard the word "mold," he'd be down here moving like his tail was on fire. He'd come in and take over everything. He was no doubt hoping I'd call him in such distress that he would have to send a crew to rescue me from my own ambition.

It would take more than a few mold spores and leaky pipes to make me give in.

"It's OK," I said to the dog. She was lying under the hammock again, staring at me with narrowed eyes. Grant had given me the phone number of a "mold guy" and a plumber, and said, "Just tell 'em I sent you, and they'll fix you right up." I had a bad feeling this was going to take the entire budget and leave me justifying it to my father. But I'd have to push that aside for now. Like that old saying, *Better to ask for forgiveness than permission.*

Problem was, I didn't want to ask for either.

Jack came back to the porch—this time with a plaid shirt—and leaned on the banister.

"So what's the damage?"

"You don't want to know."

He frowned. "Sounds like my to-do list just got a little longer."

I needed him more than I'd anticipated, but I hated to tell him that. With the number of repairs piling up, it would take serious effort to finish in six weeks. As much as it pained me to admit it, I couldn't do it without Jack.

"Guess we better get started then." I tried to sound nonchalant.

He sipped his coffee, barely hiding a smile. "We might need to renegotiate the terms of our agreement."

"First let's see how efficient you can be."

He slid his fingers along the porch rail. "Fair enough. I like a challenge. What's first on your agenda today?"

"We've got a couple more rooms left to paint."

"What's this doing here?" He stepped to the corner of the porch and picked up the tiny bag the dog had brought up.

"Who knows? The dog was chewing on it."

"It was here by the door?"

"Out in the yard. Why? What is it?"

"Probably nothing." Something in his tone said otherwise.

"But if it wasn't nothing, what would it be?"

He shrugged. "The old folks call them gris-gris."

"As in voodoo? Let me see that again."

"It's just a bunch of leaves and spices," he said, handing me the bag. "Nothing to worry about. Somebody probably lost it out in the swamp. People carry them for luck. That dog'll drag up anything."

I turned the small pouch over in my hand, pulling the strings loose to open it. Inside were some leaves, what looked like herbs, and a few beads. When I dug to the bottom, I pulled out something that looked like a bone from a small mammal. I winced, holding the bone out for him to see. "Isn't this stuff used for hexes too?"

"Don't tell me you believe in that," he said.

"Don't you?"

He laughed. "Give me a break. That's from one of those voodoo tourist shops that take your money."

"But what if it isn't? What if it's real?"

"You've been reading too many ghost stories. Ain't no such thing as black magic."

"Four hundred years of history say otherwise." I tied the strings back together, sealing the pouch.

He laughed again. "Come on. Get serious. You can't put hexes on people with chicken feet and coffee grounds." He turned to go back in the house. "Tell me which paint color you want to use so I can get started, chief."

I followed him inside and stuffed the pouch into my pocket.

IN JACK'S ROOM, we took the bed apart and slid the mattresses into the hall. I tried not to imagine him pinning me to that very mattress, his lips moving against my ear as he told me all the ways he longed to touch me. We pushed the dresser, the bookcase and the massive cedar chest into the center of the room, creating an island of mismatched wood. We spread the drop cloths out again, and Jack shoved a heap of clothes into his closet.

We had an efficient system going. He was good with a roller, covering the large areas quickly and evenly. I applied painter's tape around edges of chair rails and window frames, and followed him with a brush to get the areas that needed more attention.

He still squeezed the roller too hard, which resulted in his whole body getting covered in a fine dappling of paint. But the walls looked great, so I didn't critique his method. I caught myself staring though, as he rolled with one arm and let his weight shift to his opposite hip. Each time the taut muscles of his arms flexed, I thought of how they'd felt under my palms.

"Hey," he said at last. "What are you going to do about that list of repairs you got today?"

I snapped back to the present. Inspections. Codes. The endless list of broken things.

"I need to think that over tonight and crunch some numbers," I said.

"Tough break. But we'll manage."

"Yeah."

As soon as Grant had left, I'd told Jack about the damage. It was more than I should have disclosed, but it was one of those times when you spew everything you're thinking because of your utter shock at the ridiculousness of it all.

Jack eased the roller into the tray. "Well, you let me know what you decide. I know lots of folks around here who could help. A few of them even owe me favors."

"Thanks," I said, wondering how many favors it was going to take to pull off this flip. My father was a stickler for staying within a dime of his budgets. He had this uncanny ability to create one based on his own appraisal of a property plus the official one from an inspector. He'd get list prices of comparable homes, factor in his buying price and the cost of updating, and if the profit margin was high enough, he took on the project. For all of his faults, I admired his ability to calculate risk versus profit. If he had seen Vergie's house himself, he might have spotted one of these things that had made the top of Grant's list. He might have decided to sell it "as-is" instead of risking his own money against a return.

But I'd insisted he let me do this one, and he had skipped his own inspection and given me what he thought was a reasonable budget of $8,500. Every time I started feeling anxious about it, I reminded myself that he would get his money back regardless:

The house would sell, and since he was only out the taxes he covered for my inheritance of the property plus the repair budget, he would recoup his money even if this ended in disaster and I sold the house under market value. If I did this right, I'd have a profit too. And I'd take on bigger moneymakers that came my father's way—historic ones with some character.

This house was my set of training wheels. And with my father, you only got one shot to prove you didn't need the assistance.

When Jack had rolled the last empty spot on the wall, he poured the remaining tan paint from the tray into the pail. Then he peeled the tape from around the door and windows.

He stood back to admire the room. "I used to think all those off-whites and tans were basically the same, but you proved me wrong, Miz Parker."

"It's looking good," I said, climbing down the ladder.

"I think a celebration is in order," Jack said.

"How's that?"

He dunked the roller in a tray of water and said, "Two rooms in two days. Not a bad average."

"This is the warm-up, remember?"

He grinned and closed the paint buckets, stepping on them to seal the lids. "I think we should go have a nice celebratory meal. Can I take you to dinner, chère?"

A dinner date with Jack was hardly the way to keep him out of my zone of distraction, but it was impossible to say no to him. His eyebrows had that hopeful arch to them, and when he unleashed that crooked smile I said, "Sure you can."

"I'm just going to jump in the shower and try to scrub off this layer of butternut or pecan or whatever this lovely shade is. I'll be back in a few."

"Take your time," I said. *I will not picture Jack in the shower. I will not. Will not.*

He smirked as he stepped into the adjoining bathroom and shut the door behind him. When the water started running, I imagined him peeling off his jeans and T-shirt. I grabbed the roller and paint tray, and took them into the kitchen to wash them in the sink.

When I was finished, I went upstairs and quickly changed clothes. I considered a hot bath, but decided to do that later, when I could stumble down the hall to bed and not have to be social and chat through dinner. A bath had a way of relaxing all of my parts—especially my brain.

I hadn't packed a variety of clothes, since I hadn't planned on evenings out. Jeans, paint-splattered shorts, T-shirts: These are the things I packed for work. I didn't want to look like I was reading this as a date, so I went for a low-key nice fit—jeans that had no paint smears and a slim-fitting scoop neck T-shirt that normal gals might sometimes wear on dates. I ran a comb through my hair and tamed it back into a ponytail, pulled on my favorite vintage boots and called it done.

Downstairs I paused by Jack's door when I heard the buzzing of an electric razor. Outside, the dog barked, agitated. When I opened the front door, a woman was standing on the porch, one arm raised to knock. In her other arm was a covered dish. Her mouth opened into a tiny O.

I stared at her for a few seconds, but she said nothing.

"Hi," I said, because it seemed like I had to. "Can I help you?"

Her big hazel eyes narrowed. She looked a few years older than me, with heavy mascara and platinum hair. She wore a blouse so tight across the chest, the most critical button looked like it would pop the next time she inhaled. Her denim skirt was short and frayed, as if she'd cut it to make it shorter. She wobbled on her pink high heels, and I frowned as I thought of them leaving little divots in the floorboards of my porch.

"I was looking for Jack," she said, drawing his name out into two syllables, *Jay-yack.*

Bella growled from the corner of the porch.

"Oh, he's, uh, out right now. Can I take a message?"

She looked past me into the house, then gave me a long once-over. "His truck's here. Isn't he off today?"

Heat rose in my chest.

"I'm Enza," I said. "And you are?"

"Bringing him a casserole." She smiled then, blinking at me slowly, the way a cat does when staring you down. "I know he had a bad night, and I usually drop by after the hard days to cheer him up."

"Ah, that's thoughtful of you to bring a casserole."

"Yeah, some nights I bring him dinner. Sometimes we get around to eating it." She pursed her lips.

My cheeks burned. I wanted to shove that casserole right into her face. Bella growled again, and I thought, *Good dog.*

"Well, sorry you missed him." I moved to shut the door.

The woman smiled her fake smile again and thrust the dish into my arms. "Tell him I'll see him next time," she purred. "And tell him I said thanks again for last time." She winked at me, and then turned and strutted down the porch steps. I cringed at the clack-clack of those high heels and fought the urge to slam the door. She was no doubt waiting for that, so I shut it gently and then stormed down the hall and flung open the door to Jack's room, still carrying that damned covered dish against my ribs.

The door banged against the wall, and Jack turned toward me, dropping the shirt he was holding to just below his waist. His hair was wet from the shower, and he was completely naked.

"Jeez," he said. "Don't you knock?" His big blue eyes were wide. They shifted from me to the casserole, and he cocked his head. "What's that?"

"Dinner." I tore my gaze away from his chest. "From your girlfriend." He must have thought I was so naive. "How long did you think you could hide that from me, Jack?"

His eyes got wider. He held the shirt against him. I tried to ignore his broad shoulders, his muscular thighs, the tattoo of the bird that covered his arm from elbow to shoulder, wrapping onto his back.

"Who?" he asked, and he looked genuinely puzzled.

"About five-four, bottle blond, skintight wardrobe. I'm not that kind of girl, you jerk."

I shoved the dish at him. He dropped the shirt as he caught the dish, and I stole one last look as he held it as skillfully as he could manage. Of course he'd be fucking perfect all over, with a body like one Michelangelo chiseled out of marble.

"Now hang on," he said. "I do not have a girlfriend. I'm not that kind of *guy*."

"Well someone headed down the driveway might beg to differ."

"Enza," he said. He smiled like he was stifling a laugh, and I wanted to clock him.

"This is funny to you?"

"Miranda is not my girlfriend." He stepped behind the dresser and set the casserole on top, then pulled a pair of boxer shorts from the nearest chair. "It's absolutely not what you're thinking." Hiding himself behind the dresser, he slipped the shorts on.

I scowled, turning toward the door. "How stupid do you think I am? Does any woman ever fall for that line any more?"

"Listen," he said, grabbing my arm. "That woman has been after me forever. We went out a few times, I broke up with her, and she just keeps coming back like a damn weed. I keep telling her it's over, but she doesn't get it."

I pulled my arm free. "She said she came over all the time."

"She does. In that way that people do right before you get a restraining order against them. She shows up at work, she shows up here. I even caught her inside once, waiting for me to get home. But I swear, there is nothing between us."

"Oh, for heaven's sake." I turned again, and he rushed to the door, blocking me from leaving.

"You don't believe me," he said, sounding truly hurt.

"Jack Mayronne, you let me out of here this instant." I glared at him, picturing a little voodoo doll with his stupid perfectly mussed hair. I imagined sticking pins into the middle where its heart should be. Then sticking a few in some places lower down.

He placed his hand on my arm, sending a rippling current along my skin. "I wouldn't lie to you like that."

"Don't," I said. When I reached for the doorknob, he leaned into me. I could feel the heat from the shower coming off him in a wave. Under different circumstances, I would have buried my face in his hair, but I just tensed up, waiting for him to move.

"Trap me in the bedroom?" I said. "That's your plan?"

He grinned that damned crooked grin and said, "There are worse places to be trapped with me, *non*?"

That was it. I stomped his toes, and he sprang back, a yelp filling the air between us. I flung the door open and said, "I want you out of here by the time I get back."

"Dammit, Enza. Come back here!"

I stomped down the hall, my boot heels pounding the floorboards hard enough to leave a few dents of my own. As I strode out the front door, I could still hear him calling my name.

Chapter Seven

OUTSIDE, the air felt less charged. The sky was turning to violet, like the whole world was about to start over from scratch. I hated the idea of being in the house with Jack just then. So I climbed into my Jeep and started driving.

The back roads all looked the same after a while, and I couldn't tell if I'd gone in a big circle or led myself out into the middle of nowhere. It was soothing, driving alongside the cool green-gray water of the canal. The katydids had started again, their buzzing louder than the car engine. When at last I came to a familiar intersection, I realized Vergie's house was only about five minutes away, to my right. I turned left and drove until I came to a diner with a neon sign in the shape of a catfish.

It was a clapboard shack, all weathered wood with peeling paint, and had an earthy kind of charm. It sat nestled in a grove of huge oak trees, their limbs draped with white lights that twinkled in the branches like fireflies. A few cars were parked out front, and a couple of smokers lingered by the door. A sign read "Cold Beer, Catfish Special," with a hand-painted arrow pointing toward the shack from the road. There was no sign that indicated the name.

There weren't any other places between here and Vergie's—

not along this little highway. I was tired of driving but still didn't want to go back and face Jack. Pushing thoughts of him aside, I climbed out of the Jeep. The two men by the door, both with gray beards and baseball caps, nodded a greeting as I stepped inside.

The place was dark except for lanterns hanging over the booths. Some tables were crammed together on one side of the room, and there was a bar in the back with red lights above it. The tables and chairs were mismatched, all different colors of vinyl likely reclaimed from 1950s diners. In the back, a group of men were playing pool. The air split with the sound of balls cracking on a break, followed by hoots and whistles. Smoke hung in clouds above me.

A few heads turned as I slid into a booth near the bar. I was hoping to hide there for a while and get myself together.

And give Jack enough time to leave.

A waitress with a short skirt and beat-up red and black cowboy boots came to the table. I could hear her boot heels, even over the jukebox.

"Hi," she said. "Get you something to drink?"

"Bourbon. A double, please."

She smiled and set a menu in front of me, then headed to the bar.

There was an empty corner in the back, a space where two couples danced to an old country song I remembered from when I was a kid. Watching them tangled together made me think of Jack, and I shook my head, like that might knock the thought of him away. But skin has a memory of its own. I could still feel his hands as he held me tight against him, and his lips as they moved along my neck.

The waitress brought my drink and asked if I wanted something to eat.

So I ordered a burger. I had to eat, even though my stomach was churning. Bourbon with no food was a bad idea.

The couples danced on as the music changed to some modern country tune filled with false twang. By the way people looked at me, it was clear this was a local hangout that didn't get many outsiders. I knocked back the last of the bourbon, hoping the pleasant tingling in my toes might move to my brain and push away the image of Jack pinning me against that newly painted wall.

When I'd finished my burger and my second drink, a voice from behind me said, "It pains me to see a lady with an empty glass."

I turned, ready to let this guy have it. It took a minute to recognize him, but then he tugged on his suspenders, and the memory fell into place. Buck, from the hardware store.

"Didn't mean to startle you," Buck said. "Just saw you over here and thought I'd say hello. What are you doing here all by yourself?"

"Needed a break. Have a seat if you like."

He squeezed into the other side of the booth. When the waitress breezed by, he said, "Hey, Sheila, can we get two more of what the lady's having?"

"Just a single this time," I said.

Sheila nodded and sauntered back to the bar.

"You look like you could use another one," he said. "If you don't mind me saying."

"Nope. I imagine I do."

He smiled a sad smile. "That Jack giving you a hard time?"

"My house is giving me a hard time."

He stared at me, raising one eyebrow. There was a twinkle in his eye.

"There really are no secrets in this town," I said.

Sheila placed two drinks in front of us and winked at Buck.

"Cheers!" He clinked his glass against mine. "Can't live with 'em, can't shoot 'em without doing time."

I took a long swallow.

"He's a good guy," Buck said. "Just makes mistakes sometimes, like the rest of us."

"I suppose that's one way to look at it."

He smiled in that way that uncles do. "I'm sure you got a good reason to be mad, darlin'. You seem like a sensible woman. But knowing him, if he knows you're this upset, he's as mad at himself as you are. Don't hold it over him for too long."

I felt my cheeks flush from the bourbon. Maybe from something else too.

"Things always seem better in the morning," he said. "And they always seem worse at a place like this."

"Sounds like you've been in this predicament once or twice."

"Yep. Once or twice… You gonna be OK?"

I snorted. "I'm fine."

"I mean to get home, honey."

"Oh, sure. I'll be here a good long while. Next one will be coffee."

He finished his drink and eased out of the booth. "I'll leave you be, then. You get yourself home safe now, OK?"

I raised my glass as he ambled back to the other side of the room. Maybe Buck was right—maybe I was being too hard on Jack. We'd only known each other a few days, so why should I be surprised to learn he had baggage? Lord knows I had my share. I cursed out loud, shoving myself against the back of the booth.

When I heard heavy footsteps again, I thought Buck was coming back. To look at him, you wouldn't think he was such a softy. He looked like he could break a man in half with his thumb and index finger. "Really, I'm fine," I said, leaning my head against the booth.

"I'd say so." A man slid into the seat across from me. Remy. "Little Miss Firecracker." His voice was cool. "What are you doing in here all alone?"

"Being alone." I gave him a hard stare.

He had cleaned up considerably since that day at Buck's. It was criminal for such good looks to be wasted on an ass like him.

He raised an eyebrow and clasped his hands together on the table. "Looks to me like you could use some company."

"Let me save you some time," I said. "Whatever you think is going to happen here, it isn't."

He smiled so his dimples showed and leaned so close I smelled faint traces of aftershave. His eyes narrowed like he was about to trust me with a secret. "I just came to apologize, sugar. I think you and I got off on the wrong foot the other day. I was hoping I could make it up to you."

His knee pressed against mine under the table, and I didn't pull away.

"Let me guess. You love a good challenge."

There was that wolfish smile again. "I lost my manners that day, and I worry you got the wrong idea about me. I can't bear the thought of you thinking I'm such a jackass."

I laughed. "Why do you give a damn what I think?"

Without blinking, he said, "I know an extraordinary woman when I see one."

I took a sip from the glass. Part of me wanted to slap his cheek and walk away, but the wicked part of me wanted to stay a little longer.

"Come dance with me," he said, his eyes steady on mine.

"Don't really feel like dancing."

He flashed a mischievous grin, then stood and took my hand. "Come on, sugar, let me give you a proper apology. I'm not the big loup garou you think I am."

I was pleasantly numb, and bored with arguing. So I let him pull me from the table and lead me to the far corner of the bar. As an old blues song blared on the jukebox behind us, he raised my arms and placed them around his neck. He lowered his hands to the small of my back, pulling me against him, and I didn't exactly want to pull away.

"Now," he said, his lips moving against my ear, "that's not so bad, is it?"

His voice was gravelly and low, his breath warm against my neck. He smelled like tobacco and musk, like he'd been working in the sun all day. His hand was firm against my back. I started to pull away, but he drew me closer, his thumb barely sliding under the hem of my shirt to stroke my bare skin. My skin tingled beneath his fingers, and I stopped thinking of prying myself loose. Instead I leaned into him, sliding my fingers along the line of his collar.

"I feel bad for offending you the other day. Mayronne and me, we just don't get along. My temper sometimes gets the best of me when he's around."

"That's an understatement."

He laughed. "Fair enough."

"What did he ever do to you, anyway?" As soon as I asked, I felt him bristle.

"Aw, you don't want to hear about all that. We just don't see eye to eye. Never have, and we go back a long time."

The sad look in his eyes made me think that maybe he wasn't the bad guy I'd first taken him for. It was beginning to feel like my instincts were completely off-kilter down here, so much so that I couldn't tell the sheep from the wolves any more. The more he talked, the more I wondered about what had happened between him and Jack to create such a rift.

He spun me and then pulled me close again. "What do you say, sugar? Think we can be friends now?"

At the table behind us, Buck leaned back in his chair. From the look on his face, I half expected him to come split us apart.

The music changed to a fast song, and Remy squeezed my hip. "Come on, next round's on me."

He set our drinks on the table and slid next to me in the booth so that we were barely touching. "So tell me something about yourself," he said. "What brings you down to the bayou?"

I told him about Vergie and how I spent my summers there, how I rode billy goats through the thickets and fished in the swamp with a bottle cap on a hook.

"Now I'm trying to fix Vergie's house," I said. "But you don't want to hear about all of that."

"Sure I do." He draped his arm across the back of the booth behind my head.

I knew I was tipsy because I was talking too much, going on and on about preserving the architecture and keeping it true to what Vergie would have liked. When I finally stopped myself, he said, "And then you're handing it over to Mayronne?"

I stopped, puzzled. "What do you mean?"

He raised his eyebrows, sipping his drink. "Oh, maybe I misunderstood."

"Misunderstood what?"

He shrugged. "I heard him telling Buck he was staying in that house once y'all were finished with it. Said it was his when the work was done."

I felt my cheeks burning. "He said what?"

He stared at me for a long moment. "Well, maybe I got that wrong. Never mind."

"That son of a bitch. What else did he say?"

He finished his drink. "Sorry, sugar. Like I said—I might have misheard the whole thing." He moved the glass in a tiny circle. "Forget I said anything. Let's talk about something more pleasant."

I shook my head, thinking I'd go back to the house, throw all of Jack's stuff into the yard and pray for rain while I did it. "Bastard," I hissed, tossing back the rest of my drink.

"Sorry. We were getting along so well. I don't like to make a lady mad." He brushed a lock of hair behind my ear.

I leaned back against the booth. "It's fine. I'm not mad at you."

He slid closer. "Good. I'd hate to wreck our evening." His hand traveled along my thigh, high enough to refocus my attention. When I glanced down, he said, "I could take your mind off all of that nonsense."

"Yeah, I bet you could."

"Let me show you what the Big Easy's all about, jolie."

Before I could say anything, he leaned over and brushed his

lips against my neck, drawing a line from my ear to my collarbone. The roughness of his cheek made me shiver.

I lay my hand on his chest, more to steady myself than anything else, and he kissed me hard on the mouth, sliding his hand along my jaw. I glanced over his shoulder to see if anyone was watching, but quickly decided I didn't care. The jukebox was still blaring, and the couples were still swaying in the pool of light in the corner. His hand seemed heavy on my collarbone, holding me in place. I imagined what it would be like if we were alone, and for a solid minute, considered the likelihood of that happening. When he suddenly broke away, I opened my eyes.

Jack was pulling him out of the booth by his collar.

"What the hell!" Remy said.

Jack dragged him into the cluster of tables. "Was I not clear the other day?" Couples scattered as Jack spun Remy around and shoved him face-first into the bar. "What part of 'stay away from her' was so hard to understand?"

Jack turned to me and said, "We're leaving."

Remy laughed, dabbing blood from his split lip. "I don't think she wants to go anywhere with you, son. And now you're gonna get your ass kicked."

He rushed at Jack, throwing a punch that caught him on the chin. Jack staggered backwards and swung as Remy came closer.

The bartender shouted, pulling a baseball bat from under the register. "Oh hell no," he yelled. "Take that outside!"

They kept swinging at each other, falling against a table. Beer bottles crashed to the floor, sending a spray of glass beneath their feet. The fight was so fast it was like it couldn't be happening. I had to convince myself that, yes, it was. Then I realized I should be doing something to stop it, since I was just sitting there watching slack-jawed while two guys beat each other into lumps.

Over me.

"Hey," I said, scrambling out of the booth. "Cut it out." I stumbled toward them, only then discovering how drunk I actually was. Buck grabbed me around the waist and corralled me against the bar as the crowd moved out of their way.

"It's gonna take more than you to bust them up," he said.

The bartender rushed over, pulling Jack off Remy as he dodged one last punch. He held the bat between them, his face reddening. "Outside," he yelled. "Now!"

Remy stood, grinning as blood trickled from his lip. He stepped closer to Jack and leaned down into his face. "I hope you're getting used to the flames, Mayronne," he said. "There's still room enough for you in hell, and I'm gonna see to it that you get there." He turned and spat a mouthful of blood on the floor as he walked to the door. He flashed his wolfish grin back at me, one that said he wasn't giving up just yet.

"Out," the bartender said, giving him a final shove. The door slammed behind him, and the bartender turned to Jack. "And you too. Don't come back until you can be civilized." He brushed his hands off on his jeans, muttering to himself as he walked back around the bar. He downed a shot of something dark, and then took out a broom and dustpan.

I pushed my way through the crowd and went outside. In the parking lot, Jack and Remy were circling each other like a couple of junkyard dogs.

"You really want to do this?" Jack asked. "Let's go."

Remy laughed, the blood on his face black in the moonlight. "I've been waiting for this for a long time."

"Stop!" I shouted, grabbing Remy's arm.

He yanked his arm free, and I fell backwards onto the gravel.

"Son of a bitch," Jack said, and clocked him in the eye. Remy staggered backwards, then rushed him like a quarterback and put him in a headlock.

I scrambled to my feet, so mad I'd almost sobered up. Before I could get to them, the door opened, and Buck rushed across the parking lot, barreling toward them like a bull. He pried Remy off and twisted his arm behind his back. The big man made it look easy. He had forty pounds on Remy and Jack. He could have knocked Remy flat on the ground if he wanted to.

"That's enough," Buck said.

Remy gritted his teeth. He struggled to free himself, but Buck's grip was like a bear trap.

Jack rubbed his eyebrow and winced as his fingers came away red.

"Are you gonna leave now?" Buck asked Remy. "Or do I need to break your arm to convince you that you've worn out your welcome?"

Remy grimaced and muttered something I couldn't quite make out. Buck loosened his grip, and Remy stepped away, shrugging his shoulders and shaking his head like a boxer going into the ring. I thought for a second he'd take a swing at Buck, but he only trudged across the parking lot. As he climbed into his truck, he yelled, "This ain't over, Mayronne. Not even close!" He peeled out, spraying gravel in an arc.

Jack walked over to me, his face stern.

"What are you doing?" I asked. "What's wrong with you?"

"I came to take you home," he said, irritated.

"I'm not going anywhere with you." I crossed my arms over my chest and wobbled a little, feeling the full punch of the bourbon now.

"I thought you might say that."

"Well congratulations on your outstanding powers of reasoning." I sneered as the words came out slurred.

He cocked his head. "You going to make this difficult?"

"If you didn't already look like hell, I'd slug you myself."

He took a step closer, his jaw rigid. In one swift motion, he scooped me up and heaved me over his shoulder.

"Hey," I hollered. "Put me down!"

He ignored me and wrapped his arms around my legs, pinning me against him as I pounded my fists against his back.

"Jack Mayronne, you put me down this instant," I yelled. I looked around for help and saw Buck leaning against his old blue pickup truck, smoking a cigarette. "Buck!" I howled. "Help me!" But he just smirked and waved at me.

"Jack! I'm not kidding. You put me down or—"

"Or what?"

"Just put me down!"

He carried me across the parking lot and slipped me off his shoulder when we reached his truck. I stood dumbfounded as the earth seemed to tilt sideways, and I felt sure I'd hit the ground again. He reached behind me, opened the door and motioned for me to get inside.

I slapped him across the cheek. "How dare you! You can't just come in here and drag me away like you're some kind of Neanderthal."

"Don't make me tie you down in the back," he said calmly. "Because I've got the bungee cords."

I glared at him, but he stared me down, his hands on his hips.

"You can hit me again if you want," he said. "But you're still getting inside."

I was too tired and too dizzy to fight. Grumbling, I climbed into the seat and slammed the door just as he pulled his arm away. He slid into the driver's side and started the truck, then waved at Buck as we drove past.

Suddenly nauseated, I leaned against the window, closing my eyes. I didn't think I'd had that much to drink, but now the entire earth seemed to be pitching from one side to the other, tossing me around like a pebble.

After a couple of miles, Jack asked, "What got into you back there?" His voice was cold. "You can't go teasing people like Remy."

"I wasn't teasing anyone. And I don't need you to protect me."

As he shifted gears, my brain seemed to crash against the inside of my skull. I rolled down the window to get some air. The stars were bouncing around like pinballs. I closed my eyes again.

"You're just jealous," I mumbled.

"Maybe."

"You thought you were so smart."

He said nothing, shifting again as we hit the curvy stretch of road. If he was trying to make me carsick, he was about to succeed.

I rolled my head toward him, waving my finger in the space between us. "You're trying to get close to me so you can stay in the house. You think if I fall for you, I won't be able to kick you out."

"That's ridiculous."

"It almost worked, but I'm onto you now."

"You're drunker than a wildcat, honey." He shifted again, punching the gas. "And now you're just talking nonsense."

"Am I?"

"Yes, you are." His tone was cool and even, but he clenched his jaw as he gripped the wheel.

I leaned my cheek against the door. The warm breeze eased my pounding head. "Had me going for a while too," I said. "But Remy told me what you had planned."

He stared at the road. "Do you have any idea how stupid that was? How dangerous that guy is?"

"He told me what you said about getting the house. You had this all planned out from the start. Thought you had me."

"Christ almighty," he muttered.

"But you can forget it. Our deal's off. Nobody makes an ass out of me."

"Yeah, you don't need any help with that," he grumbled.

"You're evicted! Immediately." I stumbled over the words and laughed. "Evicted. Such a weird word. I think it's Latin for 'out on your ass.'"

"We'll talk about this tomorrow. You're blitzed."

"And you're a jerk. A house-stealing, fake, seductive jerk."

He sighed. "Darlin', you just don't get it. For such a smart woman, you do some stupid things."

"Don't lecture me." My voice rose. "You've got no room to talk about stupid things. Got no room to talk about anything."

He downshifted suddenly and pulled off into the grass. The truck rumbled along the shoulder, halfway off the road, and then came to a stop. I braced myself with one hand on the dash, a little too late.

"Are you crazy?" I said.

He turned sideways and stared at me. "Dammit, Enza, this is no joke. That guy's a shark. He destroys people like you for fun. And to see you just wandering right into his arms—how can you not see what he's up to?"

I froze, my hands now gripping the seat. This was the first time I'd seen him so frantic, his cheeks flushed. That look was enough to sober me right up.

"He's a felon, Enza. He's got a rap sheet that could stretch across the lake. He's left dozens of gals like you broken and in pieces, and there's not one single reason he ought to be walking around a free man."

I didn't know what to say. I didn't know what to believe or who to trust.

"You're lying," I said.

He slammed his fist into the steering wheel. The horn blared, echoing in the darkness.

I jumped, sliding against the door as I reached for the handle. But we were miles from the bar, and being out in the bayou at night was like being in a labyrinth.

"Good God," he said. "Are you completely blind?" He lowered his voice, taking a deep breath. I thought he was going to lose it completely, but he sat still, staring at me. "Go down to the police station. It's public record."

My head throbbed. I was going to be sick.

"How could you believe him over me?" he asked. "I thought you trusted me. I thought we had something here."

"I don't know what to think any more." My voice sounded like a squeak.

He shook his head, staring out into the night. When he spoke again, his voice had softened. "This is about before. About Miranda."

The silence was stifling. All around us, fireflies were blinking out over the water. Under any other circumstances, it would have been a beautiful night. But there I was, stuck in a swamp with a guy who was leaning toward crazy, who could easily drive off and leave me there to become the latest missing person. I just wanted to go home and pretend this night hadn't happened.

"I don't know how I can convince you," he said.

"Don't. I don't want to talk about this."

"Of course you don't."

"Can we just get out of here?"

He stared straight ahead for so long it made me nervous, thinking he might snap after all.

I slid my hand along the side panel of the door, pausing when I found the handle.

He shook his head, shifting the truck into gear and pulling back onto the road. "I don't know what to do with you," he said. "How to make you see."

We rode in silence the rest of the way home. I sat curled up in the seat, my face resting against the doorframe. I knew Remy was trouble. There was no rational reason for what I'd done. Even in my sloppy state, I knew I'd done it to get back at Jack. And even though I might blame it on something else tomorrow, I felt like a teenager trying to avenge her broken heart with the baddest boy in town.

Jack kept glancing at me. I could feel it, just like I could feel the waves of disappointment rolling off him. But I had nothing left to say, so I kept my eyes closed. I was afraid of what else he might see if I looked too long in his direction. Vergie said once that the eyes were the easiest way to let folks see into the hidden parts of yourself.

"You'd better be careful who you let go peeking around in there," she'd said. "Sometimes it's hard to see in, like looking into a house in the daylight, but other times it's easier than you'd think—like when it's dark outside and your neighbor's left his shades up."

I figured Jack Mayronne had seen enough of me for one day.

When we pulled into the yard, Jack climbed out and opened my door. I stalked past him to the porch. I expected him to leave, because it's what I would have done. But he followed me up the steps as I fumbled for my keys. I swore under my breath, jamming the wrong key into the lock.

He reached around me, taking the keys. "Here, let me."

When he pushed the door open, I stepped past him into the house, avoiding his stare. He hesitated in the pale light, as if he wasn't quite sure what to do.

"Just go," I said. I couldn't get away from him fast enough.

"I'm not leaving until you talk to me," he said, his voice cool and even.

"I've got nothing else to say to you, Jack."

He held me to him and said, "Just listen to me." His lips moved against my ear, and I felt my whole traitorous body relax.

I tried to ignore how good his arms felt around me.

He turned me toward him and nudged me against the wall so that his body was pressed against mine, as if he knew I needed him to hold me steady. "What were you thinking back there at the bar? You could have been hurt."

I scoffed. "I was upset about Miranda, sure. But then Remy told me you were trying to steal my house."

"Remy lied to you. I never said any of that."

I swallowed hard.

"Look at me," he said, and I did.

"Why didn't you kick me out when you first met me?" he asked.

My legs felt like they would buckle at any second. Jack was the only thing holding me up. "I felt sorry for you. That's the only reason I agreed to any of this."

"That's a lie," he said, staring me down. "You need me. And you want me."

"What I want is someone who isn't trying to con me."

"If anybody's conning you, it's Remy. And if you can't tell the difference, then you're not half as smart as I thought you were."

"I never should have let myself—"

He gazed at me, his eyebrow arched. "Never should have let yourself what?"

"Never should have let you stay."

He lifted my chin and pushed my hair behind my ear. "That's not what you were going to say."

Before I could argue, he slid his hands into my hair and kissed me. I moved to turn away, but he deepened the kiss, his teeth pinching my lip. His taut chest pressed into mine, and I shivered as he tugged at my hair. I grabbed his hips and dug my fingers into his back until he groaned.

When he finally pulled away, I felt dizzy, out of breath. He stared at me, as if waiting to see what I'd do. My hand rested at his waist, my fingers sliding over his belt. Before he could say anything, I pulled him to me, kissing him with a fierceness I hadn't felt before.

I felt the tension in his arms as he slid his hands along my skin, holding me tight against him. I gripped his shoulders, hoping to make him ache for me the way I did for him.

When I slid my hands into his hair, he stopped and took a step away from me. My lips tingled, and I could still taste him. It was getting harder to breathe.

"Hang on," he said, his hand barely resting on my shoulder.

"Just get over here." I grabbed him by the collar and closed the space between us.

He stepped backwards, biting his lip. "Not like this."

My head was spinning, but all I could think of was the way his hands would feel as they traced the curves of my shoulders, my hips. "Stop toying with me. Isn't this what you wanted?"

He let me kiss him, but then pulled away. "I can't," he said. "You're still drunk." With little effort, he lifted me into his arms and carried me up the stairs. He set me down on the bed in Vergie's room and flipped on the lamp.

"Jack," I said, pulling him closer. I slid one hand in the waist of his jeans as I kissed him. He groaned, pushing my hands away.

"Sleep it off," he said, easing me onto my back. He pulled my boots off and set them on the floor, then swung my legs onto the bed.

"You're leaving me again?" I said. "What are you so afraid of?"

He leaned over me, pulling the sheet up, and pinned my hand to my side when I reached for him again.

"Stay," I said, already feeling my eyelids getting heavy.

He kissed my forehead and whispered, "Good night, Enza. We'll talk tomorrow."

I struggled to keep my eyes open, reaching for him again. But he was already standing at the door, turning off the light.

"Jack," I said. My voice sounded so distant. "Wait."

"What?"

"How'd you know to come there tonight?"

"Buck called me."

He started to close the door, but I called out to him again.

"What?"

"I'm sorry I hit you. I don't want you to leave."

I thought he said something else—I was sure I heard his voice, but it was so distant now, like a bird calling from across the swamp. I heard the click of the door, felt the breeze from the open window tickle my hair. Then there were only his footsteps thumping down the stairs, echoing in the dark.

Chapter Eight

MORNING. Vergie's bedroom. Bourbon headache.

These facts registered while I lay watching the threadbare curtains waver in the breeze. My head was pounding, and already the room was too warm.

What I didn't remember was how I got into my own bed and why I was still wearing jeans and a T-shirt. What I did remember was meeting Miranda, yelling at Jack, going out for a drive, getting hungry and going to the seafood shack. Then things got fuzzy. There was bourbon at the bar—lots of bourbon. And then dancing. With Remy.

Remy. I wished that had been a bourbon-induced dream. I shook my head, as if that might straighten out my tangle of memories. Then I saw a flash of the scuffle out in the parking lot. Remy's bloody lip. And then Jack brought me home and put me to bed.

Alone. After I begged him to stay with me.

I slid under the covers and groaned.

Eventually I called up enough courage to haul myself out of bed and into the shower. When I glimpsed myself in the mirror, I cringed. It only took that one glance to convince me that everything I was afraid had happened actually had. I was doomed to a walk of shame in my own goddamn house.

～

AFTER WHAT SEEMED LIKE HOURS, I crept down the stairs, preparing myself for the awkward conversation that surely awaited me. Jack would be in the kitchen, making coffee, and I'd have to apologize for acting like an idiot, as much as it pained me to do so. But when I got downstairs, there was no Jack. No coffee.

I searched the house, but it was empty. The furniture in his bedroom was still shoved together in the center like an island of maple and antique walnut. His bed was still in pieces—we'd forgotten to put it back together. And then we'd had that fight, and I'd left.

My stomach tightened. I'd screamed at him and told him to leave.

In the living room, a blanket and a pillow sat on the sofa. He'd stayed, but where was he now? I peered out the window but didn't see his truck in the yard. Puzzled, I went to make my own coffee. His shirt was on the kitchen table.

When I picked it up I saw the flecks of dried blood and felt sick as the rest of the night came rushing back. Trying to break up the fight in the parking lot, Jack throwing me over his shoulder and hauling me to his truck. I would be that person everyone was talking about today. I shoved my palm against my forehead, cursing myself for acting like I didn't have a lick of sense. What on earth was happening to me?

There was a whining at the door, followed by persistent thumping. When I opened it, Bella pushed the screen door against the frame with her paw. When I cracked the screen, she rushed in and skidded behind me, then sat down and blinked at me, her tongue lolling.

"Don't look at me like that."

She lay down next to my feet and let out a heavy sigh.

"You're the one that started dragging up voodoo, and look where it got us."

She stared up at me, and I swear that dog rolled her eyes.

"I could do without the attitude," I said, carrying a paint can into the kitchen. I might as well get to work, with or without Jack. If he'd been called out to a fire, I'd be waiting a long time.

THE KITCHEN DIDN'T HAVE a lot of wall space to paint. It had huge cabinets, a picture window and white paneling under the chair rails. I was hoping my pale yellow paint would brighten it up a bit and also take my mind off the night before.

Maybe it was best I couldn't remember any further details.

I washed the walls down with a sponge, then let them dry while I had my second cup of coffee. Sufficiently caffeinated, I laid out drop cloths and stirred the paint. When I came back with my tool box, Bella was sniffing the paint can.

"Hey, no."

She sneezed into the can.

"Outside," I ordered. She snorted and then walked to the door. When I opened it, she bolted. She didn't stay miffed for long, that dog.

I skipped the painter's tape and used a brush and a putty knife to paint against in tricky spots. As I worked my way around the cabinets, those memories of Remy came creeping back. It was silly to have believed him for a nanosecond. He was clearly trying to take me home, and I very nearly let him. Jack had been there when I didn't even know I needed him.

And then I'd behaved like a child.

And he'd stayed here with me anyway.

Standing on the counter, I strained to reach the places just below the crown molding. I was nearly done over the sink when there was a knock at the door.

"Hang on," I yelled. Holding the handle of the brush in my

teeth, I backed down into a chair, then onto the floor. I balanced the brush on the paint can, and the knocking came again.

"Christ," I muttered. My head was pounding hard enough as it was.

I opened the door and saw that it had started to rain. Miranda held the screen door wide open.

Before I could speak, she said, "Oh. You're still here."

"Well, I do own the place. Miranda, is it?"

She smacked her gum. "That's right. Guess Jack told you about us." She smiled a tight smile, planting one hand on her hip. Today she had chosen extremely short cutoffs and a tank top that showed far too much cleavage and the top of a lacy red bra. I had a hard time picturing Jack even talking to her, let alone touching her.

That thought nauseated me all over again.

"I guess you came back for your dish," I said. "Let me get it for you."

She glared at me and popped her gum.

I retrieved the dish from the kitchen, the untouched casserole still inside. When I came back to the door, she had stepped into the hallway, the screen closed behind her. "Here you go," I said, thrusting it at her.

She stumbled backward, teetering on her heels as she stepped down onto the porch through the screen door. I boxed her in at the threshold, standing with one hand on the doorknob.

"I don't know who you think you are," she said, "but Jack doesn't give a shit about you. He only cares about me."

I started to slam the door, but Miranda wedged her foot in the threshold and threw her shoulder into the door, knocking me off balance enough to push her way inside. She may have been rail thin, but she was quick—no doubt accustomed to squeezing her way into places where she didn't belong.

"You think you can come here and steal him out from under me?" she said, her voice rising in pitch. "You think you got something I don't?" She waved her finger in my face, her bright pink nails flicking in the air between us. Her heels clacked on the floor until she'd backed me against the stair rail. One more step and she'd crash into me—then we'd both be wearing that damned casserole.

"You should go now."

"I'm not going until I see Jack."

I balled my hand into a fist and said as calmly as I could, "He's not here. And unless you want me to call the sheriff, I suggest you leave."

I figured I could take her if I had to, but she looked like the kind that scratched and pulled hair. That wasn't my thing. I could use what I remembered from college judo and kung-fu movies, though. She'd be easy to topple in those ridiculous heels.

Miranda laughed. "You're a liar, just like him. I don't feel anything but lies in this room." She held one arm out, as if invoking a spirit, and I thought for the first time that she might actually be crazy. "Nope," she said, closing her eyes. "No truth. Not at all. You think you can—"

"Miranda!"

We both turned toward the voice as the screen door opened.

Jack held a paper bag to his chest, his shirt dappled by the rain. "What are you doing? You're not supposed to be within five hundred yards of here."

"Baby," she said, her voice breathy. "I came to see you. I miss you."

"Miranda, the judge said if you did this one more time he was sending you to jail. Is that what you want?"

"Honey, please," she said, sauntering toward him, her hips swaying. "We can fix this. I know we can."

He set the bag down. "No, Miranda. You need to leave. Right now, or I'm calling the sheriff."

"Oh, Jack," she purred, pouting. "You don't mean that." She reached out to touch him, and he recoiled. Behind them, a bolt of lightning streaked across the sky.

"I told you not to come back here, and I meant it."

She glared at him, then looked back at me. "I see what's going on here. But you'll get what you deserve." She stepped toward me, but Jack grabbed her arm and pulled her back onto the porch. The spring in the screen door popped, and it stood wide open. The rain poured down, blowing a mist through the open door.

Miranda pleaded as Jack pulled her down the porch steps. The dog rushed by him, a blur of gray and brown, and streaked through the house like a bullet.

"Hey!" I shouted, and was torn between chasing the muddy dog and calling the sheriff myself. Outside, Jack had dragged Miranda onto the lawn. She had tossed the covered dish on the ground and was flailing her arms above her head, like she was calling down all the spirits to help her, but Jack turned his back and returned to the house. She stood as still as an oak, the rain pounding against her skin.

For a minute, she seemed to not notice the storm at all, but then picked up the dish and walked back to her car.

Jack paused on the porch steps. He looked at me with a pitiful expression, one that said he didn't care to talk about this but knew he had to. His shirt clung to his skin, soaked from the rain. The clicking of the dog's toenails caught my attention again as she bounded past me. From the kitchen, there was a clatter and a snort, then the yellow-streaked dog raced up the stairs, leaving buttercream paw prints in her wake.

"Dog! Get back here, dog!" I yelled, and then bit my lip to hold in a string of curses. The pounding of Catahoula paws rolled overhead. In the kitchen, the paint pail was on its side, a lake of yellow spreading across the floor. I squeezed my eyes shut, like I could stop time if I tried hard enough. If only I could take back the last hour, the last couple of days, and start over again.

When I opened my eyes, Jack was standing by the stairs. He placed two fingers in his mouth, ripping out a whistle loud enough to shake the roof. Bella came running back down the stairs and out the front door in a blur. Jack shut the door and flipped the bolt.

"I'll take the kitchen," he said. "You get the stairs."

We stumbled over each other in the kitchen, him sopping up yellow paint with a sponge and a dustpan while I filled a bucket with water in the sink. As I ran into the hallway with the soapy water, he fished a mop out of the closet and went to work on the huge yellow splotch on the floor. The overturned paint can had not been full, but it had enough paint in it to spread three or four feet across the floor.

I scrubbed the yellow paw prints off the stairs. They were drying fast, but the water-based paint would come up with some effort. The trail of prints went all the way through the upstairs hall but had quickly faded out. This was nothing a quick polish wouldn't fix.

Thunder rumbled overhead. I shut the windows in the bedroom and then trudged down the stairs, dreading what I'd find in the kitchen.

Jack was on his hands and knees, scrubbing the floor with two wet dish sponges. I knelt next to him, scrubbing the trail of paw prints that led into the hallway.

"I'm sorry about all of this," he said. He had that sad arch in his brows again.

"I know," I said. The paint was coming up, but it would leave a stain. The floor would definitely have to be refinished. Maybe painted instead of stained.

"That's the best we can do," I said.

He kept scrubbing.

"Hey," I said, placing my hands over his. "Enough. This floor needed to be redone anyway."

He stopped and sat back on his heels. "I'm sorry you had to deal with Miranda again. Sometimes she won't take no for an answer, and—" He shook his head, staring at the floor. "She's just had too hard a life."

"You don't have to explain if you don't want to," I said. But I hoped he would.

"She cared more for me than I did for her. That's pretty much it."

But he did care. He cared enough not to embarrass her, not to be cruel out there in the rain—and that made it impossible to be upset with him.

"How long ago was this?"

"More than a year," he said. "Part of me thought she was finally over it, since she hasn't tried to see me in months."

He tossed the sponges into the pail of water, then stood and dusted himself off. He pulled me to my feet, and I said, "I should be apologizing. I wish I'd dreamed half of what happened last night."

His eyebrow arched.

"You were kind to come and get me, and save me from myself."

He shrugged. "It's OK."

"It's definitely not OK. I said some unkind things."

"You do have quite the temper."

"When I got up this morning and you weren't here, I was afraid you'd really left."

A smile touched the corner of his mouth. "I just went out for beignets." He stepped into the hall to get the bag, then pulled a plate from the cabinet. As he dumped the contents of the bag, a cloud of powdered sugar floated in the air between us.

He popped one of the beignets in his mouth and pushed the plate toward me.

"I'm really glad you stayed."

"Oh yeah?" He paused as he bit into another one.

I nodded. "I seem to remember asking you to stay in bed with me."

He held one of the pastries to my lips. "Try one."

I took a bite, my lips brushing over his fingers. It was like a little puff of heaven rolling on my tongue.

"Did you want to?" I asked.

His stare turned to smoldering. "I couldn't. You were pretty drunk."

I rose from my chair and slid onto his lap, straddling him. He inhaled sharply as I brushed my finger over his lips to sweep away a streak of sugar. "And if I hadn't been?"

He caught my finger in his teeth. "I think you know the answer to that."

He slid his hands over my hips, and I bent to kiss him. His tongue teased mine, and then he was biting my lip in the most delicious way. I tugged at his hair, and he kissed me harder, sliding his hands under my shirt and pulling me against him.

He broke free and said, "I thought you wanted to keep this professional."

"I did."

"What happened?"

I tugged at the collar of his shirt. "Do you care that much?" I couldn't stop thinking about him. Naked. With his hands all over me. It was impossible to get anything done.

That's what had happened.

"Yeah," he said. "Actually, I do."

I shifted on his lap. "I was thinking we could bend the rules, this one time," I said. "Is that OK with you?" I couldn't stop kissing him, touching him, wanting him. Maybe getting him out of my system would dislodge the thoughts of him from my brain.

He raised one eyebrow, as if thinking it over. Then he grinned wickedly and said, "Yes, ma'am. Those terms are agreeable."

He slid his cheek along my neck, his teeth pinching me as he left a trail of kisses down to my collarbone. I sighed as he wound his fingers in my hair, and then he was standing, setting me on the table. I wrapped my legs around him, and he leaned back just far enough to lock his eyes with mine. His hair was tousled, standing on end, his shirt half unbuttoned. The way he looked at me made me ache all over.

He said, "Just this one time, huh?"

"Make it count, Mr. Mayronne."

He shoved the plate out of his way and lowered me back onto the table. I slid my fingers into his hair, and he grabbed my hands, placing them firmly above my head against the table top. He slid my shirt over my head, then unfastened my jeans and eased the zipper down.

"God, you are beautiful... all laid out here ready to eat."

My breath caught in my throat as he pulled my jeans down to my ankles and onto the floor. Slowly, he kissed a line along my thigh. My heart pounded as he slid his fingers over my hips, then slipped my panties off.

I sat up, and he let me undo the last few buttons of his shirt. He sighed as I unfastened his belt and unzipped his jeans. I gave them a tug, and he said, "Easy, chère. I take my time with you, remember?" He grabbed my hands, brought them to his face and kissed them.

"I certainly hope so," I said, sliding my hands along his chest.

He kissed me hard, biting my lip. In one quick move, he unhooked my bra and peeled it away. "Do you know how incredible you are?" he whispered, his lips moving against my ear. His thumbs slid over my nipples, and he traced tiny circles, forcing me to focus my thoughts only on where he touched me.

"I've thought about this so many times," he said, and took my breast into his mouth, his tongue lingering as it traced each curve. I felt the pinch of his teeth again and gasped. He gave a throaty chuckle and pushed me back onto the table, pinning me with his taut body. I squirmed under his weight but only to feel him press harder against me.

"Jack," I breathed, "how sturdy is this table?"

His laugh was muffled against my skin. "It survived at least six hurricanes, chère. I think it can withstand you and me."

One of his hands roamed through my hair while the other slid under my hips, pulling me closer so I could feel how hard he was against me.

"I've been dying to feel you again," I murmured, my hands drifting across his back.

Sleeping with Jack would complicate matters, but I didn't care. All I wanted was to feel his hands all over me, feel his hair brush over my skin as he kissed me.

"Is that a fact?" he asked, his voice ragged.

I gripped his shoulders, urging him on. He took his hands away just long enough to slide his jeans and boxers down over his hips. Kicking them off, he moved against me again, spreading my legs apart. He slid his cheek against my belly, his fingers trailing along the inside of my thigh. I shivered, waiting for him to seize me in his tight grip again.

"Jack," I said, and he eased inside me, as if he'd simply been waiting to hear his name on my lips. He moved so slowly at first that I ached for more of him. I cried out, shocked by the ways my body responded to his touch. His eyes stayed on mine as his hands traveled along my ribs, down my thighs, teasing me with their light touch. He moved harder then, faster, and I struggled to keep my breaths even. My muscles tightened, and he groaned, his hands gripping my hips so fiercely that I thought surely there would be bruises.

I loved to feel him holding me down. I called his name over and over as he picked up his rhythm, breathing hard. My hips bucked toward him, and my legs tightened around his waist. I couldn't get him close enough, couldn't get enough of him. My hands clawed at his back—he'd given up on pinning them above my head—and he leaned down to kiss me, stifling my cries.

His movements slowed again, and I caught my breath, raking my fingers through his hair. I pulled his face close so my lips moved against his ear. "I love the way you make me lose control," I said, my voice hoarse.

He nuzzled the spot below my jaw that made me shiver, then squeezed my hip with his hand as he altered our angle and pushed deeper inside me. He moved faster, placing his other hand on my cheek.

I squeezed my thighs, clenched around him, and he gasped. "God, Enza," he breathed, and the longing in his voice made me come undone. He slid his fingers between us, stroking the soft folds of my skin. There were so many sensations at once that I thought I couldn't withstand his touch a minute longer. When he kissed me again, I felt my whole body shudder like it would crumble into bits.

"Let yourself go," he said, his mouth moving against my ear. "You're so stunning like this."

He slid one hand under my head and the other to the small of my back, pulling me against him as he pushed harder. I struggled to take deeper, slower breaths to stop myself from shattering.

"Look at me, chère," he said, and when our eyes locked, my whole body trembled. His jaw clenched as his chest went rigid against mine, and I moaned his name into the hollow of his throat. Then he looked down at me, touching his nose to mine. He rested on one forearm, sliding his free hand along my cheek.

I felt more connected to him than I had to anyone, ever, in that moment I wished would never end.

Too bad we couldn't do it again.

"THERE ARE STILL A FEW BEIGNETS LEFT," he said, reaching for the plate. He'd pulled his boxers and jeans back on and was sitting in the chair next to me, tracing his fingers along my thigh.

I brushed powdered sugar from the front of my shirt. "I can't believe you just ravaged me in my kitchen."

He grinned, holding a beignet out to my lips. "You can have me in every room of this house, chère."

I caught the tiny pastry between my teeth, let my lips linger on his fingers. I tried to stop myself from imagining him making good on that promise.

He kissed me, his tongue sliding over my lip. "Delicious," he said, and my skin tingled down to my toes.

"We should get back to work," I said, taking his chin in my fingers.

He groaned playfully. "You're the boss." He gave my hip a squeeze. "In the kitchen, anyway."

I HAD every intention of doing some actual work on the house, but every muscle in my body was limp. I had to settle for calling the repair guys listed on the scrap of paper Grant had given me. I'd helped Jack get his bedroom into some semblance of order, putting the furniture back where it belonged. And now he was busy cleaning out closets upstairs and washing down the walls of the next room to be painted.

I was busy trying not to think about how all of my muscles had been so thoroughly exhausted. It helped to call and talk to the carpenters, since their mention of thousand-dollar repairs was the surefire antidote for ecstasy. I'd scheduled two estimates and was on my fourth phone call when Jack hurried down the stairs.

"Hey," he said, "you up for dinner tonight? Buck just called and asked us over."

"Um," I said, thinking this was not what people in meaningless relationships did, meeting surrogate parents and whatnot.

"It's no big deal. They wanted to welcome you, or welcome you back, as it were. Josie's been itching to meet you. That's my aunt."

I stared at him, thinking of Buck talking to me in the bar, then calling Jack when he saw me with Remy. I was mortified all over again.

"That's really nice of them. But I can't imagine Buck has a very high opinion of me right now."

"Relax," he said. "They've seen me do far stupider things, I promise you. They just want you to feel at home."

"OK," I said. It was rude not to accept an invitation, but I doubted they thought I was anything but trouble.

Buck and Josie lived right behind the hardware store. A grove of cypresses separated the two buildings, so to get to the house we had to turn into a driveway past the store.

"Buck likes an easy commute," Jack said.

At the end of the lane was a clearing with a big yard. A Craftsman-style house sat back near a pond dotted with herons. The house was two stories, painted tan with red trim. A black and white tuxedo cat emerged from the porch and perched on the banister as we walked up the path.

Jack ambled up the steps ahead of me, and the screen door banged open. A stocky woman with pale blond hair stepped out, her arms spread wide. She wore a tank top and jeans, a frilly apron and harness boots. Her hair was piled high on her head and held in a bun with a pencil.

"Jack," she said, "it's been too long. Where have you been hiding yourself?"

Before he could answer, she stepped around him and said, "And you must be Enza."

I held my hand out, but she grabbed me in a bear hug and said, "Vergie was such a sweetheart. It's so good to meet you."

"You too." My voice came out staccato as she clapped me on the back.

"This is my aunt, Josephine," Jack said.

She waved her hand at him and said, "I'm Josie. Only my mother called me Josephine."

"It's great to meet you. Thank you for having me."

"Oh, honey," she said. "You're practically family."

Leading us both inside, she took my hand. "Let me show you around."

Jack grinned. "Josie and Buck built this house. They love showing it off."

"It's beautiful." I eyed the staircase. They'd done an excellent job of re-creating Craftsman style: clean lines, dark wood, elegant simplicity. Even the windows had arched muntins, one of my favorite features of the period. "I'd show it off too."

Josie smiled. "We love refurbishing. We salvaged a lot of original woodwork from houses that were condemned after the last hurricane. Many people replace windows and doors with the new stuff, so we're always on the hunt."

I took mental notes as I followed Josie through the house. She finally led us to the backyard where Buck was stirring a giant metal pot on a propane burner.

"Hey, kid," Buck said to Jack. "I see you finally let this gal take a break."

"It's not easy." Jack winked at me. "But 'crawfish boil' were the magic words."

"I knew it," Buck said. "No one can resist."

Based on their questions, Jack had obviously filled in the blanks prior to dinner; I felt like Josie and Buck already knew everything about me. Josie wanted to learn more about my house-flipping adventures, saying she'd thought about trying a couple of her own. She and Buck did some carpentry on the side. In addition to running the store, she painted, and Buck could build just about anything.

"You want to help me with the biscuits?" Josie asked.

"I'm not much of a cook," I said, following her to the kitchen.

"Honey, please. Everybody can make biscuits."

She quickly tossed the dough together and rolled it out on the counter, then used the lid of a Mason jar to cut them out.

"I sure am glad you found Jack," she said.

I paused, placing the biscuits in the iron skillet like she'd shown me. "Yeah, that was a lucky surprise," I said. "He's been a huge help with the house."

She smiled, more to herself than at me.

"He's one of the good ones," she said.

Josie grabbed another skillet and filled it so the biscuits were touching, then slid both into the oven.

OUTSIDE, when Buck had declared the boil perfect, we all gathered at the picnic table and filled our bowls. Josie told me stories about Jack that made him blush so hard I thought he'd crawl under the table. They practically raised him after his parents had died, and now they were telling me all the things he'd never tell me about himself.

"Jack graduated cum laude from Tulane," Josie said. "Went on a scholarship."

"Is that right?" I turned to Jack and made a mental note to ask him more later.

"Lord, Josie," he said, running his fingers through his hair. "Enza doesn't want to hear about all that."

"He never did sing his own praises," she said.

I was envious of him, having Buck and Josie. They were just the kind of people I imagined everyone else in the world having back when I realized that I didn't. He'd gotten a second chance with parents, and that made me both happy for him and sad for myself. I could have been that way with Vergie, but I didn't know it at the time and didn't have someone to tell me.

We stayed there until well after dark, until the only lights were the tiny white bulbs strung in the oak trees by the picnic table. The low-hanging limbs created a canopy over us, filled with buzzing katydids.

"Well," Jack said at last, "we'd best be getting back. I have to go in later tonight, and this one will be up early to start more repairs."

"Don't be such a stranger," Josie said. "And bring this gal back, will you?" She hugged me again, squeezing me tight.

"Thank you," I said, "for everything."

Buck hugged me too, slapping me on the shoulder. "If you need anything, you just give us a call. I mean anything." It was a reference to the night before, most certainly. I hated that I'd gotten so close to Remy, so carelessly, but it was worse that Buck had to see it.

"Thanks."

Jack placed his hand on the small of my back as we walked toward the front of the house—a gesture that Josie did not miss—and then quickly dropped it when she smiled at us.

"Sorry," he whispered, as we headed for his truck. "Reflex, I guess."

"It's OK," I said. "I just wouldn't want to give them the wrong idea."

He nodded.

What I didn't say was that was the most at home I'd felt since I was a kid. Having dinner with Josie and Buck, hearing stories about Jack as a wild teenager, feeling the warmth of his hands spread through me every time we touched—these were things I hadn't expected to experience. Not that evening and maybe not ever again.

Chapter Nine

THE NEXT DAY, I went into Vergie's room with the intention of boxing things up. The room itself didn't need much work, but it would help to pack her things. I'd scheduled a couple of the repair guys Grant had recommended, but they couldn't come until Friday, which meant they'd start work Monday. The worst thing about repairs was the waiting.

Jack had gone in early in the morning to cover for a friend and would be back late. He was supposed to have two days off, but they'd been shorthanded for several weeks. The arsonist was making them all work extra shifts.

I had two boxes filled with books and knick-knacks by the time I got to the closet, but then my packing turned to snooping. I found an old record player on the top shelf and pulled an old zydeco record from its sleeve. The needle plopped into the groove, and music rolled through the room. I grabbed one of Vergie's straw hats and put it on. It was a little tight, and the big brim flopped down in front of my eyes. It seemed to catch the sound from the record and funnel it straight into my ears. Pushing the clothes aside, I caught the faintest hint of Vergie's magnolia-scented perfume. It was like being snatched backward in time, to when we sat sipping tea together on the porch.

The closet shelves were full of boxes and stacks of books. It hadn't occurred to me until right then that Vergie might have kept some things of my mother's. "I sure hope you were a packrat," I said, emptying the first box onto the floor.

Photos and little notebooks, letters and trinkets—I arranged them all like a collage and then sat back to look at them. It was like they were parts of an equation that only made sense if you saw all the components together. In one pile was a tiny doll made of corn husks and scraps of cloth. Staring into its blank face, I thought of Miranda standing in the storm, still as a fence post as the rain beat her hair against her face. I wondered what had drawn Jack to her in the beginning. It was fascinating to imagine how unlikely couples stayed together—what it was that bound them so tightly to one another, despite their dissimilarity.

My parents had been two of those people. My father was practical, responsible and reliable as a hammer. He found comfort in solid calculations and stone-cold statistics. He liked predictability in all things, and my mother had been about as predictable as a tornado in a square state. She'd been a painter and taught art in middle school before I was born. Then she stayed home with me and sometimes painted when I was keeping myself busy catching frogs to put in my dollhouse. She'd sit outside to work sometimes, watching me from the corner of her eye.

After my mother left us, some days I imagined tracking her down. But I always chickened out. After all, she could have found me any time if she'd wanted to. I figured she didn't care any more —maybe never did to begin with—because why else would she vanish from my life? The act of leaving made it clear she didn't want to know anything more about me. So I decided I didn't want to learn anything else about her either.

My father rarely talked about my mother. On one occasion years ago, he'd said, "She went all new-agey and metaphysical on me and then walked out." He said she was like a hummingbird in that she never stayed in one place very long, and so he wasn't at all surprised when she left. I'd often wondered how much truth there was in that, because I'd caught him crying once or twice shortly after she took off. He would never admit to that, of course, and tried to be this stoic figure, like that would somehow make it easier. He seemed to think that if he made her sound flaky enough, we wouldn't blame ourselves. He made a point of telling me she had started reading tarot cards, drawing up astrological charts, and had one day decided that they were no longer compatible according to their numerology, the Chinese calendar and the tea leaves in the bottom of her china cup. My father sneered when he told me that, calling her ridiculous, saying she'd finally crossed the edge of reason. But as I grew older, I began to think they had finally just grown apart, like limbs in the fork of a tree. After a long enough time, they could no longer fit together.

That didn't mean I excused her behavior. She could leave him —but she didn't have to leave me too.

There had always been tension between them. On the bad days, I'd wondered how they'd made it as long as they had. On the worst days, I wondered if every relationship was doomed to that fate—if all couples realized at some point that they were more different than they'd thought at the start, and so different they had no hope of staying together.

The saddest part for me was how quickly I'd forgotten the little details about my mother once she'd left. It hadn't occurred to me that the memories were slipping away until I was in my twenties. After a while, I couldn't conjure the image of her face—I could imagine her eyes and her freckles, but I couldn't put the pieces together in one continuous shape. It scared me to think of how this had happened so quickly. Sometimes it seemed like the people I cared most about in my life were destined to leave me, and I seemed destined to forget them. It made me want to cling tight to the last memories I had of my mother and Vergie. Some nights, I imagined the more vivid ones, playing them over and over in my mind as I fell asleep. Maybe if I thought about them hard enough, I could train my brain to remember them.

Sifting through Vergie's photos and trinkets, I wondered why she had never remarried. She'd married her high school sweetheart—but not until she was twenty-five. My grandfather, Jay, had waited and waited for Vergie, who refused to marry him while her own mother was in poor health. It was only after her mother died that Vergie reclaimed her own life and married Jay. They had a year and a half together before he died of an aneurysm, coming home from the late shift at the textile mill where he'd worked since he was sixteen. That story hadn't affected me much at the time, but now, staring at the photos, I cried as I thought of Vergie, a widow so young after a marriage so short, and a grandfather I'd never met. It seemed there was never a convenient time for the things we needed most.

Near the bottom of a shoebox were some snapshots of Vergie and Jay. In one, with "Niagara" scribbled on the back, they both wore bright yellow slickers, their faces streaked with mist from the falls. Both grinning like the Cheshire Cat, they looked like they fit perfectly together, like tongue-and-groove boards. Rather than staring into the camera, as most people do, Vergie and Jay were always staring right at each other, as if nothing around them was nearly as interesting as the person right in front of them. From those pictures, it was clear why she'd never married another man. Some people find their match only once.

Things like that made me wonder if I'd met my match and lost him, too busy or preoccupied to recognize him.

My cell phone rang, and my whole body shivered.

Jack.

I climbed up from the floor and scrambled to find it, following the ringing into the hallway. By the time I answered, I was out of breath.

"Sounds like you're busy," my father said, and I held the phone farther from my head. "That's what I like to hear." His voice boomed in my ear, and I furrowed my brow.

"What can I do for you, Dad?"

"Just checking in. How's everything going?"

"Fine."

"Can you elaborate?"

No need to mention Jack. My father was liable to drive down here himself to personally kick the man out, and he'd never trust me with another job. Ever. He'd see Jack as a freeloader, and he'd let me have it for allowing him to stay. Even worse, he'd know in a second there was something brewing between us. He could read me as easily as *The Wall Street Journal.*

"Everything's on schedule," I said. "Repairs are going great. The house is in good shape. Nothing I can't handle."

"You sound like something's amiss," he said. I could hear his pen tapping against his desk.

Only my father used words like *amiss.*

"All is fine. There's some mold that has to be taken care of. And a leaky pipe, but otherwise it's nothing big."

"Mold?" he bellowed. "How much? What did you do?"

I told him about my appointment with the specialist, and there was a pause on the other end of the line. He was no doubt pulling up a spreadsheet and punching buttons on his calculator.

"And what will that set you back?"

"Two to three thousand, give or take," I said, but it was closer to four. The specialist gave me a ballpark based on the size of the house, but I knew it could climb higher depending on the extent of the damage.

"Give or take? What kind of accounting is that?"

"Twenty-six hundred and eleven dollars and thirty-nine cents. Is that more helpful?"

"Don't be a smart-ass. The budget is what drives these projects. You lose track of the numbers, you screw yourself over."

I sighed, glad he couldn't see the face I was making.

"Enza, what have I told you about big investments? What about this pipe?"

"Twelve hundred."

"Are you out of your mind? You can't throw that much money around on single repairs."

"It had to be done, Dad. The mold is a health hazard. The water bill is twice what it should be."

"Let the next owner worry about that," he barked. "You're not supposed to make the house new again. You're supposed to make it *look* new."

"I find that a little unethical, Dad."

He groaned, and out of reflex I held the phone from my ear as he grumbled about losses and money pits. At last he snapped, "This is a business, Enza. It has nothing to do with ethics."

Before I could answer, he slammed the phone down. Part of me feared he'd show up the next day, his phone in one hand and hammer in the other, but it was possible he'd wait it out. He needed to test me and see if I'd cause my own destruction.

I threw the phone, aiming for the bed. But I'd never had a good arm. It sailed toward the window, then caught in the curtain for a split second before dropping out into the yard. I thought I heard it ring just before it crashed to the ground.

"Dammit!" I rushed to the window. Below, the dog came bounding across the grass, pausing to sniff the phone.

"Hey," I yelled. "Drop it!"

Bella cocked her head, then took the phone in her mouth and pranced away.

I ran down the stairs and out onto the porch. Bella gave me one quick look and streaked across the yard.

"Dog! Get your furry ass back here!" My feet squished in the spongy ground as I ran, but Bella cut a zigzag path toward the swamp. She was teasing me on purpose. That dog hated me. I chased her anyway, thinking she might at least drop the phone while she was overcome with glee. The ground turned to mud, and she paused under a cypress tree. I slowed to a walk. She turned, and giving me the closest thing to a smile that a dog can have, bounded farther into the swamp.

"You get back here!" I stuck two fingers in my mouth and tried my best to whistle like Jack had, but I sounded like a balloon losing its air. Briars snagged my shirt, tearing my skin as I kept one eye on the dog and the other on the ground. I stumbled over a tangle of roots and reached for a tree to steady myself. The dog dropped the phone, panting, and looked straight at me.

"This is because we threw you out, isn't it?" I said. The mud clung to my feet as I walked along the edge of the stream. The dog looked away as if she were finally bored with me. When I was within a few feet, she snorted and snatched up the phone again. I moved to grab her, and she leapt toward the water. The mud gave way under my feet, and I slipped and landed in a puddle. The smell of decaying vegetation made me gag, and my ribs throbbed from where they'd smashed against a tangle of roots.

My ankle stung. My side ached. Mud covered my jeans and blouse. I cursed that dog to pieces, but she only trotted farther into the woods, the water splashing behind her. I limped back through the brush to the house, cursing the whole parish in general and this patch of ground in particular.

At last I collapsed on the porch steps and pulled my boots off. They were caked in mud, and the left one was already tight on my swollen ankle. I tossed the boots to the side of the steps, and that's when I saw it.

Lying in the grass was a tiny doll-like figure. I slid closer and reached into the weeds. It was a humanlike form that looked like it had been fashioned out of an old sock, with little stumpy arms and legs tied on. It was impossible to tell if it was meant to be male or female, but it definitely had a face and hair. At first I thought it was a child's toy, but then I realized there were sewing pins stuck in it—so far that their colored round heads were all that protruded.

Only one kind of doll wore pins. The question was whether it was real or just a prank.

I pulled myself up with a groan and leaned against the rail. I peeled my shirt and jeans off on the porch and stumbled into the house in my panties and bra. My ankle hurt more with every step. My skin was streaked with dirt and blood, and my arms crisscrossed with cuts from the briars.

I tossed the doll on the kitchen table and hobbled into Jack's bathroom to fill the tub. After fishing a bottle of red wine out of the pantry, I limped into the study and searched the bookshelves for a book that had caught my attention earlier. I'd forgotten about it until the mojo bag appeared, then got sidetracked again before I could read it.

Voodoo in New Orleans. I plucked the thin paperback from the shelf and took it with me, wincing each time I put weight on my ankle.

I stripped and eased myself into the hot bath. The cuts from the thorns throbbed when the water touched them, and I took a long drink of wine to tamp down the pain. My ankle was already purple and swollen, and as I lay back in the tub, I muttered, "What else could possibly go wrong?"

I knew as soon as the words echoed against the tile that I should have kept that thought to myself, because as soon as you tempt fate, it will absolutely come to bite you in the ass.

BY THE TIME I was halfway through the bottle, I'd skimmed the first three chapters of *Voodoo in New Orleans.* So far I'd learned basics about how one mixes up a gris-gris. It was a tiny object made to attract good fortune, love, money—the usual desires people had. The author discussed anecdotal evidence of these objects providing what the maker wanted, plus examples of how they'd been used to attract negative energy to a person. I skipped ahead to a chapter on voodoo dolls and cringed as I read some of the cases related to those—people had actually been prosecuted and jailed back in the day for creating dolls that brought havoc to their victims. There were cases of broken arms, poisoning, heart attacks and worse. I felt myself getting sucked into the lore and for a moment wondered just what the gris-gris and the doll in my yard could be bringing to me. I tallied up the little problems that had arisen this week—the roof, the mold, Miranda, Remy—but then shook the thoughts away.

That was silly. Wasn't it?

It was the wine, I thought. It was late, I was exhausted, and the wine was making my brain too susceptible to folklore. I dropped the book onto the floor and sank deeper into the water. Jack was right. There couldn't be anything to this voodoo business. There might have been something real about the practice back in its heyday, but now it was just a mystery that created allure for tourists.

I'd just added more hot water to my bath when I heard a truck come up the drive. A door slammed, the headlights streamed into the window, and the truck went back down the road. For a second I froze, but then I heard a key in the lock and Jack's footsteps in the hall.

"Enza," he called, "Are you up there?"

"Down here," I said, taking another drink from the bottle. It was nearly three-quarters empty now, and my ankle felt light and tingly, just like every other part of me.

The door to the bedroom opened. "Enza?"

"In here," I said, sloshing a handful of bubbles toward my feet.

"You're working awfully late," he said, and the door swung open.

I shifted slightly, instinctively covering my breasts with my arm.

"Jeez," he said, averting his eyes. "I thought you were painting in here or something."

"Nope," I said, relaxing again. "Off the clock."

He glanced in my direction, still not letting his eyes rest on me. It was cute, the way he was suddenly shy.

"Why are you in my bathtub? Is something wrong with yours?"

I giggled. "Why are you staring at the wall? It's not like there's anything in here you haven't seen already."

"I'm trying to be a gentleman."

I laughed. "My tub is upstairs."

He looked at me then, and saw the wine bottle and the paperback. "I see."

"Your dog crippled me and made it impossible for me to climb stairs."

"What?"

I motioned at my purple ankle propped on the rim of the tub, and he cringed.

"What happened?" he asked, kneeling at my side. He slid his fingers over the bone, and I winced.

"Your dog happened. She stole my phone and went tearing through the swamp, so I of course had to chase her. I tripped and then *whammo*, busted ankle."

"Christ," he said, sliding his fingers along my calf. "I'm sorry. She does have a bad habit of stealing things."

"You owe me a new phone."

He gently moved my ankle to the left, then to the right.

"Ow! Easy!"

"Sorry." He rubbed his fingers over the bruise. "Looks like a sprain. Nothing too serious, but you should stay off it a couple of days." His eyes darkened as they came to rest on mine. "You know, stay in bed."

I felt a ripple of heat wash over me. "Thanks, Dr. Mayronne."

He leaned over the edge of the tub and kissed me on the lips, his tongue finding mine. "I'd climb in there with you if you weren't wounded," he said. Part of me wished he would, ankle be damned. This man could clearly heal me in a thousand different ways.

"It's a bit chilly in here," I said. The water was barely warm now, and I felt goose bumps all over.

"Then let me get you out and warm you up." He pulled me to my feet and handed me a towel, turning his back as I dried off.

"Hey," I said, "who was that bringing you home?"

"One of the guys from the station."

"Why?"

He wrapped his big plaid bathrobe around me. "Someone slashed the tires on my truck today."

"Tires? Plural?"

"Yep. All four."

"Oh my God. Maybe the doll was you!" My head spun a little as I stepped out of the tub into his arms. I should have had dinner before wine.

"What?"

"There was a voodoo doll in the yard today. I thought someone was trying to freak me out, but maybe it was meant for you."

He rolled his eyes, fighting back a grin. "Was there a pin stuck in its ankle?"

"Very funny," I said, looping my arm in his. "But you have to admit, things are a little weird around here."

He scoffed, leading me into his bedroom.

"I'm serious! Think about it."

"I don't have to. I'm sure Miranda was the one who slashed my tires, getting back at me after her little scene the other day."

"Maybe Miranda's into voodoo. Maybe she's trying to put a hex on you and me both. The tires, the house, the dog that is clearly possessed by a demon—it's a lot of coincidental disaster."

"That's crazy," he said. "Your problem is a house that hasn't had any major repairs in forty years. My problem is an obsessive ex. This is not voodoo, chère. This is the universe telling us to make better decisions."

"Doesn't explain the dog," I said.

"You've been mixing wine and heavy reading. The only one putting a spell on me is you."

He tugged at my hair, wet from the bath, and kissed the spot just below my ear. I thought of the day before, the way he'd spread me out on the kitchen table, kissing me and stroking me until I'd come for him. I'd spent the day trying to push those thoughts aside, but all I wanted was for him to lay his chiseled body on mine and make me his again and again.

So much for one time. So much for getting him out of my system.

"Let's get you to bed," he said. "You can sleep in my room tonight. You know, because of the stairs."

I almost protested, mainly out of reflex. But then I thought of sleeping next to Jack, his arm draped over my hips, and quickly reconsidered.

He helped me over to the bed, and I sat. "Can I get you pajamas or anything from upstairs? Frilly girl things?"

"No," I said. "Don't need them."

He kissed me on the forehead and turned to leave.

"Hey, where are you going?"

"I'll take the couch," he said.

"You're leaving me in my hour of need?"

He walked back over to the bed and stood in front of me. "If you want me to stay, chère, just ask."

I slid my hand under his shirt, tracing the taut muscles there. "Stay."

When he slipped off his T-shirt, I saw the cut on his upper arm, the sutures. There were bruises on his shoulder, a bandage below his collarbone. "Oh my God."

"It's not as bad as it looks." He eased into the bed next to me.

"What happened to you?" I felt like an idiot for complaining about a lost phone and a sprained ankle.

He shrugged. "A big warehouse. Abandoned, thankfully. Lost cause, though. Burned up before we could save it."

"That's terrible."

"They think it was the arsonist again."

I slid my fingers along his arm, careful to dodge the wounds. It sickened me to think of Jack in these buildings with rotting floorboards and century-old beams. Ceilings and walls collapsed so easily, and things that were there one instant were gone in the next.

"Do they have any leads?" I asked.

"Not yet," he said, irritated. "This is the sixth one. They should have caught this guy by now."

I curled myself against him as he told me the rest, falling asleep as he stroked my hair. I felt safe there, wrapped in his arms, but how long could it last?

IN MY DREAM, I was surrounded by red-orange flames in a house that was Vergie's—but then was not. The rooms were the same, but their placement was all wrong. Frantic, I ran from room to room, trying to find the stairs, to find the way out. The dog was barking outside, but I couldn't see a door or a window. Smoke filled my lungs and burned my chest. Flames lapped at my skin. I felt like I was catching fire myself, and Jack was nowhere to be found. I called and called for him, but there was only the dog, barking behind me, the sound growing softer in the distance. I crawled along the floor, holding my shirt over my nose. Beams creaked overhead, and the walls crackled and popped. Then the fire was everywhere. I was trapped in a room with no windows, and around me was nothing but orange light and dense smoke. When I looked down at my hands, I saw they were square and callused. The reason I couldn't find Jack was because I *was* Jack.

I sat up in the bed, gasping for air. The covers were crumpled at my feet, and my hair was wet and plastered to my face. Next to me, Jack was sleeping soundly, his breaths deep and even. I lay back down, trying not to wake him, trying to slow my own breaths. But my heart felt like it was being squeezed like a fist. This was no ordinary nightmare. Vergie would say this was the kind meant to send you a message.

Chapter Ten

I WAS KILLING time until the roofers started. Because they were friends of Jack's, they would be coming over tomorrow, on a Saturday—unheard of in these parts. I'd planned to work on the porch floor today, but since there would be carpenters both above and below in less than twenty-four hours, it was smarter to push that to later in the week. With my luck, they'd have to bust through the floorboards after I painted them, so I might as well put off doing anything until the dirtiest work was complete.

My ankle was still sore, but I was able to walk without the shooting pains I'd felt earlier. Jack was on duty, so I was on my own. I had my morning coffee (not as good as what he made) and sat down to make a new timeline. The roof and mold problems would set me back a few days, but with some extra effort I could still meet my deadline.

The end of week one, and things were moving fast with Jack and slow with the house. Frankly I'd have been happier if the reverse were true. Whatever was happening with Jack was fun— there was no denying that—but I couldn't dwell on it too much. I liked him—more every day, it seemed—but I couldn't see what would happen with him when the house was finished. I liked having plans, goals, prescribed outcomes. This thing with Jack had none of those, and it made me nervous. Would I just pack my things and leave him? Shake his hand, and thank him for his expertise?

Once satisfied with my new calendar for repairs, I opened my laptop and did a little research while I ate my toast and eggs. A quick Internet search led me to several tourist-trap voodoo shops, but there was also a museum that had useful information online. I'd spooked myself last night, probably due to the wine and *Voodoo in New Orleans*. But part of me wondered: Was it so far-fetched that someone could want to do me harm? Or Jack? Remy hated him and probably had it in for me now too. Miranda was nutty enough to combine her stalking with something more serious. It was unlikely that either of them could actually channel the dark arts and torment us with magic, but they could certainly pose other threats. These are the things you heard about in the news—warning signs that escalated into physical violence. Was there reason to think these were more than pranks?

Finding out if one could really unleash voodoo on a gal to make her life fall apart or make a lover come back to her, well, that would be useful to know too. I went up to Vergie's room and opened the nightstand. Inside were the gris-gris and the fabric doll with the pins, right where I'd stashed them. I shoved both into my pockets.

THE FRENCH QUARTER was just like I remembered it. Tourists scurried on every sidewalk, fanning themselves against the heat. The street musicians sang and strummed on the corners, chatting up people who gathered to listen to them as they wandered from one bar to the next. Every restaurant had its doors open, music pouring out with the air conditioning, luring people from the midday sun.

To gather proper intel, I first went to the historical society, claiming I was doing research for a book. People are always intrigued by the prospect of contributing to historical research, and perhaps being thanked on the acknowledgements page, so they tend to be forthcoming with information. A woman who led the tour out at the old Number Seven cemetery had directed me toward a side street not far from the French Quarter.

She got a serious look on her face and said, "Now, if you want to learn about the real thing, you need to go see Duchess." She drew me a map and told me to mention her name so that the woman wouldn't turn me away. "She's got no patience for people seeking out love spells and souvenirs," the woman said, her eyes narrowed. "She only talks about it with people who respect it as she does."

I'd spent a few hours in New Orleans when I'd returned for Vergie's funeral, but it had been years since I'd truly walked down those streets. I found that most things hadn't changed. The same apartment buildings were there, old Mardi Gras beads draped on the iron railings. The doors were painted different colors, and the names of some of the shops had changed, but the cornerstones remained. I turned onto Bourbon Street and into a crowd. All around me, people walked with hurricanes in plastic flutes almost as tall as they were, gawking into dimly-lit doorways. I glanced in one window and saw a flurry of pale skin and garters, the slim legs and high heels of a woman dancing on a tabletop.

When I turned off Bourbon, the crowd thinned. Three more blocks and I was away from the tourist traps, by the Faubourg Marigny. I stopped to re-read the address I'd scribbled on a scrap of paper. The shop should be another block away, on a back street. You couldn't throw a rock without hitting a voodoo shop in this part of town, but most were for the tourists. They were filled with alligator feet, gris-gris packed with rose petals and thyme, and voodoo dolls that couldn't conjure any more than a salt shaker could. The shops drew in curious travelers who wanted an "authentic" souvenir from a culture that seemed exotic and mysterious—and they'd made enough money to stay in business for decades. People never got tired of mystery.

Vergie hadn't been a stranger to voodoo either. She had taken me to see Marie Laveau's tomb when I was a child. Back then I'd tried to make my own voodoo doll to get back at a neighborhood bully, but Vergie had stopped me quick as a hawk, telling me I was messing with something I didn't understand. We'd wandered around the old cemetery where the Voodoo Queen was buried, and I'd been surprised by the makeshift shrine believers had erected in her honor—a collection of flowers, beads and bottles of colored liquids. There were small piles that looked like junk at first, but once I got up close, I saw they were little works of art—layers of flowers, cards and candles, dolls made like effigies of real people who wanted help from the priestess. People left strange pieces of themselves, like garters and ties, watches and high-heeled shoes. And then there was the food. As a little girl, I couldn't understand why people left glasses of wine and honey with wafers, but Vergie had explained that spirits get hungry too. The whole idea, she said, was to keep the spirit as content in death as she had been in life.

As we stood in the cemetery that day, the sky a crisp blue overhead, Vergie told me that voodoo really had nothing to do with revenge and evil spirits. The tourists were getting a twisted story that sold a lot of souvenirs and tickets to the cemetery tour, but it wasn't what the real religion was all about.

"It's important that you realize when you're being had," Vergie had said. "You have to be able to separate the truth from the lies." After that, I quit making voodoo dolls to get back at girls who'd picked on me at school. It still seemed like there was some truth in the talk of vengeful spirits, though. Even at that age, I understood that for every ounce of good in the world, there was an ounce of bad.

I stopped in front of a pale yellow building with green awnings. There was no sign out front, but it was the right number: 88 ½. A bell clanged above my head as I opened the door, and a gigantic orange cat stepped right in front of me, swishing his tail along the floor like a dust mop.

The room was dark, filled with the smell of dried herbs and flowers. Shelves lined the walls from the floor to the ceiling, packed with relics that I paused to look at only briefly before a voice bellowed from the back of the shop.

"We're closed," the deep female voice said. "Try the one on Bourbon. They got anything you want."

"Jacinda said you were the only one who could help me," I said, trying to locate the voice.

"Jacinda sent you?" A woman stepped out from behind a bookcase, wrapped in a bright blue and purple muumuu that seemed to glow in the dim light. Her skin was light brown, and she wobbled slightly when she walked. She was a stout woman; not fat, but simply well-built, like she could withstand any kind of storm.

"Miss Dauphine?" I asked, extending my hand.

The woman stood with her hands on her hips, her bracelets jangling when she moved. "Mmm-hmm." She stared down her nose at me. "Everybody calls me Duchess. How you know Jacinda?"

"I just met her today," I said, shoving my hands into my pockets.

"Why is that girl sending you down here? Some fella gone and broke your heart? Cause I ain't in the business of love potions. Ain't in the business of revenge neither. She knows that."

"I need someone who will tell me the truth."

She laughed. "The truth, she says. Child, you gonna look a long time for that."

I pulled the velvet pouch and the doll from my shoulder bag, and Duchess peered into my hand.

"What you got there?" she asked, her tone lightening.

"I was hoping you could tell me what these mean. I found them in my yard."

"Somebody been leaving you offerings?" Duchess pulled a

pair of silver-rimmed glasses from a fold in her dress and placed them low on her nose. She wiggled her fingers, motioning for me to give her the items. Pushing her bracelets up on her arm, she emptied some of the contents of the bag into her palm. It looked like a fistful of potpourri, but I knew by the arch in the woman's painted eyebrows that it wasn't so benign.

"Why you want to know about this? What you plan on doing?"

"I just want to know what it's for." I watched her eyes, trying not to say the wrong thing. "I want to know if this is cause for worry."

Duchess stared at me, her gaze shifting above my head. I got the feeling I couldn't have hidden anything from this woman even if I wanted to.

She pushed her glasses up on her nose. "You got a good aura," she said. "Pale, but good color." Her plum-colored lips tightened, and then she turned, gliding toward a room in the back. "Well, come on," she said over her shoulder. "Let's see what mojo somebody's putting on you."

She nudged her elbows through a beaded curtain, dodging the strings of tiny beads that clinked and rattled like bells. A massive wooden desk sat in the center of the room, covered with books and a collection of objects that looked much more ominous than anything for sale in the voodoo shops on Bourbon Street. There was a small skull that might have been a cat or a raccoon, and a painted one that was definitely an alligator. The teeth were bright yellow, glimmering in their sockets. Covered in vibrant red and green designs, it looked like it belonged in a museum.

Duchess sat behind the desk, emptying her hands over a square of glass the size of a cutting board. She brushed the flecks of herbs from her palms, then motioned for me to sit across from her.

"This could take a while," she said. Her eyes were wide and brown.

"I've got nowhere else to be," I said, offering a smile.

Her lips were a taut line. She reached for a magnifying glass and tweezers, and sorted through the heap of herbs and leaves, picking out pieces and making tiny piles. Occasionally she sniffed them. I picked up a doll with hair made of Spanish moss, wrapped in a red scrap of cloth. Tiny stitches covered the doll, nearly impossible to see without holding it close. It felt surprisingly soft.

"Careful," Duchess warned. "That one ain't been baptized yet."

"Baptized?"

"In the loosest sense of the word," she said, a glint of laughter in her eye. "You got to wait for them to tell you their names. That one's said nothing yet. Likes being all mysterious."

"What's she for?" The doll had a pale brown face, with no indication of eyes or a mouth, and yet she still seemed to be smiling somehow. She was similar to mine, but more refined, crafted more deliberately.

"Hasn't told me that either. But whatever it is you want, it's liable to rub off on her. Then you'll be the only one that can use her. And she ain't cheap."

I placed the doll back on the desk, but still felt its blank face staring into me. I tried not to think too hard about anything in particular.

"Somebody's got a broken heart," Duchess said at last. "You got blue violet, chickweed, red clover. All of these are meant to attract faithfulness, commitment. Things of that nature." She clicked her tongue, as if she'd seen this far too many times before, then plucked a dried petal from the glass and held it in her fingers. "Some folks carry these around with them, hoping to attract a lover, but then you got lovesick fools who are all the time leaving these things near their beloved," she said. "This one's in love bad."

I gestured to the pile. "Is that a bone?"

"Snake rib. Meant to bind you to your intended."

"How do I know who left it?" I asked.

"Child, I can't tell you that. Don't you know who's all broke up over you?"

"It's not for me."

She raised an eyebrow. "You sure about that?"

"Pretty sure."

She stared at me as if scanning my face for lies.

"Somebody left it at my—" I hesitated, not wanting to explain my living situation to her. "At my friend's house."

"Mmm-hmm." She plucked a tiny twig from the glass. "Devil's shoestring." It looked like dried honeysuckle vine. "One of the strongest herbs for attraction and desire—the sweaty, nasty kind. Somebody's got it bad for your friend." She dragged out the last word as if she knew it didn't accurately describe what had passed between Jack and me. "And see this?" she said, "This is yohimbe bark. It attracts dark passion. Lust. It's meant to make a body ache for you." She pushed the flecks of dried herbs around the glass. "Whoever left this is serious about making their unrequited love requited."

She reached for the doll I'd brought and turned it over in her hands.

"Is that what I think it's for?" I asked.

She snipped the belly of the doll with manicure scissors and a similar heap of herbs spilled out. "Lots of different uses for dolls. This one's meant for pain, though. Got pins stuck in the heart, in the belly, in the brain."

I cringed. "So this really works?"

She laughed, a low smoky laugh that sounded like it came from deep within a cave. "It depends on faith, child. It works if the person doing it believes in it. So I guess the question is, does this poor lovesick fool believe. And that's an easy answer, based on all the trouble they went to. When did you find this?"

"The doll was yesterday. The pouch a couple of days before."

"Full moon two nights ago. Best time for love spells."

It had to be Miranda. The only question was: How far would she go?

"So what should I do?" I asked.

She nodded toward the corner of the desk where I'd left the blank-faced doll. "You might think about holding on to that doll until she tells you her name. Otherwise, I wouldn't want to be in the path of the person leaving these."

"How about my friend? What's he supposed to do?"

She leaned back in the chair, scratching her chin. "I can mix up a little gris-gris for your fella, try and keep this poor soul away. But like I said, you got to believe. He got to believe. Otherwise, it's like a handful of salt and pepper."

I stared at the doll for a moment.

"What makes you so sure it's for your friend and not for you?" she asked, leaning back in her chair.

"I've only been back a little while," I said. "I hardly know a soul here any more."

"It only takes one," Duchess said.

"I've been here less than a week and met less than half a dozen people. No way this is meant for me."

"Mmm-hmm." She laced her fingers over her belly and said, "I've heard that one before."

DRIVING HOME, I considered what Duchess had said. Was Miranda focusing on Jack, or had she made that doll for me instead?

That night, I let Bella inside and slept in Jack's room again. The upstairs felt like a separate building entirely, and if someone came into the yard tonight, I wanted to know it. I slipped the gris-gris that Duchess had made for me under the pillow (where she said it would be most effective) and laid a kitchen knife on the nightstand. I kept telling myself this was silly, but I couldn't quite convince myself. Compiling lists sometimes put me to sleep, so I made a mental list of repairs I could do the next day: painting, washing down walls, repairing the window in the upstairs bathroom. Then I made a list of reasons Miranda might be leaving these voodoo tokens around: to lure Jack back to her, to harm him, to get me out of her way.

That was no good. *New list, Enza.*

I thought about Jack. Made a list of reasons he was a good idea. Or a bad idea. (There's nothing like a good pro/con list to wear you out.) The dog lay snoring on my feet while I stared at the blue light that filtered through the curtains. With the windows shut tight, the house was stuffy. The more I thought about Jack, the more I wished he was there. Maybe something casual with him wouldn't be such a bad idea. Simple was what I needed, right?

Chapter Eleven

THE DOG WOKE me in the morning as she leapt down from the bed. Trying to hide under the covers and ignore her was no use; she only circled the room, the click-clicking of her nails sounding like hail. Finally I gave up and let her outside, catching a glimpse of the sunrise, and went straight back to bed. My sleep had been fitful, interrupted by nightmares of a house falling to pieces as it burned with me inside. The roofers would be there soon, but I was certain I'd hear them when they drove up. So I buried my head under the covers, trying to doze a little longer. I didn't hear another thing until there was a knock on the bedroom door. When I lifted the covers, the room was bright with late-morning light.

"Hey, Enza," Jack said. "You all right in there?" He'd cracked the bedroom door, just barely.

"Fine. What time is it?" The birds were going full throttle outside—I'd have thought since starting at six, they'd be exhausted by now. But they never were.

"It's a little after ten," he said, stepping inside. "You sure you're OK?"

"Couldn't sleep last night," I said. "Are the roofers here?"

"I talked to them already. I didn't want to wake you, and they'd just started unloading when I pulled up."

I couldn't believe I'd slept through all of that.

Three carpenters were stomping on the roof, ripping up shingles. The noise made me think again of the nightmare that had kept me awake for half the night. Sounds of cracking beams and collapsing walls had seemed real enough to wake me and send me vaulting out of bed twice to check for smoke and flame. I heard their muffled voices and shivered, thinking of the way the voices had drifted through the burning walls in the dream.

Jack leaned against the doorframe, a hint of a smile on his lips. "You need me to come carry you out of there?"

His offer was tempting, but I climbed out of bed and said, "Think I can manage."

He saw me wince as I put weight on my ankle. "Suit yourself. I've got coffee when you're ready."

I tried to ignore the pain as I wrapped his robe tight around me and hobbled into the kitchen. I half expected to find Jack making breakfast, and was already thinking fondly of his omelets and beignets.

Instead, I found him kneeling on the floor with a paint brush. The doors to the cabinets were scattered around the room, propped against the walls, the table, the refrigerator.

"What are you doing?" I asked.

He froze, paint dripping from the brush onto the door below him. "Thought I'd get started early."

"You're painting the cabinets."

"Didn't feel like sleeping when I got in. And with the new wall color, they looked pretty bad. I was hoping to be done before you got up."

"Why would you do all of this without asking?"

"Thought you could use the help," he said.

The walls were the same yellow as the bedroom, but it seemed much warmer in this room, with light streaming in from so many windows. The brightness was almost too much.

He frowned. "You don't like them."

"They're white."

"I thought it would brighten the place up." He put the brush down and wiped his hands across his jeans. He was down to the last cabinet.

I sat down at the table, feeling like the wind had been knocked out of me. "I don't dislike them. It's just not what I'd planned." Outside, a heap of shingles crashed to the ground. "They do look better, though."

Now the cabinets blended in with the white paneling below the chair rail, and it seemed cohesive. With the exception of the huge yellow splotch on the floor.

Jack crawled across the floor to where I was sitting. He rested his forearms on my bare knees and said, "A little surprise here and there is good for you." He kissed my knee, and for a moment I forgot about the team of roofers above us.

He stood slowly, then brought me a cup of coffee. As I raised the cup to my lips, a crash upstairs shook the whole house. I felt the vibration in my feet as the coffee splattered in my lap.

Jack ran upstairs as I limped after him.

He stopped in the doorway of Vergie's room and blocked me with his arm. I leaned around him, my hands on his shoulders.

"What is it?" I asked. "Let me by."

He tried to stop me, but I ducked under his arm.

"What the hell?" I felt the blood rush to my cheeks.

One of the roofers was lying on the floor, surrounded by shards of plaster and wood. The space around him was covered in a layer of white dust. A gaping hole above him was bleeding sunlight. He climbed to his feet, brushing the splinters from his clothes.

Two faces peered through the hole in the ceiling. "Hey, Wayne," one said. "You all right down there?"

The man waved in the direction of the hole. "It seems there was another bad place in the roof," he said, shaking the plaster out of his hair. "Don't know how we missed that one." He seemed perfectly calm, as if this happened every day.

"Are you OK?" I prayed this was not the beginning of a lawsuit.

He laughed. "Oh, sure. The ceilings are shorter up here. I didn't fall far."

I cinched the robe tighter around me. A hundred curses rippled through my head.

Jack grabbed me by the shoulders and steered me back downstairs to the couch before I could say anything more. All the while I felt like I was choking on words I wanted to scream.

"This is a nightmare," I said. "How can it get any worse?"

"Sit. Finish your coffee. I'll go talk to them. And put that ankle up."

I leaned back into the cushions, staring at the ceiling. Cracks stretched from one doorframe to the other, like the roads on an atlas. If this place was a map, it was one that would only lead me in circles. That was becoming clearer by the day.

Above, the voices volleyed back and forth. The roofer's was calm like a breeze. Jack's was more agitated but still too low for me to make out his words. I topped off my coffee and walked outside. It was already a hotbox, the air so thick it felt like I was trying to breathe underwater.

Two roofers peered into the hole, scratching their heads and pointing. I pretended not to watch them as I paced around the yard, imagining the story I might cook up for my father. He'd lose it if he knew everything that was going on, and he'd be able to tell in one phone call. Parents are eerie that way, how they can tell what's really happening with you, no matter how good a liar you are. And if you're a terrible liar, like me, then you don't stand a chance.

I left the roofers to their quarreling and wandered into the front yard. The Jeep was where I'd left it, but something looked wrong. I walked closer and then saw that the tires on the driver's side were completely flat. I walked around to the other side and saw that those were flat as well.

"Shit!" I dropped the coffee cup in the grass and kicked the back tire with my good foot, feeling my chest twisting into a knot. I screamed, stamping my feet in the grass, but the sudden jolt sent a shock of pain through my ankle. "Stupid Jeep, stupid ankle, goddamn stupid house!" I yelled. When I turned, Jack was standing with Wayne on the front walkway. They both stared at me slack-jawed.

They'd just seen my tantrum. Mortified, I cinched the robe again and turned back to the Jeep, arms crossed.

"What's the matter?" Jack asked as he walked up behind me. Wayne ambled along behind him, momentarily distracted from the roof.

"My tires." I turned to face them. "All four."

Jack walked around the Jeep, surveying the damage. His jaw clenched.

"Somebody must be real mad at you," Wayne said. He scratched his head, staring at the Jeep.

Jack shot him a look, and he cleared his throat, adjusting his cap.

"Guess I should get back to that hole," he said, leaving us with the Jeep.

Jack was on his knees, examining the back tire. "Looks like a screwdriver, maybe." He dragged his finger over the side, where there was a quarter-inch hole.

"You care to expand on what happened to your truck at the station?" I asked.

"Well, first I thought of Miranda. Then I figured it was likely Remy getting his rocks off." He traced his fingers over the hole. "Did you hear a car come up here last night?"

"Don't you think I would have gone outside to check things out if I'd heard something?" I said.

He frowned. "I wish you wouldn't."

"That son of a bitch," I said. "I'm going to break his face." I shuddered, thinking of Remy creeping into the yard, so close to me while I slept. And Jack so far away.

"Not a chance." He stood, brushing his jeans off. "I don't want you within a hundred yards of that guy. You hear me?"

I stood up straighter to glare, but I was still looking up at him.

His brow arched. "Enza? Promise me you're not going to do anything stupid."

"Somebody needs to call him out for being a jackass."

"That somebody doesn't need to be you. Don't go stirring up trouble."

"I'd say it's pretty well stirred."

He stared at me like he might sling me over his shoulder again and lock me up in his closet. "You are one stubborn woman."

"I'm a big girl, Jack. You worry about you, and let me worry about me." I turned and stalked toward the house.

"Would you let me handle this?" he said, and muttered something that sounded vaguely French.

"You could at least have the courtesy to curse at me in English," I shouted over my shoulder. I could still hear him mumbling when I got up to the porch.

A LITTLE WHILE LATER, Jack came back to the house. "One of the boys is coming to give me a ride to town," he said, pulling his boots on. "My truck's ready, and I thought I might get four Jeep-sized tires while I was out. That is, if you'd like me to worry about you for a brief moment."

I bit my lip to hide a smile. "Suit yourself."

He smiled too, just barely. "But I suppose you want to put them on yourself."

As badly as I wanted to stay mad at him, he sure made it hard to do.

He glanced over at me and winked. "Maybe we could trade favors," he added.

Before I could answer, he turned away. A rusted-out pickup truck pulled up in the drive and blew the horn. A long tanned arm waved out the window, and Jack stood. "See you in a while, sugar. Try to stay out of trouble."

"That's funny coming from you."

He sauntered through the grass to the truck. As soon as he climbed in, the engine roared and sputtered, and they rumbled through the cypress grove, a cloud of dust following them.

WITH VERGIE'S room full of plaster and shingles, there was no hope of working on it. Instead I focused on the other rooms, trying to ignore the pounding of boot heels on the roof and the scream of saw blades. When I'd finally had all I could stand, I went outside and stared up at the roof. The sun was beating down, and the breeze had died. This was one of those days that made me want to lie in a tub of ice and drink spiked lemonade. I filled three glasses with ice water and took them into the yard. I didn't know how those guys were still on the roof, since it must have felt like simmering in a giant frying pan, but there they were. Two of them were hunched over, the saw still whining. I walked to the spot just below them, stepping over the pieces of rotted lumber that had been flung from the roof. They were scattered all around, like debris from an explosion. I yelled as loud as I could, and when the saw stopped, I yelled again, flailing my arm until one of the guys waved.

"Hey," I called out. "How's it going up there?"

Randall, a friend of Jack's from high school, walked to the eave and leaned over, cupping his hands over his mouth. "It's fine. We're just cutting out the bad spots now." He'd taken his shirt off and was already red.

"I brought y'all some water," I shouted.

"Thanks," he said. "We'll be down in a few."

I set the tray on the little glass-top table that was situated between two lawn chairs.

It was nearly two. They'd said it would take a few hours, but if they were only now pulling out the rot, this was going to stretch into the next day. There was no way they'd stay up there when the afternoon heat set in.

"This seems like more than just the corner," I hollered, motioning to the pieces by my feet.

"It was a little bigger than we first thought. Not to worry, though. We'll get you straight."

"How big?" I asked, but his partner, Mike, started the saw up again, drowning me out. Randall waved and turned back to the hole. As I walked back to the porch, I thought of the bill doubling, tripling. The dog grunted from under the hammock, her paws over her ears.

It seemed like every time I fixed something in the house, something bigger fell apart. I hadn't expected it to be easy, but I thought I'd been making steady progress until all of this happened. During my first walk through, I hadn't seen structural damage or anything that indicated I'd be falling down this kind of rabbit hole. But now this house felt like it was buckling under its own weight and dragging me down with it. For the first time, I thought of calling my father and asking him to send reinforcements, or telling him to take care of it his way because I'd been too earnest. I hated the idea of confessing this to him, though, because I knew he'd already thought it. He'd humored me, sending me down to Bayou Sabine, and he was probably sitting in his office right now, waiting for my phone call. Hell, he'd probably even made a bet with the rest of the staff to see how long I could hold out down here.

That thought alone made me want to tough it out and finish.

And then there was Jack. If I gave up, he'd be out on his ass. I needed to hold up my end of this arrangement just as much as he did. I wanted him to stay, and as long as the house needed work, he would. I just needed to make myself a little less crazy about him, because that was the fastest way to complicate things.

～

JUST AFTER FOUR, the roofers started loading up the truck. Wayne came to the porch, where I sat sanding banister rails.

"Miss Parker, we'll see you in the morning," he said. "It won't take too much extra time to fix that mishap. We found a couple more weak spots, but we'll have her fixed in no time."

"But tomorrow's Sunday."

"We've got another job starting Monday. I want to get you finished up before that one starts."

I thanked him. Working on Sunday was completely unheard of.

"Mike got that bedroom all cleaned up," he said. "Most of it anyway."

"I really appreciate it," I said, still a bit dumbstruck. These guys must have owed Jack big time. I made a mental note to thank Jack properly. What exactly that would entail, I wasn't quite sure.

Mike, who looked all of nineteen, approached, carrying something under his arm. "You know this was back there?" he asked. He held out his tanned arms, holding what appeared to be an alligator skull.

"Mike!" Wayne scolded. "What have I told you about snooping in people's yards?"

"You going to tell me that was in the roof?" I said, and the older man laughed.

"No, it was out back," Mike said. "Half-buried. I saw a jawbone sticking out and got a little curious—I sort of collect skulls and things."

Wayne shrugged as if to say, *Kids these days.*

I turned it over in my hands. Green and red dots were painted around the eye sockets, faded but still visible. It looked like something had been carved in the snout, but I couldn't make out anything legible.

"You want to keep it?" Mike asked. "You mind if I take it?"

"Mike," Wayne said. "What did I tell you about bumming things off people?"

"I guess the dog dragged it up," I said, eyeing the skull. "But let me hang on to it for the time being."

Mike's brow furrowed.

"Son, you got a hundred of those things," Wayne said. "Where would you put one more?" He rolled his eyes and gave me a smile. "See you in the morning," he said, steering Mike away.

I turned the skull over in my hands, staring at the empty sockets, the ragged teeth. Bits of dirt clung to it, though it looked bright enough to have been bleached. I shivered, thinking of the animal it had belonged to and the last place I had seen one like this.

It had been resting on a shelf in Duchess' voodoo shop.

Chapter Twelve

I **WAS** in Vergie's room, sweeping bits of plaster and tar into piles when I heard Jack open the front door. I'd worked myself into a frenzy by then, worrying about that stupid skull and how it ended up in the yard. When Jack called my name I was already coming down the stairs, stuffing it into a duffle bag.

"I need a favor," I said, rushing past him to the door.

"So you want those tires on?" Holding a jack and a wrench by his sides, he looked like the poster boy for Triple-A roadside assistance. "I figure it's probably my fault, so—"

I slung the bag over my shoulder and said, "There's no time."

"Say what?"

"I need you to take me somewhere." I pulled on his arm, but he didn't budge.

"It won't take but a little while to put them on," he said.

"We have to go now." I pried the wrench and the jack from his hands. "She won't be there much longer."

He raised an eyebrow. "Who won't be there? What's going on?"

"Come on," I said, hooking my arm in his. "I'll explain on the way."

"Darlin', what's got into you?"

"Give me your keys," I commanded. If he moved any slower, I'd have to dig them out of his pocket myself. An enjoyable task, I thought.

Focus, Enza.

"Look," he said, "if you're thinking of going out looking for Remy, you can forget it. I don't know what you're—"

"I'm not going after Remy, you big lug nut. I have to see Duchess. Now will you please just come on?"

"Who?"

I tugged on his arm until he started walking.

He muttered under his breath as I ran along ahead of him and climbed into the truck.

He slid into the driver's side with what had to be a deliberate ease meant to teach me some sort of lesson regarding patience. Nobody moved in a hurry down here, especially when you asked them to.

Turning the key slowly, he asked, "And where to, ma'am?" drawing out every syllable.

"Don't make me regret letting you drive," I said. "The faster you hit the highway, the faster I'll explain."

He smirked as the gravel churned beneath us. "Oh, sure," he said. "Now you want to move fast."

HE SHOOK his head each time he looked at me, but he drove down into the Quarter anyway.

"You're cracked," he said.

"There was a skull lying in the yard. We need help."

"One of us does," he said flatly.

When we got out of the car, he slung the duffle bag over his shoulder, still frowning. As I led him around the corner to the little yellow building, he said, "You don't actually think this is going to help, do you?"

"How do you explain the sudden influx of crazy?" I hissed.

"The house is falling down around us, and it was fine when I got here. Now I've got gris-gris and skulls and dolls and all kinds of weird shit turning up in the yard—and all hell breaks loose! You, Remy, the house, Miranda. How the hell else do you explain it?"

He eyed the duffle bag. "This is nonsense. Skulls and dried flowers do not make a house fall apart. Rot and hurricanes do."

"You have to admit, this is a strange conjunction of events."

"Welcome to the bayou, chère. That's our whole history in a nutshell."

I shoved the door open, and the bell clanged overhead.

Jack shook his head as I parted a beaded curtain and the strings flopped back in his face. The beads tangled around his neck, and he swatted them like gnats.

"Good grief." He scanned the rows of potions and the baskets full of dolls, then picked up a chicken foot and waved it at me as he spoke. "You seem like such a rational gal, and then you drag me to a place like this. Talk about a strange conjunction."

"Shhh… Have some respect."

He paused, running his finger along an alligator skin that was hanging by a row of shelves. "It's your money, darlin'."

I went to the back of the shop, carrying the alligator skull in the crook of my arm.

"We're about to close," Duchess said, her voice trailing out from the back room. "Come back in the morning."

"It's me again," I said, peering in the back. "It's kind of an emergency."

Duchess looked up from her work table, staring at me over the rim of her glasses. "Oh, Lord. Thought that gris-gris would've lasted longer than this."

"I might need something stronger," I said, laying the skull on the table.

There was a clatter in the front room, and I winced, following Duchess' gaze as she leaned past the doorframe to peer into the store. She frowned and turned back to me.

"Sorry," Jack said, catching a bottle just as it wobbled on the shelf. He shoved his hands in his pockets and turned away.

Duchess raised an eyebrow and said, "So this is the fella, then?"

I nodded.

"Mmm-hmm." Duchess looked back at the skull. "This ain't good. Ain't good at all." She pushed her chair back and hoisted herself up. Her bright green dress billowed as she sashayed into the front of the store. Squeezing past Jack, she paused, looking him up and down. "Mmm-hmm," she said, then continued to the front door. She flipped the lock and turned the sign in the window to *Closed*. "This is gonna take a while, sugar," she said to Jack. "Try not to break anything."

He smiled. "Yes ma'am."

She raised one eyebrow, as if she'd seen the kind of damage that sort of smile could do a hundred times over.

"Come on, child," she said to me. "Let's have a look at that thing."

Duchess sat stone faced while I told her about the slashed tires, the way the house seemed to be falling apart more every day. I felt like I was talking to a shrink, spilling all the details about Jack's fight with Remy, the rash of fires, the sudden appearance of Miranda. I wasn't holding back any more.

"Sorry," I said. "That's probably way more than you wanted to know."

"Now, you wouldn't go to a doctor and only tell them about one of your ten symptoms, would you?" She leaned back in her chair and pushed her glasses up into her hair. "You got to tell me everything. And believe me, it ain't nothing I haven't heard already."

"This just turned up today," I said, pointing to the skull. "At my house. Where Jack lives too."

Duchess picked it up and handled it for a good long while. She was so quiet that she made me nervous. Nothing good ever comes of people being that quiet. The only other sound was Jack's boot heels thumping along the floorboards in the other room.

Finally, Duchess sat the skull on the table between us. "Somebody's got it in for a body in that house, big time," she said. "Maybe you. Maybe the fella." She paused. "Maybe both."

I glanced at the skull. "What do you think?"

She shook her head. "I couldn't say. But this is bad business right here. Somebody wants one of y'all to suffer."

"What can we do?"

"Well, lucky for you, this ain't the first time I've seen somebody this riled up."

There was another crash out front, followed by a flurry of French curses. The big orange cat bolted into the office, his ears flattened.

Duchess raised two fingers to her temple and sighed. "How 'bout you go keep an eye on that bull you brought in here and I'll get something ready for you."

I thanked her and parted the beaded curtain.

"Mmm-hmm," Duchess said.

It was dusk when we left the shop.

"I still can't believe you bought all that," Jack said, his eyes shifting from the road to the bag in my lap. "But I suppose it's good of you to support small businesses."

"We need all the help we can get."

I unzipped the duffle bag and took out the skull. Duchess had painted a different pattern on it with red and orange paint, then stuffed bundles of dried flowers in the sockets. It reminded me of skulls decorated for the Mexican Day of the Dead, how the blend of bright colors and flowers turned the ghoulish into something beautiful. Duchess said this would reverse the original spell brought on by the skull.

"Would you put that thing away?" Jack said. "It's giving me the creeps."

I held it out to him, wiggling the jaw.

He shivered, turning back to the road. "Lord, have mercy."

"You heard what she said. We both have to believe in it to keep the house safe."

"You can believe enough for the both of us."

"Jack, you can't deny there's something weird going on around here."

"Weird, yes. Voodoo, no."

"Would it hurt to give this a try?"

He downshifted as we entered the cypress grove, his knuckles white in the moonlight. "I don't like to see you taken advantage of."

His eyes met mine for a second before resting on the road. I shoved the skull into the bag and leaned back against the seat.

"Don't worry," he said. "I won't let that bastard within a mile of you."

"Who? Remy? You think he did this?"

"He likes to screw with people. And he's got it in for me, but he won't lay a finger on you. I'll see to that."

All this time, I'd been convinced it was just Miranda, lovesick and broken-hearted. But to think of Remy skulking around the house, trying to sabotage Jack—that was enough to ensure I never slept again. Miranda might want Jack back, but I didn't think she'd really do us any harm.

Remy was a different story entirely. There was no denying the hatred I'd seen in his eyes when he'd stared Jack down at the bar. The thought of him behind all of this made my stomach twist in on itself. He'd use this as a distraction for something else—I was sure of it. And it made me sick to think of what that something else might be.

~

Back at Vergie's, Jack wandered into the kitchen and opened a bottle of wine. "Have a drink with me, jolie? Help chase those bad spirits away."

"Sure." I pulled my boots off, wincing as pain shot through my ankle. It had swelled again, aching after having walked on it so long.

He handed me a glass and took a long swallow from his, nodding toward the cabinets strewn across the floor. "I'll take care of those tomorrow. They should be dry by now." He turned the radio on, and the room filled with a scratchy blues song, the whine of washboards and steel guitars.

I felt bad for fussing at him earlier. The truth was, the room looked better already. "They look great," I said. "I'm sorry about before. I was being a jerk."

He shrugged, leaning against the counter. "Yeah, you kind of were. But it's OK. I should have asked."

"It was nice of you to do."

"Just part of our agreement, right, chère?" His voice had a sad lilt to it that I didn't quite understand. Deep down, he seemed as vulnerable as the rest of us. He just wanted the same things we all did—to be needed and appreciated.

I slid my hand over his shoulder as I passed him, limping a little as I walked to the sofa.

He came out of the kitchen with a bag of frozen peas and the bottle of wine. Sitting next to me, he pulled my feet into his lap. "Here," he said, laying the peas on my ankle.

I leaned back into the cushions, closing my eyes, letting the music wash over me like a breeze. Finally, Jack said, "I'm sorry I dragged you into all of this."

"What do you mean?"

He shook his head, pouring more wine into his glass. "You wouldn't need gris-gris and gator skulls if it wasn't for me. You wouldn't have all these messed up people in your life."

"It's all right. My life was a bit dull."

"Something tells me you didn't want this particular kind of

excitement." He slid his hand along my ankle, drawing tiny circles with his fingers. "My life's a real mess, darlin'. And I feel like I just pulled you into it blind. And now you've got the scratches and bruises to prove it."

"If you hadn't noticed, my life was already a mess. Now it just spans a couple of extra states."

He frowned. "I should have left when you first got here."

Hearing him say that caused a twinge in my chest. That's when I knew for sure: I needed his help, but I *wanted* him to stay. And not just because of repairs.

There was no way I'd let him walk out of this house now.

He slid his fingers along my shin, drawing a line from my knee to my toes. It about set my skin on fire, but I tried not to let him see. I still thought it best not to let him know how much of an effect he had on me. It was better if he thought this was a casual fling. Better if I did too.

So I sipped my wine, hoping he'd think the flush in my cheeks was from the Shiraz.

"You might drive me crazy," I said, "but I still like you."

"Is that right?" He finished his wine and set the empty glass on the floor.

"If I were completely honest," I said, sitting up straighter, "I would say it's a shame, this rule we have about not mixing business with pleasure."

He leaned closer, sliding his hand along my thigh. "It does seem to put unnecessary stress on you."

"I'm beginning to think so, yes."

"Right. But we have this agreement." His eyes seemed blue enough to drown in.

"We could maybe add an amendment to this agreement." I poured the rest of the wine into my glass and took a sip.

"Go on." His other hand rested on the back of the couch.

"Here's my problem," I said, sliding my fingers along his hand. "I can't handle any more complexity right now. And this thing with you and me, it's all kinds of complicated. So if there was a way to make it simple, maybe that could work."

"And how do you propose we make it simple?"

"It involves another agreement."

"I'm listening." A smile touched his lips as his fingers slid farther along my thigh.

I felt my cheeks turning red, but I went on. "We agree to keep this casual," I said. "No strings. No worrying about where this is headed. Just take it day by day, moment to moment."

He stared at me, as if weighing the thoughts in his mind. "Keep it casual, huh?"

"I'm not in a place for something serious," I said, raising an eyebrow. "Some days I feel like I'm barely holding it together, and if one more thing swings out of control, I'm going to lose it."

He took the glass from me and finished the last bit of wine.

"What do you think?" I asked.

The way he looked at me then sent a shiver down to my toes.

He slid closer, bracing one arm behind me, cupping his hand under my cheek and said, "I think you're too far away, chère." He kissed me, gently at first, then caught my lower lip with his teeth as he wound his fingers in my hair.

Maybe by making this casual, I could consider it resolved and focus on the house. Sometimes you just need to feel another person. All the things that come before and after, they don't matter so much.

"Does this mean you're OK with our new terms?" I asked.

"Simple. Casual. Got it." He pulled me close, his hands sliding along my hips.

I slipped my arms around him and kissed him until he groaned. The warmth of his hands made me want the weight of his body on mine again. I didn't care any more about fear or regret. I just wanted to feel him.

He stopped for an instant and gazed at me, as if trying to decide if this was some sort of trap, if I was teasing him. I pulled him against me, kissed his neck from his ear to his shoulder, and trembled as his scratchy cheek grazed my skin.

As I tugged at the buttons on his shirt, his hand caught mine, squeezing my fingers, sending a current through my arms.

"I like this new agreement," I said. Forgetting my ankle, I swung my leg around him, straddling his lap. He watched me trail my fingers along his chest, and then he pulled my shirt over my head and tossed it to the floor.

His breath tickled my throat as he said, "You're about to like it a lot more," and kissed me deeply, sliding his hands along my back. He lay back on the couch and pulled me on top of him.

His fingers traced my ribs, tickling as they slid down to my hips. He pulled me closer and kissed the hollow of my throat, drawing a line from my chin to my breasts with the tip of his tongue.

"I think about doing this to you all day long," he said.

I pinned his hands above his head. "Go on," I said, nuzzling his ear.

He chuckled in the way that meant he was about to do something deliciously wicked. The warmth of his breath made me shiver as he mumbled something half in French, and I gasped as his hand slipped inside my jeans.

I flattened myself against him. His grip tightened, and he no longer needed to say anything.

In one quick move, he rolled us over. I trembled beneath him, my skin burning where we touched. Like a reflex, I wound my legs around him, drawing him closer. I peeled his shirt from his body, and he leaned up for a minute and paused, like he was deciding what to do with me. I couldn't wait for him to touch me again.

"Tell me what you want," he said.

My fingers slid down to his belt. "I want you so bad I can hardly stand it."

Grabbing my hands, he inched backward so that his weight

was over my hips. My skin tingled from the warmth of his hands. His fingers roamed over my belly, found the curves of my breasts.

He pinned my arms by my sides and said, "Stay." He pulled my jeans slowly down to my knees, then over my ankles, and I sighed as he traced his tongue along the inside of my calf, up to my thigh. "I'm going to kiss all of these freckles," he said, his voice gravelly. "One by one."

I reached for his belt, and he let me unfasten it, unzip his jeans. He wriggled out of them slowly—his boxers too—and then kicked them out of the way. As his lips brushed the curve of my hip, then the swell of my breast, he laid himself on me again, and I wrapped my legs around him. I loved the way he moved his hands so deliberately, as if committing every contour to memory.

"I don't usually do this sort of thing," I said, "just for the record."

He slid his thumb along my collarbone as he kissed my neck, the roughness of his cheek making me shiver. "I can't imagine why you make an exception for me, but you can tell me later." And his mouth closed on my breast, as softly as rain, his tongue flicking against my skin.

I gasped as he slid his hand between my thighs, moving his thumb in tiny circles. Dizzy, I closed my eyes, gripping his shoulders as if I was about to fall from a great height.

He paused long enough to make me ache for his touch. I'd never wanted a man's hands on me so badly in my life.

"You make me crazy, you," he whispered. "I can barely control myself."

My heart pounded so hard he must have felt it in his teeth.

"Then come here," I said, and pulled his face to mine. As I kissed him, I felt his tongue and teeth, and wanted him to devour me, taking his time. Sliding my hands down his back, I grasped his hips. I felt him hard against me, and I squeezed him tighter. "Jack," I murmured, knowing I didn't need to say anything more.

Hearing his name seemed to set him on fire. He nudged my

thighs farther apart, and then was inside me with one slow, unraveling maneuver that shook me to the tips of my toes.

I felt him everywhere at once, within me and around me; I felt desired, protected when his eyes locked with mine. And I imagined those eyes fixed on mine for the rest of my days.

"Enza," he said, his voice low. "Tell me what you want."

I tugged his hair, pulling his face to mine. Bracing his hands by my shoulders, he moved deeper—a slow, steady rhythm that made my heart pound in my ears.

I moaned his name, despite my greatest effort not to, my lips moving against his ear. "Jack, don't stop. Don't ever stop."

His lips curved into a wicked smile. "Anything you say, chère."

When I squeezed my legs tighter around him, he gasped. It felt like tiny waves were rippling through my body, radiating to my feet and the ends of my hair. Though I felt him in every part of me, it didn't seem enough. I wanted more of him and didn't want this moment to end. His deep, slow movements were the ones that unraveled me, and as he looked into my eyes, he teased me, making each roll of his hips last as long as possible. He closed his eyes, still mumbling words I couldn't entirely hear. I felt more alive than I ever had.

Pinpoints of light burst around me, like a meadow full of fireflies. As he thrust harder, sliding his rough cheek along my neck, his fingers wound in my hair, and I felt a jolt that threatened to rupture my heart. I cried out, feeling myself tighten around him. My voice didn't sound like my own.

His movements slowed, and when I opened my eyes, I saw his faint smile.

He kissed my lips, lightly this time. I slid my hands along his arms, feeling his muscles tense with each movement.

He groaned, pressing his forehead against mine as he went rigid as stone, his muscles quivering. Then his body relaxed, and when he fixed his eyes on mine, he traced a finger along my cheek and said, "You are the foxiest landlady ever."

I laughed as he leaned up on his elbow.

As the muscles in his arm quaked, I traced my fingers over the feathers of the tattooed bird.

He stared at me for a while, then at last said, "Say something."

I brushed my lips over his shoulder and said, "Two rooms down, six to go, Mr. Mayronne."

He laughed a raucous laugh that made me want to pull him on top of me again.

"I like this new amendment," I said, sliding my hand back into his hair.

He pulled my fingers to his lips. "I like it too, darlin'. Very much."

Chapter Thirteen

STORIES about the arsonist had moved from the front page to the third of the local paper, replaced by an exposé on the new candidate for governor. Today there was just a tiny one-column report. Eight fires, and no suspects had been named. In a photo of the most recent blaze, smoke tumbled from the windows of a warehouse. A half a dozen firefighters were in the frame, but if one of them was Jack, I couldn't tell.

I was stretched out in the hammock on the porch, watching Jack work on the Jeep. It felt like I was living someone else's life—I'd woken up thinking that surely I'd dreamed everything that had happened the day before with him. But there he'd been, tangled in the sheets next to me, his arm draped around my waist. I'd lain there awake for another hour, listening to him breathe, not wanting to break the spell. He hadn't woken up until the roofers had started up the circular saw outside.

Now, across the yard, he was on his knees changing my tires. He'd shed his T-shirt back on the second one. Midmorning, and it was already so hot I didn't feel like lifting more than a coffee mug. Learning about car maintenance wasn't a terrible way to start the day, I figured. I might need those skills one day, so it was important to watch him very carefully. Especially once he'd lost the shirt.

When Jack stood and brushed himself off, I lifted the paper again, turning a couple of pages just so he wouldn't think I was lazing around staring at him. In the back section, where the classifieds were, he'd circled a half a dozen ads for houses to rent. Skimming over the ads, I felt my chest tighten. Across the way, he set the jack under the last tire and started cranking. I tucked the paper under my arm, grabbed my glass of water and walked over to him.

"How about a drink?" I asked.

He turned and smiled. "You finally joined the living."

"I feel bad watching you do all the work."

His eyebrow arched, a definite sign that some wicked thought had passed through his head.

"Thanks, chère." He took the water and sat back in the grass, wiping his hand across his brow. He had streaks of grease across his chest, down his forearms.

"How's it coming?" I asked.

"She'll be good as new in no time. Like a pony with new shoes."

I sat down across from him. "I see you beat me to the morning paper."

He took a long drink of water and said, "How's that?"

"You're checking out other houses to rent."

He nodded. "Time's slipping away, chère. I'm going to be out in the cold soon."

I felt the stab of something like dread and tried to make my voice sound chipper. "Found any prospects yet?"

"I found some of the sketchiest houses in the parish, and they were still asking too much. I've resigned myself to the fact that I may be going to a cot in the firehouse." He shook his head, then said, "Unless, of course, you were to take on the position of landlord, and keep this beautiful house for your own, and rent it to a fine upstanding citizen who can also be persuaded to pay you in your favorite kind of favors."

I liked thinking of those favors. "Jack, we've had this conversation." But then I had another thought. "We've never talked about you being the new owner, though."

"What?"

"If you like the house so much, why don't you buy it?"

He shook his head. "Doubt it'll be in my price range."

"I wouldn't be so sure. I hear the seller's quite motivated."

He smiled, then said, "New subject. Did you see the other news in the paper?"

"You mean page three?"

"This arsonist is making us look like idiots," he said. "How is it possible this guy keeps slipping through our fingers?" He turned back to the Jeep, twisting the lug nuts off. "They had a press conference yesterday and gave us about ten minutes' warning. We were babbling like shorebirds in front of half the town. We'll be punchlines by sundown."

He glanced at his watch as he wiped his hands on an old rag. "I've got to get to the station in a little while. Have to do a two-day shift."

"Maybe those tires will still be working when you get back."

His eyebrow arched. "You see anybody skulking around here with a screwdriver, you have my permission to shoot them."

"Will do."

He pulled his cell phone from his pocket and handed it to me. "Call me at the station if you need anything. And I mean anything."

"You mean like if any more skulls show up in the yard?"

He frowned. "I'm serious. The number's programmed in there." He whistled as if calling for a cab. The dog crawled out from the shade of the cypresses and trotted over to us, her tail wagging. When she sat at Jack's feet, he knelt down and scratched her ears. He muttered to her in patois, phrases I could only half understand.

The dog barked.

"I hope you told her to go dig up my phone."

"I told her to watch out for you," he said. He stepped over to me and kissed me lightly on the lips.

"Really?" I said. "That's all I get?"

He grinned, sliding his fingers down my neck, his other hand drifting along the small of my back. "Any more and I won't be able to tear myself away. If I've got to suffer for a couple of days, so do you." He pecked my lip, catching it lightly in his teeth. "The best things are worth waiting for," he said, his lips moving against my ear. "Didn't you learn that yet?" He swatted me on the behind and walked back to the house.

I SPENT the rest of the day on the porch, working on the old banister rails. Pale and crackled, they looked as spindly as fish bones. The house was coming together on the inside, but from the outside, it still looked brittle, like it might collapse if you stared at it too hard. Scraping the old paint off was soothing—like shedding an old skin, making way for something stronger. The roofers worked above me, their hammers pounding like a giant metronome, counting down the days, the hours I had left to finish the house. I hadn't talked to my father since the dog ran away with the phone, and he was likely itching for an update.

I wasn't too upset that the phone was submerged in the swamp.

When the afternoon sun had moved to the far corner of the sky, the roofers climbed down, their shirts wrapped around their heads. Though they were already deeply tanned, their backs and shoulders were red.

"I think we've got you all fixed up," Wayne said, climbing down the ladder. "She ought to make it another ten years or more."

"Perfect," I said.

Randall appeared with three plastic cups I'd brought out earlier. "Thanks for the water," he said, raking a hand through his damp dark hair. "We went through ours fast." He had a warm smile, like Jack.

"This is my least favorite part," Wayne said, pulling a cigarette from his pocket. He lit it with a match and said, "I'll go get the bill while the boys pack up."

"If I'd been on the roof all day, that would be my favorite part," I said.

He took a long drag on the cigarette. He couldn't have been more than ten years older than me, but he already had deep-set wrinkles around his eyes, no doubt from baking in the sun. "This is usually the time when folks cuss me to pieces—when I'm driving away."

I took the cups to the kitchen while the roofers loaded their gear into the pickup. The two younger men climbed in the back and popped a couple of beers while Wayne pulled a shirt on and strolled over to the porch to bring me the bill.

The rot had cost much more than I'd planned for, but it seemed fair. Especially since they'd stayed through the hottest part of the day to finish on time. When Wayne fell through the roof, I thought for sure the bill would double, if not triple, but Jack must have worked a little magic on them after all. Maybe there was something to be said for knowing a fella who was in the boys' club.

"Thanks for doing it so quickly," I said, writing him the check.

"No problem. A friend of Jack's is a friend of mine."

He tucked the check in his back pocket and touched the brim of his hat. "You call if you should need anything else," he said, and strode back to the truck.

I walked to the back of the house and stared up at the roof. The sun was just sinking below the roofline, making it difficult to examine the work, but I could see that the new patches of shingles had blended nicely. As I picked up a few stray pieces in the yard, the dog came around the corner of the house and let out a half-hearted bark. She stared off into the swamp, and when I followed her gaze, I saw movement down in the cypress grove. At first I thought it was a trick of the sunlight, but then I noticed a shape that looked like a person. A person who was skulking.

I took a few steps toward the tree line. Shadows from the cypress limbs moved on the ground like serpents. The way the light played on the bark made it impossible to tell what was real and what was not.

Then the figure dashed out from the brush and slipped into the cover of trees. There was no mistaking the silhouette this time —tall, lanky and two-legged.

"Hey!" I yelled. The head turned in my direction for a split second, and then the figure was gone. The dog bolted to the grove, barking as her feet thudded in the grass. I followed, not thinking of who I might find when I caught up with her. My ankle throbbed after a few steps, but still I ran. It could have been a teenager or someone out fishing in the creek, but I had a feeling it was more sinister than that. Pain shot through my foot with every step, and finally I stopped a few yards short of the tree line. Whoever it was had vanished into the swamp.

The dog's barking was fainter now. There were tracks in the mud, big holes where feet had sunk down deep. I hopped from one patch of weeds to another to keep my own feet from sinking. I whistled for the dog but didn't see her. The forest was swallowing the last bits of the afternoon, the insects already humming as the fading light lured them out. Calling once more for the dog, I turned and limped back to the house, wishing I didn't have to spend the night there alone.

Inside, I ran myself a hot bath and dialed the station using Jack's cell phone. Then I hung up. I leaned back against the tile, thinking of how adamant he'd been. I dialed again, and when he answered, I told him about the roof being finished. Then I told him about the person in the swamp.

"I'm coming back. I'll get one of the guys to cover for me."

"You don't need to do that. I'm fine."

He insisted, stubborn as a goat. But I knew he needed the money.

"Really," I said. "I'll be OK."

There was a long pause. Then muttering that was half French.

"Please promise me you'll stay inside," he said finally. "Do not go outside again."

"Fine."

"I mean it, Enza. Promise me."

"OK, OK. I promise."

"Call the police if you see anything else." The chill in his tone made me shiver in the warm water.

EVEN THOUGH I knew it would keep me up all night, I searched the Internet for anything related to voodoo. By dark, I'd combed through dozens of websites, scrolling through shopping lists for spells, instructions for incantations, and a variety of price lists for anything from simple consultations to all out lay-the-whammy-on-you rituals. Most sites were clamoring for business from the lovesick and the frightened. But every once in a while I came across one that wasn't meant for amateurs, or vengeful lovers, or people looking to get even. A few offered some history of voodoo and explained what some of the things that had turned up in the yard might mean. This also gave me the chance to check facts against what Duchess had told me. So far, she was right in line with the more reputable online practitioners, which was equal parts reassuring and unsettling. Yeah, she seemed to be the real deal—but who wanted these things to be real?

There was a thump on the porch, and my whole body jerked. When it happened again, I realized it was the dog. She pawed at the screen door, banging it against the frame.

"For heaven's sake, dog," I said, trudging to the door. "You nearly scared the life out of me."

She peered through the screen, tongue lolling. When I didn't unlatch it fast enough, she pushed the door again.

"I'm coming already." I opened the door, and she bounded inside, skidding on the floor as she ran into the living room and dove onto the couch.

"You'd better enjoy your last few days of this," I said.

As I walked back into the kitchen, I heard Jack's phone vibrating on the counter. Pulling a beer out of the fridge, I ignored it, but then it went off again. After it buzzed a third time, I thought it might be Jack trying to call me.

I pressed the button on top and saw it was text messages. The first said, *miss you baby, wish you were here.* I flushed, thinking about how his hands had roamed over my body the day before. Try as I might to deny it, something about that man made me want more than a casual fling. I scrolled down.

I think about u all the time, the second said. I grinned.

The third said, *Want to know what i'm thinking right now?*

He must have borrowed a friend's phone. I quickly typed back, *Do tell.*

I stared at the screen, waiting. Then it buzzed. *Why don't u come here and i'll show u.*

"If only," I said, and typed, *Somehow I don't think the fellas would like that.*

The screen lit up. *Fk em. I need you more.*

I stared for a minute.

Don't make me start without u baby, it said.

I liked Jack's naughty side. An image of us in the firehouse flashed through my mind. My heart beat faster.

U have a fire that needs putting out? I typed.

There was an agonizing pause. Such a tease, this man.

Come see 4 yrself, it said.

No fair getting me all riled up, I typed, *when you can't put yr hands all over me.*

Come over, it said. *I'll put them anywhere u want.*

My skin tingled from the memory of his touch. Before I could answer, it buzzed again. *R u hard yet? Better get over here b4 u miss all the fun.*

I stared for a moment, confused. Then I felt sick.

The phone buzzed again. *Come rescue me*, it said.

I started to type again, and then stopped and touched the "call" button.

"Hey, baby," a woman's voice said. "I knew you missed me."

My throat tightened.

"I hope you're on your way over," she said.

It was Miranda. I was sure of it.

"Jack?" she said. "Are you there?"

I hung up, feeling like someone had punched me in the gut. What if she came over here looking for him? Could I call the police and have them arrest her?

The phone rang, and I pushed it across the table. I couldn't stay here. I didn't want to find out what Miranda would do next. Jack would be at the station two more nights. One more full day. If I called him, he'd insist on coming home. If he didn't, he'd worry himself sick all night, and if he was called out to a fire, he didn't need to be thinking about me.

I should have been able to handle this on my own—especially since I'd gotten myself into this mess by answering those stupid texts. Pretending to be naughty never got me anywhere. Ever.

The phone buzzed with another text, and I picked it up, my hand shaking.

Wtf?? it said.

It rang again, and I tossed it into the sink and grabbed my keys. I didn't know where to go, but I couldn't stay in the house. Outside, the air was still like the inside of an oven. I climbed into the Jeep and rolled the windows down. The tires squealed as I punched the gas, grinding my way down the drive. I turned onto the two lane highway, heading south toward New Orleans. I passed a couple of the local restaurants and the bar where I'd had that run-in with Remy. With my luck, if I walked into any place that was open around here, I'd walk right into Miranda. Or worse,

Remy. That was the thing about small towns—you couldn't avoid people when you needed to.

Then I thought of Josie and Buck, and turned the Jeep around.

I STOOD at their front door, my stomach in a knot. When I rang the bell, Josie answered.

"Enza," she said. "What a surprise. Come on in."

"I'm sorry to show up unexpected, but I'm sort of in a predicament," I said, following her inside.

"Is Jack OK?" she asked, her eyes widening.

"Oh! Yes. Sorry. He's fine, but I've got this situation where I don't—I can't be alone at the house tonight, and Jack's at the station. I hate to ask, but is there any way I could stay with you?"

"Of course you can, sweetie." She wrapped her arm around my shoulders just as Buck walked in.

"Is there something we can do?" she asked. "Jack said y'all had trouble with the roof."

I shook my head, feeling like I might cry at any second—partly from fear and embarrassment and partly from relief.

"Everything OK, Enza?" Buck asked.

Josie told him what I'd said. She looked more serious, like she knew this had nothing to do with troublesome repairs. "Come on upstairs," she said to me. "We'll get you situated in the spare room."

"What's the kid done now?" Buck asked.

"Hush," Josie told him, turning me toward the stairs.

The spare room was cozy, painted pale green with light wood trim. It was filled with antique furniture, most notably an old trunk with leather straps. I made a mental note to ask her later where she'd found such a piece. A double bed was made up with a patchwork quilt, a framed print of Audubon's blue herons hanging over the headboard.

Josie pointed out the bathroom, then opened the dresser

drawer and pulled out an oversize T-shirt. "You can sleep in this, and I'll get you a toothbrush."

"Thank you so much," I said, giving her a hug. Her perfume smelled like lily of the valley.

"Oh, honey," she said, patting my back. "Everything's going to be fine."

She didn't ask any questions, and part of me hated to confess that I'd been careless. There was no way to explain it that didn't involve Jack. And it didn't seem right to tell them this had to do with Miranda. Whether they knew about her or not, I had no business talking about Jack's ex-girlfriends.

Still, I felt bad being so mysterious. It was bound to make them think things were much worse than they were.

"Why don't you come downstairs and let me make you a toddy," Josie said. "I've got six kinds of Kentucky bourbon, and every one of them will knock you out like a hammer."

Chapter Fourteen

THE SMELL of coffee and butter woke me up, and I felt completely disoriented. It took me a full minute to realize I wasn't in North Carolina, and I wasn't at Vergie's either. A thick curtain covered the tiny window, making it impossible to judge the time by the light in the room. When I drew the drapes, the brightness surprised me. I threw my clothes on and went down to the kitchen.

"Hey, sunshine," Buck said. "Sleep well?" He was frying bacon and sausage, and sipping a glass of orange juice.

"Like a brick. Josie was right about the toddy."

Josie turned from her scrambled eggs. "Morning, hon. We're just about ready here. Help yourself to coffee."

I poured myself a cup and sat at the table, watching them reach over each other, seamlessly making breakfast together. I felt bad for not telling them what was going on, but how could I?

Josie brought two plates to the table and sat next to me. Buck followed with a tray of biscuits.

"Jack called a little while ago," Josie said to me. "He asked you to call him back at the station. He said not to wake you."

"How'd he know I was here?"

"Said he couldn't get you on his cell," Josie said. "He asked Buck to go check on you, but we told him you were here."

"You told him I was OK?"

"Yes, but he was worried. He wanted to know what happened to make you come over."

"Not that we aren't pleased to have the company," Buck said.

I smiled. "It seems silly this morning."

They looked at me, curious. I tore into a biscuit and said, "What do y'all know about voodoo?"

They listened as I told them about all the things we'd found in the yard. I left out the part about Miranda and the casserole, but I told them I'd seen someone skulking around the house and that the tires on my Jeep had been slashed.

"Who in the world would do such a thing?" Josie said.

Buck raised his eyebrows.

"It came to a head last night," I said. "The more I thought about it, the more nervous I was about staying there alone. But it's probably nothing. I shouldn't have bothered you."

"Doesn't sound like nothing to me," Buck said. "I don't put much stock in voodoo, but hoodlums are a different story."

"Nonsense," Josie said. "It's no bother. You'll stay here until Jack's off duty."

"Oh no. I'll go home today. I'll be fine."

"I insist," Josie said. "You can help me make the bourbon balls for the Daughters of the American Revolution luncheon tomorrow. It'd help me out tremendously, since Buck's way of helping is to taste them until there's none left."

Thinking of going back to Vergie's made my heart thump so hard I felt it in my ears. The workaholic part of me was screaming to get my lazy ass back to the house and get back on task. But another part of me, the part that couldn't forget Miranda's breathy voice and unwanted house calls, insisted it was smarter to stay away. I wasn't exactly afraid of Miranda, but I'd prefer to not be at the house alone if she felt the need to stop by.

"I'd be happy to," I told Josie. "I've never made bourbon balls."

"Oh, your world's about to change," she said. "Just wait and see." She slid a plate of eggs and sausage in front of me. "Now have some breakfast and fortify yourself. This is serious business we're getting into."

I CALLED THE STATION, hoping Jack wouldn't be able to talk and I could leave a message. But the guy who answered called out for him, and Jack picked up, breathless.

"What's happened?" he asked. "Are you OK?"

"I'm fine. I just freaked out. It was nothing."

There was a pause on the other end of the line.

"Obviously it's not nothing."

"I'll tell you everything when you get home."

"Tell me now."

"Jack," I said, trying to keep my voice down, "it's fine, really. I'm staying at Josie and Buck's tonight, and I'm good."

"Tonight too? Enza, tell me what happened."

"Miranda sent some texts, and it just rattled me. That's all."

"What?" His voice was louder. "Did she come over there?"

"No, but I thought she might, so I came here." I peeked into the kitchen. "Listen, I have to go make bourbon balls for the DAR luncheon. Break a leg, and I'll see you tomorrow."

"Say what?"

I hung up quickly, despite his protests.

Josie poked her head around the corner, holding a bottle of bourbon in one hand and another frilly apron in the other. "Hey," she said. "You ready to get this show on the road?"

"Absolutely."

As it turned out, bourbon balls were the most miraculous thing I'd ever seen made in a kitchen. I followed Buck's method, which was to taste and re-taste. We had to make several extra batches because of all our sampling, but also because Josie said Jack would throw the tantrum from hell if I didn't take some back for him. By dinner time we had every cookie tin and plastic container in the kitchen filled with bourbon balls.

"You know," Josie said, "I'm glad you're here. It's great to see you fixing up Vergie's house. It's good for Jack too."

I wasn't sure what he'd told her about our arrangement and if she knew the house was going on the market.

"He's been a huge help," I said. "Just about everything that could have gone wrong has. I'm lucky he's here."

"He's good that way. He's a fixer, he is." She smiled a knowing smile. "He's lucky too, though. He'd given up on finding a nice gal."

I didn't know what to say to that, so I blurted, "Oh, we're just friends."

She raised an eyebrow.

"I mean, Jack's great," I added. "But we've just got a business arrangement."

She smiled again, like she didn't believe that for a minute.

WHEN I LEFT the next morning, bourbon balls in tow, Josie said, "Now you come back anytime, hon. With or without Jack."

I thanked them again and then drove to the next town to pick up a new cell phone. My father had probably left an array of messages ranging from curious to wrathful, but I couldn't blame him too much since this was technically his money I was spending. When I turned the phone on, I expected it to light up with voicemails—weren't these things saved in a cloud somewhere?—but there was nothing.

No messages.

No checking up on me.

Maybe he was starting to get it.

When I pulled into the drive, I was surprised to see Jack's truck parked under the oak tree by the house. It was barely noon.

Inside, he was making pasta.

"You're back early," I said.

"You, my dear, scared me to death."

"I have bourbon balls," I said, holding out the tin.

He looked at me skeptically, then turned back to the pasta. "Are you going to tell me what happened?"

I'd really hoped to avoid the Miranda conversation. "Try one," I said, opening the tin. "These have orange liqueur."

"You can't distract me with boozy truffles. I was worried about you."

"Sorry," I said, sitting down at the table. "I didn't want to get into details when I was with Josie and Buck. I didn't know how much they knew about the Miranda situation."

"What is the Miranda situation? What's with these text messages?" He scrolled through them on the phone, and I felt ill.

"It was stupid. I didn't want to bother you over this."

"Go on." His calmness was unnerving.

"That first text came, and I thought it was you being cheeky. So I answered."

He raised his eyebrows and said, "OK."

"Then I realized it wasn't you. So I called the number to find out who it was. And Miranda answered."

His eyes widened.

"I know it's silly, but after the phone call I was worried she'd come over here again. So I went to Josie and Buck's."

"Jesus, Enza. Why didn't you call me?"

"You don't need to babysit me."

He groaned, running his hands through his hair. "You're impossible."

"I got to visit your family. Not a bad day."

He stood, aggravated, and began to pace.

"I'm sorry. I should have told you."

"Damn right." He leaned toward the window, gripping the frame.

"I wanted to avoid another scene."

He shook his head, staring into the yard. "Miranda is my problem," he said firmly. "She shouldn't be yours too."

"I didn't want you to worry."

"I'm supposed to be helping you, looking out for you. Not making your life more complicated."

Complicated had happened the second I walked up and found him in the hammock, but I kept that thought to myself.

"It's all right," I said at last. "Let's forget about the whole thing."

"It's not all right!" he said, his voice rising again. "I made a promise."

He bit his lip like he'd said too much.

"What does that mean?" I asked. "What promise?"

He sat down across from me at the table and reached for his coffee. I'd never seen him so flustered before.

"Jack?"

He rested his elbows on the table and gazed at me. "I should have said something sooner. But it just seemed weird. I thought it would scare you."

"What's going on?"

He sighed. "I promised Vergie I'd look out for you, that I'd help you any way I could."

At first I thought I misheard him.

"I wanted to tell you, Enza. But I knew it would make everything between us seem—contrived." Beneath the table, his knee brushed against mine. "She knew she was sick." His voice lowered to almost a whisper. "She knew you'd come take care of the house—after—and she asked me to stick around and help you however you needed. I promised her I'd look out for you."

My breath caught in my throat. "You knew I was coming?"

He nodded.

"She knew she was dying?"

He nodded again, his eyes sad.

"Why didn't she call me? I would have come down here. I could have helped her."

He shook his head. "That's not what she wanted. She didn't want you to be sad or feel burdened. But she knew what this place did for you. She wanted you to have it."

My eyes stung with tears. She'd been thinking of me all that time, and I'd been so oblivious. My chest ached as I held back sobs that would surely crack my heart in half.

Jack brought my hand to his lips. "She loved you so much. And she knew you loved her the same."

"Why didn't you tell me all of this before?" I asked.

He shrugged. "I knew you wouldn't believe me. I mean, why would you? You didn't know me at all."

He was right, of course. I wouldn't have believed him.

"And after, I just didn't know how. I didn't want you to think I was only here because Vergie asked me."

What exactly did that mean? I started to ask him, but he spoke up first.

"I loved her too," he said. "I know I'm not her kin, but she meant the world to me. And even if you're madder than hell at me, I intend to keep my promise to her. So if you tell me to piss off and just show up with a hammer to finish all these repairs and never say another word to you, then that's exactly what I'll do. But I really hope it doesn't come to that."

"I'm not mad at you."

My head was pounding but not from anger. Under other circumstances, I probably wouldn't have believed any of this. But people here were tangled in ways I couldn't predict, and every time I thought I had them figured out, another loose end led somewhere I couldn't imagine.

He held my hand in both of his. "Please say something," he said.

"Why else would you be here?"

"What do you mean?"

"You said you didn't want me to think the only reason you're here is because of Vergie. Why else would you be here?"

"Oh," he said, shifting in his chair. "I meant our agreement. The repairs."

I stared at him, hard. Whatever he was hiding, he'd shoved it deep beneath the skin. He released my hand.

"Right," I said.

We sat in silence for a few minutes. Finally I said, "I'm glad you told me."

"I hope this doesn't make things awkward between us," he said.

"It doesn't have to. Though it's certainly unexpected."

"Are you OK?" he asked.

I laughed. "I'm not some delicate orchid, Jack. I'll be fine."

He smiled at that, seemingly relieved. But he didn't look convinced.

"What are you going to do about Miranda?" I asked.

"Let me worry about her."

I nodded, standing up from my chair. "I'm sorry I made you worry," I said, ruffling his hair.

"I know."

"How about we tackle this gnarly kitchen floor?" I said, eager to change the subject. "I've got a couple of days to make up for."

With the dog banished outside, we set to work. The giant yellow spot from the spilled paint was far too stubborn to pull up without stripping the floor. I decided instead to paint it in a muted checkerboard pattern of blue and white. If we did it right, it would look farmhouse chic and blend with the rest. It was a technique I'd used only once before, and I'd forgotten the agony of sanding and laying strips of painter's tape out with a T-square. It took two hours to sand and wash the floor, then another hour to get the tape just right, crossing at precise right angles to avoid any rhombuses or rectangles. Still, it was preferable to stripping and staining.

We'd moved the furniture onto the porch. The refrigerator was in the hallway, but I'd left the stove in its nook.

Jack and I started in opposite corners of the farthest row, painting toward the hallway so we wouldn't trap ourselves inside. He painted blue, and I painted white, so every few minutes we leap-frogged over each other to continue down the row. He hummed a little as he painted but was mostly quiet, like something was on his mind. I wanted to ask him more about Vergie and if he ever worked for her the summers I was here, but I didn't. I was afraid it would embarrass him, and I wasn't entirely sure I wanted to know.

When we were halfway across the floor, he blurted, "So you really thought I was texting you those messages?"

My brush wavered, crossing over into one of his blue squares. "Damn," I said, wiping the smudge with my finger.

He smirked, his brush stopping as he glanced at me from the corner of his eye.

"Yes," I said, with an exaggerated sigh.

He tried to hide his widening grin. "Didn't know you had that in you, chère."

"I'm just full of surprises."

He moved to the next square so we were shoulder to shoulder. "Wicked little vixen."

"You're distracting me."

He turned and dragged the brush slowly over the wood. "What are the chances you'd text me like that for real?"

"Help me pull off this miracle, and we'll renegotiate our terms."

He chuckled. "Fair enough, chère. But I'm holding you to that one."

WHEN WE FINALLY FINISHED, I was starving. The floors wouldn't be dry for another hour at least, so we wouldn't be able to cook anything.

"The bad news is we're stuck with what's in the fridge," Jack said. "The worse news is I left the bourbon in the kitchen cabinet, way over there."

"Looks like we're having sandwiches," I said, peering into the fridge. Inside was a loaf of bread, some deli meat and a jar of mustard.

"Or I could take you out to dinner."

My arms were smeared with paint. My hair was frizzy and full of dust from the sanding. "It would take forever to get cleaned up and semi-girly. What about take-out?"

"Sure, I can get something at Brenda's." He pulled out his phone and started to dial. "You think of a way to get to the bourbon while I'm gone."

"Roger that."

He walked outside, ordering two specials as he sauntered to his truck.

It was sweet, the way he was so careful with everything we did. As soon as he was gone, I padded over to the cabinet barefoot. This floor was meant to be rustic, after all.

With the bourbon in hand, I slinked back into the hallway, keeping to the squares I thought were most dry. I made it across without pulling up more than a few flecks of paint. After some light sanding, those spots would blend right in.

I poured myself a shot—Jack would just have to catch up— and collapsed on the couch. Everything was aching from crawling around on my knees.

After a short while, my phone rang.

"Hey," I said. "Forget something?"

"The station just called," Jack said. "I have to go."

"What? You're joking."

"Afraid not," he said. "There's a big fire across the canal. Probably the damned arsonist again."

"You just got back. Can't someone else fill in for you?"

He sighed. "We're shorthanded as it is. It's all hands on deck until they catch this bastard." He paused, then said, "I left Brenda's a few minutes ago. I have dinner, but I've got to go straight to the station."

"It's OK."

"I'm sorry, chère. Raincheck?"

"Sure. Just please be—" I stopped myself before I jinxed him. "Break a leg. In a big way."

He laughed. "Will do. I'll see you soon."

Chapter Fifteen

I MADE a sandwich and ate it on the porch while the dog stared at me. Tossing bits of ham to her seemed to buy her affection, at least for the time being.

"Don't think I'm not still mad at you about the floor. That was unacceptable behavior."

Her ears flattened.

"That checkerboard pattern turned out all right though."

I tossed another slice of ham, which she snatched mid-air.

"It wasn't a terrible turn of events, but you could be more graceful with your suggestions."

She coughed.

We sat on the porch until the dark rolled over us. Me drinking bourbon and tossing deli slices to a dog, the dog likely plotting how to wreck the next room.

I stood to go inside and felt shooting pains in my back and shoulders. When I reached for the screen door, Bella sat up and stared at me, ears pricked forward.

"Come on," I said, holding the door open. "I could use some company."

She darted inside, then followed me as I poured myself another glass of bourbon.

Upstairs, I filled the tub with hot water and put an old blues record on Vergie's turntable in the bedroom. The dog cocked her head, watching me light a few candles.

"What? No judging." I slipped out of my jeans, and she sat on the floor, her eyes still fixed on me. The bathroom was one of the only rooms that didn't need much repair. An old clawfoot tub was surrounded by a mosaic of white and cobalt floor tiles. Pale blue walls provided a respite from the scorching Louisiana summer. And a window sill above the tub held a row of candles.

As steam rose from the water, I tossed my shirt on the sink and stepped into the tub. Bella blinked at me, her expression a mix of curiosity and contempt. I was glad to have her in the house. It seemed less empty that way.

I leaned back in the tub, trying to forget the rotten roof, the painted skull, the figure in the woods. Harder still, I tried to stop thinking about Jack. We'd agreed this could be a casual affair, but it was getting harder every day to keep thinking of him that way. I'd let him get close to me, unlike most men before. I liked having him around, and—also unlike past experiences—I wasn't already picturing how my life would be when he left.

I got out of the bath to turn the record over, and the dog whined. Music filled the room as I splashed back into the water. The old house was casting its spell on me once again—the smell of magnolia, the echo of the music. Everything reminded me of how free I'd felt all those years ago. For a long time, I'd convinced myself I couldn't have that again, but now I was beginning to think that I might.

That I *should*.

I closed my eyes and sank deeper into the water. I thought of the way Jack had kissed me, slid his hands along my skin as if I was this rare creature he didn't quite know how to handle. One moment, he was gentle, like I might break in his hands, and the next, he was wild with desire. No man had ever made me feel the way he did, and I wondered just how rare that feeling was.

The dog sat up abruptly, her toenails clicking on the tile. She turned to the door and growled. "Relax," I said, but she only growled deeper, stepping out of the room. I sat up just as the lights blinked out. The record slowed to a stop. The candles flickered in the window, and the dog disappeared down the hall. I sat still, listening for any sound from downstairs. But there was none.

"Damn. I thought they fixed this." I climbed out of the bath and cinched my robe around me, not even bothering to towel off. Bella whined and came back to the door.

"Come on," I said, grabbing one of the candles for light. "Let's go flip the breaker back." She followed at my heels.

The flame flickered as I padded down the stairs, and the dog raced past me. Outside, the bayou was completely black. With no close neighbors, there was never any ambient light. The darkness stretched for miles, and the swamp always felt closer at night.

I opened the closet under the stairs and held the candle to the breaker box. When I flipped the main breaker, the house remained still and dark.

I cursed and flipped the other breakers two by two. None of them appeared to be tripped, but I tried them anyway. When I got to the bottom row, my skin tingled from my neck to my ankles. My throat tightened at the thought of spending the rest of the night in total darkness, total silence.

I jumped when I heard a thump in the hallway, and I clung to the doorframe. "Jack?" I whispered.

Finally, the dog crept around the corner and looked at me, her head hanging low.

I clutched my robe to my chest. "Dammit, Bella," I said, walking back into the living room. "You've got to quit doing that."

I'd left my phone upstairs. Who would I call at this hour anyway? Jack was likely still fighting the fire across the canal and might not be back for hours. I trudged back up the stairs, the dog right behind. There was nothing to do but tough it out and call an electrician in the morning.

When I reached the top of the stairs, I heard what sounded like breaking glass, and I froze, my hand on the banister. The dog bounded back down the stairs, barking like the devil was after her. I ducked into the bedroom, my heart banging against my ribs. I held my breath, waiting for another sound, wondering how to get away. The crash had been real—I couldn't have imagined it. Someone must be outside on the porch, smashing a window, unlocking the door. I tried to hold myself together, thinking of how to escape. I could hide upstairs, then sneak out if someone came up. I could crawl out the window and wait on the roof.

I felt around for a weapon. There was a pencil, a vase, a wrench. The wrench would have to do. I'd have to make it through the yard and down to the highway without being intercepted—and I'd have to make it in the dark. I strained my ears, listening for footsteps, for any other sound besides the pounding of my heart. But there was only silence.

I had to move. Frantic, I found my phone and shoved it in the pocket of my robe.

I blew out the candle and eased into the hall, tightening my grip on the wrench. Still hearing no sound, I paused at the top of the stairs. With blood pounding in my ears, I slipped down the steps on my tiptoes, wincing as the boards creaked. I continued, but stopped when I saw a light flickering in the corner of my eye.

Flames lapped at the curtains in the living room. An eerie orange light was cast over the room, smoke billowing toward the ceiling. I choked back a scream and ran into the kitchen, forgetting about intruders. The crackling of the fire filled my ears, but I dug through the cabinets under the sink, throwing everything onto the floor, searching for a fire extinguisher. I knew there was one in there, but as I dragged my hands along the wall by the refrigerator, along the cabinets, I couldn't picture where I'd seen it. Everything had been jumbled in the chaos of repairs. I turned the faucet on full blast and grabbed a pot from the stove, filling it with water. The smell of smoke was stronger now, permeating the kitchen. I ran back to the living room and threw the water on the curtains.

That, of course, did nothing.

The fire had spread to the rug, to the chair by the window. I ran back to the sink and filled the pot again. "Come on!" I willed the water to come out faster. Running back to the fire, I threw the water on the worst of the flames, but they only flickered. It was spreading too fast. I pulled a quilt from the sofa and wrapped my hands in it, then grabbed the curtains near the bottom and yanked them down from the rods. A ripping sound split the air as the curtains pooled on the floor. I tossed the quilt on top of them, trying to smother the flames.

The dog barked wildly in the doorway. My gut told me to run. But how could I leave the house to burn? I swore as I threw the quilt on the burning carpet, trying to stamp out the fire. But it continued—fueled by sheets and drop cloths, it now covered more than a quarter of the room. I backed away from the heat, covering my nose and mouth, feeling my whole body shaking.

Bella tugged at my robe with her teeth, pulling me off-balance, her eyes orange in the light. I scanned the room one more time, but there was nothing I could use to put out the flames. They were rising to the ceiling and rippling across the floor. I ran into the yard, the dog behind me, her barks piercing the night air. My last hope was the spigot in the flower bed by the porch. I twisted it on and grabbed the hose as I dialed 911.

My voice didn't even sound like my own as I gave the operator the address. "Please hurry!" I cried, dragging the hose to the side of the house. With flames licking at the window frame, I sprayed water into the broken window along the wood siding, but it seemed like only a trickle.

Smoke poured from the window, and I ran back into the house, dragging the hose behind me as far as it would reach. The living room glowed orange. From the doorway, I aimed the stream of water at the ceiling, hosing down the walls. I pulled my robe over my nose, spraying the furniture, the carpet, the curtains.

My throat burned as I coughed, and I sank to my knees to stay under the worst of the smoke. Now the fire touched all four walls of the room. The heat burned my skin. The crackling of the wood filled my ears. Still I aimed water at the ceiling, backing into the hallway, bracing myself to run when the flames got too close. If nothing else, the water might slow the fire and stop it from spreading to the rest of the house.

When I heard the siren, it sounded faint, as if it were still on the main highway. The next crash made me flinch and instinctively cover my head—I was sure it was the ceiling collapsing, that I had made a horrible mistake. But then I felt an arm clamp around my waist and another across my shoulders, and I was being dragged backwards into the night.

"Have you lost your mind?" Jack's breath was hot on my neck. He pulled me down the steps and into the yard, swearing all the way.

I collapsed at his feet, gasping and coughing. My eyes stung from the heat and the smoke. This had to be a nightmare. I shook my head, squeezing my eyes shut. *Wake up,* I thought, *Wake up!*

"Shit," Jack said. He was on his knees in the grass, cupping my face in his hands. "What were you thinking, Enza? You could have been killed!"

He scooped me up and carried me to the picnic table in the yard. Bella followed and folded herself under the table with a huff. Every time I took a deep breath, I coughed. Jack sat next to me, wrapping his arm around my shoulders. Still, I trembled.

Across the yard, a half a dozen firefighters were spraying the flames that lapped at the side of the house. Another strode over to me and gently placed a blanket over my shoulders. "Hi, Enza." He knelt in front of me. "I'm Zane." He glanced at Jack and then said, "You OK?"

I nodded, though I was far from OK.

"Any idea how this happened?"

My chest felt heavy from the smoke. I pushed the itchy blanket away and said, "I don't know. The power went out, and I went downstairs to check the breakers. Then I heard something break, like a window, and the next thing I knew the living room was on fire."

The men exchanged a look. A flash of anger shot through Jack's eyes.

"The worst of it's out now," Zane said, nodding toward the guys gathered by the truck. They were passing off axes and other equipment and filing into the house. Thin trails of smoke still rose from the window, but the eerie orange glow was gone. "You probably saved the house, doing what you did." He stood and handed me a bottle of water.

"Don't encourage her," Jack said. "I can't decide if that was brave or stupid."

"Hell," Zane said. "Tough as nails, I'd say."

I turned to Jack. "I had to."

"It's just bricks and wood. It can be rebuilt."

"It wasn't that bad in there. I'd have gotten out when it got too dangerous."

He raked his hands through his hair. "The ceiling could have fallen. You could have been trapped. If we'd been five minutes later—"

"I couldn't just stand there and watch it burn to the ground."

"Christ almighty," he said. "Stubborn as a mule."

Zane opened his medical kit. "We should check you over," he said, placing a stethoscope against my chest. I inhaled deeply and coughed again.

"Did you have any unattended flames in the house?" Zane asked. "Candles, incense, anything like that?"

"Not in the living room. Just upstairs."

"Any old lamps or things with old wiring?"

"They worked on the wiring a week or so ago, but they said it was all fixed and up to code."

He nodded, glancing at Jack as if he was holding something back.

"It wasn't storming out this way, was it?" Zane asked. "You see any lightning?"

"No," I answered. Suddenly aware that I was only wearing a robe, I pulled it tight against me, crossing my arms over my chest.

"You said the window broke," Jack said.

"That's what it sounded like." I tried to recall that moment on the stairs. I'd been so frightened, it was possible I'd imagined it. It was possible the dog had knocked something over. But I knew she hadn't. "I could have sworn I heard somebody in the house. I was sneaking down the stairs when I saw the fire." Shivering, I pulled the blanket back over my shoulders. "Then I went to get the hose and forgot about the rest."

Jack's jaw clenched. His fingers were kneading the fabric of his turnouts, his knuckles white. He opened his mouth to say something, and one of the others whistled for him to come over.

"You sit tight, chère," he said, his voice gravelly. He squeezed my shoulder and jogged over to the others.

He stood with his hands on his hips, nodding as the other man spoke. His face looked hard and angular in the moonlight. I couldn't make out what they were saying, particularly with Zane still fussing over my scratches and asking questions.

The dog snorted under the table, then crept out toward the swamp. She took a few steps and then stopped, her ears pricked forward.

Zane dabbed something on a cut on my forehead, and I heard one of the guys say, "accelerant."

The dog growled and dashed into the swamp.

"Hey," I yelled.

"Sorry," Zane said, drawing his hand back.

"No, it's the dog. She went after something."

Zane stared in the direction of the swamp.

My whole body tensed again as he stood, his hand on my back.

"Stay here," he said, his eyes still on the woods. "I'll check it out."

Jack trudged back over, fixing me with a worried look.

"What is it?" I asked. "What's happening?"

He stared past me, biting his lip. "It's not good, darlin'. Not good at all."

"That much is clear, but I need details."

"You can't stay here. This is my fault."

"What?" None of this made sense. It was becoming more and more like a nightmare.

"I was supposed to be here tonight," he said. "I took that shift last minute."

"You think someone did this trying to get to you?"

He sat beside me, shaking his head. "All this arson business. It's been old abandoned buildings, and now all of a sudden it's a firefighter's house. The guys think it's some kind of grudge."

"Well they came to that conclusion awfully fast."

He nodded. "We thought it was someone with a grudge against the department, but now it's evident it's about me. And I've put you in danger."

I opened my mouth, but no sound came out.

"This wasn't an accident, Enza. They found proof inside. Traces of accelerant, an intense point of origin, just like the others. Probably tossed something through the window."

I felt faint. The possibility had crossed my mind of course, but to hear him say it aloud, so matter of fact, meant it wasn't as unlikely as I'd thought. Tears stung my eyes, and I couldn't hold them back any more. All the fear and anger broke free and rattled inside my chest.

Jack wrapped his arms around my shoulders. His lips brushed against my temple as he said, "You're all right. I'm not leaving you alone again."

One of the guys walked over and stood next to Jack. He was stout with short dark hair and spoke with a thick Louisiana drawl. "I'm taking the rest of your shift," he said. "You got somewhere you can go?"

"Thanks, Robbie," Jack said. "We'll go to my uncle's."

Robbie smiled at me and clasped Jack on the shoulder before walking back to the truck.

Zane emerged from the woods and returned to the others.

"Hey," I called out. A cough tore through my chest, and Jack's hand went straight to my back to steady me.

Jack whistled and waved Zane over.

"Sorry," Zane said. "No sign of the dog." He glanced at Jack. "No sign of anyone else, either."

"Let's get you out of here," Jack said to me.

"What about Bella?"

"She'll be fine. This isn't her first night out in the woods."

I saw a look pass between the men, but what it meant, I couldn't quite tell.

"I need to go in and get some real clothes," I said.

"I'll grab some things for you," Jack said. "Stay here." He jogged across the yard to the house, casting one last look in the direction of the swamp.

"Thanks for patching me up, Zane."

He smiled. "Any time. But let's not make it a habit." He crossed his arms over his chest, looking back to the house. Standing guard.

"Sorry you had to go through all of this," he said. "But the worst is over."

I smiled warily. I didn't believe him for a second.

Chapter Sixteen

JACK CALLED Buck as we were driving past the canal. I could hear Buck shouting on the other end of the line.

"She's OK," Jack told him at last, sliding his hand over my knee. "Shaken up, but not badly hurt."

He'd changed out of his turnouts, but he still smelled like smoke. I inhaled as much of the night air as I could.

At their house, Josie hugged me so tight I flinched. She and Buck were both sleepy-eyed, wearing pajamas.

"Oh, honey," she said to me. "We're so glad you're all right. Both of you."

She hugged Jack, and he said, "If you don't mind, we'll turn in and talk in the morning."

"Of course, dear," she said. "You know where everything is. I've already made up the bedrooms for you."

We thanked them, and Jack led me upstairs.

I heard Josie and Buck whispering as we climbed the stairs. The lamps were on in the two bedrooms, the sheets turned down. Jack took my bag into the green room I'd stayed in before. "This one's got the better mattress," he said. "I'll just be next door."

He kissed me on the forehead, folding his arms around me.

"I don't think I can sleep." I leaned my cheek against his chest. "Will you stay up with me for a while?"

I hadn't noticed I was trembling until he held me tight against him.

"Hey," he said. "You're safe here."

I nodded, trying to relax my grip around his waist. He slid his hands up and down my back.

After a few minutes, he said, "I'll be right back."

When he went downstairs, I pulled one of his shirts from the duffle bag and slipped it on. As I climbed into bed, I heard a muffled exchange between Jack and Josie, the rattle of dishes in the kitchen.

I closed my eyes but saw only orange.

After a little while, Jack came back with a bottle of whiskey and two glasses.

"Thought this might settle your nerves a bit." He poured a shot into each glass.

He handed me one and sat next to me on the bed.

"Thank you," I said. "For saving me. It sounds stupid to say, because thank you isn't enough."

He turned to me and slid his hand over mine, then brought it to his lips and kissed the inside of my wrist. He held it there, pressed against his face, as he laced his fingers in mine.

"I thought I'd lost you," he said, his lips brushing my palm.

I moved closer to him then, and he released my hand so he could gather me against his chest, winding his arms around me.

I lay my head on his chest, listening to the thumping of his heart.

"Getting a call to your own house is bad enough, but when I didn't see you outside—" He squeezed me tighter, sliding his hand down to rest on my hip.

I sank into him, draping my arm around his waist.

"I don't ever want to feel that again," he said.

There was a scratching noise outside the window, and I jumped, clutching Jack's shirt.

"Hey," he said. "It's OK. It's probably just a raccoon." His lips brushed against my ear as he spoke.

I eased back against him. It was hard to stop the thoughts from churning.

"Do you think it's Remy?" I said at last.

His body tensed, though he tried to hide it as he slid his fingers along my skin.

"The guy might hate me, but I don't see him going to all this trouble."

"He said he hoped you would die in a fire."

"People say a lot of stupid things." He reached for his glass and downed the drink in one swallow.

"Yeah, and sometimes they do stupid things. Why would he do this to you? What happened between you two?"

He said nothing, stroking my hair.

"Jack, you can tell me. Whatever it is."

He reached over to the nightstand and refilled his glass.

"Is this because of me? That night at the bar?"

"No," he said quickly. "This is not your fault." He slid his hand along my cheek. "But he could have been planning to hurt you that night as a way to hurt me."

I swallowed hard. Remy was a jerk, sure—but I thought I'd seen a crack in his facade that night. I'd seen a glimmer of the wounded part of him, something that made me think he was only pretending to be a brute. It was hard to think of him actually trying to hurt me.

"Why would he do that?"

He stared into his glass. "Because he wants me to suffer, Enza. As much as I made him suffer."

I sat up straighter, squeezing Jack's knee. He took another long drink and stared at my hand.

"His brother Luke worked with us, back when I was in the New Orleans unit," he said. He wouldn't look at me.

"Hey, it's OK."

"Believe me, it's not. It's not something I'm proud of, Enza."

I lay my hand on his shoulder. "You can tell me anything."

After a long pause, he shook his head. "There was a big warehouse fire, and Luke and I pushed into a back room. The windows blew out, and we got caught in a backdraft. Everything was red, so hot you couldn't breathe." He stared at the space between his feet. "Part of the roof collapsed on us, and Luke was pinned under a beam. I tried to pull him out, but I wasn't strong enough. When the rest of the roof started to come down, another guy, Derrick, pulled me out before I could get Luke free. I fucking hated him for doing that."

"Oh, Jack." I didn't know what else to say.

"I couldn't save him," he said.

We sat in silence, staring into the darkness.

"It wasn't your fault," I said at last. It sounded less trite in my head.

"Of course it was. How could it not be? The first thing you learn is to take care of your own."

I put my arm around him, but he shrugged it away. The pain and guilt seemed to roll off him in waves.

"And his wife," he said. "She never got over it. I couldn't face her after that. I knew she wished it had been me who died in that warehouse, and most days I did too."

"Jack," I said, my eyes brimming with tears. I had no idea what words might comfort him. What can you say to someone who hurts so deeply?

"Those two were the happiest couple you ever saw. I mean the kind that couldn't keep their hands off each other, always smiling and laughing, making you jealous deep down in your soul, then making you feel bad for feeling jealous, and wishing you could be so lucky." He glanced at me with glassy eyes. "She drowned herself in the lake behind their house a few months later."

"Oh my God," I said, and regretted it immediately.

"All because of me," he said.

I wound my arms around him, but his body was rigid as an oak.

"It wasn't your fault," I said. "It was a horrible accident, but it was just that—an accident. You can't blame yourself."

"I couldn't stand to see those guys. I had to leave the parish, find another department and start over."

"Hey," I said, but he wouldn't look me in the eye.

I grabbed his chin in my fingers and tugged his face toward mine. His brow was furrowed, his eyes glassy. "Look at me. You're the bravest man I know."

He shook his head. "Remy has every right to hate me. We got into our fair share of fights over the years. He put me in the hospital once, and I had him arrested one time, but then it died down. I figured he was getting over it."

He grabbed my hand and pulled it to his lips, squeezing it tight. His eyes darkened. "I'd kill him if he hurt you. And I won't give him another chance." He kissed my palm and said, "I won't leave you alone again."

"You have to go to the police."

"I've got no proof."

I felt my cheeks burning. "We can't let him get away with this. He's got to pay for what he's done."

His grip tightened. "This is my fight. Not yours. I don't want you tangled up in this any more than you already are."

"You have to tell someone. He has a motive."

"Everybody has a motive, darlin'. If you look hard enough."

"So what's the plan? Sit around and wait for him to try again?" My eyes teared up. The thought of Remy walking around free, hanging this over Jack's head and making us both live in fear was too much for me to take.

Jack slid his arm around my shoulders and pulled me close. "Don't worry. We'll fix this."

"How?"

"Let me worry about that. Why don't I run you a bath?"

I was coiled so tight, it felt like I'd burst. It would take more than a hot bath to unwind from all of this, but the gesture was sweet. I nodded, and he kissed me on the forehead.

When I heard the water start, I finished my drink and poured another. My hands still trembled. I stared at my fingers and cursed Remy, wishing that hexes were real, that I could get something from Duchess to dole out revenge. But wasn't a thirst for revenge how we all got here?

In the bathroom, Jack was sitting on the edge of the old clawfoot tub, dragging his hand through the water.

"Maybe this will help you relax," he said, standing. "I'll leave you be."

I slid my hand along his cheek. "I thought you said you wouldn't leave me again."

He stared at me for a long moment, his eyes filled with hurt and longing.

My fingers drifted down his neck, down the center of his chest, following the trail of buttons on his shirt. His body tensed as I reached his belt and pulled him closer to me.

"I just want to forget about today," I said. "At least for a little while."

His hand rested at the small of my back.

"I know things have gotten more complicated, but can we go back to simple for a minute?" I asked, slipping my hands under his shirt.

"A minute, huh?" He squeezed my hip.

"A night."

He traced his finger over my lips and said, "You know I want you desperately, but I feel like I'm taking advantage."

I moved my hands into his hair and gave it a firm tug. "You're not," I said, staring him down. "I need you, Jack. I can't stop thinking about you."

He leaned down and kissed my neck. "You know I'll do anything you ask, chère. I've become helpless that way."

"It's too bad your aunt and uncle are downstairs."

"I can be quiet. Can you?" He drew me tight against him, deepening his kiss, catching my lip with his teeth.

I pulled back to catch my breath and murmured, "Undress

me." I lowered my hands to my sides, and he stood there blinking at me.

"I like the way my shirt looks on you," he said, undoing the buttons. When he reached the last one, he slipped the shirt from my shoulders and dropped it to the floor.

He slid his fingers along my collarbone, down over one breast, drawing a line to my hip. As he sank to his knees, he pulled my panties over my hips.

My breath caught in my throat as his eyes met mine. The mingling of tenderness and wickedness in them made my chest clench. He rose to his feet, his fingers sliding up my thighs, over my ribs, pausing over my breasts. I loved watching him look at me. I'd never been comfortable naked in my whole life, but with Jack, it was different. I wanted to stand before him, unflinching, with everything bared as I soaked up his gaze.

"You're curvier than any man deserves," he said, his voice husky. "I could spend all night touching you." His hands roamed up and down my back as he spoke, leaving my skin tingling.

My hands rested on his shoulders as he pulled me against him. "I thought I lost you tonight," he said. "I don't know what I'd do if that happened."

"I'm right here… All yours."

He unbuttoned his shirt, saying, "Get in," and nodded toward the tub.

I sank into the water as he unbuckled his belt, shoving his jeans and boxers to the floor. His eyes were fixed on mine as he climbed in with me, sloshing water onto the tile.

The water was steaming, soothing my aching neck and shoulders.

Jack sat opposite me as he maneuvered his legs around mine. I sank deeper into the warmth as I took him in: his broad shoulders, his chiseled arms and chest. Each movement of his bicep caused the feathers of the bird to ripple.

I wanted to catch those feathers on my tongue.

"How'd you get so lovely?" he said. "I feel like I'll go blind if I stare too long."

"Stop," I said.

"Don't you know what a knockout you are?" He slipped his hand under my heel, his thumbs massaging my foot. "You could stop my heart with one look."

I smiled, leaning my head against the rim of the tub.

"Mmm," he said. "That's the one."

I flicked my hand in the water, splashing him.

"I always wanted to crawl out of my skin and into someone else's," I said. "I wanted to be thinner, prettier, have better hair."

"Good God, why?" he said. "I can't imagine you any other way."

I shook my head. "That's a long, boring story."

"Tell me," he said, his fingers still sliding along the arch of my foot. "I want to know everything about you, Enza Parker."

I smiled, feeling my cheeks burn again. "I was a tomboy. I was invisible. Guys never liked me."

"I might have a thing for tomboys," he said. "Good thing you didn't know me when I was nineteen."

"I bet you were a hell raiser at nineteen."

"I plead the fifth," he said, bringing my foot to his lips.

"No fair dodging. I told you."

He grinned, his lips brushing against my toes. His stubbly chin tickled, but his kisses held me still. I loved the way his eyes drifted over me, as if drinking me in. I felt beautiful when he held me in his gaze, and that was something I'd rarely felt—if ever.

"That feels incredible," I said, and he grinned, fixing me with a sly stare.

"Tell me something else about you," I said.

"Like what, chère?" His tongue was soft as a feather, tracing an achingly slow line along the arch of my foot.

I closed my eyes. "Anything. Where you went on vacation as a kid, what your favorite movie is, the first girl you ever kissed."

"Orange Beach," he said, sliding his teeth along my big toe. "*Chinatown*. A girl named Caroline."

"Tell me the wildest thing you ever did, Jack."

He grinned. "What if I said you?"

I splashed him as he slid his fingers up to my knee. "Seriously," I said. "I want to know all about you."

After a long pause he rested my foot on his shoulder and said, "You know, your grandmother saved me, in a way." His fingers drifted along my calf. "I was a wreck in high school. And one day I showed up to cut her grass. I did an awful job the first few times, and then one day she brought me inside and gave me a glass of sweet tea."

He slid his thumbs behind my knees. "She said, 'Mr. Mayronne, you're going to have to straighten up if you want to do better than what people think you capable of.' She had my number."

I nodded, thinking of those times she'd straightened me out too.

"I started helping her around her house and supported myself during college. She always knew what folks needed to hear. She was a hell of a lady, your grandmother."

"What'd you study, mister cum laude?"

He smiled. "Geology. I was a rock hound."

"How'd you go from rocks to fighting fires?"

He shrugged. "I worked for the Forest Service for a couple of years. One summer when there were wildfires burning, they needed everyone they could get. You had to have a red card to help, so I took the pack test, got certified as a firefighter and did a couple of rotations in Texas."

"That's amazing."

"I liked it a lot more than geology. And I felt like I was doing something good."

"Do you ever miss it?"

"Sometimes. It's hard being gone all the time, but every once in a while I think of doing it again."

He slid his hand behind my knee, and I thought of him out in the wild, surrounded by flame and acres of tinder. I couldn't imagine the fearlessness that would take.

"How is it that we never met, if you were working for Vergie in high school?" I asked.

"She knew me too well, darlin'. She knew that no matter how much I'd straightened myself out, I'd still be bad for you. I'd have been all over you like fleas on a hound." He laughed a throaty laugh that made me want to climb in his lap. "And she wasn't letting you near the likes of me."

"Come on," I said, but the look in his eyes said it was the truth.

"I saw you a couple times. I sometimes brought groceries over when you were practicing piano. You were banging those keys like Jerry Lee Lewis one day, and Miss Vergie caught me with my face pressed against the window. I thought she'd fire me for sure."

I laughed. "I'd forgotten about the piano lessons. What did she do?"

"She just gave me that mama bear look and raised one of those penciled-on eyebrows, and I knew that was a line I dare not cross."

"I wish I'd met you then," I said, trying to picture a teenage Jack.

He grinned. "No ma'am, you do not."

"I'm awfully glad I met you now."

He eased my feet into the water, sliding his hands up to my knees. "Come here," he said. "You're too far away."

I slid to him, water sloshing over the edge of the tub. He turned me so my back was to him and pulled me against his chest, folding me in his arms.

I wanted to stay that way all night, until the water grew cold, feeling his breath against my neck as he nuzzled me with tiny kisses, soft as rain. I sighed as his arms tightened around my waist. One hand slid beneath the water, between my thighs, and his teeth pinched my ear as he moved his fingers in tiny circles.

"Jack," I whispered, squeezing his thighs under the water.

"What is it, chère? Tell me what you like. Tell me what you want."

I felt like I was leaving my body as he moved his fingers slowly, so deliberate in their grace. As I leaned my head back into his chest, he slid his prickly chin along my neck and closed his lips over my earlobe as he said, "Anything, chère. Anything."

I shut my eyes, pressing my body closer to his. "It scares me, the way I feel about you," I whispered, placing my arm over his. I shuddered as the pressure in his fingers increased. "I don't have the best luck with men."

His lips moved against my ear. "Your luck's about to change, darlin'. Believe me."

And I did.

His arm tightened across my chest. I could feel him hard, pressing against my lower back. Still he teased me, sliding one hand along the curve of my breast, his fingers pinching the nipple. I gasped as his other hand moved beneath the water, and I thought of how he'd appeared in my life in such a haphazard way. I'd never imagined meeting a man like Jack, and it saddened me to think of the little time we had left together. When the house was finished, I might never see him again.

I pushed those thoughts aside, and told myself to relish this time we had together and stop overthinking everything. As he murmured in my ear, telling me the things he longed to do to me, I at last let myself relax in his grip, let him bring me the pleasure I'd denied myself for so long.

He was the kind of man I'd once thought was too rare to ever find.

He slid his fingers inside me as he nuzzled my ear, his scratchy cheek making me flinch with delight. Teasing me mercilessly with his fingers, he groaned as I ground my hips against him. With one arm still locked across my chest, he slid his legs over mine, pinning me against him.

"You drive me crazy like this… so wild." His teeth pinched my neck as his fingers quickened. "Come apart in my hands."

I dug my fingers into the hard muscle of his thighs as he began to move his thumb in tiny circles again. The more I squirmed, the tighter he held me, until my back arched and I saw tiny pinpoints of light. It was so hard not to cry out—I gasped as he held his lips against my neck, his hand stroking my thigh.

My heart banged against my ribs, my skin tingled all over. I turned my cheek against his and whispered, "Jack, I love the way you touch me."

He folded his arms over my chest and said, "I could touch you every day of my life, and it still wouldn't be enough for me."

I WOKE UP GASPING. My throat felt like it had been squeezed shut, and my skin tingled as if singed by fire. In the dream I was back in the house, the room bright orange, the flames rippling over the walls and ceiling. But this time, there was no door. The orange washed over me in waves. All around, the beams creaked, the plaster crackled, the glass shattered.

Jack sat up and slipped his arms around me. "Hey, it's OK, darlin', you're safe." His lips brushed my ear as he held me to his chest.

My heart pounded so hard against my skin that it hurt. When I closed my eyes, I still saw smoke and flames.

"It's all right," he said, stroking my arm. "I'm here."

I took a deep breath, hoping to drive away the smoke that lingered. "I was in the house but couldn't get out. Couldn't find you."

He lay back, pulling me toward him.

"Go back to sleep," he said. He draped one arm over my hip, sliding his fingers in a tiny soothing arc.

For the moment, I did feel safe. Even though my house had nearly burned down around me, there was no other place I'd rather be. There was no other person I'd rather be tangled up with.

Outside, the swamp pulsed with the thrumming of katydids and night birds. Jack's breaths came slow and even, and soon my chest rose and fell with his, relaxing under the weight of his arms. I knew then that I didn't want to rush through the rest of the repairs.

I didn't want to leave Bayou Sabine.

I didn't want to leave Jack.

Chapter Seventeen

MID-MORNING,we went back to Vergie's. My stomach twisted up like a pretzel as we parked in the yard. The back of the house was still covered in ash, but the dog was stretched out on the porch like it was just another day.

"You still want to tell me this place isn't cursed?" I said.

"It's got nothing to do with curses," Jack said.

Curses might be easier to deal with.

"When's that inspector supposed to be here?" he added.

I lifted his wrist to look at his watch. "Right about now." I climbed out of the Jeep and walked to the porch. Jack had a distant look in his eyes, scanning the edge of the tree line.

Inside, the living room was blackened from floor to ceiling. Bits of the hardwood floors and painted walls just barely peeked through the char. Holes from the firefighters' axes gaped like wounds. It was much worse than it had seemed last night. The door frames in the hall and kitchen were blackened, the ceiling charred. It would take weeks to repair this damage—if it could be salvaged at all.

Now I saw why Jack had been so angry when he'd found me with the hose. I was shocked the whole house hadn't gone up like kindling. I fought back tears as the door opened.

Jack entered with a man wearing a shirt and tie with jeans. The man was already sweating, his cuffs rolled to his elbows. His bald head was pink with sunburn.

"Miss Parker," he said, shaking my hand. "I'm Nick Jacobs. Sorry to meet you under these circumstances." He looked over my shoulder, already assessing the room.

A surge of nausea hit me, and I thought for sure I'd vomit right on his shoes. Jack gave me a concerned look as I excused myself and returned to the porch.

Outside, I took a deep breath, exhaling slowly. It seemed my breathing was the only thing I could control. Stumbling down the walk, I sank to my knees and then lay back in the grass, imagining how it might feel if the ground ripped open and covered me. Overhead, clouds floated like cotton balls on a pale sky.

After a few minutes, I heard Jack's boots thumping on the porch, scuffing in the grass as they came nearer. He sat next to me, but for a long while he said nothing.

"Just when I think it can't get any worse," I said, "it always does."

"We'll fix this," he said.

I scowled. "Part of me wants to pack up and leave. Get in the car and drive."

He plucked a weed from between his feet, twirling it in his fingers as he stared out over the yard.

"My father would love that, though. He'd love to rub my nose in this for the next decade."

"You worry too much about what your father thinks."

That's when the tears started. The ugly tears that come with the angry cry that comes when you finally see the truth you've been avoiding.

I couldn't hold back any more.

Jack stared across the yard, chewing his lip.

Men never understand the angry cry.

"I don't know why I care so much what he thinks. Sometimes I wish I could leave everything behind—my job, my home—and start over with no father to impress."

"So do it. Start over."

I frowned. "You make it sound so easy."

He stripped the leaves from the stem one by one. "The only person who can make you carry all of that burden around is you. We let it go when we're ready, though."

"I can't quit. Quitting is giving up. Then he wins."

"Sometimes toughing it out isn't the answer," he said. "Sometimes cutting your losses is cutting yourself free."

"I just wanted to do this right," I said. "For Vergie."

"You're good at this, chère. And she would have been proud."

I snorted, yanking fistfuls of grass from around my hips. "This is a disaster."

"You were doing fine with this place. It's not your fault some asshole set it on fire. You're beating yourself up for nothing."

He lay down in the grass next to me, lacing his hands behind his head. How could he be so relaxed? I felt like I would burst apart at the seams the second I quit forcing myself to hold it together.

But he was right.

I couldn't leave this house unfinished. My father was my weakness. I could see that when I talked to Jack. My father had expected me to fail, but I wouldn't do it. Not this time.

"I'm finishing this," I said, my voice raspy.

"That's my girl."

"I'm serious."

"I know you are."

After what seemed like hours, the inspector walked outside and cleared his throat. His tie was loose now, his shirt sticking to his skin. He pushed his glasses up onto his head and said, "Well, Miss Parker, the good news is that much of this can be saved. It could have been a lot worse."

I scrambled to my feet.

He held his hand over his eyes to block the sun. "The bad

news is, it was definitely arson, so that means more complicated paperwork. Might take longer for your insurance claim to go through."

I sighed, brushing myself off.

Nick motioned for us to follow him into the house.

Inside, he took his pen from behind his ear and pointed toward the corner—a scorched spot that had burned deeper into the floor than anywhere else. Bits of glass lay all around it, melted into pebbles. "That's the point of origin," he said, pointing to the black mark. "Most of the glass fragments are melted and misshapen, but a few large fragments are curved. Clearly not from the window."

"A Molotov cocktail," Jack said.

"That'd be my guess."

"Unbelievable," I said, though it wasn't much of a surprise.

"Usually, these things work out in your favor," Nick said. "It just takes longer than we'd like."

He tucked his clipboard under his arm and stepped outside. "Good to see you again, Jack. We'll get you a report as soon as possible, Miss Parker."

"Can we start the repairs?" I asked.

He tugged at his tie. "Unfortunately, you have to wait for your insurance adjustor."

Jack walked Nick to his car, leaving me standing in the rubble, imagining how I might begin to make Remy pay for this. I picked up some of the biggest chunks of plaster and debris, and made a pile by the door.

When Jack returned, he said, "You should leave that. We may need photos for evidence."

Tears stung my eyes again. Remy—or whoever did this—was out walking around in the summer heat, driving to work or loafing on his couch drinking a beer. Or planning his next fire. And that made me furious.

"I have to do something," I said, my voice shaking.

"Listen, nobody expects you to start right back to work like nothing happened. Let's get out of here for a while."

I laughed. "Now I really can't afford to lose any more days."

He rested his big hands on my shoulders and turned me so he could stare me in the eye. "You need to get away from this and relax. Let me help you, OK? We'll sit down and get a plan together. But I'm not going to let you stay here and work yourself up into a frenzy."

"Jack, I appreciate what you're trying to do, but—"

"No buts. The house can wait one more day."

"It can't. It's been almost three weeks, and this is going to set me back even further."

I felt a surge of panic as I looked around the scorched room. There wasn't much I could do, aside from sweep up piles of rubble. "I can't just sit around and do nothing."

He pulled me against him, holding me tight. It seemed like he was the only thing keeping me together.

"Come on... let's go."

Before I could argue, I heard footsteps on the porch. I dabbed at my eyes, figuring Nick had forgotten something, but as I stepped away from Jack, I felt my heart twist into a knot.

A deep voice bellowed from the doorway. "Just what in the hell is going on here?"

My heart clenched and I said, "Oh, hell."

Chapter Eighteen

I FROZE, not wanting to turn around. I told myself that I was imagining the voice, that I was finally cracking from this disaster. But then I heard it again.

"Enza!" my father yelled, his voice reverberating through the house. "Why the hell aren't you answering your phone?"

My father stood in the doorway. He looked as if he'd just stormed out of a board meeting, wearing an expensive charcoal suit with a hideous red and purple patterned tie. He snatched his aviator shades from his face and stuffed them in his suit pocket.

"Dad, what are you doing down here?"

"As per our last conversation, I thought I should come see how things were going. Since I called two dozen times and left messages, to no avail, I naturally began to wonder whether you were avoiding me or had ended up in a gutter." He gave Jack a long, disapproving look and then went on. "It seemed that if I wanted to talk to you I was going to have to come do it in person."

Jack's brow furrowed.

"It's only been a few days," I said. "Batteries die. Phones get lost. I hardly think that warrants getting on a plane."

He glared at me. "Are you going to tell me your battery was

dead? You couldn't go pop a quarter in a pay phone? Avoiding calls is no way to handle a business, but I think you know that. You drop off the radar, I start to think you're doing something foolish."

"Nobody has pay phones any more," I said.

His face hardened.

I glanced over at Jack. He had that same look on his face that he'd had when he'd slugged Remy in the bar.

My father brushed past me and stomped into the burned room, his narrowed eyes taking in every detail, every singed surface. "Holy hell," he said. His frown was like a scar.

"I wasn't avoiding you," I said. "I actually lost my phone. I guess your messages didn't get passed on to the new one."

"I'd ask how things were going, but that seems painfully evident. You neglected to mention fire damage. Anything else you left out?"

"There wasn't any fire damage when we talked. As usual, your timing is exceptional."

He stalked through the other rooms. "This is a disaster! A money pit."

"It's not that bad," I said. "It won't take much to wrap it up." As the words came out, I realized it sounded like a plea. It sounded ridiculously optimistic, even to my ears. But I knew I could finish it.

My father snorted. "It won't take much? Look around you, Enza. That's delusional."

"You should have seen it before she started," Jack said. "She's worked a miracle on it already."

"And who the hell's this?" my father asked, poking his thumb at Jack.

Before I could answer, Jack stepped closer and extended his hand. "Jack Mayronne," he said. I could tell from his clenched jaw that he didn't really want to shake my father's hand, but his politeness won out over his anger. He looked like he'd rather be anywhere but here.

My father had a knack for making people want to leave a room just by walking into it. He took Jack's hand and gave it one hard shake, purely as a formality, and said, "You're one of the carpenters?"

Jack raised an eyebrow.

"Yeah," I said, before he could answer.

Jack shot me a look.

My father paced between us, his expensive loafers echoing on the hardwood. "When did this happen?"

"It's not as bad as it looks," I said.

His eyes rested on mine. "Forgive me if I have a hard time believing that, dear. Now how did you manage to catch this place on fire?"

"Christ," Jack muttered under his breath.

My father whipped his head around. "Something you want to add, son?"

"Jack," I said, but he didn't even glance at me. His eyes were steady on my father's. This was about to get bad.

"Your daughter was trapped in the house," Jack said. "She could have been killed." His eyes were bright with fury, but he kept his voice steady and low.

"I wasn't exactly trapped. Let's not blow things out of proportion."

"Oh, right," Jack said. "If I were going to be completely accurate, I'd tell you Enza stayed in the burning house in order to hose this room down and keep it from burning to the ground before the fire department got here."

My father's jaw tightened. "I knew this place would be more trouble than it was worth."

"I'll finish it," I said. "I just may need a few extra weeks."

"Honey, you need to cut your losses, go back home, and let me get some folks in here that know what they're doing." He pulled at a piece of charred wood trim. "Or just sell it like it is and get out while we can still break even."

"No. I said I'd finish it, and I will."

"Time is money," he said, frowning. "And this is money we don't have."

"I'm not leaving." I felt the blood rushing to my head again.

He planted his hands on his hips, glaring at me. It took every ounce of my focus not to look away.

"You're impossible," he said. "Never know when to back down."

"Sorry to disappoint you," I said, my voice rising. "But I'm not going to hand this over just because you came down here in your fancy suit on your big white horse."

I felt like screaming, but I knew he'd be hoping for that—it would be another example of how I'd lost control. So I said, "I'm not going to quit just because you said so. You gave me a job to do, and you wanted me to prove myself, and now you're telling me to quit before I have the chance to."

"I'm not telling you this as your father. I'm telling you as your boss."

"I think you are telling me as my father. Because I'm telling you this place can be salvaged and you can still turn a profit on it —and you're willing to throw that away. Would you do that with anybody else on your crew? You sure wouldn't do it to Sam or Jeffrey." I knew I was pushing him, but enough was enough. He'd taken the guys that worked for him under his wing and pretended to do the same with me—but he didn't give me half the latitude he gave them. And he knew it.

"This is a bad business decision," he said. "You're letting your pride get in the way, as usual. And I'm not losing money because of your pride."

"This is about finishing what I started."

He stared at the ceiling, shaking his head. For what seemed like forever, he didn't say anything. Finally, he put his glasses back on and said, "You always were as stubborn as a goddamn goat." He stepped between piles of rubble as he made his way to the door. From the porch, he turned and said, "I should just sell it as-is."

"You can't," I said, unflinching. "It's in my name."

"Need I remind you who's covering the cost of these repairs?"

"We have an agreement. Or does that apply to everyone except me?"

His face was twisted into a scowl, but I refused to look away. He strode out of the house and climbed into his boat of a rental car, slamming the door. When the car disappeared at the end of the driveway, I slid into a heap on the porch.

I was furious that he would come here under the pretense of being worried about my safety. He hadn't batted an eye when Jack told him about how I tried to fight the fire. He didn't care about all the work I'd already done. All he saw were the flaws, how I hadn't stayed on the schedule he'd made.

Jack stood with his arms crossed, his eyes on the driveway. "Hard to believe you came from that stock."

"Sometimes I think I'm more like him than I'd like to admit."

In the distance, a car horn blew. Jack shook his head. "You OK?"

"I will be."

He raised an eyebrow. "Now would you like to get out of here for a while?"

What I really wanted to do was drive my fist through the wall. But the lovely arch in his eyebrows made me smile. "Yes, Mr. Mayronne, I believe I would."

He pulled me to my feet and said, "Good. I know just the place."

WE CLIMBED INTO THE JEEP, and he said, "Brenda's has the best gator tail in the state. And the bourbon's not bad, either."

I grimaced at the thought. "Do I look like a woman who eats alligator tail?"

"It's a delicacy," he said, mock offended. "You can't leave here without trying it."

I cringed at the thought of leaving here. Leaving Jack.

Brenda's didn't look like much from the outside. Locals flocked to it, but it probably didn't see many new faces. It was bright yellow clapboard with a wood shingled roof. An alligator skull hung over the door, a halo of flowers draped over it. I shuddered, thinking of the skull we'd found in the yard.

As Jack held the door for me, the people inside turned to see who was coming in. Several diners sat at the bar, and some were sprinkled in booths and tables. It looked like a cross between a pancake house and a hunting lodge. The paneled walls were a jigsaw puzzle of old framed photos and road signs. Red vinyl booths sat like islands on a scuffed hardwood floor. Jack waved to a woman with red hair pulled up in a bun, and we slid into a booth. She brought two glasses of water over and said, "Hey, Jack. Saw you on the news."

He winced. "Hope it wasn't for very long."

"I was wondering why we hadn't seen you around here in a while. But I guess you got your hands full." She glanced at me and half-smiled. "Hope y'all catch that arsonist soon."

"Brenda, this is Enza," he said. "She's Vergie's granddaughter."

"Well, how about that. We sure miss her." She smiled, then returned to business. "What can I get you today? Your usual?"

"Sure," he said. "Make it two."

"You gonna trust this devil to order for you, hon?" she said to me.

"He's a pretty good guesser," I said, and she grinned.

Brenda walked back to the front and yelled into the kitchen. The fry cook waved his arm at her, stubbing a cigarette out against the doorframe.

As she came back with two beers, the bell above the door clanged, and she turned like it was a reflex. "Dammit," she said, frowning. She plunked the beers down in front of us and strode to the counter.

Remy ambled toward the bar and eased onto a stool at the

end, leaving several empty seats between him and the nearest diner. He glanced around but didn't seem to see us. As a young blond woman appeared to take his order, Brenda intercepted. She handed the girl a coffee pot and sent her to a booth in the back.

Brenda sidled over to Remy herself, her arms crossed over her chest. She looked like a mother hen protecting her brood. He was grinning, holding his hands out beside him as if to surrender. Her stare didn't seem to faze him. At last she yanked a pad out of her apron pocket and scribbled his order on it. She slapped the ticket on the ring by the window and nodded to the cook.

Jack sipped his beer. "Some days you just can't win."

I started to get up from the table, but he dropped his hand on my arm. "What do you think you're doing?"

"I'm going to give that cowardly son of a bitch a piece of my mind."

He squeezed my arm until I sat back down. "My mother used to say that if you go around doing that, you'll soon have no brains left for yourself."

"How can you sit here all calm and cool, drinking a beer like nothing happened?"

"I'd love to go bust this bottle over his head and drag him out into the swamp, but that ain't gonna fix anything. If he's the one behind all this, then we'll get him. But not here."

I turned my wrist, trying to free myself from his grip.

"Spook him now," he said, "and we'll never catch him."

At the bar, Remy still had his back to us. I leaned into the booth, dragging my fingernails along the vinyl seat. "So I'm supposed to smile and go on like everything's fine."

"Put the bad guys at ease, and it makes them slip up."

I took a long drink. "Come on. Let's go someplace else."

"And miss Brenda's grilled shrimp and gator tail? No ma'am." Jack glanced around the other tables. The place was nearly full now, the lights dim and the room buzzing with chatter. We were a good twenty feet from the bar, tucked in a corner. "I'm not letting that jackass ruin our day any more than he already has."

"I'm not sure I can sit in the same building with him," I said, resting my head in my hands.

"Just pretend he's not here."

I rolled my eyes. "Right."

"New subject," he said. "I talked to the chief, and he said it was safe to stay in the house tonight."

"Did he say if we could start fixing that room?"

He shook his head. "Don't worry. I know some people. When we get the OK to move ahead, they'll take care of it."

The way he looked at me now, I felt like an idiot for having doubted his intentions. It made me think I was becoming too cold, like my father. Here was Jack, devoting all this time and energy to helping me, and my first reaction had been to think he must have an ulterior motive. Had I really trusted Remy's word over his? Tears welled in my eyes again, despite my greatest effort to hold them back.

"Hey." He lifted my hand to his lips. "No more. It's killing me, seeing you so sad."

"Angry tears," I said, my voice cracking. "I'm not sad. I'm furious. It just comes out this way."

His lips moved against my fingers. "We'll fix this. It's going to be fine."

"I hope so. Because right now I feel like I hitched a ride on the Titanic."

He smiled. "You'll see."

Behind us, a familiar voice growled, "Well, ain't that sweet." My whole body stiffened.

Remy stood next to the table, his hands on his hips, so close I could see the dirt on his fingernails.

My stomach churned. Jack stared at me and gave me the slightest shake of his head.

"Saw you on TV, champ," Remy said to him. "Doing the whole city proud, aren't you?"

Without raising his eyes, Jack said, "We're trying to have dinner here, Broussard. Or didn't you notice?"

"Well, where are my manners," Remy said, his voice deep. "Am I interrupting something between you and Miss Firecracker here?"

I kept my eyes steady on Jack's. They seemed to darken to the color of spruce.

"Really, darlin'," Remy said to me. "You didn't strike me as the desperate type."

He pulled a chair from behind him, shoved it up against the table and straddled it, leaning his elbows over the back. "I got to tell you, sweetheart, you're wasting your time with this one. I was hoping he'd be out of the picture by now so you and I could pick up where we left off." He winked at me, and I dug my fingers into the edge of the booth. I wanted to beat his face into the floor.

"Leave us be," Jack said, his voice low. "I'm only asking once."

"Or what?" Remy said, laughing.

"You're wasting your time," I said. "All these games of yours."

His laugh, hollow and deep, raised the hair on my arms.

"We know what you've been doing," I said. "Don't think for a minute you'll get away with it."

Jack kicked me under the table, but I stared straight at Remy.

"Don't know what you're talking about," he said.

"It's only a matter of time until—" I said.

Jack stepped on my foot and interrupted. "Don't make a scene here," he said to Remy, his voice cool and even. "I like Brenda." Jack looked at me, willing me not to say anything else.

Remy grinned. "I didn't come to make a scene, Mayronne. I came to say I hope y'all find that crazy arsonist soon. It's a shame y'all can't seem to catch him."

I couldn't stand that smirk any more. I stood and poured my glass of beer right into his lap.

Remy jumped up out of the chair. His shirt and pants were soaked. He leaned close to me, and for a second I thought he'd hit me for sure. But he just grinned and said, "Is this your way of trying to get my clothes off, sugar? I do love a gal that likes to play dirty."

"Get out of here," I said, my voice low. "Before I think of something to do with this empty glass."

"You should listen to the lady," Jack said, standing.

"Hmm," Remy said. "You know what they say about gals with hot tempers." He slid his finger along my jaw, and I grabbed his hand and twisted it backward as hard as I could. He struggled for a moment against my grip, clearly surprised. But he slipped out of my grasp easily when he put his weight into it and squeezed my wrist so hard it stung. He gave me a look that chilled me down to my toes.

Jack stepped between us, forcing Remy to drop my arm, and said, "You know, your brother got all the brains in the family." He kept his voice quiet, but it didn't make a bit of difference. We were the most interesting thing in that diner, and everybody stared at us like they were soaking up the details so they could run home and tell all their friends later.

"Don't you dare talk about him," Remy said, his eyes turning cold. The muscles in his arm tensed as he gripped the back of the chair.

"Hell must've been full," Jack said, his eyes narrowed. "That's the only way he'd go before you."

In a blur, Remy grabbed Jack by his collar and spun him into a headlock. The chair tipped over, and I moved to separate them, but they crashed into the next table, knocking the ketchup bottles and salt shakers to the floor. A group of diners stood, backing away from their table as Jack wriggled free of Remy's grip. Remy pulled his fist back by his hip and swung, catching Jack right below the eye. When he swung again, Jack blocked his fist and nailed him in the jaw, knocking him backwards. Remy stumbled, but caught his balance and lunged again, his teeth gleaming against his skin. Jack ducked his punch and backed into a booth. Plates crashed to the hardwood floor, glass splintered. Remy drew his fist back, but before he could throw another punch, the cook came barreling down the aisle and grabbed him from behind, locking his arms by his sides.

"Brother, how many times we got to throw you out of here?" the cook said, a cigarette dangling from his lip. His face was red, his short hair damp with sweat.

"This ain't got nothing to do with you," Remy growled.

The cook, his apron splattered with grease, grinned as he cranked Remy's hand toward his shoulders until he winced. "That's where you're wrong," he said. "My diner, my business." He held Remy easily, one hand drawing the cigarette from his lips and thumping the ashes into a cup on the table. He glanced at Jack as Brenda sidled between them.

"You two want to roll around like a couple of alley cats, you take it outside," she said. "Unless you want to spend the night in jail."

"You want me to call the sheriff, Brenda?" the cook said. "You just say the word."

"Sorry," Jack said to her, smoothing his shirt over his chest.

"You ain't begun to know sorry," Remy said. "But you will."

The cook tightened his grip and pushed Remy toward the front door. "That's it," he grumbled. "I've had enough of this shit."

I stood behind Jack, one hand gripping the back of the booth, one over my mouth. All around us, diners stared, their forks frozen in midair. It seemed I'd never be able to have an uneventful night out anywhere in this town.

"What is wrong with you, Mayronne?" Brenda said, waggling her finger at him. "You are better than this. What's gotten into you?"

"I'm real sorry, Brenda," Jack said again. "We'll go. Send me a bill for the damage." He glanced around the room, his head lowered. Part of me wanted to crawl under one of the tables and hide, but part of me wanted to kiss him right there in front of everybody.

The diners stared as the cook shoved Remy out the front door. Jack was still red from his shirt collar to the roots of his hair.

"I'll get you a couple of doggie bags," Brenda said, her voice still stern. "That boy deserves a knuckle sandwich every now and then." Walking past him, she paused, then said close to his ear, "But next time, don't do it here."

Jack nodded and left a few bills on the table that would have covered dinner three times over. He placed his hand on my elbow and steered me to the door. The customers' eyes followed us as we passed, then quickly turned back to their plates. The chatter started up again only as we reached the door.

Outside, it felt twenty degrees cooler. "Way to pretend he's not there," I said.

"The circumstances changed."

"I really wanted to deck him while you had him distracted. You think fighting dirty makes me a bad person?"

Jack opened the Jeep door for me, giving me a look that said he wasn't entirely put off by that idea. "One of us in a brawl is bad enough. That wasn't exactly the relaxing dinner I had in mind."

"So we'll have it at home." I leaned toward him as he climbed in. "How's your eye?"

"Fine," he said.

A cut over his eyebrow was bleeding. When I touched it, he winced. "It's starting to swell."

"I've had worse."

He cocked his head, staring past me into the parking lot. A soft rain was falling. At the back corner of the lot, Remy leaned against a rusted-out pickup, smoking a cigarette. When Jack started the car, he turned his head in our direction, smoke swirling around him. We pulled onto the road, and I watched him in the side mirror, growing smaller in the distance. The rain fell harder, but still he leaned against the truck, one foot propped on the tire, like he was waiting for the rain to wash something away.

"His first punch is always a left hook," I said.

Jack turned to me, his brow furrowed.

"Just for future reference." I pulled the box of shrimp from the bag and popped one in my mouth. "It's a pattern with him. He's fairly predictable."

He looked at me like I was some puzzle he was missing a few pieces for, and his lips tightened in a thin smile. "Don't eat all those without me," he said, nodding toward the bag. "We can't exactly show our faces in there anytime soon."

"Oh please. Not one of them would have complained if you'd knocked him out cold."

He raised an eyebrow.

"These, by the way, are fabulous," I said. "Might be worth a brawl."

"This isn't a joke, Enza. Remy's not a guy to take lightly."

"Don't you think I know that? He nearly burned the house down with me in it."

"You shouldn't have accused him," he said, his voice low. "The last thing we need is for him to get desperate."

"Well if he knows we're on to him, maybe he'll get scared and back off."

"Guys like him don't get scared." He said this like there was no room for argument.

We rode in silence. At last he said, "I don't want you going out by yourself any more. Not until this is settled."

I laughed. "What are you, my mother now? Come on."

"I'm serious," he said. "If he's coming after you, it's to get back at me. And there's nothing he wouldn't do to make me suffer. If he thinks you're important to me, then that puts you in danger."

I opened my mouth to speak, but the stern look on Jack's face made me stop. He wasn't just being protective—he was worried. I shivered at the thought of just how far Remy might go to hurt one of us. Rage was nothing to be taken lightly.

Then I wondered exactly how important I was to Jack. He meant more to me than I was ready to admit. *One thing at a time*, I kept telling myself. Finish the house before resolving whatever this was between Jack and me. I'd been foolish to think I could have a simple fling with him. The feelings I had for him were growing stronger by the day, but I had to tamp them down long enough to finish the job I came here to do. I needed to separate these two forces that were vying for my attention or else they'd rip me apart. And if that happened, I'd likely lose them both.

WE WENT BACK to Buck and Josie's to spend the night. The two of them had gone over to their friends' house for poker night—at first they'd threatened to cancel, but we insisted they go. I didn't want anyone else being put out. Now I was glad they weren't home to see Jack come in with his bruised face.

After we ate, I poured myself a bourbon and curled up on the couch while Jack took a shower. I closed my eyes, letting the hum of the katydids lull me into a stupor. A giant moth beat its wings against the screen behind me, fighting to get to the lamp light.

At last Jack came out of the bathroom, his hair wet. He was wearing a clean plaid shirt and a pair of jeans with a hole in the knee. He poured himself a drink and sat next to me on the sofa.

"You should let me take care of those cuts," I said.

"Ah, it's nothing," he said, touching his eyebrow. Remy had landed a couple of good punches before the cook had pulled him outside, still grappling and swearing. Jack had come out with a bruise on his cheek and cuts on his chin and eyebrow.

I went into the bathroom and dug in the medicine cabinet until I found the barest of first-aid essentials. Jack waved me away when I tilted his chin up and dabbed some alcohol on his eyebrow.

"A couple of these are deep," I said, looking at them under the lamp light.

"I'm fine," he said, turning his head away.

I climbed onto his lap, my knees by his hips. "Hold still," I said. His body tensed beneath me, and he stopped squirming.

"Only scratches," he said, his eyes steady on mine.

"I know, tough guy. Just humor me." I dabbed the cut on his jaw first. "Does that hurt?"

"No." He rested his hands on my thighs, and a tickling heat traveled over my skin like an electric current.

I swabbed some ointment on his eyebrow, and he flinched. "Sorry," I said. They didn't look bad enough for stitches, but I put a tiny bandage on the deepest one to hold it together. "How about this?" I asked, touching the bruise around his eye. "Does that hurt?"

"A little."

I kissed his brow lightly, just above the cut. "And here?"

"No."

I kissed him on the neck, just below his jaw. "What about here?"

His hands slid beneath my skirt, up to my hips. "No."

With my lips barely touching his, I said, "And here?"

He sat still, but didn't kiss me back. "What's the matter?" I asked.

He placed his hands back on my knees and said, "Maybe we've been thinking about this backwards. Maybe I need to get as far away from you as possible."

"What happened to 'I'm not letting you out of my sight'?"

He sighed. "If Remy's after me, then the worst thing I can do is stay near you. That just keeps you in danger."

"So you don't want to stay with me, and you don't want me alone. That doesn't leave a lot of options."

"You could stay here."

"Jack," I said, frowning. "I'm not putting Buck and Josie out like that."

"They'd love to have you."

"No. I need to get back to Vergie's. I'm done being scared." I already felt silly not going back tonight, despite the nausea that hit me every time I pictured sleeping upstairs in the house.

"I could send one of the guys to stay with you and keep an eye out," he said.

"Absolutely not. It's you or no one."

"While I'd be thrilled to hear that in any other situation, I think in this one you need to reconsider."

"I don't need bodyguards," I said, pushing a lock of hair behind his ear. "Besides, they won't take care of me quite the way you do."

"It's nothing to take lightly. Whatever this is," he gestured in the space between us, "we need to put it on hold. Just until everything blows over."

I stared at him, my jaw slack.

He took my hand. "It's not safe for you to be so close to me. And I can't stand the idea of you being hurt because of me."

"Jack," I said. "Don't."

"I can't be with you if it puts you in danger. I couldn't live with myself if something happened to you."

"I'm a grown woman, Jack. I get a say in this. You don't get to decide without me that it's best you leave."

He squeezed my knee. "It's the only way to keep you safe."

"I'm not about to let somebody like Remy decide how I live my life. Or who I spend it with. If he wants to come after me, then fine. I'll be ready."

"It most certainly is not fine," he said, his hands tightening. "If he's gunning for me, I want him to come after me when I'm alone. Not when I'm with you."

"But I—"

"End of discussion," he said, his voice gruff. "I won't have you in the middle of this." He lifted me off his lap and set me down as he stood, like he expected me to stay wherever he put me.

I couldn't believe he was saying this, that he was leaving me. Especially now.

"Don't you 'end of discussion' me," I said.

He sighed, running his hands through his hair.

"Don't you dare leave," I said. "We're in this together." My voice started to crack, and I felt a surge of panic, like I had when the flames had reached the ceiling, when it seemed like I'd made a fatal mistake. My throat tightened. It hurt to breathe. "I don't know what I'd do without—" My voice broke with a sob.

He strode to me so quickly that I thought he would bolt past me and through the door. But he slipped his arms around me and pulled me tight against him. "Easy," he whispered. "It's OK." He held me so close I could feel his heart hammering against my chest. He stroked my hair, whispering in my ear.

Still, I trembled.

"Shhh," he said at last. "If you want me to stay, I'll stay."

Shivering, I wound my arms around him. I couldn't get him close enough.

"I'm sorry," he said. "I just want you to be safe."

"I only feel safe with you."

He kissed me on the forehead. "Come on. You're exhausted."

I let him lead me up the stairs to the green bedroom. He pulled back the sheets and eased me onto the bed. Climbing in on the other side, he slipped his shirt and jeans off and tossed them onto the chair in the corner. I turned onto my side, and he pulled me to him. He slid his leg over mine, holding me in place, and at last I felt like the world wasn't going to explode around me. His lips brushed my ear as he said, "Get some rest, chère. You're safe now."

I felt the sting of tears as I closed my eyes, listening to the night birds calling outside. Lying there with him, feeling the warmth of his body encircling mine—there was no other place I wanted to be. But in a couple of weeks, this would be over. I would leave. He would leave. For the first time, I thought of the house not as Vergie's, but as another place someone else would live in, a place I could never go again.

And I hated the thought.

Chapter Nineteen

MY FATHER'S visit had given me renewed purpose. I was ready to tackle the next round of repairs and prove this was only a minor setback. Nothing I couldn't handle.

Jack, after insisting on stopping for coffee and beignets, drove us back to Vergie's. He licked powdered sugar from his fingers as we pulled into the driveway, and I knew he did it just to punish me for sliding out of his grasp when we first woke. Buck and Josie had already left for the hardware store, so we had the house to ourselves. He'd threatened to keep me in bed all day, whispering his plans in my ear with his limbs tangled around mine. If it hadn't been for my father's threats the day before, I would have stayed there and let him make good on all of his delicious promises.

But my father had hijacked my brain, and with his voice ringing in my ears, there was no way I could spend the day in bed with Jack. I could deal with a lot of different kinds of weird, but not that kind.

Now Jack took great delight in torturing me, staring at me as he sucked the sugar from his fingertip.

"Come on," I said. "Enough already."

"I don't know what you mean, chère."

"Whatever." I climbed out of the Jeep, grinning to myself as he followed me up the porch steps.

Because the insurance agent had instructed us to leave the damaged room alone for a few days, I started back on my list, pretending there was no burned room to contend with.

Instead, Jack and I started painting the first room upstairs in "Virginia Beach," the shade of blue he'd chosen. He'd left the room as a spare, with hardly any furniture. There was a roll top desk, a love seat and an oriental rug. Built-in bookcases boasted an array of books and knickknacks. With little wall space, it was a cinch to paint. We'd made our now-standard island of furniture in the center of the room, draped some cloths over everything and rolled up the rug. I'd plugged in the record player outside in the hallway, and Jack had surprised me by dropping the needle onto an early Al Green record. He surprised me even more by crooning along.

We were nearly halfway finished with the walls when the dog started barking in the yard.

I went into Vergie's bedroom to look out the window and saw a car in the driveway.

"Hey, Jack," I called, "someone's here."

He met me in the hallway, still holding a paintbrush. "I'll go," he said, brushing past me down the stairs. Just like that, he'd shifted back to protective mode, all business and no more Al.

The doorbell rang when we were midway down the steps.

"Jack, really. I think it's safe for me to open the door to my house."

He tossed me an annoyed glance and beat me to the door.

A man in a bright blue shirt and suit pants stood on the porch, his finger hovering above the buzzer. He held a small notebook and clipboard under his arm. His salt-and-pepper hair was gelled into a kind of wave.

Jack leaned against the door, almost blocking my view. He braced his other arm against the door frame in a way that meant no one was coming through him.

"Hi," the man said. "I'm looking for Miss Parker. Mr. Parker asked me to come over and take a look around. I hope now is a good time. He asked me to work this in today."

I squeezed past Jack and extended my hand. "I'm Enza Parker. And you are?"

"August James," he said, shaking my hand a bit too firmly. "Your father said you were looking to sell as-is and sent me to get some information from you and work up some comps."

"He what?"

"He explained you were on a tight schedule," he said. "I can give you an idea of asking price by tomorrow."

"I think there's been some mistake," Jack said.

But I knew there had been no mistake. I felt everything in me tighten like a spring.

"Mr. James," I said, my voice even, "I'm sorry my father wasted your time, but he's not in charge of this sale. I'm afraid I'm not selling this house as-is. Maybe I could contact you in a few weeks when the repairs are finished."

His lips parted.

Jack's hand came to rest at the small of my back, and I relaxed.

"I'm very sorry for the confusion," I said.

He looked stunned. "I don't understand. You don't want comps?"

"No, but please leave your card," I went on, "because I'll be handling the sale and will be looking for a real estate agent in a few weeks."

He pulled a business card from the pocket of his shirt and handed it to me, his brow furrowed. "Don't you want me to just look around and give you a ballpark?"

Jack crossed his arms over his chest.

"Well, please call me if you change your mind," August said. "This is a lovely property."

"Thank you," I said. "I'm sorry for your trouble."

He gave us a quick look over his shoulder as he walked back to his car, an impossibly shiny black sedan with a sunroof.

After I closed the door Jack said, "I can't believe that just happened."

"Oh, I can." My father had left after one conversation, and that was never a good sign.

WHEN THE PAINTING WAS FINISHED, I finally approached the burned room. Right after the fire, Jack and Zane had taped plastic over the windows and the doorway. I pulled it back and stepped inside.

Before, when I'd looked in this room with the investigator, all I'd seen was black. Now I saw the freshly painted walls were gray with spots where the fire had had a burst of intensity. Clumps of charred plaster were scattered on the floor, holes in the walls left thin backing boards exposed like ribs. The floorboards were blackened and dull; the ceiling was dark like a thunderhead. Springs popped out of the wingback chair like broken bones. Everything would have to be replaced.

I truly was in over my head. I'd always felt pressure from my father, thinking my work wouldn't be good enough—but now I felt like I might not be able to finish at all.

I pulled the real estate agent's business card from my pocket and stared at his name, embossed in gold ink, and wondered if I'd have to concede that my father was right. How could I ever finish the house now? Walls needed to be rebuilt. A floor needed to be replaced. How could I finish this in two more weeks?

"Hey," Jack said, coming up behind me. "You OK?"

"Sure," I lied. "Just wanted to take a real look around."

He slid his arm around my shoulders. "It's going to be OK, you know."

I nodded, though right then that was the last thing I thought to be true.

"I know some guys, friends of Buck's. They can knock this out for you inside a week, and meanwhile you and I will tackle the rest."

I nodded again, and he kissed me on the forehead.

AFTER LUNCH, Jack called me upstairs.

"I found something for you," he said. He was standing in the closet of the room we'd just painted—the one that looked like it hadn't been used in years.

"There was a box of Vergie's things in here," he said, placing a faded pink hat box in my hands.

"Did you just find this?"

"I'd honestly forgotten it was here," he said. "I was going to clear my stuff out of the spare rooms and remembered there were some things stashed in the closets."

I thanked him as I opened the box.

He shrugged. "I'm going to repair a few of the tiles in the bathroom. I'll leave you to it."

I hardly heard him as I was too busy digging through the contents of the box. Photos, a couple of journals, and a stack of letters with a rubber band around them. I didn't recognize the return address. I opened one of the envelopes, addressed to Vergie, and when I turned it over, I saw it was signed "Martine."

My mother. I read the first letter, dated a year after she'd left my father and me. In it, she talked about a trip she'd taken to New Mexico, how she'd traveled to Carlsbad Caverns and seen some unusual rock formation at a place called Plaza Blanca. She talked about working on a ranch, the crazy things the tourists did. She talked about when she'd be home next.

Home.

I opened one of the journals and saw it was Vergie's, dated ten years earlier. I started to read but then stopped. I wasn't sure how much I wanted to know. About her, about my mother, about everything. For so long, I'd wished I had the missing parts to the story, but now that it was here, it was too much. Too fast.

The answers might not be details I wanted to know.

I brought the box back to her old bedroom. Jack was in the bathroom, tapping tiles into place with a rubber mallet. The floor had been missing a few. They formed a simple pattern, tiny hexagonal tiles that were popular in the 1940s, and were mostly white, with a smattering of cobalt. Jack must have gone out and found replacements without telling me.

"Hey," I said.

"Find anything interesting in there?"

"Yeah, but I can't look at all of it just yet. How's it going in here?"

"Lonely." He popped a cluster of tiles into place and tapped them with a mallet, smiling sweetly at me. He carefully applied the adhesive, filling in a tiny area under the sink. The tiles matched perfectly.

"That looks great." I reached down and ran my fingers through his hair.

"You're distracting me, chère," he said, slipping the tile into place.

"Mm, that's me. Very distracting."

"You have no idea."

Part of the allure of having a fling was having nothing at stake and no strings attached. It was safer that way. But now I felt something different. As much as I was willing myself not to, I was falling for him. Hard. I hadn't really let myself believe it until now.

He set another tile into place and tapped it with the mallet.

"What do you think?" he asked.

If the grout had been down, I couldn't have pinpointed which tiles were replacements. "Homey. Vintage. Perfect."

He stood, brushing himself off. "Good." He gave me a quick peck on the lips and said, "Now, git, before I forget how to do the rest," and swatted me on the behind.

"Is that any way to talk to your landlady?"

He narrowed his eyes and pointed to the door. "Out, vixen. You want the grout to match, don't you?"

I grinned and backed out of the doorway. "Suit yourself."

OUTSIDE, I walked around the house and made a list of repairs titled "Exterior." There was this problem of landscaping that I had to tackle—my least favorite part of flipping. I was a jinx to all things verdant. Always had been. Planting flowers, bringing in hedges, planting trees—I could do it, but they could easily die before the house was sold, and there I'd be with a yard full of despair. Nobody liked to see dead flowers. It was off-putting.

After scribbling my notes, the dog following at my heels, I went back inside to find Jack standing over the stove, tossing an arc of green and yellow vegetables in a skillet.

"What's all this?" I asked, leaning over his shoulder to peek.

"I was starving," he said. "Thought maybe you were too."

"Why haven't I been letting you do this all along?" I said, and he smiled, laying two fish fillets into another skillet.

He popped the cork off a bottle of white wine and filled two glasses to the top.

"Are you trying to get me hammered?" I asked, taking the glass.

"Cheers," he said, clinking his glass against mine. "You look thirsty."

He slid his hand around my back, pulling me against him. He kissed me lightly at first, but as I tightened my arms around him, he parted my lips with his tongue. I tasted the sweetness of the wine, the saltiness of him, and he deepened the kiss until my fingers curled in his hair. When he finally let me go, I said, "What was that for?"

He held my face close to his. "We've got some time," he whispered. "That needs to simmer a while."

"Sneaky," I said. "Luring me into the kitchen with the promise of dinner."

Sliding his hands beneath my shirt, he pulled me back against him, his lips grazing my neck. "We could work up an appetite," he said, his hands slipping under my skirt. He took my glass and set it on the counter, then nudged me against the wall. The warmth of his hands on my bare skin made me shiver.

He didn't seem to think of this as casual any more, either. That thought terrified me.

With his hips pinned against mine, he traced a line along my collarbone with his tongue. I kissed his rough cheek as his hands tightened around my waist. His touch made me lightheaded, like I was floating away into some point far on the horizon, and when the phone's ringing pierced the air, I barely heard it at all, still raking my fingers through his hair, drawing him even closer.

He pulled away from me, fumbling to reach my phone on the counter.

"Leave it," I said, sliding my hands along his chest, down to his hips.

"Could be important," he said, looking at the screen.

"You answer it then," I said, gripping him tighter. "My hands are full."

When he answered the phone, I caught his free hand and brought it to my lips, catching one finger in my teeth. He blinked sleepily, then said, "Just a minute," and handed me the phone.

I took it, trying to read his expression.

My father's voice boomed from across the Mississippi. "Well, at least someone's answering your phone. Who's that man?"

"Hi, Dad," I said. Jack frowned as he slid his arms around me again.

"Who is that man answering the phone?"

"He's my carpenter." Jack raised his eyebrow, nodding as he tugged at the buttons of my shirt. I brushed his hands away. He dropped them to my hips.

"You sound out of breath."

"I was hurrying to take this call." Jack slid one finger between my breasts, sending a shiver down my arm.

"Why do you have a carpenter over there this time of day? Overtime will cost you a fortune. Is this that Jack person that was over there before?"

I glowered, trying to keep my voice cool and even. Only my father could set me to fuming this fast. "This is a favor," I said. "He was a friend of Vergie's."

Jack stepped closer, leaning his body against mine. I rested my hand on his hip, trying to keep him at bay. My head was already spinning, and my father could sense weakness like a predator.

"Nothing comes for free, Enza. But enough about this. I want to know why you sent my real estate agent away. A perfectly good real estate agent who was set to get that place on the market pronto. If you're trying to piss me off, you're doing a damn fine job."

Jack eased his fingers into my shirt, undoing the buttons.

"I told you I could finish on my own."

I held the phone away from my ear as my father yelled. Jack jokingly shook his finger at me and whispered, "Bad girl. Very bad." He slid his fingers down my arm and added, "Have to straighten you out later."

I swatted his hands away, turning my back to him. "Dad," I began, but it was impossible to get a word in edgewise. He was in full tirade mode, bellowing about responsibility, and planning and anything else he could toss at me as an insult. The man seemed to think I was lacking in everything.

"I just don't understand what you're thinking," he said. "Every day you spend down there is money lost."

"Dad, relax."

"Don't you tell me to relax. I knew you couldn't do this on your own. I knew I should have stopped this a long time ago, before you got out of control."

"Now hang on," I said. Jack took a step back as I got louder. "I can manage just fine. This place looks great, and it's going to sell fast."

"Then sell it. As-is. Right now."

"That's a mistake. We'll get much more if you give me time to finish."

"You should have called in a crew to help you. We're going to end up losing a ton of money on this, and it's your fault."

"We're not losing money," I said. Jack's eyes were wide. He turned back to the steaming skillets, leaving me to pace by the table. "I know what I'm doing."

"Clearly that's not the case," he said. "I'm not sinking one more day or one more dime into that place. It's going on the market as-is, immediately."

My hands began to shake. "Dad, I didn't want it to come down to this, but the fact is, Vergie left the house to me. Not you. You've got no right to sell it out from under me, and I won't let you bully me into it. If this is how you feel, then I no longer work for you."

Jack turned back to me, his eyebrows raised. There was silence on the other end of the line.

"Did you hear me, Dad?"

"After all I've done for you," he said, "this is how you repay me."

"You're the one making it this way."

He grumbled something I couldn't hear, and then said, "If that's the way you want it, then fine. But I'll expect you to pay back every penny I've provided for these repairs, or else I'll see you in court. I expect payment in thirty days."

"Dad, I hardly think that's necessary."

"You have no idea what a disappointment this is," he said, "but I can't say I'm all that surprised."

Before I could answer, he hung up.

I stared at the phone, gritting my teeth so hard I thought surely one would crack. I tossed the phone onto the table. "Bastard," I said, and trudged onto the porch, letting the screen door slam behind me.

The air was thick and stifling. June in Louisiana was as relentless as my father. I felt like crying, but I was determined not to let him get the best of me again. I was tired of crying. I hated crying.

Jack followed me, and before the door even shut behind him, I said, "Please, just leave me alone for a minute." If he showed his typical tenderness I would fall to pieces.

My back was to him, but I could feel him staring at me. After a long moment, the door squeaked as he went back inside. Tears spilled down my cheeks, and I walked down the steps and into the yard. The grass was soft and damp against my bare feet, and part of me wanted to melt right into it like rain. When I stopped at the edge of the yard, I sat down, raking my hands through the lawn like it was the fur of some gigantic cat.

The katydids had started up, so loud they made the whole night vibrate. They were like some huge mechanical beast, buzzing for hours on end. In the tall grass, the lightning bugs flickered in a frenzy, a million little dots of light that zigged and zagged, just as lost as I was. This really was a beautiful place, and the longer I was here, the longer I could see myself staying. If I wasn't going to work for my father, did I have a reason to go back home?

There was no way my father would let me work for him again —that bridge was torched. He'd forgive me eventually, probably, but suffering through his wrath in the meantime was not an appealing option. And besides, did I want to keep fighting against his expectations of me? Why not start my own flipping business? I had a little savings and might be able to get a loan. It was a possibility I hadn't considered before.

I heard footsteps in the grass behind me and quickly brushed the tears away, grateful to be in the dark. Seeing me cry was nothing new for him at this point, but I still hated it. Jack sat down, stretching his feet out, wiggling his toes. He turned to face me for a minute, then lay down and put his hands behind his head.

"Want to fill in the blanks?" he said.

The silence was like being under a spell. I just wanted to watch the twinkling fireflies, listen to the buzzing of the katydids and hear the woeful calls of the owls in the woods.

At last I said, "My father is displeased."

"You have a real gift for understatement, you know that?"

I stretched out in the grass next to him. It felt good to lie back in the darkness. "I think we've reached the end of our partnership," I said.

He turned toward me, his brow furrowed. "What?"

"My dad and me. We're done for real this time."

"Oh." He turned back toward the stars. He slid his hand over his chest, like he was making sure it was still intact. "Right, your dad."

I turned to him, resting on my elbow. "You thought I meant you."

He shrugged, his eyes sad.

"No, sir. I'm not done with you yet." I traced one finger along his arm.

"I hope not," he said, sliding his hand behind his head. "For the record, I'm glad you held your ground. You shouldn't let him bully you." He found my hand in the grass and squeezed.

I hated that my father could still make me so angry, that I still cared so much about his approval. As much as I wanted to not need it, a part of me did—and I wanted that part to disappear.

"As a side note," he said, his voice lighter, "you're stone cold foxy when you're all riled up."

I smirked, and he pulled my hand to his lips, kissing my knuckles. "You're doing a great job with this place. Vergie would be proud."

"That's sweet of you."

"Don't worry," he said. "This will work out fine. You're stronger already for it."

"I pushed him too far."

He snorted. "I think you said exactly what you needed to.

Your father is a bully, and he needs to know when he crosses the line with you. Nobody deserves to be treated the way he treats you."

"You should have heard the disgust in his voice."

"chère, the whole parish heard it. If you hadn't gone off on him, I would have said everything you said to him and more."

I smiled a little at that—the image of Jack going toe to toe with my father.

He leaned up on his elbow and leveled his eyes with mine. "I'm a firm believer in calling people out on their bullshit, regardless of whether they're your kin. Hell, sometimes especially because they're your kin."

"But I think he might be right, and that's what kills me. I am in over my head."

"So what? Nobody ever got ahead by not taking risks. And the things worth doing, they're usually not all that easy."

"You've got an answer for everything. It's sort of irritating."

"I learned a lot by screwing up." He brushed my hair away from my neck and leaned down so his lips moved against my ear. "You're tougher than you give yourself credit for," he said, his voice deepening. "And I, for one, am glad you ended up down here. Even though you're kicking me out of my house."

"Is that right?"

"God's honest truth," he said, holding one hand up like a Boy Scout. "Besides, don't you feel better after telling him off?"

My father had completely crawled under my skin. Right then, he was likely sitting at his massive wood desk, crunching numbers and tallying up my mistakes like I was some kind of balance sheet. *Screw him*, I thought. I was perfectly capable of surviving without my father's approval. It was time to start living that way.

"Yeah," I said. "Actually, it felt damn good. I should get pissed and yell at people more often."

He laughed, rolling onto his back.

I lay still, listening to his laugh mingle with the calls from the night birds. Sometimes I was tired of being the planner, being on a schedule. Sometimes I wanted someone else to take control for me. I wanted to be one tiny thing in this vast expanse of darkness.

I sat up quickly and straddled him so that my knees were on either side of his chest. He slid his hands along my thighs and said, "Well, hello there."

"Hello, yourself," I said, and leaned down to kiss him. His teeth pinched my lip in the way that always sent a shiver along my skin, and I slid my fingers into his hair. His hands moved down my back as he pulled me against him. "What's all that for?" he said, when he finally took a breath.

"Cheering me up." I stood up slowly, easing out of his grasp.

"Hey, where are you going?"

"It's awful hot out here." Taking a few steps toward the water, I slipped my shirt over my head and tossed it at him.

Raising one eyebrow, he said, "What's gotten into you, chère?"

I slid out of my skirt and dropped it on the bank.

He leaned up on his elbows, smiling a wicked smile.

"Are you coming, or are you just going to gawk at me?" I asked.

He was on his feet in one fluid motion, sauntering toward me in that easy way of his that was so disarming. "Come here, you."

"You have to catch me first," I said, stepping into the water.

"Hey," he said, jogging toward the bank. "Get back up here."

The creek was deep in this part, over my head in the widest bend. The water was usually still here, except when there was a torrent of rain. Bends like this one were like lagoons, holding warmth from the heat of the day. Paddling around on my back, I grinned in the moonlight, splashing and giggling. It was the most relaxed I'd felt in days, like some crazy baptism that washed away all the things that left me scared and worried. It felt good to stand up to my father.

Jack came to the edge of the water, the waves lapping at his ankles. "Would you come back? The gators in there'll eat you up."

I laughed, staring up at the big round moon, loving the way

the light bounced across the water and skimmed across my skin. "Then you'd better come eat me up first."

"Enza, I'm not kidding."

I paddled farther away. "Come and get me, you big chicken."

He stood with his hands on his hips, like he might will me back to shore.

It was heaven, that warm water under the moon. Like being in some other time, some other place, where the things that shouldn't matter didn't.

I turned when I heard a splash, thinking for a second it might actually be an alligator, but then I saw the ripple of waves, the flash of skin. Jack surfaced next to me, smirking as he moved closer.

"Nice, isn't it?" I said.

His eyes narrowed. "Do I have to haul you away on my shoulder again?"

I laughed, splashing him.

"Oh, now you've done it," he said, and lunged toward me, wrapping his arms around me before I could swim away. I slid my hands down his back, below his waist, delighted to discover he'd left his clothes on the bank. He tightened his grip as he kissed my neck. I squirmed, giggling, but it was impossible to wriggle out of his grip. Not that I wanted to anyway. I let him pull me back toward the bank as he waded through the dark water.

"Oh, come on, Jack. Swim with me."

"You do like to tease me." He slid down into the water, pulling me with him, his hands drifting to my hips.

I wound myself around him. "You wouldn't have it any other way."

His eyes were wide, nearly black in the moonlight. Standing in the waist-deep water, he pulled me against him, my body cool in the water, warm where his skin met mine. He kissed me hard as drops of water fell from the ends of his hair, rolling down my cheeks and my neck, drawing a thin tingling line. My hands traced the curve of his back, then rested on his hips. The pinch of his teeth made me grip him tighter, stroking him until he whispered my name, his voice ragged.

He slid his fingers up from my waist, his thumbs drawing a line to my breasts. His lips trailed down, down, as he nudged me toward the bank.

"Time to get you out of here," he said, his lips moving against the hollow of my throat. "I don't want anything nibbling you but me."

He gripped the backs of my thighs as he lifted me, wrapping my legs around his waist. His body tensed as I tightened myself around him, winding my arms around his shoulders as he pressed his lips to my neck. He traced every contour with his tongue, his teeth, until I could hardly stand it. I kissed him harder then, tugging at his hair. I dug my fingers into his back, trying to coax out the rougher side of him, and when at last he called my name, I knew he was trying to do the same. His breath was hot against my skin; his hands held me with a firmness that made me shiver. I could never have enough of him.

"Why are you holding back?" I said, my lips brushing his ear. "I'm not so delicate."

His breaths came deep and fast, his hands gripping me harder. "Thank God for that," he said, moving toward the bank.

He carried me the last few steps to the shore, and we fell into the grass. My body ached to feel his weight, and I arched my back, drawing him closer as he settled on top of me. His hands pinned mine in the damp grass as he kissed me, harder now, as if something inside him was fighting to escape. I locked my legs around him, but he slid out of my grasp, smiling wickedly. He traced his tongue along my ribs, inching his way down, and then sat back on his knees as he pulled my ankle to his lips. He stared at me as he slid his teeth along the line of my calf, my thigh. My breath caught in my chest as his hands rested on my hips. He caressed me with his thumbs, saying, "Relax, chère," and then slid his tongue along my softest skin. I cried out as he traced tiny circles with his tongue, tasting and teasing. I loved the way he took his time, making me long for more of his touch. Helpless, I dug my fingers into the grass as I felt the pull of his lips, the slight pinch of his teeth. I closed my eyes, dizzy, and whispered his name as my breath turned ragged. He pushed me further and further, his hands kneading my hips. My heart pounded so hard it hurt to breathe, and then I buckled, trembling beneath him. His palm traced a line from my hip to my neck as I struggled to catch my breath, and then he was on top of me, his hands on either side of my shoulders, his taut body sinking into mine.

"Jack," I said, my voice wavering.

He kissed one corner of my mouth and said, "Say my name again."

"Jack," I moaned, and repeated it again and again.

His grin made me shiver. He shifted his weight, pinning my hips with his, and I thought for sure I would come apart again.

"I can't get enough of you," I murmured.

He slid his cheek along my neck, down to my shoulder, and said, "I'm not done with you yet, chère. I've been thinking about this all day." The darkness of his voice drove me wild, and I ached to feel him inside me again.

I tightened my legs around him, and he said, "Darlin', when you do that, I want to take you a hundred different ways."

Squeezing, I said, "I wish you would."

"Mmm," he said, closing his eyes for an instant, and then his mouth returned to mine in a kiss that I felt all the way to my heels. With one long, slow motion he was inside me, and I gripped his shoulders tight. He groaned as I pulled at his hair and called his name, and he moved deeper, achingly slow. My hands drifted down his back, and he quickly rolled me in the grass, leaving me straddling him, my knees by his sides.

He grinned, wriggling under me, his hands gripping my hips, steering me into place. "Your turn," he said, his voice bewitching. As his fingers slid along my skin, I closed my eyes, tilted my face toward the stars, and smiled as my name fell from his lips again and again, piercing the stillness of the salty air.

When I felt him getting close, I eased off him and slid my hands along his chest. He sighed as I traced a line to his navel, his hip. "Wicked, you," he said.

"Just thought you needed to catch your breath."

"We'll see about that." He rolled on top of me, and I laughed as he pinned me down, tickling my hips with his fingers. I wiggled beneath him as he rubbed his cheek along my neck but stopped when his hands gripped me like a vise—one in my hair and one at my hip. He held me firmly in place, the way he knew I liked, and slid inside me in a move that made my whole body shiver.

"Jack," I said, breathless.

"You make me so absolutely crazy," he said.

I felt wild as he moved faster, harder, urging me on. His body tightened, and his muscles tensed against mine. I dug my fingers into his back, feeling myself unravel.

"Don't stop," I whispered. "Don't you dare."

He grinned, his hands sliding along my skin, stroking and squeezing. He slowed for a minute, teasing me, until I groaned. He laughed his wicked laugh, sliding his cheek along my jaw. With so many sensations at once, I thought I would surely explode, but he held me as he moved harder again. "Is this what you want, chère?"

My body quaked beneath his. He tensed again, then shifted his weight. I locked my arms around him and said, "Just stay like this. I love feeling you all over me."

He slid his hand along my cheek as he whispered, "I think you like it almost as much as I do, darlin'."

IF SOMEONE HAD TOLD me a few weeks before that I'd be rolling around on a riverbank in the middle of the night with a guy like Jack, I would have told them they were certifiable. But I was beginning to think I was the crazy one for keeping a distance between us.

"Shit," I said. "Our dinner's probably blackened."

He stood up, grabbing his jeans, and offered his hand to help me up. "I left it warming in the oven for us."

As I gathered up the rest of our clothes, I heard movement in the brush. A cloud passed over the moon, making it nearly impossible to see in the darkness. There was more rustling in the scrub brush, and a twig snapped. Something was out there.

"Did you hear that?" I asked, struggling to get my shirt buttoned.

"Told you the gators would get you," he said, nipping at my shoulder. He pulled his jeans on and led me toward the house.

I clutched the clothes against my body and followed him, my heart thumping. We were halfway to the house when the moon came out from behind a cloud, and I saw the shape of a person moving through the cypresses, just on the other side of the river.

I stopped. It couldn't be real. I blinked and looked again, and there was nothing.

"Hey," Jack said, "You all right?"

"Yeah," I said. I scanned the tree line but saw nothing unusual. The moon shone brightly again, casting everything around us in blue.

It wasn't hard to imagine Remy's lanky silhouette passing between the trees as he crept along the edge of the water. He could be out in that curtain of cypress, waiting. I shivered. Could it really be Remy, or was I being paranoid? The thought of him getting to me like that made me sick to my stomach.

"You sure you're OK?" Jack asked.

"Come on," I said, taking his hand. "I'm starving."

Chapter Twenty

THE NEXT MORNING, I stumbled into the kitchen to find Jack making omelets with an ungodly amount of sausage and cheese. He didn't have to go in to work until noon, but he was never one to roll out of bed and split anyway. This was something I appreciated about him: his ability to be fully functional first thing in the morning. Mostly because I was nothing like him in that regard.

"How did I manage to find a man who can repair houses *and* cook?" I said.

"Guess you just wandered into the right swamp." He poured a cup of coffee, then tousled my hair and kissed me. "Did you find anything interesting in the hat box yesterday?"

"Didn't you look inside it?" I asked.

"No."

"Really?"

"Well, aside from just peeking inside when I first found it... I wasn't going to read Vergie's letters."

"I'm not sure I can read them yet either," I said. "It looks like most of them are from my mother."

He stared at me, stone-faced. "I had no idea."

I shrugged. "It's OK. I don't think about her a lot."

"You must be curious, though."

"Yes and no. Someday I'll read them." I smiled, sipping my coffee. "Just not today."

His eyebrows turned upward in a sad arc.

"There were also journals that Vergie kept," I said. "And it means the world to have those."

He smiled then. There was really no way I could ever repay him for giving that box to me.

"So listen," he said when he was halfway through his eggs. "I'm leaving in a little while, but I've arranged for a friend to come stay with you until my shift's over."

"That's not necessary."

He shot me his don't-start-with-me stare. "I told you I'm not leaving you alone again, and I meant it, Enza."

"Jack, I'm a big girl."

"I already called. He owes me a favor."

I gave him my hardest glare.

He stared right back and said, "This isn't up for negotiation. You'll like Andre. He's got a ton of good stories and cooks up a mean jambalaya. And he'll protect you from any unwanted houseguests." He waved his fork at me, like it might drive his point home.

"Fine."

He smiled. He was even more stubborn than me. But it wasn't so bad having him looking out for me. I wasn't used to having someone care so much.

AS IT TURNED OUT, Andre was a fabulous cook. He was also the sheriff. Since he was off-duty, he was wearing a T-shirt and jeans. That, combined with his wild red hair and stubbly beard, made him look like any ordinary guy in the parish. He was shorter and heavier than Jack, with broad shoulders and muscular arms. *The better to catch the bad guys with,* I thought. He wasn't much older than me and had a sense of humor so dry that I couldn't ever quite tell when he was joking.

"Almost done," he said, tossing some sausage in a skillet.

"You didn't have to do all this."

"You've been working outside all day. Makes you hungry, *non*?"

His accent was even stronger than Jack's. I felt like we had a ten-second delay, where I needed time to decode his words. He got a big kick out of that, I could tell.

Earlier, he'd stayed downstairs in the kitchen (front of the house, where he could see anyone entering the drive from the woods) and read the local paper, while I worked on finishing the spare room upstairs. I'd emptied the closet where Jack had found Vergie's hat box of mementos and found little else I wanted to keep. My progress was slow, but I had to keep myself busy both to stay on track and to stop my mind from churning over Martine, my dad and Jack.

That afternoon, after standing guard in the kitchen, Andre had wandered around the yard, looking for any clues that might explain the weirdness that seemed to hover over us. When I'd started stripping the cracking paint off the porch rails, he'd grabbed a putty knife out of my toolbox and began working right alongside me. Every time he leaned way over, I caught a glimpse of the pistol tucked in a holster in the back of his jeans. Even without it, he looked like he could take just about anybody down in a fight.

Now he whistled quietly, stirring something in a tiny pot and taking a taste.

"Thanks for the help," I said. "You didn't have to paint, either."

"What, you think I'm going to lie in the hammock all day and watch a lady work? Come now." He winked in that way that must be reflex down here. He'd no doubt left his own trail of broken hearts. "Sit," he said.

I wasn't used to having men cook for me and look out for me, and frankly I was getting a little spoiled. Every once in a while, I'd forget he was there on guard duty—but then I'd catch him peeking out the window with a look on his face that showed, despite his friendly banter, he was on high alert.

Maybe he and Jack knew something I didn't.

Andre put a plate in front of me and sat down with one for himself. "Hope you like it hot," he said, deadpan as ever.

"You got any leads on the arsonist?" I asked. I'd spent all day fighting my curiosity.

"I probably shouldn't discuss it," he said. "But don't you worry. We'll catch him."

"This is delicious," I said, trying to muster all the charm I could. It seemed to get you a long way in these parts. "Might be the best I ever had."

"Well I never get tired of hearing a lady say that," he said. His smile suggested he might have spent some time on the other side of the law, back in the day.

"Come on. Can't you tell me anything?"

He pushed the sausage around on his plate. "Don't you think you're in this deep enough?"

"I just wondered if you had any suspects, that's all."

He stared at me, his eyebrow raised, and I almost told him to forget I asked. This was probably the same face he made in the interrogation room.

"Unofficially," he said, "we've got a few folks we're keeping an eye on."

His phone rang, and he dug it out of his pocket while I poured myself a glass of water.

"OK," he said, turning away from me. "Where's Theo?"

I strained to hear the voice on the other end of the line, but Andre stood and walked into the hall.

"Is anybody else around?" His voice was gruff. Sheriff mode.

Although I liked being cared for, I hated being baby-sat. I wasn't this fragile little thing that couldn't be let out of anyone's sight for fear of getting broken, and I didn't like men making me feel that way.

Andre came back in, sliding the phone into his pocket.

"Duty calls?" I said.

"There's been an incident. But I can't leave you here by yourself."

"For heaven's sake. I'll be fine."

"I swore I'd look out for you," he said. "I'm not leaving you alone."

"Then I guess you have to take me with you."

"I can't take you to a crime scene," he said.

"Unless you can split yourself in two, you're gonna have to."

He grabbed one last sausage link and glared at me, his brown eyes narrowed. He tossed the fork in the sink and said, "You stay in the car."

"Deal," I said. It was certainly better than sitting all alone in the house, worrying about my deadline, my budget and the situation with my father.

He walked outside first, scanning the yard as I locked the front door. He led me to his cruiser and said, "I'm sure I'll regret this, but it won't be the first time a woman impaired my judgment."

He opened the back car door for me, and I scoffed.

"Sorry," he said. "Habit."

He opened the front passenger door and stopped himself.

"How about we don't tell Mayronne about this little field trip," he said.

"Deal."

WE PULLED into a parking lot shrouded by trees. The ramshackle bar was for locals only—not a place outsiders would easily find. It looked like a shack with a porch. A hand-painted sign in the window read "liquor, cigarettes, bait," illuminated by a couple of dim porch lights. I could barely make out the silhouettes of men standing around outside. A patrol car was already there, its lights still flashing. And an ambulance.

"Wait in the car," Andre said. He tucked a bit of his shirt into his jeans, just enough so the badge clipped to his belt was visible.

"Yes, sir."

I slouched down in the seat as he strode into the bar. A deputy was outside, talking to bystanders as he scribbled on a pad. I rolled the window down a couple of inches, straining to hear what they were saying, but I only caught bits and snatches—nothing that explained what was going on. The folks outside took turns lighting cigarettes and scuffing their toes in the dirt, clearly bored and hammered.

I sat up when two medics wheeled a gurney out with a body covered by a sheet. At first I thought I wasn't seeing right, but when they pushed it closer, over to the ambulance, there was no doubt. This was a murder scene.

I was so focused on the sheet that I didn't see Andre until he was a few feet away, ushering a roughed-up Remy right past me toward the other patrol car. Remy's hair was tousled, his shirt ripped, his hands cuffed behind his back. He paused by the window, looking confused for a minute as it seemed to register that I was sitting in a police car. A familiar sneer spread across his face, and he gave me a salacious wink.

Andre shoved him onward, and I jumped out of the car, my pulse pounding in my ears.

"You son of a bitch!" I yelled, stomping across the parking lot.

Remy half-smiled, and I wanted to knock that smirk right off his face.

"You think you can terrorize us?" I said.

Andre spun around. "What do you think you're doing? I told you to stay in the car."

The other officer took Remy while Andre steered me back to the cruiser. "It's him!" I said. "He tried to burn my house down." I sidestepped Andre and moved toward Remy. I'd have given anything to be six inches taller so I could stare at him nose to nose. "I know it was you, and so help me, I swear—"

Andre grabbed my elbow and pulled.

"Don't know what you mean, sugar." Remy's voice was so calm it was sickening. "But that temper of yours is awfully cute."

I yanked my arm free and swung with my other, and my fist caught Remy right in the nose. It hurt like hell, and I thought I'd broken my hand for sure.

Remy chuckled, a thin trail of blood trickling from his nose. "Sheriff," he said coolly, "are you going to stand there and let this woman assault me?"

I shook my hand by my side, cringing at the sight of Remy's blood on it.

"I didn't see any assault," Andre said flatly, turning back to me. "But Miss Parker, I think you ought to go back and wait in the car while I talk with Broussard here."

"He tried to kill me!" I said. "And Jack! You've been tearing this town up looking for the arsonist, and he's standing right here!"

Remy stared at me, his eyes darkening. "I think they call that slander, Miss Parker."

"And I suppose you don't know anything about the slashed tires and people creeping around the house, either."

"That's real sad somebody tried to hurt your boyfriend," Remy said, his voice still cool. "But he's made enemies around here."

"You bastard," I said, stepping closer.

Andre grabbed my arm again and said, "Come here, Enza." This time there was no getting out of his grip. He walked me over to the car and said only loud enough for me to hear, "Don't make me lock you in the back."

"You have to arrest him! You can't just let him walk away. I know it's him, Andre. I know it."

His jaw was rigid. "Do I need to remind you, Miss Parker, that I am the sheriff? When I tell you to wait in the car, that's not a suggestion." His eyes were cold, not like they'd been the rest of the day, and it made the hair on the back of my neck stand up. He was all business now. I'd pushed him too far.

I climbed in the front seat and closed the door, still glaring at Remy. He puckered his lips in a mock kiss, and I felt the blood rush to my head again.

Andre wrote in a small notepad as they talked. Remy occasionally shrugged as if to say, *Who, me?* It made me want to jump out of the car again because I knew he was lying. But if I did, Andre would probably handcuff me and drive me to jail himself. So I sat, fuming, hoping Andre was smart enough to see through this act.

WHEN ANDRE GOT BACK in the car, I was ready for a tirade. At first, he remained motionless, watching the ambulance lights disappear down the gravel road, and then he turned to me.

"Now, just so I can continue to improve my communication skills with the public," he said, "what part of 'stay in the car and keep out of trouble' was unclear?"

"Sorry," I said. "I lost it."

"You can't go around taunting people like Broussard." He sounded just like Jack.

I balled my fists by my sides. "But he's behind all of this, and seeing him standing there—cocky as hell—I snapped."

"That may very well be, but you can't interfere with ongoing investigations. We have a much higher rate of success when the criminals don't know we're onto them. And it's safe to say the element of surprise is lost when you call them out in front of the sheriff."

I thought he was messing with me again, but I didn't want to push my luck. My mouth had gotten me in enough trouble lately.

"I'm sorry," I said. "But he's just arrogant enough to think he's still getting away with it, right? Don't guys like him keep doing what they're doing, pushing everybody's buttons until they get caught? I mean, he probably wants to get caught, right?"

"I think you've been watching too many cop shows, Miss Parker. How about you let me handle the bad guys like Broussard, since that's what the great state of Louisiana pays me to do."

I sighed as he started the car and pulled back onto the highway.

With the faintest smile, he said, eyes never leaving the road, "You've got a mean right hook, though, I'll tell you that."

When it seemed he'd thoroughly cooled off, I said, "What happened to that guy in the bar?"

He shot me a sideways glance. "It seems he took a knife to a gunfight."

"Did Remy shoot him?" I shuddered, dreading the answer.

"If he did, no one's saying so. Broussard gave us enough of a scuffle inside that I sent him down to the precinct to think about his error in judgment. Folks said a stranger came in, and then Broussard and the guy started arguing out back. Then they heard gunshots and went outside and found him."

"You believe that?"

He shrugged. "I suppose there's about a four percent chance it happened that way. That no one saw a thing." He glanced in the rearview, probably out of habit, and said, "To read our reports, you'd think the parish was overrun with drifters with hot tempers and bad aim."

AT THE HOUSE, Andre was back to his jovial self—mostly. He sat down in the study with a beer and laid his gun on the coffee table. "I'll stay down here for the night."

"I'm turning in," I said. "Got to get up early and get back to the repairs."

He propped his feet up on the coffee table. "Go ahead, chère.

You ain't got nothing to worry about. You get yourself a good night's rest."

"Thanks, Andre."

The chances of that were slim under the circumstances, but I nodded and went upstairs. I was so tired I could hardly keep my eyes open—but as soon as I closed them, I'd see Remy sneering at me like he wanted to swallow me whole. It wasn't entirely bad, knowing that Andre was downstairs with a pistol. I just hoped he wasn't a heavy sleeper.

In the dream, I was painting a dollhouse, gluing shingles to the roof. Vergie was passing me miniature paintings, telling me they were some my mother had made especially for the house. We stuck them to the tiny walls next to photos of my mother and me. I rearranged the furniture as Vergie hummed along with the record player. Then my father appeared with a sledgehammer and a hard hat, bashing the house to pieces. When I turned, there was another house, so I started painting it too. My father laughed, still wearing a crisp Oxford shirt and pleated pants, a thin layer of sawdust clinging to his skin. *You know what your problem is,* he said to me, raising the hammer over his head, *All wind-up, but no follow-through.* He swung the hammer like a five-iron and smashed the house to bits. I stood, pounding my fists against his chest. He laughed again, but when I looked up at him, it was Remy. A grin stretched across his face as the dollhouse splintered in front of me, tiny shingles and windowpanes scattering across the room. His laughter made the room shake.

Then there was a burst of orange flame, and my throat closed as the smoke filled my lungs. The dog howled, and I ran toward the door, but I slammed into a wall that crackled with flames. Big arms tightened around my shoulders, arms that must have been pulling me to safety. But then they shoved me against the wall so the fire burned my skin.

I snapped awake, gasping as I sat up in the bed. The sheets were damp. My hair stuck to my forehead. My heart raced. Outside, the barking was louder, right by the window. I froze, terrified that Remy was in the house, that he had muscled his way through with a jug of gasoline and a match, bent on doing it right this time. I strained my ears, listening for footsteps, for anything, then heard the door open downstairs.

The feeling drained from my legs as I stood. I grabbed a screwdriver that was lying on the dresser and crept into the hallway. The floorboards downstairs creaked. Holding my breath, I eased down the stairs.

At the bottom, the dog rushed past me, her fur brushing my bare legs. I screamed without meaning to, then felt a hand on my shoulder as the screwdriver clattered on the floor.

"Enza," Andre said, "it's OK. It's me."

He put his other hand on my arm, steadying me. "It's OK," he repeated. "I just let the dog in. She was having a fit out there, and I didn't want to wake you."

I shivered, leaning against the wall.

"Easy, darlin'," he said, pulling me against his chest. "I'm sorry. I didn't mean to scare you."

Tears stung my eyes.

"Shhh," he said. He hesitated, then draped his arms around me. "Take it easy. You're safe. I'm right here."

He led me into the kitchen and sat me down at the table. I held my head in my hands as he sat next to me and poured some bourbon into a glass.

"Here," he said, pushing it toward me. "My grandma used to give me a shot to help me sleep. Worked like a charm."

My hand shook as I sipped.

"You all right?"

I nodded. "Just a nightmare. Then I heard a noise down here."

"Sorry. That fool dog was barking her head off." He gestured toward Bella who lay on her side as if this was a perfectly routine event.

"She does that." I didn't think there was enough alcohol in the whole state to get me back to sleep, but it was worth a try. At the very least, it might ease my nerves and stop my blood from pounding in my ears.

When I could feel my knees again, I stood and walked toward the stairs. "I'm going to try this one more time," I said, and Andre stood with me.

"You got nothing to worry about." His eyes were steady on mine. "Nobody's gonna get through me."

I nodded and headed upstairs. "Hey, Andre," I said, and he stepped into the doorway. "Thank you."

"You're welcome," he said, and watched from the bottom of the stairs until I closed the bedroom door.

Chapter Twenty-One

SUNLIGHT STREAMED THROUGH THE WINDOWS. Cinching my robe over my pajamas, I trudged down the stairs, concerned only with finding coffee.

Andre sat at the kitchen table, reading the newspaper.

He'd already made coffee. I pulled a mug from the cabinet and poured myself a cup.

"You get some sleep?" he asked.

I sat down across from him. "More than I thought I would. It was easier knowing you were here."

"Glad I could help." He dropped the paper and went over to the stove. "I left some breakfast warming for you." There was a clatter of silverware as he kept his back to me, moving like those chefs do on television, dropping salt and bits of parsley from chin height.

He slid a plate in front of me—an omelet with sausage and fruit on the side.

"Jeez," I said.

He shrugged. "I got bored waiting for you to wake up. And what sort of public servant would I be if I didn't make enough for you too? By the way, Jack's already called twice this morning, checking up on you."

I paused, mid-bite. "You didn't tell him about our little ride-along, did you?"

"No, ma'am, I did not. I would prefer that information stay between you and me."

That made two of us. Jack would go through the roof if he knew I'd had another encounter with Remy.

I turned back to my omelet, trying to eat like a lady, even though I was ravenous. It was only then that I heard the chewing sound coming from the hallway. I leaned back in my chair far enough to see the dog stretched out by the front door, gnawing on something that looked like a stick.

"What's that dog got now?" I muttered.

Andre shook his head, turning back to the paper. "Don't know. Probably brought it in from the yard. I let her out this morning, but she came right back a few minutes later. Can't say I blame her. It's already hotter than hell out there."

I wished the heat would hold off a couple of days so I could finish the work outside without feeling like I was in a greenhouse. But the universe wasn't up for cutting me any breaks.

"Anything in there about the shooting last night?" I asked.

"Nothing we didn't know already."

The dog sneezed, making me jump. There was a loud crack, followed by a string of sneezes, and I pushed the plate aside. "What is she into?"

She wasn't chewing on a stick at all. I reached down and swiped the thing from her while she was racked by another series of sneezes. She shot me a disapproving look as I turned the object over in my hands. It looked like it was made from something like grapevines—like those decorative woven wreaths. It was stuffed with straw and corn husks, and was shaped like a snake. My stomach turned just looking at it. I didn't know what it meant, but there was one person who would.

"Looks like my plans for the day have changed," I said.

Andre lowered the paper and reached for his coffee. "What is that thing?"

"You feel like taking a drive into town?"

His eyes narrowed. "What for?"

"Errands?"

"I'm afraid you're going to have to be more specific."

"Promise you won't make fun of me."

He frowned, picking at the vines and leaves. "I would never."

"I need to go see the voodoo priestess."

He shook his head a bit, like he had water in his ear. "You what?"

"You heard me. She's the only one who can tell me what this means."

"What it means is that fool dog went out and found the grossest thing she could to try and eat. There's nothing mystical about it. It could have come from a mile away."

"Or it could have been right outside the door, like every other freaky cursed thing that showed up here."

"What other freaky cursed things?"

"Jack didn't tell you?" I shook my head. "Of course he didn't. Because he thinks it's not real."

He glanced up at the ceiling, muttering something I couldn't make out. But that didn't matter—the look on his face told me everything he was thinking.

"But I still need a ride into town."

"You're wasting your time," he said. "Those people are just looking to separate tourists from their money."

"This lady's different. She told me about all the other stuff, and she'll know what this is too."

He laid the snake on the table and sighed. "I get the feeling I'm taking you whether I want to or not."

I smiled my sweetest smile.

"Fine," he said with a sigh. "Let me get my gun."

THE DOOR WAS LOCKED, but I rapped my knuckles against the glass anyway. Duchess' big orange cat was sitting in the window, his yellow eyes narrowed into slits. I pressed my face to the glass and thought I saw the beaded curtain swing.

"I think you're out of luck," Andre said. He had his back to me, scanning the street. His badge was hidden under his shirt, clipped to his belt, and I got a glimpse of it every time he crossed his arms over his chest.

"She's here," I said, and knocked until I heard footsteps.

"Cool your heels," Duchess said through the door. "If something's ailing you that bad, I probably can't help no way."

She pulled the door open and stood blocking it, her hands on her hips. Her hair was swept back against her head, held there by a bright blue scarf. "Well, if it isn't Miss Love Triangle," she said, her eyebrow arching. "What's got you so on fire, child? Can't you read?" She pointed a long pink fingernail to a sign that read *Closed for Lunch*.

"This couldn't wait, Miss Dauphine," I said, still out of breath from rushing through the Quarter. "I need your help. Please."

"Girl, you look like you being chased by the devil himself. And what'd you bring the po-po for?"

Andre turned, frowning.

"Long story," I said. "But he's off duty. Just gave me a ride is all." She shot me a wary look, but I went on. "I just need a minute, please. You have to tell me what this means." I yanked the snake out of my bag and held it out for her to see.

"Ho, now," she said, stepping back. "Don't be waving stuff around when you don't know what it is." She held her hand over her heart and opened the door wide. "Come on," she said, peeking around the doorframe, "before anybody sees you and that thing."

Andre paused, looking down the street, and she said, "You too, Mr. Po-po, before somebody sees you and starts all the tongues around here wagging."

I stepped inside, Andre at my heels, and followed Duchess back to the room with the bookcases. It smelled pungent, like something had died. A large mortar and pestle sat in the middle of the desk, along with an array of tiny bones.

"I don't have much time," Duchess said, pushing the bowl to the corner of the desk. "My niece is getting married today, and I've got things to get ready for the ceremony. So how 'bout you give me the abridged version."

I held the snake out carefully. "This was in my yard this morning."

Duchess took the snake and laid it on her desk. She pulled a magnifying glass from the drawer and leaned closer to it.

"You know what snakes do?" she asked.

"Aside from the obvious?" Andre said.

"Snake is a gateway," she said, pulling a twig out of the tightly knit bundle with a pair of tweezers. "It's like a bridge between two worlds, or in this case, who you are and who you want to be." She paused, picking through the straw inside. "Somebody was performing a ritual. Snakes are used to seal rituals, to make them stick."

"Great," I said.

Duchess clicked her tongue, pulling another twig from the bundle. "It's mostly swamp vines, but there's some devil's shoestring stuck in here. See this?"

I studied the green flake between us. Andre rolled his eyes, and I shot him a look.

"This is spikenard," she said. "Keeps you faithful. There's vetivert reed here too. And Adam and Eve root."

"Adam and Eve?"

"It comes from an orchid. Not easy to find," she said. "Binds two lovers for eternity."

I sat back in the chair and frowned.

"Is this meant for your same mister, or has our triangle become a square?" She glanced over at Andre, who had pushed his dark aviator shades up into his hair. His eyebrows shot up.

"No, ma'am," I said. "He's just looking out for me today."

"Mmm-hmm," she said, her eyes drifting over him. She

turned back to me and said, "You better not cross this girl, honey. The whole thing's soaked in Black Sampson oil. She's working some serious mojo on your fella, but this is the dark kind."

"How dark?" I glanced at Andre, who stared out into the shop as if he was ignoring us.

She peered at me over the rims of her glasses. "The if-I-can't-have-him-nobody-will variety."

I felt sick.

She clicked her tongue, shaking her head. "Mercy, I do hate love triangles. But they keep me in business." With a pair of scissors, she cut through the dried vines and pulled out a tan cloth. "Bet we'll find something of your fella's in here," she said as she unrolled it.

Inside were more herbs and dried flowers—and a watch. I didn't recognize it, but it had to be Jack's.

"Would she make it herself, or would someone like you have to make it?"

She raised her eyebrows and said, "Well, it's stronger if it comes from a priest or a priestess."

"You know who might have made it for her?"

She glanced at Andre and shook her head. "Lots of folks around here could have."

I leaned back in the chair.

"What you need is some protection," she said. She opened the bottom drawer of her desk and dug out a handful of small packets. "I'll mix up something for you. This girl don't have far to go till she gets to the bad place."

She paused, her hand in the drawer, and stared at Andre. "But non-believers need to wait outside. Their energy takes the power out of the gris-gris."

He raised one eyebrow, but she didn't make another move.

"Then I'll just be outside," he said.

When he was past the beaded curtain, Duchess scooped pinches of herbs from three different packages and dropped them into a velvet pouch. From a large jar, she scooped a tablespoon of loamy black soil and dropped it in too.

"What's that?" I asked.

"Graveyard dirt."

"From a real graveyard?"

"Well it ain't from no country club," she said. "Reverses bad magic." She looked at the bag, then back at me. "Maybe just one more scoop."

"So this will keep her away?" My eyes drifted back to the snake, with its hollow little eye holes that seemed to stare right into me.

"No," she said, cinching the bag tight. "This is going to keep her bad mojo away." She nodded toward the front room and said, "Probably gonna take Mr. Po-po out there to keep her away."

She stood and leveled her eyes to mine. "I hope that fella's worth all this trouble."

When I didn't answer, she said, "Come on out front, and I'll ring you up."

"A HUNDRED BUCKS!" Andre exclaimed. We were speeding over Lake Pontchartrain, the wind whipping my hair across my face. "Are you nuts?"

"It's Miranda. It has to be. For a while I thought it might be Remy, just screwing with me, but it's her."

Andre turned toward me so I could see my reflection in his shades. "You got any hard evidence of that?"

I almost blurted that Miranda had accosted me at the house, but instead I said, "Just what Duchess said."

"That won't exactly hold up in court. Besides, why would she go to all this trouble?"

"You heard Duchess. She wants Jack. She's trying to get him back with voodoo." It sounded ridiculous when I said it out loud.

"And you really believe that?"

"What do you know about Miranda?"

"She's been in some trouble before. Nothing too serious, though. She and Jack used to go out, but that burned out pretty fast. From what he told me, she didn't want to break it off and kept trying to get him back."

"What if she's the one who set fire to the house?" I said. "What if it wasn't Remy?"

Andre smirked. "She's a wildcat, but she's no murderer. It wouldn't surprise me if she's the one leaving all this voodoo shit in your yard, but she's not homicidal. She's just lovesick."

"How can you be so sure?"

"I went to high school with her. Besides, if we're going with what your voodoo lady says, she focused all her energy on Jack—none of that stuff was directed at you."

"So you believe Duchess?"

He snorted. "I believe in the hard evidence that is human behavior. She's obviously focused on him and not you. She might be annoying, but I don't think she's dangerous. And if she wants Jack that bad, she wouldn't be setting fires everywhere trying to burn him up in one."

I shuddered at his bluntness. I didn't want to think about fires.

He took the exit that led back to the house and said, "But Remy? He's a different story. A little gris-gris in your pocket won't do a bit of good with him, unless you got a nine millimeter in the other."

I shuddered, watching the swampland whiz by. He was right, of course, but I hated the idea of never feeling safe alone until Remy was caught.

"Don't worry," he said. "He'll screw up sooner or later. And when he does, I'll be there waiting."

I spent the afternoon painting banister rails on the porch, trying to focus on anything but voodoo tokens. The rails were as spindly as bones, and there seemed to be a hundred of them. The radio, tuned to a local zydeco station, was the only thing keeping me sane. That and Andre, who had picked up a paintbrush out of sheer pity once he walked out and heard me cursing. Painting was one of those things that brought me a zen-like calm for about an hour, and then it turned torturous. Andre was humming along with the radio, slapping the rails so hard he splattered a fine spray of paint all over himself. He even had flecks of white in his beard.

It turned muggy after lunch, which only magnified the tedium of painting, and I'd become far less precise than usual. About forty rails in, it became clear this was going to be one of those less-than-perfect jobs that gave the house what the real estate agent would call "character."

It didn't help that I was fixated on what Miranda might be planning next. She couldn't actually win Jack over with voodoo, but what happened when she finally came to understand that? Then what would she do to him?

What would she do to me if she thought I was in her way?

I dropped the brush in a container of water and said, "Andre, I need another favor."

Chapter Twenty-Two

ANDRE SAT ON HIS HEELS, forcing white paint into the crevices of the porch banister. As soon as I said Miranda's name, he went on high alert. "No way," he said, avoiding my stare.

"Come on, Andre," I said. "I just want to go talk to her and sort this out."

He snorted. "I've heard that one before. Right before I slapped the cuffs on."

"I'm not looking for trouble."

He glanced at me as he refilled his brush.

"What could go wrong? You'll be with me."

He laid the brush down on the rim of the paint can and stood up so we were almost eye to eye. "You need to leave this alone, Enza. She'll get over Jack, just like she did all the others."

"It's only getting worse. This is one of those times where after something terrible happens, when the story comes out in the paper, everybody says, 'All the signs were there! Why didn't they see the signs?'"

"I know you're rattled," he said. "But you have to trust me on this. This is what Miranda does. She gets all worked up over somebody until another guy comes along. And that's assuming this is even her."

"You expect me to believe there's another woman out there obsessed with Jack and dark magic?"

He lowered one hand to his side. The other he planted firmly on the wet banister. He quickly lifted his hand, cursing when he saw the paint on his palm.

"Hang on," he said. "I'm going to wash this off."

When I heard the water come on in the kitchen, I slipped inside and grabbed my car keys from the table in the hall. I ran down the porch steps and climbed into the Jeep.

By the time I had it cranked, Andre was hurrying toward me. I thought briefly about slamming the gas pedal and tearing past him down the drive anyway, but I knew he'd catch up in a mile or two. And I'd be better off staying on Andre's good side.

He stopped a few feet from the bumper and put his hands on his hips. "Really?" he said.

I leaned out the window. "I've got to do this. You want to come with me, or you want to chase me?"

"Enza, Jack will never speak to me again if I handcuff you."

I smiled. "Guess you better come with me, then."

"This is a terrible idea."

"I have to talk to her."

Scowling, he stared at me.

"You can keep an eye on me, same as you would here. If you think about it that way, there's really no difference."

"Your logic is somewhat flawed, jolie."

I revved the engine, giving him my warmest smile. "Come on, Andre, help a gal in need."

He looked at the ground, then kicked a rock in the dirt. Finally, he climbed into the passenger seat and slipped his sunglasses on. "Jack can never know about this," he said.

I pulled onto the driveway. "Where do we find Miranda this time of day?"

He looked at his watch. "She's probably at work. Take a left at the end of the drive."

A<small>NDRE HARDLY SPOKE</small> as we drove, except to give me directions. His jaw was set in a hard line. After a while, he said, "Slow down. It's up here on the right."

He pointed to a clearing with a cinder-block building. Painted a deep shade of red, it had a porch of rough-hewn beams. Railroad ties were laid end-to-end along the ground in front to indicate parking spaces. At the corner of the building was a life-size likeness of a mule, painted white with big X's where its eyes should be.

I parked in a far corner of the lot, in the shade.

"Welcome to the Dead Donkey," he said. "My least favorite dive bar in the parish. And yet somehow I end up here every other day."

As I gazed at the front of the building, I was suddenly horrified by the idea of talking to Miranda.

Andre turned to me and said, "You have five minutes, and then I'm coming in."

"That's hardly long enough to sort this out. I need fifteen at least. This is a delicate situation."

"Six," Andre said.

"Ten."

He stared at me over his glasses. "Six," he drawled. "And then I'm coming in to start making arrests."

I wasn't sure he could arrest me, but I thought it best not to cross him further. "OK," I said sweetly. "I'll be right back."

He bit his lip, staring straight at the front door.

T<small>HE GRAVEL CRUNCHED</small> under my feet as I walked up to the porch. Neon beer signs flickered in a couple of small windows, but there was no other indication the place was even open. I stepped over a smattering of broken glass and went inside. Light poured in behind me, and the customers, mostly men, squinted like they'd been in the dark for days. Dartboards lined the paneled walls. A lone pool table sat in the corner. Around it, a cluster of men in dirty jeans and T-shirts stood drinking beer from cans. An old jukebox sat against the far wall. A guy pounded his fist against it as he fed it quarters.

Miranda was in the far corner, balancing cans and glasses on a tray by her head. In that instant, a tiny voice of reason told me to leave, that it wasn't too late—I could slip back out, and she'd never know I was there. But then she turned, and her eyes narrowed, and the window passed.

Trying to look more together than I was, I took a deep breath and walked toward the bar. The bartender was a tall guy with shaggy blond hair and a fading bruise around his eye. He nodded without smiling. "What can I get you?"

"A shot of whiskey, please."

He poured a generous shot, and I laid a ten on the bar. "I need to talk to Miranda."

He took the bill, then disappeared through the swinging kitchen door and yelled, "Hey, Miranda! I need you up front."

I downed the shot and winced.

A minute later, the kitchen door swung open and banged against the wall. Miranda came out with the bartender right behind her. He stayed back, pouring a couple of beers at the opposite end of the bar while she sauntered over, her high heels clacking on the tile. Her hair was piled high on her head. Gold hoops as big as bracelets bobbed in her ears.

Her face tightened when she saw me. "What do you want?"

"I needed to tell you something."

She crossed her arms, glaring.

I glanced at the bartender. He pretended to ignore us.

"What you've been doing," I said, keeping my voice low. "It has to stop."

She cocked her head, frowning. "What's that supposed to mean?"

"Coming to my house. Leaving things in the yard. It's not going to work. I'm not going anywhere."

She scoffed, glancing behind her. The bartender started drying glasses, looking up at us every now and then.

"I don't know what you're talking about," she said, and turned to walk away.

"I think you do," I said, raising my voice. "And I just came to tell you—"

"Tell me what?" she snapped.

"Look, I know about the restraining order. I don't want to call the sheriff, but you're not leaving me any choice. You have to stop what you're doing. You can't actually think it's going to bring Jack back to you."

"You don't know anything about us."

"Men who want to be with you don't file restraining orders."

She glared at me, biting her lip. "How dare you come in here."

"He's not the guy for you. Just leave him be."

Her lip trembled, though I wasn't sure if it was from fury or sadness. I couldn't help but feel sorry for her.

"Don't you want to be with someone who wants to be with you?" I said. "You don't want to chase someone who doesn't love you."

"Get out of here," she said, flushed.

"This is the only time I'm going to ask you. I was hoping we could resolve this like adults."

"I said get out!" she yelled.

"Hey!" the bartender said, walking toward us. "There a problem here?"

"Yeah," Miranda said. "But she's leaving."

He crossed his arms over his chest, stepping to Miranda's side.

"I'm going," I told her. "But think about what I said."

She sneered, then glanced at the bartender. "Thinks she can come in here and threaten me."

The bartender stepped forward. "You'd best be on your way," he said.

"No more," I said to Miranda. She was still muttering to the bartender as I walked to the front door and bumped into Andre.

"Jesus," I said. "Nice lurking."

"Your six minutes were up," he said, holding the door for me.

I trudged outside, squinting in the light.

He led me back out to the Jeep and said, "Was that the outcome you were hoping for?"

I frowned, starting the engine. "Not exactly. But at least she knows we know it's her."

∾

BACK AT THE HOUSE, Andre insisted on cooking dinner again.

"It relaxes me," he said, tossing potatoes in olive oil. "You know, after an event has put me on edge."

I poured two glasses of wine, but when I offered him one, he shook his head.

After a while, he said, "You certainly have a way of setting your mind on something."

"Stubborn, you mean."

He shoved the tray of potatoes in the oven. "It's not entirely unlikeable."

When he turned, I grabbed him and hugged him. "Thank you for helping me today."

"Oh," he said, stiffening. "Um, you're welcome."

He held his arms by his sides, oven mitts on both hands.

"I just can't have everything falling apart at the same time," I said.

He patted my shoulder, the mitt thumping against me. "I know, sugar. I know."

∾

AT TEN O'CLOCK, Jack still wasn't home. Andre assured me

everything was fine, that sometimes being late just meant the next guy hadn't shown up for his shift on time.

"Go on to bed," he told me. "I'll stay until he gets home."

Still worried, I climbed into Jack's bed. I lay in the dark for a long time, thinking about what Duchess had said and the way Miranda had glared at me. I hoped Andre was right, that she would find someone else to get hung up on and forget about Jack, but it was hard to push aside the thought of her doing something else—something worse—in the meantime. Jack seemed to think he could keep me safe by having Andre around, but they couldn't always be with me. I hated the fact that I fell asleep each night wondering what Miranda was planning and what Remy was planning. It made me furious that they had squeezed themselves into my life, and it seemed the only way I could escape them was to leave Bayou Sabine.

And Jack.

IT WAS late in the night when Jack came home. I woke when he bumped into the nightstand while stripping out of his clothes.

"Sorry," he said, nuzzling my ear. "I was trying not to wake you."

I kissed him, and he pulled me against his chest, winding his arms around me.

"How was it?" I asked, barely awake.

"Quiet," he said. "No calls."

"Is that unusual?"

"It didn't used to be."

I slid my arm around his waist, and he sighed.

"I could get used to coming home to this," he said. He slid his fingers along my hip as he spoke. "I've never met anybody like you, Enza Parker, and here you are, in my bed. How'd I get so lucky?"

"That's a good question."

"Smart ass," he said, swatting my behind. "With a lovely ass." He pulled me closer and kissed me as I laughed.

"Is this your way of saying you missed me?" I asked.

"A little bit." When he kissed my neck and slid his teeth along my shoulder, I felt an urgency in him that I hadn't felt before. Yet he was holding something back.

As I gripped him tighter, I tugged at his hair, trying to coax the rougher side of him out. He groaned and rolled on top of me so fast it startled me. The force of his body pinning me down made me wild, and as he moved his hips against mine, I knew he wouldn't stop until I was completely unraveled. He knew exactly how to touch me, exactly where to place his hands, his lips, his tongue.

I wound my legs around him, feeling the hardness of him pressing against my hip, aching to feel more of him.

"I think this means you missed me too," he said, his lips moving against my ear.

"You have no idea." I dragged my fingers down his back. He squeezed my shoulders as he kissed me, hard, and I cried out as his cheek slid down my neck to my breasts.

I loved the roughness of his chin, the hard edges of his teeth, and I gripped him tighter as my own touch became rougher. The friction of his body moving against mine made me dizzy. In one swift move, he rolled onto his back, pulling me on top of him so my knees were on either side of his chest. The way he moved so fast and with such force only made my heart pound louder in my chest.

I'd never been with a man as passionate as Jack, a man who seemed intent on making me feel so much pleasure. He took control of me in the best way, guiding my hands over his body, pressing them into his skin as if hoping to leave traces he'd see the next day. I squeezed his hips, and his eyes darkened in the most delicious way. I leaned in to kiss his chest, moving down as slowly as he had with me, but as I reached his hips, he rolled me onto my back again and held me fast in his grip. My breath quickened. I wanted him to take me roughly, to make me feel his strength, and when I stared at him, I knew he could see it in my eyes.

He moved his fingers in small strokes, teasing me with kisses that stole my breath. I thought my lips would surely bruise, but I needed to feel this desire that seemed to grow within him with each passing moment. A groan came from deep within my throat, and I wound my fingers in his hair, surprised by the thoughts that crept into my mind. I wanted him to take me every way he could, over and over, until I was too tired to breathe. When I could stand his teasing no more, I tightened my legs around him and said, "Jack, I can't wait another second."

"Oh, yes you can," he said, half-smiling.

"You're making me crazy."

"That's the idea."

I dug my fingers into his shoulders as I pressed my mouth against his neck to muffle my cries. When I looked back at him, he smiled in that devilish way of his that said he knew exactly what he was doing and had no intention of stopping. Turning his attention back to my breasts, his chin barely touched my skin as he traced small circles with his tongue.

"You taste so sweet," he said.

I leaned back into the pillows, closing my eyes. The room was spinning like I was drunk. Jack's breaths came hard and fast; when he pressed himself against me, I could feel the thumping of his heart against my chest. My skin tingled where it touched his, like static electricity, and still I wanted more.

"You drive me wild looking at me like that," he said.

I grabbed his hair and pulled his face close to mine. I felt like some other, freer version of myself. "Come here, you're too far away."

"Yes, ma'am," he said. His smile said he was about to give me everything I wanted and more, and as he moved inside me, I cried out, unable to control myself.

"Enza," he said, his voice going hoarse. "Do you have any idea what you do to me?"

"An inkling," I said, my breath catching in my throat.

He laughed, his teeth pinching my neck as he kissed me. He lifted my hips, taking me by surprise so that I cried out again, helpless under his spell.

"Do you like it this way," he whispered, moving hard and fast, and my voice cracked when I spoke.

"Don't stop," I breathed. "Don't ever stop."

Digging my fingers into his back, I whispered things I never thought I'd say aloud, and his movements became bolder, a staccato rhythm. He could sense exactly what I wanted, and as my voice deepened, so did his thrusts.

"I knew you were a rough and tumble gal, chère," he said, nearly out of breath.

I locked my knees around his hips, drawing him in farther, until he cried out himself, as if touched by a firebrand.

"Enza," he said, calling my name again and again. No one had ever called my name like that, but then Jack wasn't like other men I'd known.

His hands roamed over my skin, and as he watched me respond to his own pulsing rhythm, he moved harder, faster, until we were as close as two lovers could be. When he kissed me again, he shifted his weight in a slow, deliberate move that sent us both reeling.

"Jack," I said at last, my heart pounding. My body seemed to move all on its own, as unpredictable as jazz. When his own movements slowed, he slid over to lie next to me. His breath tickled my ear as he nuzzled my shoulder, sliding his fingers along my skin, as if drawing a map that would lead him back to this moment that he would dare me to forget.

I reached over and ran my fingers through his hair. It was so tangled and wild I couldn't help myself. My eyes were heavy, but I wanted to sear that image of him into my memory.

After a while, he said, "You'll put me to sleep doing that."

"You must be exhausted."

He tightened his arm around me and whispered, "In the best way."

"That was a little inconsiderate, mauling you right as you came through the door."

He mumbled, half-asleep, "Yes, that was terrible of you. Please don't ever do that again. Especially in a few days when I come home from my next shift."

I slid my hand along his chest, and he turned, locking his arms around me. He kissed my cheek, his eyes closed, and muttered, "I don't want you to go, chère."

"Why, because your life will go back to normal?"

He mumbled something I couldn't quite make out.

"What?" I whispered, nearly asleep.

"Because I love you," he said.

"You what?" I said, thinking I'd surely misheard him, but he was quiet.

"Jack?" I whispered.

He snored softly, and I lay my head against his shoulder.

I love you too, I wanted to say, but even though I knew he couldn't hear me, the words wouldn't come out.

Chapter Twenty-Three

WHEN I OPENED my eyes in the morning, I was alone. I lay in bed for a while, thinking Jack might come back. It was already bright out. It baffled me that he could get up early after working so late, but he always woke around the same time, regardless of what he did the day before. I admired that kind of resolve. When it became evident he wasn't coming back, I went to look for him.

The kitchen was empty, but the French press was half full. I poured myself a cup of warm coffee and walked through the house, but there was no sign of Jack. It was already hot, the air heavy with humidity. And it was just past ten. I dreaded the thought of working on the house in the heat. Even though I wasn't defending my timeline to my father any more, I still wanted to finish as soon as possible. I opened the door and cringed, feeling the wall of heat that was late June in Louisiana.

When I stepped onto the porch, I saw the dog bound across the lawn, a little brown blur in a field of green. A whistle cut the air, and I followed the sound. Jack was down near the water, Bella rushing toward him with a stick in her mouth. She dropped it at his feet, and he tossed it into the yard again in a graceful arc.

The dog thundered through the grass, the tall weeds rippling in her wake. Jack waved at me as he tossed the stick again and grinned in the way that made my toes curl. Even from a distance, he could set my mind reeling with all sorts of naughty ideas.

When the dog didn't come back, he whistled again, calling her name. She was down by the water, nose to the ground, ignoring him completely. He finally walked toward her, still whistling and clapping his hands. He leaned over and tried to wrestle something away from her, and I shivered, thinking it was no doubt some disgusting dead thing.

Fantasy ruined.

After a tug-of-war style scuffle, Bella won out, and Jack fell backwards into the grass. He stood, and the dog took off again like a bolt of lightning. I laughed, taking great delight in watching him saunter toward the house.

He smiled as he reached the porch. "Taking it easy, are we?" he said.

"Just admiring the view."

"Hmm." He kissed me, catching my lip.

"Keep that up, and I'll want to go right back to bed."

"That could be arranged." He sat in the porch swing and pulled me down with him. "I think I fell asleep on you last night."

The egrets had taken their usual places in the cypress trees, calling to each other across the water. They made it seem like life was so easy around here—it almost made me forget about things like arson.

"You did. Mid-sentence. But I forgive you."

"I'm sure I can think of a suitable way to make it up to you."

I grinned, ruffling his hair. "I don't doubt that."

Part of me wanted to laze the morning away, but I knew I should get to work on my outside tasks. With two weeks left, I couldn't afford to slow down.

"Hey," I said, "when do you think Buck might be able to start on the living room?"

Jack looked surprised. "I don't know. Next week, maybe?"

"Any chance he could start sooner? I was hoping I might still get the house on the market right by the middle of July."

"Oh," he said. "That fast?"

"It'll probably take him a week to ten days for the repairs. Then I'll need a few days to paint and spiffy up. I might still make my deadline."

"I thought you weren't worried about that any more."

"Well, I've still got to sell the house as soon as possible. I want to be done with my father, and that can't happen until I've paid him back the money he used for all this."

"Oh." He stood then, walking to the other side of the porch.

"Could you ask him?"

"Yeah," he said, the word clipped. "Fine." He slid his fingers along the banister rail, staring off into the yard.

"What's the matter?" I asked.

"Nothing." He turned and whistled for the dog.

"Clearly it's something. Just tell me. Do you think Buck won't want to do it? Should I not ask him?"

"No, Enza. He'll do it."

I waited for him to go on, but he didn't. He went inside and let the screen door slam behind him.

I FOUND him leaning against the counter in the kitchen, drinking a cup of coffee. He didn't look up.

"Jack," I said. "Talk to me."

He shrugged. "I just thought you were going to slow down. Take your time finishing now."

"The sooner I finish, the sooner I can pay my father back. And then I can move on."

He turned to me, his eyes sad. "Move on where?"

"I don't know. But I can't do anything until I'm square with him. He won't wait long for me to pay him back. He'd take me to court just to make a damn point."

"I don't want you to hurry up and finish. I've been trying to stop counting days, to stop picturing you driving out of here. I feel terrible about it, but I'm not entirely unhappy when something else goes wrong in this place so you have to stay a while longer."

"I'm sorry."

"I hate the idea of you leaving."

I walked over to him and placed my hand on his arm. "I know. But I have to finish. I owe him a lot of money. More than I have."

He sighed, sliding his hand around my waist. "But I'm crazy about you, chère. I want you to stay."

"I know you do."

"You can't tell me you don't feel something here."

I bit my lip. "That doesn't change anything."

"Of course it does. Stay with me."

"I can't, Jack. And the more you ask me, the harder it's going to be."

He looked at me like I'd slapped him. It sounded easy, the way he said it. *Stay*. As if I could forget about my house in North Carolina, forget about my debts, forget about my father. I thought I loved Jack, but what if this was just something that felt like love? What if I left everything behind, stayed here, and it turned out to be a disaster? People didn't relocate after month-long flings. Did they?

"I'm sorry," I said again, sliding my fingers along his cheek.

He turned his head and said, "So much for simple and uncomplicated, I guess."

"We both knew this wasn't simple. But I still don't regret it."

He scoffed, brushing past me as he walked outside onto the porch and into the yard.

I felt like the wind had been knocked out of me. I'd never met a guy like Jack, never felt this way about anyone before. It was easy when I kept relationships casual. If I didn't let men get too close, then it didn't hurt so bad when they left. And they always left. Sometimes I wanted them to. But with Jack, it had been easy to let him in close, and being close meant I let myself feel things for him I had never felt before. But being close meant being vulnerable. As long as I thought of us as casual, then I'd be able to walk away when I was finished.

But it was getting harder to convince myself that was true. Unlike the men before him, I didn't want to fix him and send him on his way.

FOR THE REST of the day, I tried to keep myself busy so I thought less about this battle between my brain and my heart. There was no longer any need to leave the living room in its decrepit state, so I started filling trash bags with anything that was damaged beyond repair: remains of the curtains, lamps with stained glass shades, books with blackened pages. We'd had the sofa, chairs and coffee table hauled away to the dump after the fire, but we'd left everything else in place. Some of Vergie's things had been on the bookshelves in this room, but most of their contents had been Jack's. I put anything that looked like it was his in a cardboard box and set it aside.

Jack came back inside just long enough to get a bucket of paint from the sitting room and to change his shirt. It was scorching outside, but he'd said he wanted to replace a few of the bad shingles on the front of the house. Probably because it meant he could put a few walls between us and not have to talk to me. I knew I'd hurt his feelings earlier, but I didn't know what to say to him now. So I focused on cleaning out the burned room and let him concentrate on the outside of the house. The wood shingles were pale blue, shaped like the scales of a fish. It was a pain to replace them, but Jack had removed one himself to use as a pattern. He'd cut them out with a jigsaw, getting the curve just right, and painted them to match the house. When I'd peeked out the window earlier, he'd been sanding them a little, so they wouldn't look brand new next to the old ones.

Jack went back outside without saying a word.

I hesitated, then poured a glass of water and joined him. Jack stood on a step ladder, nailing the shingles back into place. He pulled one from the pouch tied around his waist, took a nail that he held in his teeth, and hammered it into place with three solid hits.

"Hey," I said. "Looking good."

He'd replaced a dozen or more already, in two separate areas by the windows. He pulled another nail from his teeth and drove it in with three strokes, heavier this time.

"I thought you might be thirsty," I continued.

He glanced at me, pulling another shingle from the pouch. "Thanks. Just leave it by the sawhorse."

"I wish you'd talk to me. Let me explain something."

Another shingle. Another nail. Three hits with the hammer.

"Can you come down for a minute?" I asked.

"I think you made yourself clear already."

"It's complicated," I said. "I could explain it better."

"I'm a little busy right now," he said, driving another nail in.

I waited a short while, but when he placed another shingle and plucked another nail from his apron, I gave up. "OK, I'll be inside."

VERGIE'S ROOM was the only one left to paint. I was saving it for last. I opened the trunk at the foot of the bed and took out the hat box Jack had given me. I'd left all of the letters and journals inside like he found it. I'd only peeked at a couple of the letters from my mother, addressed to Vergie.

They felt heavy in my hands. I might never learn everything I wanted to know about my mother. Maybe it was better that way. I didn't need to know everything, but I needed to know *something* about why she had left me. At last I untied the ribbon holding the letters I'd been too afraid to read a few days before. Each envelope had the same oddly slanted handwriting, and most were dated the year my mother left us. I shuffled them into order and pulled the top letter from the stack. My pulse quickened as I opened it.

There were fourteen letters in all. I read them in order but still only had a glimpse of whatever had driven my mother away. She talked a lot about me, which was surprising. She told Vergie about the games we played, about how she was teaching me to cook, how she'd tried to sew a patchwork quilt for me and failed. She'd been so frustrated over not finishing that she made it into a pillow just so she had something to show for her efforts. She mentioned a vacation we took to the beach, playing in the ocean. She talked about being homesick for Louisiana. The only thing she mentioned about my father was that they "continued to grow apart." I read the letters twice, trying to decipher something that lay between the lines, something that might indicate an affair, or fighting, or some other event that would have made her want to leave. But there was no mention of any single incident. She often talked of feeling trapped, like she was in a life she was not meant to live, but she didn't elaborate. I could tell she was unhappy, even as she wrote about the daughter she loved. She often asked Vergie, *What should I do?* And I imagined her alone, frustrated and scared—pretending to be happy in a life she didn't like.

In the last letter, she said she'd come to a decision and knew what she had to do to live the life she wanted. She wrote that she would see Vergie soon and that she looked forward to coming back.

Had she come here all those years ago? Had she come back to live with Vergie in this very house? Tears welled in my eyes as I thought of my mother, here, in this room and in all the others, feeling the same way I felt about this house, this land. Feeling like it was a sanctuary, the place that would let her be the person she so longed to be.

Why hadn't she brought me with her?

I loved my father, despite his flaws, and I couldn't imagine how different my life would have been without him. But I also couldn't imagine why my mother chose to leave me behind. With her gone, and now Vergie gone, I might never know.

And now, as much as I hated her for leaving, I was doing the same thing. Why was it that when things got complicated with Jack, my first instinct was to walk away?

I hated that we had that in common.

I pushed the photographs aside and pulled the small brown journal from the bottom of the box. The ink had bled and faded on some of the pages, but the handwriting was still legible in most places. Vergie's diary. The first entry was dated twenty-three years before. When I flipped to the last page, I saw that it spanned three years. Vergie clearly wasn't a daily writer but perhaps one who recorded the most important events in her life. This would have been before my mother left me, but I wondered if there still might be some insight in these pages.

I'd made it through a half a dozen entries when there was a light knock on the door.

From the doorway, Jack said, "I just got called in. I may not be back until late."

"Oh," I said, looking at the clock. It was after eight.

"I tried to call Andre, but I can't get him on his cell." His voice was still cool. "If you want I could call Buck to come over, or you could go over to their place. They'd be happy to have you."

"It's OK," I said, waving him off. "I'll be fine."

He sighed. "I'd feel better if you weren't alone."

"Don't worry about me," I said.

He shook his head, placing his hands on his hips. "I'll worry about you all night." His eyes were sad and dark. Because of me.

"OK," I said, giving in. "I'll go over to their house."

"Now?"

"Yes. I'll just get a few things together and head over there. I won't be far behind you."

"OK," he said, running his hand through his hair. He turned to leave.

"Jack, wait."

He paused. "What?"

"I was hoping we could talk later. About this morning."

He slid his hand along the doorframe, avoiding my gaze.

"Please. There are some things I need to tell you."

He nodded. "OK. In the morning. You should plan to spend the night at Buck's. If I finish in time, I'll join you over there."

"Break a leg."

He walked quickly down the hall, his footsteps heavy on the stairs, and out on the porch. And then he was gone.

I turned back to the journal, just to read a few more entries before I left. Reading Vergie's words, I saw a whole new part of her that had never existed for me before. It made me wonder if there were other journals in the house, packed up in closets, stashed in trunks, hidden on the bookshelves between her paperback westerns. And what about my mother? What if she'd kept journals here and I hadn't found them yet? There were so many secrets here, I wondered if I could ever stay long enough to untangle them all.

The next time I looked at the clock, it was nearly ten.

"Shit," I said. I hated to call Buck and Josie that late. Jack would be furious at me if I didn't go over there. Downstairs, I found my phone lying on the kitchen table, the ringer turned off. There was a voicemail from an hour ago, plus two other missed calls.

I pressed the play button. It was Josie.

Hey, sweetie, she said. *Jack called and said you needed to come stay with us while he went to work. I just thought you'd be here by now, so I wanted to make sure everything's OK. Call me when you can. We'll be up.*

She'd be worried about me by now. Bella whined, scratching at the door.

I called Josie back, and she answered on the second ring.

"I'm so sorry," I told her. "I was doing some cleaning and lost track of time. Is it all right to come now?"

The dog barked, pacing.

"Of course," she said. "We'll see you in a few minutes."

Bella barked again, and I opened the door. She bolted across the yard.

"Thanks, Josie." I shut the door and flipped the bolt.

I left the phone on the table, and fished my keys and wallet out of my messenger bag. Then I hurried upstairs and threw my toothbrush and a change of clothes into my duffle bag. I took the other journal from the hat box, skimmed a few pages, and put it in with my clothes. Now that I'd started reading, I couldn't stop. I took a quick look in Vergie's closet and the back sitting room to see if any stray journals were lying around. I hadn't checked the bookcases yet, but I'd go over every square foot of that house to be sure my mother hadn't left a notebook somewhere. I made a mental note to comb through the books when I got back. Something told me I'd find more of Vergie's journals sandwiched between her novels.

Glancing at the clock on the dresser, I cursed under my breath. I had to get over to Josie's—it had been twenty minutes already. An idea popped into my head, and I checked the trunk in the upstairs room Jack had left as a study. But I didn't find anything more. Defeated, I grabbed my bag and went downstairs.

I stopped on the bottom step. The smell of cigarette smoke hung in the air.

In the time it took for the smell to register, I saw the figure by the front door and felt a surge of panic.

Remy stepped into the light from the kitchen, plucking a cigarette from his lips.

"Going somewhere, darlin'?"

Chapter Twenty-Four

I FROZE, my heart hammering in my chest.

Remy Broussard stubbed his cigarette out against the kitchen doorframe, blowing a stream of smoke in the air between us.

"How did you get in here?" I asked, dropping the duffle.

A sly grin touched the corners of his mouth. "Back door was open," he said. "I called, but there was no answer. I was concerned for your safety, so I let myself in."

The kitchen door was most certainly locked. But it had glass panes.

"What do you want?" I said, trying to keep my voice calm.

"I just figured it was time we talked. About these little outbursts you seem to have, and this propensity of yours to slander me in public places, in front of civil servants." He cocked his head. "It's really a nasty habit."

He was blocking the front door. I glanced toward the kitchen, thinking of knives and frying pans, but I was too far away. He would easily cut me off.

I couldn't outrun him. He was twice my size. I needed another tactic.

"I'm sorry," I said. "I shouldn't have said those things. I was just upset." I leaned against the newel post at the stairs. "I'm sure you understand."

He took a step toward me. "Ah, so this is just a misunderstanding."

I tried to sound pleasant, to smile, even. "I didn't mean any of those things. I'm sorry."

"You said that already." He stared at me, his eyes dark. "What's the matter, darlin'? You're shaking like a kitten."

"I feel bad about all of this," I said, swallowing hard. "And you're right. I shouldn't have said anything that night with the sheriff. I'll talk to him. He thought I was crazy anyway." I laughed a little, like I might shrug it off.

His eyes narrowed, and I felt the hair on my neck rise.

"Let me make it up to you," I said. "Can I fix you a drink?" I nodded toward the kitchen.

"Fair enough," he said.

I eased past him, and he followed me into the kitchen, eyeing me closely as I pulled two glasses from the cabinet and poured the bourbon. There was a knife block at the end of the counter, just out of reach. He could easily overpower me if I made any sudden moves, and I shuddered thinking of what he'd do to me.

I handed him the glass, willing my hand to stay steady. His fingers brushed over mine. Behind him, I saw the broken pane of glass in the door but quickly looked back to him.

"How about we start over?" I suggested, holding my glass to his. "I gave you a second chance, right? Now I'm asking you to forgive my bad manners."

He raised one eyebrow, as if that was a fair statement. As I took a sip of my drink, he knocked his back with a flick of the glass. His eyes rested heavy on mine.

"I've been thinking about you," I said, stepping closer to him. "Ever since that night at the bar."

"Is that right," he said. It didn't sound like a question.

I took another sip of bourbon and lay my hand on his chest.

His eyes rested on my hand.

"We could have fun together, you and me," I said, sliding my finger along the buttons of his shirt. As long as my hand was moving, it wasn't trembling.

"Oh, I don't doubt that," he said.

"How about you let me make this up to you?"

He grabbed my hand, squeezing it hard. "You're a terrible liar, darlin'." His face hardened as he leaned closer to me. His other hand came around me quickly, grabbing a fistful of my hair. I yelped as my glass hit the floor and shattered.

"Come with me," he said, his lips brushing my ear. He twisted my hand behind my back and shoved me against the wall. His body pressed hard against my back, holding me in place.

"I thought you wanted to talk," I said. With my cheek pressed against the wall, I could just see him out of the corner of my eye.

He laughed. "You are a firecracker all right," he said, pushing my wrist into the small of my back. My shoulder throbbed as he leaned against me, his breath hot near my ear. "You mostly just need to listen," he said.

I closed my eyes, cursing myself for not leaving sooner, like Jack had wanted me to.

"Jack will be home any second. He'll murder you for this."

He laughed. "Your boyfriend's stuck in a fire. A big one that he likely won't make it out of. Some warehouse that went up like a tinderbox." I could smell the bourbon on his breath. "It's tragic really, the way he left here to fight a fire, only to leave you to die in one."

My heart pounded. I squirmed under his grip.

"This old place will go up in no time too," he said. "You just got lucky before."

"There's no need to do this. I'm leaving town. You'll never see me again."

"It's a little late for bargaining, don't you think?" He grabbed my free hand and pulled it behind me. "Now hold still, or I'll make this hurt a lot more than it has to." With both of my wrists in one of his hands, he fumbled in his pocket for something. His weight shifted, and I slammed my head backwards as hard as I could.

There was a loud crack and a bolt of pain in the back of my skull, but his grip loosened long enough for me to whirl myself around and punch. My fist landed at his throat, and he gagged. He reached for me, stumbling, but I yanked my arm free from his grasp. I fell against the table and then felt his hands on my back. My hammer was by the corner of the table, half buried by the newspaper.

He grabbed a fistful of my hair and pulled my head back as I fumbled for the hammer. When my hand found the handle, he spun me around to face him, and I swung.

He jerked his head back, missing most of the blow, but the hammer caught him on the jaw. He lunged at me then, his eyes dark with fury. One hand locked around my wrist as he slammed me back against the wall. I saw tiny pinpricks of light as my head hit the wood. Still clenching the hammer, I willed my arm to swing, but his grip was too strong. He shoved my wrist into the wall, and the hammer clattered to the floor. Pain shot through my arm, making my eyes water.

"You're going to be sorry you did that," he said, his voice still eerily calm. He locked his other hand around my throat, and I gasped as his fingers squeezed. He leaned so close I could feel his breath in my face. I gripped his forearms and tried to scratch. I kicked him, but he didn't even flinch.

He only sneered as he squeezed tighter. I coughed, gasping for air, but feeling none. All I could think was, *I've been so stupid.*

When the room started to go dark, he turned my body again and shoved me against the wall, holding my wrists behind me. I heard the rustling of fabric, felt him fumbling with something against my hands, and then my wrists stung as they were cinched together.

His hand returned to my neck, moving my hair away from my face. I struggled to free my hands, but whatever he used was holding them fast. The more I struggled, the more they hurt.

Remy pushed his forearm into my back, still gripping my neck, and spoke close to my ear. "I'm going to sit you down now and get something from the hall." He held a hunting knife by my cheek and said, "Are you going to give me any more trouble?"

I swallowed hard, feeling my heart pounding as he leaned farther into me. "No," I said, my voice shaking.

"Good." He shoved me down into the chair at the table.

I tried to pry my wrists apart as he stepped into the hallway. He must have used a zip-tie, because it wouldn't budge. I stopped when he came back into the kitchen and a shiver went through me.

He held an old red gas can by his hip, the hunting knife in his other hand.

I looked around the room, but there was nothing to help me. "Please, don't do this."

He unscrewed the cap on the gas can and slung it to his side as he walked toward me.

"They'll know it's you," I said. "You can't get away."

He chuckled as my eyes began to water. The smell of the gasoline filled the air between us, making me gag. "It's easy to disappear," he said.

"Why are you doing this?" I asked.

He stared at me, tossing the gas can into the corner. A stream of liquid puddled under it on the floor.

"Your brother," I said.

He jerked his head toward me, pointing the knife. "Don't," he said.

"I know you blame Jack. He told me what happened."

He had me out of the chair and against the wall in an instant. His hand was around my throat, his body pressing hard against me.

I gasped, trying to catch my breath, but he only squeezed tighter, his thumbs biting my skin.

"You don't know shit," he said, his face inches from mine.

My vision narrowed as darkness seeped in from the sides of

the room. The edges of his face blurred. I tried to twist my body away, but his grip was too tight. His eyes burned into mine. My chest throbbed.

There was a crash, and Remy's hand went limp. I slid down the wall, falling into a heap on the floor. I coughed, gasping for air that wouldn't come. The floorboards were cool against my face, the sting of gasoline sharp. There was a scuffle, a banging sound, and when I looked up, I saw Jack slamming Remy's head against the counter by the sink. Remy's hands flailed behind him, but Jack shoved his face into the porcelain once more.

Remy's body went limp, and Jack pushed him to the floor.

His face lay a few feet from mine, his eyes closed.

The room started to go dark again, and then Jack was on his knees by my side, helping me to sit up. "Enza, can you hear me? Are you OK?" He was still wearing his turnouts, covered in soot and ash. His white shirt was streaked with blood.

I nodded, still coughing. My throat felt swollen shut.

He looked me over. "Are you hurt anywhere else?" His hands drifted over my body as he checked for wounds.

I shook my head, still unable to speak.

He held my face in his hands and kissed me on the forehead. He smelled like a campfire. "I thought I was too late," he whispered. "Just sit tight." He held me against his chest, wrapping his arms around me, and right then, those arms felt like the only things holding me together. I shivered as he dug his cell phone out of his pocket and dialed. He gave the police the address, said he'd wounded an intruder and then hung up.

I looked over his shoulder at Remy, still lying motionless in the corner. I wound my arms around Jack's waist and leaned my head against his neck.

POLICE SIRENS PIERCED the air outside. The sound of boots echoed in the hallway, and Jack yelled, "In here!"

Andre and his partner slipped into the kitchen, pistols raised. Footsteps moved quickly through the rest of the house.

"It's just him," Jack said to Andre, nodding toward Remy, who still lay unmoving in the corner.

Jack stood, helping me to my feet. Andre walked over to Remy and kicked his foot until he grumbled.

"Wake up, Broussard," Andre said, his voice as calm as ever. "It's time to take you to your new home."

Remy grunted, struggling to get up. He had an ugly bruise forming around one eye. The other was swollen shut. Blood trickled down his cheek into the collar of his shirt. I started trembling again as he came to.

"Might as well stay down there," Andre told him. "Just turn over on your belly."

Remy glared at me with a fury that made me want to beat him back into the floor. I took a step toward him, but Jack swept his arm around me and steered me to the back of the house.

"Hey," I said. "Let me go."

Andre cuffed Remy's hands behind his back, then pulled him up from the floor.

"Shhh," Jack said, leading me to his bedroom. "You've seen enough of him tonight, don't you think?"

"He attacked me!" I yelled, but the words sounded like a whisper.

He placed his hands on my shoulders and held me in place. "I know, chère. And I very nearly killed him for it." His eyes were wide. "Let Andre take it from here."

I slumped down on the bed, shaking with rage. Jack sat next to me and put one arm around my shoulders, drawing me into him.

"I was so stupid," I said. "I should have gone straight over to Josie's, and this wouldn't have happened."

He sighed, stroking my hair. "This is not your fault."

Maybe, I thought, but I'd certainly given him the perfect opportunity. I heard scuffling outside the room and caught sight of Andre shoving Remy down the hall and out the front door.

"How did you know to come home?" I asked.

"Josie called and said you hadn't made it over yet. She couldn't get you on the phone and got worried."

"Remy said there was a big fire in a warehouse, that you were in it."

"Yeah, it was a bad one, but we were OK. When I got out, I got Josie's message. So I came over."

I felt another wave of nausea. If it wasn't for Josie, I would have been the one bleeding on the floor.

"He set that fire," I told Jack. "He admitted it. And the one here too."

"Don't worry," he said, squeezing my shoulder. "He's going away for a long time."

Andre knocked on the doorframe. "Enza, I know this is a terrible night, but I need to ask you a few questions."

"It's fine," I said, brushing tears from my eyes. I sat up straighter, and Jack took my hand in his, sliding his thumb along my palm.

"The paramedics will be here soon, but before they get here, can you tell me exactly what happened?"

He wrote down everything in a small notebook, nodding each time I answered one of his questions. Jack's arm tensed around me as I described the broken door pane, the way I tried to talk to him, the way he shoved me against the wall.

Jack brought my hand to his lips, kissing my knuckles.

I squeezed his hand as Andre stepped aside to let the paramedics in.

"Thanks, Enza," Andre said. "I'll get the rest from you later."

WE SPENT the night at Buck and Josie's even though it meant waking them around midnight. Jack called to let them know what had happened, and Josie insisted.

Josie gave me a big hug when we got to the door. "Honey, I

know you just want to go straight to bed, so we've got your room all set. You sleep tight, and we'll see you at the breakfast table."

"Thank you," I said. "I can't say that enough times. You saved my life tonight."

"Oh, honey," she said, grabbing my hands in hers. "We're just so glad you're all right."

"It's a good thing they arrested that jackass," Buck said, his arms crossed over his chest. "Because I'd like nothing more than to go over there and break him in two."

Jack nodded, his face darkening. "Andre will take care of him."

"Not the way I would," Buck said.

Jack slipped his hand to the small of my back and led me toward the stairs. "Good night," he said to them. "We'll see you in the morning."

Upstairs, Josie had just made up one room—the larger one I'd stayed in before. She'd turned down the sheets and left a lamp on.

"Guess she's onto us," Jack said.

I smiled weakly as he walked across the hall and flipped on the light in the other bedroom.

"Hey," I said, following him to the hall. "What are you doing?"

"I'll sleep in here."

"Don't," I said, taking his hand. "Stay with me." I led him back into the room and shut the door.

"I figured you'd want some space after this morning," he said. "After everything."

I slid my jeans off and climbed into bed. He stared at me for a long moment, then unbuttoned his shirt and stripped out of his jeans. He eased into bed next to me and turned to face me.

"I was scared to death tonight," he said, holding my hand in his.

"Me too. I thought that was the end."

"I could have killed the guy, Enza. For a minute I thought I had."

"I know."

"The thought that he'd hurt you—"

"I know." I wrapped my arms around him and pulled myself tight against his chest.

His body heaved with a deep sigh. "I love you," he said. "I know you think it's too fast and too soon and too everything, but—"

"I'm staying," I said, cutting him off.

"What?" he said, shifting so he could look me in the eye.

"I'm keeping Vergie's house. I don't want to leave, either."

His brow wrinkled. "Just like that?"

"I love you too."

He smiled, kissing me lightly on the lips, just as he had that first time when we were all tangled up in the living room.

"I tried to tell you earlier today," I said. "But you were too busy freezing me out."

"I'm sorry, darlin'. It's only because you'd broken my heart."

"Well, then."

"It's OK," he said. "It's healing up nicely."

I kissed him on the neck, and he sighed, folding me in his arms.

After a while he said, "Not that I'm not delighted to hear your revelation, but what about your father and the business?"

"I'll find a way to work it out. I could sell my house in North Carolina and pay him back. I could go out on my own and flip houses down here."

"Sounds like you've been doing some serious thinking."

"I had a lot of time to mull things over while you were giving me the cold shoulder."

He slid his finger along my ribs, tickling me as he held me tight against him. "At least it made you come to your senses."

I laughed, wriggling against him until he stopped and let me go. I loved that he could still make me laugh, even on a day like today.

He looked at me, his eyes wide in the dim light.

"What?" I said.

"I absolutely love making you laugh in bed."

He slid his fingers in my hair and kissed me, pinching my lips with his teeth so that my whole body tingled.

"I love that you can," I said.

Then he looked me in the eye. "There's one more very important question I have to ask you," he said.

"What's that?"

He raised one eyebrow and said, "Are you still kicking me out of my house?"

"Are you kidding? What landlady kicks out a perfectly good handyman *and* cook?"

He grinned, kissing my neck, scratching me with his beard until I laughed and squirmed in his grip, though being out of his reach was the last thing I wanted.

"I'll happily fix anything for you, chère. Leaky pipes, missing tiles, jambalaya, you name it."

"Can I get that in writing?"

"Absolutely."

He stilled, tightening his arms around me, and lay his head against my neck. I felt myself finally relax as he kissed my shoulder and whispered, "I'm glad you're staying. I don't think I could stand to watch you leave."

I laced my fingers in his as I closed my eyes, listening to him whisper in the dark. My life was about to get a lot more complicated, but this thing with Jack was starting to feel simple after all.

I wanted to be with him. All the time. It didn't get much simpler than that.

Chapter Twenty-Five

FOUR WEEKS LATER, I had a new living room. Buck had put up drywall, built a jig to cut crown molding to match what was original to the house, and installed a new set of built-in bookcases to replace the ones damaged by the fire. He and Josie had insisted on helping me with all of it, from installing the new heart pine flooring to painting the walls and ceiling. They'd been over almost every day for two weeks, even making final repairs after I'd had the new sofa and chairs delivered.

Today, they'd called to say they had one more quick addition to make to the room. I put some coffee on, and not long after, Bella started barking and ran to the front door.

She wagged her stumpy tail at me when I got there. She liked me now that I wasn't leaving her herd.

Josie was standing on the porch with a vase of lilies and a bottle of bourbon.

"Hi, hon. We brought you a little housewarming present."

"Well, thank you," I said, taking both from her hands.

She smiled and said, "Your real present's in the truck. Wait right there."

I put the flowers and the bourbon in the kitchen, and when I went back to the porch, Buck and Josie were carrying a coffee table up the walk. I grabbed the middle as they barreled through the door and into the living room. We set it down in front of the couch and stepped back.

"This is lovely," I said.

"Buck wanted to make you something special," Josie said. "And he knew you had a particular style in mind."

"You made this?" The table reminded me of the Mission style: sleek and elegant, but rustic. The top was made of slender boards held together with butterfly joints. The boards had been stained, but still had slight variation in the color and a smattering of scars. I ran my fingers over the surface. "This is beautiful. Thank you."

"Tell her the rest," Josie said, nudging him in the ribs.

"I used some of the original floorboards from this room," he said. "The ones that weren't damaged too bad. I hope that's OK. I know you like to salvage too."

"Oh, wow," I said.

Buck smiled, resting his hands on his hips.

I startled him with a big hug, and he chuckled.

"I think she likes it," Josie said.

"I love it," I said, hugging her too.

"We're so glad you're staying," Josie said. "But then, I knew you would." She winked, and Buck shook his head.

"I haven't seen Jack this happy in his entire life," she added.

"That woman thinks she's psychic," Buck said.

She shrugged. "I just see things, dear. Call it what you like."

AFTER THEY LEFT, I went outside to plant the azaleas I'd bought the week before. It was easily a hundred degrees, but I'd started to get used to the heat again. Vergie had always been able to make anything grow; now I hoped to channel a little bit of her—just enough for my azaleas. I was starting small.

I'd made decent progress in my plans to wrap things up in North Carolina and begin a new life in Bayou Sabine. I'd formed a business plan and put my assets in order. I didn't have many, but I had some savings set aside and my house in North Carolina to sell. But before getting started with the business, I wanted to sell my house first and pay my father what I owed him. I wanted to settle as many debts as I could before flipping another house.

My new business seemed like it could have some potential. There were plenty of houses down here that had good character and needed a makeover. Jack was interested in helping with repairs to share profits, and he'd mentioned the idea to Buck too. Together we could knock out quality projects fast, and with Buck's knack for using reclaimed wood, vintage fixtures and other salvaged parts of historic buildings, we could make impressive transformations. I already had my eye on a house on Buck's side of the canal.

I spaced the azaleas out in front of the porch and started to dig. My mother's letters still gnawed at me. I couldn't help but wonder what had happened to her. Was she living near here? Had she moved a thousand miles away to start over? Sometimes I pictured her in California, or Maine, or some nondescript place where she could just disappear. I'd trained myself to think of her that way over the years, but at Vergie's funeral, when I thought I'd seen her, when I'd realized that was a real possibility—I'd thought my chest would collapse. If I asked enough questions around here, I could untangle the truths. Like Jack said, everyone knew everyone's business. Someone would know about Vergie's daughter. Someone would know if she'd come back here, and someone could tell me where she'd gone. If I wanted to look hard enough, I could find her. The question was: How badly did I want to find her?

After an hour of digging holes, my shirt was clinging to my skin. I was streaked in dirt, but I'd planted azaleas all along the front of the porch. Bella, splayed on her side like she was melting, watched me from under one by the corner. I was soaking the soil around them one last time when I heard the truck rumble along the driveway. Jack parked under the big oak tree and ambled across the grass in that slow, easy way of his that always made me feel like I was the only thing in his line of sight. He was still wearing his turnouts—the bottoms, anyway. Under the dark red suspenders he wore a tight white T-shirt that was gray with ash.

He stopped at the porch and smiled his crooked smile. "Hey, you."

"Hey, yourself," I said. "You always wear that when you're off duty?"

"Gets me lots of free drinks," he said, looping his thumbs in the suspenders.

"I'll bet."

"I was in a hurry," he said. "Just got finished with our training session, and the guys were going back to the station to eat. I knew that would take hours, and frankly I couldn't wait that long to see you."

I smiled at that, thinking of tackling him in the grass.

"Doing a bit of gardening, are you?"

"Maybe this bunch will survive," I said. The first shrubs I'd planted had died in a week. Josie had told me they were invincible, but she didn't know my history with flora. I'd crossed my fingers and hoped for good mojo as I'd poured water over these. I'd even opened up the last gris-gris Duchess had given me and mixed it in with the soil. It couldn't hurt, I thought.

His eyes drifted over me, as if he were deciding where he would kiss me first.

"That was a long two days," I said.

"Does that mean you missed me?" He stepped closer, his body a few inches from mine.

I slid my fingers down the length of the suspenders, stopping at his waist.

"Is it bad that I want to tear those pants off you with my teeth?" I asked.

He grinned, sliding his hands beneath my shirt, to the small of my back. "I'm going to hold you to that."

"I have a surprise to show you inside."

"Oh?" He had a devilish glint in his eye.

I backed into the house, inching out of his reach each time he got close. He looked at me quizzically as I dodged his hands.

"You playing hard to get now?" he asked in a throaty voice.

He lunged toward me, and I bolted. He followed me into the living room, and I pointed to the table.

"Surprise!"

"Lovely," he said, reaching for me again.

I laughed, taking his chin in my hand, turning his face toward the table. "Buck made it. From floorboards he saved from this room."

"Beautiful." He turned back to me, tugging at the buttons on my shirt.

"Hey," I said, gently smacking his hands away. "You're getting me all dirty."

"I'll show you dirty, chère." He lunged again, and I yelped, running into the bedroom as he bounded behind me. I stumbled into the room, thinking he was right on my heels, but when I turned, he was gone. I paused, listening for the sound of his boots, expecting him to tackle me on the spot.

Instead, I heard the stereo come on in the adjoining room, the volume rising as a sultry brass band pierced the air. There was the wail of a slide trombone, a slow bass line that I could feel in my chest. I heard a thump, then another, and there he was in the doorway, tossing his boots to the floor. He slipped his suspenders down, his eyes burning into mine as he walked toward me.

He took his shirt off, slung it once around his head and tossed it at me. I chuckled as he hooked his thumbs in the suspenders, swaying to the music and smiling his crooked smile.

I didn't dare move and break the spell.

"I think you missed your calling," I said.

"No, no, darlin'," he said in his husky voice, "I don't do this for just anyone."

He unfastened his pants, and he slid them to the floor,

hopping on one foot and then the other as he struggled to step out of them and still maintain a bit of dignity.

He looked as clumsy as a foal, trying to stay on his feet, but I was completely smitten. He was disarming that way—strong on the outside but not without his adorable moments of awkwardness. I laughed, and he sauntered over to me, stripped down to a pair of boxers with little red crawfish.

"Something funny?" he asked, sliding one finger along my arm.

He slipped his other hand along my ribs, where he knew I was most ticklish, and I squirmed, laughing.

He grinned and swept me onto the bed, kissing my neck, scratching me with his stubbly cheek.

I squirmed underneath him. "Cut it out," I said, laughing and writhing in his grip. "You know that drives me crazy!"

"Mmm-hmm," he said, squeezing me tighter. The more I laughed, the more he tickled me, brushing his lips over my ribs, my hips. He'd memorized my most ticklish bits and zeroed in when he was feeling merciless.

"I love that laugh," he said, his lips moving against my neck. "I want to hear it the rest of my life."

I liked the sound of that. It was a distinct possibility.

He loosened his grip long enough to pull my shirt over my head and toss it to the floor. With one forearm resting by my head, he slid his free hand along my hip.

I wound my fingers in his hair and said, "How did I get lucky enough to find you?"

He kissed me lightly on the lips, his eyes steady on mine. "Vergie's one hell of a matchmaker."

I smiled, thinking she'd managed to look out for me one last time.

"You know, I'm really glad I didn't kick you out of here on that first day," I said.

He snorted. "You couldn't have kicked me out. You were hot for me."

My jaw dropped, and I swatted him with a pillow.

"I thought you were cute too. That wild hair and those beat-up cowboy boots. I dreamed about you for days."

"Jack Mayronne, are you trying to tell me you thought you had me from the start?"

He grinned. "Not even. I just knew I couldn't let you go."

I narrowed my eyes. "You're lucky I didn't send you packing, mister. With that mouth on you."

He grinned as he slid his fingers along my cheek. "Yes, I am, chère. Luckier than I ever dreamed."

He leaned in to kiss me, and I clutched him tight. I was where I was supposed to be, and I was feeling awfully lucky myself.

Next in The Bayou Sabine Series

ENZA'S STORY continues in BAYOU WHISPERS, when someone dear to her is put in danger at a disastrous Christmas gathering. Her relationship with Jack is put to the test as she discovers the truth about her mother's disappearance—will the truth set her free or send her fleeing Bayou Sabine forever?

Chapter One

December had brought a treacherous heat wave to my part of Louisiana, but it didn't stop me from stringing two boxes of Christmas lights across the front porch. Standing on the top rung of the ladder, I reached to the corner of the ceiling and stapled the strand to the beadboard. It had been almost five months since I'd moved all of my belongings here, but I still couldn't break the habit of calling this house Vergie's. She'd left it to me, but this little Victorian would always be my grandmother's.

Lately, though, I'd begun to think of it as the house my mother grew up in. The kitchen she'd had breakfast in, the clawfoot tub she'd used for baths. I was starting to see my mother everywhere in this house, even though I could barely remember her face.

I hadn't thought about her this much in fifteen years, when she first left my father and me. But being back in Bayou Sabine stirred up my fragmented memories, like shards of a broken vase that were being pieced together to form its original shape.

The more I tried to push the thoughts of her away in the daytime, the more they haunted me as I slept. Now I woke in the night, drawing panicked breaths and clutching the sheets in my fists. My nightmares always startled Jack awake as well, but he just wrapped his big arms around me and pulled me against his chest, sliding his fingers up and down my back. The thrumming of his heart against my cheek soothed me back into sleep—but only for a little while.

Sometimes I called her name in my sleep. Not *Mom*, but Martine.

Last night was no different. I'd dreamt I was back at Vergie's funeral, standing in the pouring rain while the church seemed to split open and fill the sky with the sound of hymns being sung. The air around me vibrated with a dirge that started somewhere far off in the distance. In the flashes of lightning I saw a long line of people, walking in pairs, carrying umbrellas the way they did at the funerals in Old Saint Louis Number 1. I couldn't see the faces of the people marching by, brushing past, knocking their shoulders against mine. It was as if they didn't see me standing there, soaked to the bone. The crowd separated, passing me on either side, but still I couldn't tell who these people were. Their faces were blurred, like photographs taken with the wrong aperture.

My heart banged so hard against my ribs it hurt. My breath caught in my throat as I tried to call out for my friend Kate. She'd taken me to this funeral—she had to be there, and she could take me away—but there was only the crowd shoving against me. I started to topple in the wet grass, my heels sinking into the lawn, and still I cried out for Kate.

Lightning crashed, close this time, and I scrambled to my feet. When I stood, the crowd was gone, and I could barely see in the heavy rain. But there was a hand on my shoulder, and when I spun around I saw her. It was my mother. I was sure of it. She wore huge black sunglasses and a wide-brimmed hat. Her long hair was curly and dark, just like mine. Nothing about her face was familiar, but I knew it was her. As I opened my mouth to speak, my heart still pounding in my ears, she shoved me as hard as she could. I staggered backwards, falling from an impossible height, and awoke when I crashed to the earth.

Jack had pulled me closer, slid his fingers in my hair as he whispered in my ear. I loved that this town had brought me to him, but I hated it for dredging up so much of my mother and the parts of her I'd let myself forget.

Some people are better forgotten, but sometimes they hold fast to you with claws and teeth and refuse to let you leave them behind.

SINCE THE SUMMER, Jack and I had finished our renovations on Vergie's house and had flipped another little Craftsman in the country. I figured if he and I could survive two renovations together, we could handle having our families over for Christmas.

Well, I hadn't actually suggested to him yet that we invite my father to come down from Raleigh. I had to find the right moment to announce that part of the plan.

My father was still frustrated with me for leaving suddenly back in July, when I decided to stay here with Jack and start my own house-flipping business. In the ten years I'd worked for my father, he'd made a habit of freezing me out when I made him mad. But this past summer, I told him I was finished taking orders from him and was ready to take charge of my own projects.

Our relationship had rapidly decayed in the last year, so I

figured the best thing for us was to have some time apart. Having eight hundred miles between us didn't hurt, either.

He'd been suspicious of Jack from the first time I mentioned he was helping me repair Vergie's house, and he was annoyed when I moved here from North Carolina to stay with him. My father had given up on telling me what to do when it came to men, but he quietly seethed and never asked about him, like he figured Jack would just go away, like all the others did. My father once accused me of taking in broken men and trying to fix them, and he seemed to think Jack was just another of those men. I was hoping to convince him otherwise for the sake of whatever bits of our relationship we might salvage.

MY HAIR WAS STICKING to my forehead. I pulled a ponytail holder from the pocket of my jeans and tied my long hair back. It still frizzed in the humidity, but it was getting more accustomed to the bayou climate.

Jack's dog, Bella, was parked on the opposite end of the porch, eyeing me from the shade. Her mottled gray coat was dappled with sunlight, her front legs splayed out in front of her. She looked like she was melting into the floorboards. It was a little after five, but felt like noon in summer.

When Jack's truck came rumbling down the driveway, she raised one ear slightly, then resumed her log pose.

I stapled more lights into place and climbed down the ladder to move it a few feet over. This was my first Christmas in Bayou Sabine and my first Christmas away from North Carolina. I was determined to make it feel like a proper holiday. My father had stopped decorating for Christmas after my mom left us. I was sixteen, and after that, any decorating was up to me. My mother had loved Christmas, right down to the plastic reindeer on the roof, and my dad had enjoyed it simply because she did. But now that she was gone, he didn't want reminders of her and the things she loved.

Unfortunately, that included a lot of the things I loved.

He'd tossed out the plastic Santas and elves, and stopped hanging lights around the door. For the first few years he vetoed the holiday altogether, refusing to even put up a tree. I was in college by then, so I decorated my dorm room and got my fix before I came home for winter break.

This year was also my first Christmas with Jack. So I wanted everything to be as close to perfect as it could be. "Perfect" was a tall order, but I hoped for it regardless.

Jack parked behind the house and strode up to the porch, his dark hair standing out in tufts. He was wearing the same jeans and navy blue T-shirt he'd left the house in the day before.

I never tired of watching his slow, easy swagger, the way he fixed his eyes on me like there was nothing else in his field of vision. He moved with more grace than I'd expect from a man so tall and muscular.

"Hey," I said, stapling the next section of lights into place.

He stopped at the ladder and slid his hand along my calf. "Hey yourself," he said. "Are you getting in the spirit?"

"I'm trying, but it's hard when it's eighty degrees outside."

I climbed down the ladder, pausing on the bottom rung so I could look him in the eye. As he pulled me close for a kiss, I tangled my fingers in his hair.

When I finally let him go, he said, "I think you might have missed me."

"You have no idea."

He lifted me off the ladder and set me down in front of him, leaving his hands cinched around my hips. "Can't believe you're not sick of me yet," he said. "That's the damnedest thing."

I shrugged. "You keep this place interesting."

He laughed, swatting me on the behind. "I'm going to get cleaned up. Then I'm making you dinner."

Of the two of us, Jack was the better cook by far. I'd

occasionally cook, but Jack, having been raised by spice-loving Cajuns, easily put my dishes to shame. He'd humor me and eat what I made, but most nights he offered to cook, saying it relaxed him after a long stint at the firehouse. Apparently all of the firefighters at his engine were excellent chefs, always trading recipes and preparing meals for each other during shifts.

"No fires this time?" I asked.

"Nope, just some training sessions. Hence the desperate need for the shower."

As he stepped inside, I called after him, "You want some company?"

"When have I ever said no to that, chère?" He stripped his shirt off and tossed it at me.

I draped the string of lights on the ladder and followed him into the house. He wrapped his arms around me, squeezing me against his bare chest. I laughed, squirming as he tickled my sides, but then his grip tightened. Nuzzling my ear, he said, "When's Kate coming? Tomorrow?"

"Yeah," I said, giggling as he tickled my neck with his stubbly cheek.

"Perfect. One more night to ourselves."

He scooped me up over his shoulder and headed for the bedroom.

"Jack! Put me down!"

He laughed, his feet thumping on the hardwood. "No, ma'am, I'm afraid I can't do that."

LATER, I lay next to him, sliding my fingers through his hair. It was soft as a rabbit's fur and nearly black in the dim light.

"I've been thinking about Christmas," I said.

"Hmm," he replied, his eyes closed.

"How about we ask Josie and Buck over here for dinner?"

"They usually do it at their place. Josie likes to go all out."

"I just thought it'd be nice to have them over here, after all the help they've been."

"She loves hosting," he said. "Sometimes my cousin comes down, and she always asks the guys from the station that don't have anywhere to go."

"We could have all of them here too," I said. "And I was thinking of asking my dad to come out. It'd be nice if they all met each other."

He opened his eyes, his face still buried in the pillow. The dark blue of his eyes still startled me. "Your dad?"

"I know," I said, rolling onto my back. "But you two met under extremely stressful circumstances. I'm sure you'd get along in a normal situation."

His eyebrow arched. "Your dad hates me."

"He doesn't hate you. He hates that I moved in with a man he doesn't know."

His eyes narrowed.

"Please," I said. "I really want you to spend some time together. You're an important part of my life, Jack. And I'd like to mend things with my dad. He's the only family I have."

He slipped his hand over my hip and leaned over to kiss my forehead.

"OK," he said. "I'll tell them."

I ruffled his hair until he smiled.

"But he's not staying here," he said.

I frowned.

"I don't want your father plotting how to kill me every night when you and I retire to the same bedroom."

I laughed and swatted him with a pillow.

"And I'm not sleeping on the couch with Bella," he said.

"Fair enough."

He sighed and pulled me close against his strong chest.

~

It was after lunch the next day when I heard Kate's car coming down the gravel lane. A cloud of dust followed her little red Volkswagen as it curled along the meadow, and I stepped out on the porch to greet her.

"Good grief," she said, climbing out. "I thought the damn GPS was going to send me right into the ocean. It seems to think canals are roadways." She pulled a suitcase out of the backseat and trudged through the grass in a pair of impossibly high wedges. Kate was my best friend and had been since college. We agreed on a lot of things, but fashion was not one of them. Kate was girly—she loved swishy skirts and lipstick, high heels and hairspray. I was perfectly happy as a tomboy in jeans and beat-up cowboy boots. She'd tried to make me appreciate fashion for the last ten years, but the most I could muster was some pale lipstick and a flat iron every now and then.

"That can't be the only bag you have," I said, nodding toward the tiny suitcase.

She rolled her eyes. "Oh please. This is overflow from the trunk."

She set the suitcase on the steps and hugged me, tighter than she had in a long time. "Look at this house!" she shrieked. "It's adorable."

The old Victorian was the typical four-on-four style with a porch that stretched the entire length of the front. My bedroom, bathroom and the living room were in the front, with a hall straight down the middle and the kitchen and dining room in the back. The kitchen had a back door and walk-in pantry that had some of the loveliest woodwork in the whole house. The dining room had a built-in bookcase along one entire wall that made me want to turn it into a study. The upstairs had four big rooms and a small bathroom. We'd kept one as a guest bedroom. The others we were still figuring out: Jack liked having a room just for his things, and I liked having a room that was mine.

"How are you doing?" I asked.

"As well as I can be, after that cheating jackass," she said.

I grabbed her bag. "Come in, and let me make you a drink. I'll show you around when you get settled." I knew she'd love seeing the house's features and all the work we'd done, but I also knew what a long drive it was from Raleigh.

In the kitchen, I introduced her to Jack.

"Glad to have you with us," he said, shaking her hand.

"It's good to meet you for real this time."

She'd met Jack briefly at Vergie's funeral, before I'd even met him. She'd teased me the rest of that weekend about the handsome man in the pale gray suit. When I'd told Jack about that later, he'd laughed and said, "I only wear a suit about twice a year, but if you like it that much, I might find an excuse to wear it around the house."

KATE and I sat on the porch swing for a long time, drinking vodka tonics and watching the clouds drift across the sky. From the porch, we had a clear view of the lagoon at the edge of the cypresses. Kate had piled her honey-blond hair high up on her head and changed into a pair of jeans and a blouse.

"Thanks for letting me stay with you," she said after a while.

"Of course. You needed to get away."

"Understatement of the year." She held the glass against her face. She'd called me the week before and told me she'd found out that her fiancé, Benjamin, was cheating on her. They'd been going out a year and had set a date for May. Kate had discovered a strange cell phone in Benjamin's coat pocket and had done enough investigating to learn he only used it for the woman he was seeing in secret.

Kate had called me the day she'd confronted him. He denied everything, but he couldn't make up enough lies to convince her she was wrong. Kate was a biologist, an observer of behavior patterns. It killed her to think she hadn't been able to see his.

I told her to come and stay as long as she wanted. She never took vacation days, so she had enough time accrued to carry her through the New Year. I knew she wouldn't take more than a week though. She thought guests had an expiration date. I thought that rule didn't apply to friends, and sometimes I managed to convince her of it.

After we'd lost track of our refills, she said, "Why didn't you tell me I was being stupid?"

"Because you weren't being stupid."

She grimaced, squeezing the lime into her drink. "A year was too soon to get engaged. I should have made him pay for the deposits on the vineyard and the cake."

"He's the one who was stupid. Let's get that straight."

She raised her glass. "Maybe I'll still get the cake. Chocolate raspberry. The best I've ever had."

"Not all behaviors are predictable," I said. "You know that."

"I just feel like the worst cliché ever."

"He's the cliché."

"Maybe I'll just stick with single-celled organisms for a while."

I leaned back in the swing, feeling tipsy. "I never really liked him anyway. He winked too much, like a car salesman."

"Enza Parker!" she said, tossing her lime at me. "You said you liked him."

"You're practically my sister. What did you expect me to say?"

She was quiet for a long moment, then fixed me with a hard stare. "Did you know what he was doing?"

I sat up straight. "Of course not. Why would you ask me that?"

She studied me, as if calculating something, then looked away.

"Hey," I said. "Look at me."

She did.

"I didn't know," I said. "I wouldn't keep his cheating a secret."

"But you lied about liking him."

"Kate," I said, resting my hand on her arm. "It was only important that you liked him."

She turned away, staring out into the field. Although the humidity lingered, the air was starting to turn chilly.

"My mother used to tell me I should never get married," Kate said. "She told me I had expectations of loyalty that no man could live up to. Maybe I should take her advice."

"Mothers don't always have the answers," I said, but part of me thought I shouldn't get married either. My parents' marriage had ended in disaster.

She gazed out over the field, sipping her drink. It was impossible to read her mind. Her face never revealed her thoughts. My head was fuzzy from the vodka, and I wondered if hers was too.

"Do you ever wonder?" she said at last. "Do you ever want to find her?"

I'd told her about the letters, the journals I'd found in my grandmother's closet. When I was younger, I'd imagined meeting my mother again someday, considered what we might say to each other. But at Vergie's funeral, when it had occurred to me that I might see her there, lurking like a phantom, I'd panicked and run out of the church and into a raging thunderstorm.

"Sometimes," I said. The truth was, I wished I didn't want to find her. I wanted to not care any more, to not wonder where she was, why she left, what she was like. But as hard as I tried to bury those thoughts, they still gnawed at me, down deep where I couldn't always reach. I wished I could rip them from my head, like weeding a garden, but it didn't work that way.

"Maybe you should find her," Kate said. "Just get it over with, and then you'd no longer wonder."

"Some things might be better left unknown."

"Imagine my marriage with Benjamin if I hadn't found out he was cheating on me. The unknown never helped anybody. Trust me on that. I'm a scientist."

∼

LATER, when Kate was sound asleep in the guest room upstairs, I slipped into my own bedroom downstairs, where Jack lay with his back toward me. I stripped out of my clothes and settled into bed next to him. He rolled over and draped his arm around my waist, pulling me against him.

No matter how quiet I was, I always woke him.

"You two have a nice chat?" he mumbled, half asleep.

"Yeah."

"Figured I should make myself scarce, given the circumstances with her fiancé."

I scoffed, my head still buzzing from the alcohol. "She's hardly going to take it out on you. You'll like her."

"I don't doubt that. I just figure right about now she's wishing there were four billion less of us fellas around."

I slipped my hand over his. "She liked you from the get-go, remember?"

He muttered something I couldn't quite make out. He was drifting off again.

For a while I lay there thinking about what Kate had said. Why had I been so afraid of bumping into my mother at Vergie's funeral? For a ghost, she occupied an awful lot of real estate in my mind. My memories may have been fragmented, but it was shocking how being down here brought back so many of them. Now that Kate was here, I kept thinking back to the funeral, the way the little gray-haired lady had said I looked just like my mother, how she said she hadn't seen her in a while. It made me wonder where she'd seen her last and how long ago. She might not be as far away as I thought.

My stomach clenched, and everything inside me seemed to squeeze tighter.

"Jack," I whispered. "You still awake?"

"Hmm," he muttered, slipping his feet over mine as his arm tightened around my hips.

"Do you remember when you told me about the man Vergie was seeing before she died?"

"Yeah," he said. "George."

"Do you know his last name?"

"Don't remember off-hand. Might have it written down somewhere."

"Didn't you say he worked at the jazz museum?"

He kissed my neck. "Go to sleep, chère. Let's talk in the morning."

"I could go down there and look for him. That might be better than a phone call anyway. If you went with me, would you recognize him?"

"Sure," he said. "But why do you want to see George?"

Through the window, the moonlight sliced through the room, so intense I could see the pattern of the lace curtains on the floorboards, blue and black. My chest tightened, and I felt wide awake.

"I want to ask him if Vergie ever told him about my mother."

Read more about Enza and Jack in
Bayou Whispers, Book Two in the Bayou Sabine Series

Join My Newsletter

JOIN my team and you'll get my special author newsletter, Writing Down South. Click here to subscribe and claim your free books.

Also by Lauren Faulkenberry

The Bayou Sabine Series:

TROUBLE IN BAYOU SABINE
BACK TO BAYOU SABINE
BAYOU WHISPERS
JUST THE TROUBLE I NEEDED

Other Fiction:

BENEATH OUR SKIN and Other Stories

Sign up for Lauren's author newsletter,
Writing Down South and get two free books! Sign up at
laurenfaulkenberry.com

Acknowledgments

This book couldn't exist without the encouragement and support of my family, friends and mentors. A special thank you goes to Katie Rose Guest Pryal for being the best reader a gal could ask for; to Allen Gee for pushing me to be a better writer way back in my grad school days at GCSU; to Sonja Greentree Rossow for encouraging me to keep going, always.

Thank you to Velvet Morning Press for first publishing this book.

To my family: Thank you for believing in me and telling me to keep doing what I love. Without you, I couldn't be a writer. To my parents: Thank you for making me think I could be anyone I wanted to be, for telling me I should keep writing, and for teaching me to see all the love stories in the world. To my grandmother and my great aunt Et: Thank you for raising me on good stories from the get go. To Andrew: Thank you for reminding me that a good love story is nothing without laughter.

About the Author

Lauren divides her time between writing, teaching, and printmaking. She is the author of the Bayou Sabine Series, which includes the novels *Trouble in Bayou Sabine* and *Bayou Whispers*. Originally from South Carolina, she has worked as an archaeologist, an English teacher, and a ranger for the National Park Service. She earned her MFA in creative writing from Georgia College & State University, and her MFA in Book Arts from The University of Alabama.

She won the *Family Circle* short fiction contest, was a finalist for the Novello Festival Press First Novel Award, and was nominated for an AWP Intro Award. She currently lives in North Carolina, where she's at work on the next novel in the Bayou Sabine series. Sign up for Lauren's author newsletter, *Writing Down South*, at laurenfaulkenberry.com.

facebook.com/FaulkenberryAuthor

twitter.com/firebrandpress

instagram.com/firebrandpress

amazon.com/author/lauren-faulkenberry

bookbub.com/authors/lauren-faulkenberry